NZINGA
AFRICAN WARRIOR QUEEN

Also by Moses L. Howard:

The Sky High Road
A Teacher in East Africa
The Human Mandolin
The Ostrich Chase

Writing as Musa Nagenda:

Dogs of Fear: A Story of Modern Africa
The Ostrich Egg Shell Canteen

NZINGA
AFRICAN WARRIOR QUEEN

MOSES L. HOWARD

Jugum Press

Copyright © 2016 by Moses L. Howard

First print edition: September 2016
ISBN-13: 978-1-939423-40-5

Library of Congress Control Number: 2016911238
Jugum Press, Seattle, Washington USA

Cover by Lisa Tilton Design
Book design by Annie Pearson

Published by Jugum Press
505 Broadway East #237
Seattle, Washington 98102
Find ebook editions at www.jugumpress.com
Contact: JugumPress@outlook.com

For my mother, Missoura Bradley Howard,
whose loving quotation was,
"Can anything good come out of Nazareth?"
— John 1:46

CONTENTS

NZINGA
AFRICAN WARRIOR QUEEN

PROLOGUE

THE PORTUGUESE EXPLORERS SAILING along the west coast of Africa spotted the white beaches of what came to be called Angola. They invaded and took the coastal land in 1576—by the Catholic calendar—and built a fort and a town, which they named Luanda.

Over the years, they repeatedly brought armies and tried to conquer the whole of Angola. However, the king, who was called the Ngola, repulsed them with a strong army, and so did his heirs for years, not permitting the Portuguese to advance more than a few miles inland. The Portuguese spies watched and waited until at last an old strong Ngola died, and a young king arrived who neglected his army and did not guard his kingdom.

In 1621, the Portuguese governor saw his chance to take the country. He promised the rulers in Portugal to deliver slaves and silver and brought fast horse-soldiers from Lisbon to Africa. He had spread the rumor among the Africans in town that horse-soldiers were coming to help raise the cannon that had slipped into the river. He intended this rumor to reach the new Ngola's ears so that no one might suspect the horse-soldiers' real destination.

With stealth and speed, the Portuguese invaders unloaded their ships' cargo of guns and horses on the docks of Luanda. By noon, the horse-soldiers and a small group of foot-soldiers were far up the Lugalula River near the small ugly fort the Portuguese had built at a place called Massangano. When they neared the fort, they changed course, deserting the river and forest, striking out in the early darkness across the savannah.

The horse-soldiers passed village after village during the night without meeting anyone rushing toward them. With the first brightness of morning on the hills, they saw in the distance the Ngola's palace shining within an expansive thorn enclosure. The beautifully decorated grass-and-bamboo structures gleamed in the early morning light. Cordero, the lean leader of the expedition, stood tall in his stirrups and glanced around.

"Our spies say their army is putting down a revolt in the Kongo. We shall take the palace and other spoils. Hurry! Hurry!"

The men swept down the hillside, and the huge, strong war-horses with iron-fitted hooves charged through the palace's bamboo gates, trampling women and children. The Portuguese soldiers, protected by heavy mail and metal helmets, brandished long gleaming swords dripping with the blood of African guards who had risen to stop them with hippo-hide shields and spears. The horses reared, stomped, and raced through the catacomb-like lanes of the palace, overturning food bins, breaking down walls, neighing and snorting.

The horse-soldiers lopped off the heads of the king's guards and of old women servants who appeared in their paths. With every flash of the sharp-honed blades, blood spurted from the victims in sprayed jets, striking, discoloring, and running in rivulets down the leather breastplates and harnesses of the horses. This deadly dash into the palace grounds brought them to the king's living quarters, where they galloped through the labyrinth, coming to an area decorated with lion skins.

"See the shields with iron rings on the door? These are the king's quarters," yelled the leader. "Just as the priest told the governor."

They surprised the king's wife and mother in their separate rooms, each undressed in bed. Captain Cordero, poised on horseback beside the king's bed, deftly sliced with his sword, cutting away the cocoon of covers to reveal the naked, slender, long-legged queen, who awoke in wild-eyed terror and tried to hide her nakedness with her hands.

"Oh, ho!" said his snub-nosed orderly, who ran in on foot behind Cordero.

"Beautiful, is it not, Epejo?" the captain said. "But we have work to do. Get the king. Quickly."

"The spies say the king is out hunting." Epejo shook his shaggy head, smiling. "So, senhor, you have much time to linger here with this one."

"She is as beautiful as they say, but a little too thin for my favor." Cordero shook off disappointment. He'd wished for the king's return, because his capture meant a handsome reward. He nodded toward the queen. "The governor ordered me to bring these goods to Luanda. Undamaged. Tie her up."

"But, Senhor Cordero . . . " Epejo protested.

"That goes for all the people here. Once we're in Luanda, it will be a different story for them."

Two other horse-soldiers joined them, striking violently with their riding crops at the people they herded along in front of them. Among them were the king's mother and two lovely women.

"They're too beautiful to sell as slaves," Penote said. The horse-soldier was a slim, pale skeleton of a man whose skull-bone prints showed beneath his skin. "Let's disappear with them into the bushes."

"These two must be the king's sisters. How are they called?" Cordero asked.

Epejo said, "This slim one with the basket-weave hair is Kikambi, and this one with big breasts and wide hips is Kifunzi." He pointed with glee.

Cordero's face clouded again with disappointment. "Where is the other sister? The governor wants the one called Nzinga, who's next to the king in importance. Get her!"

"*Where is she?*" Penote shouted at the women in their Kimbundu tongue, brandishing his sword above his head like a scythe.

The king's mother shuddered in fright. "Yes, take Nzinga and leave us here."

Chala, the king's wife, a cloth now draped around her waist, screamed loudly and long, then whimpered and tried to reach her mother-in-law. The soldiers held her, slyly fondling her breasts. The two sisters, Funzi and Kambi, hugged each other. The older sister, Funzi, was defiant. "It's good Nzinga isn't here. We can't tell them anything."

"Nzinga!" Epejo shouted, listening nearby. He pounced on Funzi. "I heard that." He caught her arm, squeezing mercilessly until she screamed and knelt on the ground in pain. "Where is she? Where is Nzinga?"

"Tell us or be sold as slaves," Penote said. He helped bind the women to other captives and then herded them toward the wrecked palace gates.

"You better tell us now," Epejo said. "Cordero will beat it out of you. He'll find her." He reached for Funzi again.

Shaking her aching arm, Funzi fumed, ready for combat. She faced him, weaponless but determined to show she was not defenseless. While he was off balance, she caught the hand that held her and bit hard where Epejo's finger connected to his hand, shaking her head from side to side until the finger dangled loosely, independent of his hand. Epejo cried out and doubled over in pain.

Penote, still on horseback, delivered a backhand blow that sent Funzi reeling into the thorny hedge surrounding the palace. Kambi broke free and ran toward her sister, but soldiers caught her and held her back. Funzi attempted to rise among the thorns, which tore at her garments and pierced her arms and face. Bleeding, she knelt on one knee among the thorny branches. Cordero held the sharp point of his sword between Funzi's breasts.

"Stop that!" Kambi shouted in accented Portuguese. She fought her way to Funzi's side and grabbed Cordero's elbow.

Cordero glared at her over his shoulder, his teeth bared.

"Where is Nzinga?"

"She's . . . she's traveling somewhere else in the kingdom. And my sister, there," Kambi pointed to Funzi, "you can't kill her. She's worth money!"

As she spoke, drums around the countryside began to sound wildly. Through the palace gates, Cordero saw a few ill-equipped spearmen gathering in the distance. Sheathing his sword, he spoke in Portuguese to Epejo, who still cringed and whimpered. "Get that hand fixed." Then, turning to Penote: "Why are you waiting? Get these slaves to Luanda."

He mounted his horse and rode as if to attack the spearmen gathered on the hillside near the palace. He brandished his sword as he charged, and the spearmen fell back. He returned to the others.

"They won't attack us for fear of wounding the king's mother and wife."

The men rolled and trussed the loudly-complaining king's mother, tied up all the women in blankets, and threw them across the backs of horses. Then they hurried their prisoners over the savannah toward Luanda.

◈

PART I
IN THE TIME OF THE OLD NGOLA

1583 – 1615

◈

1.
CELEBRATION

THE OLD KING OF NDONGO, the Ngola Kilijua, returned home in the dry season, riding in a litter. The African savannah shimmered in the August sun. The mat of amber grasses swayed and sighed like gentle waves on a calm sea. On its surface the grass rippled and undulated, but deep down in the gray earth the thirsty roots of the long blades gripped like tenuous fingers, grasping and squeezing the hard soil, desperately seeking water. For months, night and day, the roots sent upward the flow that greened the savannah. But now the skin of the earth did not respond. Relief could come only from the clouds. Yet above the swaying grasses, the sky's gaze remained serenely blue, a solitary white plume of cloud playing across its face.

A fierce wave ran through the swaying grass mat, causing a steady forward motion accompanied by sounds unfamiliar to ears that cherished the music of the grasses, to those inhabitants who sang in the grasses, ate in the grasses, gave birth, lived, and died in the grasses. For them a different music played. These beings moving through the grass so briskly brought bold music, challenging and violent. Sounds drifted over the savannah, of human voices and human feet, of knives.

Ubolo, Upolo!
Plonk, plik, ple, plomp!

Whoosh, whee, clee, clompik!

Spisffff, nopffff, wheeeee zzip!

Spears remained at the ready, but were not needed for the work that feet and arms did.

Yet the grasses didn't yield at once to the sound or movement of invading feet. The strong, thick stalks fought to survive on the African veldt and refused to bow under the onrush of the first cruel steps. Only after constant battering did the grass give up its springing counter-attack, after thousands of feet marched it into submission.

This charging wave advanced swiftly, orderly, rhythmically across the vastness of the veldt, like the wind filling a void with its methodical, cyclic sweep. Warthog, dik-dik, sable wildebeest, gazelle, rhino, and lion sniffed the air, puzzled. Then the scent told all. They quickly detoured. Some sprang away in the face of this hungry, surging throng, filling the air above the grasses with their leaping escape. Others disturbed the stalks with crawling, rushing, and digging retreats from this mass that needed to feed itself as it moved. Small groups scouted out from the sides at intervals, but then, after a squeal from prey, withdrew back to the main body as if driven back by the rhythm of drums.

The voices of the callers never ceased. Chants varied, but the rhythms maintained, as though the mass traveled on cadence. And it did, unless some obstacle moved into its path; then the tempo slowed or sped to a shrill cry.

"*Mbacka! Mbacka!*"

"*Cambambe, Uuuhu, Uuuhu Uuuhuuaa!*"

This chant issued from the throat of deep-chested men with lean brown bodies that remained dry of sweat from sunrise to early afternoon under the equatorial sun. Drums hidden in the moving ranks underscored and confirmed the chant.

"*Mbacka, Mbacka, Cambambe, Uuuhuu!*"

This wave of marching warriors was ordered, disciplined, and armed with spears, knives, bows and arrows, and a few captured guns. The army was massive in depth and sweep. A soldier at the front ordered to walk back along its ranks would take at least a day to reach the end of the column. In addition to the trained soldiers, the army's numbers were swollen by captives and displaced refugees fleeing the Portuguese, forming a body that reached back toward Luanda. Others who came along were the curious people from Ndongo who joined the army as it passed through their villages.

From far back in the flowing throng, yet moving to the same rhythm, a clutch of muscular warriors pressed forward, supporting litters bearing their leader and his ministers. As the slightly bent bodies and running bearers tired, they shifted the poles to other warriors who stepped in to relieve them. From the side of one litter, a messenger was dispatched to the drummers, who at once changed the tempo. The whole army sped up its march as though readied for a great emergency. The chant raced along.

"Mbacka, Mbacka. Cambambe, Huh, Huh!"

For months, since the Ngola had left to fight a battle, runners returned daily to Mbacka, the royal village, racing with all their strength to carry news to their leader's people, to tell how the Ngola rested, how he slept, how he fought, how he won and how he lost, and why. Now the runners didn't have so far to go when they left the army to run to the Mbanza, the Ngola's palace:

"The Ngola is coming!"

"The Ngola is near!"

Finally they had only a short distance to run. Panting to catch their breath, for they ran at top speed all the way, they had only one message.

"The Ngola is here!"

The change in the movement of the army was caused by its surroundings. The grass underfoot collapsed now into a soft cushion. In the distance loomed green bushes, then trees, and finally a forest. Cool air struck them in the face. The sound that had been a murmur at midday now roared in their ears. Cutting through the chants, it had more power than the book of the drums. The marchers gave themselves up to that roar, moving almost as if in a dance. It didn't matter that their pulses pounded in their temples and they were near collapse. An inner sense of release drove them toward the Cambambe waterfalls, where the Ngola's palace, the Mbanza, stood on a hill above the Cuanza River.

The column split into equal halves as it came through the forest into the clearing, fanning out along the banks of the river some distance away from the Mbanza. People poured out of the villages and ancestral shrines along the way as the warriors, now leaping and dancing, paraded in front of them. The praise singers heralded the arrival of the Ngola, dropping to their knees to honor him.

Along the banks, and even back in the forest, the builders had already set to work with permission from spiritual leaders and the prime minister, cutting down trees to construct the Ngola's round houses. Even while the rear units were still moving, the Ngola's firebrand was brought forward and the cooks set up to prepare food.

The royal drummers with the Ngola's ceremonial instruments took over in a gigantic festival of drumming that echoed up and down the river and through the whole of Ndongo. The dancers came, women first, undulating and calling, laughing playfully, chanting and leaping in a contest, one unit striving to outdo the other. The strident, haunting sounds from the bushbuck horns broke all inhibitions, calling everyone to come and chant.

"Ngola! Ngola! Ngola! Rainmaker!"

When the eyes seeking the king could endure the waiting no longer, a wild frenzy of drumming brought him through the crowd. The army opened its ranks to a spear-bearing phalanx of warriors who bolted wildly through the crowd like lightning, cutting down a score of onlookers who blocked the way. These were left lying to the side, dying in their own blood, while litter bearers bore the Ngola forward with dazzling speed and hoisted him high above the cheering crowd. People fell prostrate on the ground, averting their eyes from his brilliance and clasping their hands above their heads.

•

While the people in the palace enclosure celebrated the return of the Ngola, the returning soldiers celebrated outside, a safeguard against the army bringing back pestilence. None of the people who came with the Ngola could enter the palace for ten days. They scrubbed in the river several times and waited. The formal celebration for their return had to come later.

In the meantime, the celebration inside the palace lasted long into the night and continued for several nights. The moon was high and bright. They told stories and reenacted battles, embraced their age mates, created the music of battles, and danced. A feast began afresh each day, with plantain beer, millet beer, and palm wines.

The merrymaking at the palace was mixed with cries throughout the kingdom of people who were related to Chief Kassa, who had betrayed the Ngola's plans to the Portuguese. Although the Ngola had granted Kassa a chiefdom that lay between Luanda and Massangano, Kassa had family and property in different parts of Ndongo. As soon as the Ngola arrived home, he held a meeting with his chiefs to give orders about the renegade Chief Kassa.

"Burn his land. Take his people and make them servants in other families. Take his cattle. Anyone who is hungry may kill and cook his goats. They may dig his yams, harvest his cassava, and winnow his grain. Let people take whatever is his tonight throughout the kingdom. Do it quickly. Let none of them flee. Leave his land bare for another chief and his people."

As soon as the order was given, people began disappearing from the celebration, heading for parts of Ndongo where Kassa was known to have property. They wanted to be present at the moment when the Ngola's soldiers arrived. Once the Ngola issued such an order, all possessions of the offender could be claimed by any loyal citizen of Ndongo. They knew Kassa's villagers had heard the news and were busy hiding all they owned. This effort would surely fail once the king withdrew his protection. So people watched and waited for the soldiers to arrive, and when their work was done, the people pounced on what was left. After that, fires blazed in the night in parts of the kingdom, and some heard Kassa's people crying for their lost possessions and lost honor.

What the Ngola ordered was the least costly price paid for disloyalty to the Ngola. The greatest price was death to the disloyal one and possibly his family. Many of the soldiers who fought alongside the Ngola were rewarded with Kassa's cows, his land, his servants, and any goods found in his houses. Kassa's punishment didn't end with this night. His army would be watched night and day.

After the Portuguese army left them, Kassa's army would be under periodic siege from the Ngola's chiefs, his fields near Luanda would be burned, and his houses raided. Anyone who injured Kassa's property in any way received the protection of the Ngola.

•

The Ngola made preparations to send parts of his army and his chiefs to their various homes across Ndongo. He visited nearby shrines to pay homage to the gods and ancestors, and he presided at rain-making ceremonies. Ten days after his return, the Ngola and his two wives sat in their private common room inside the palace at Mbacka. The royal children were brought in.

Kaningwa, the first wife, was slender with small breasts, and was known throughout Ndongo as a great beauty. She wore stylish African clothes made from many-colored kente cloth and the best fashions and cloth from the Portuguese trade. She was a favorite among many wives of the Ngola's chiefs, who copied the styles Kaningwa wore and talked of her constantly. She invited them to visit in the palace and spoke freely with them of her family and the Ngola's business.

Kaningwa took the lead in welcoming the Ngola. She ordered servants to bring drinks and then was the first to drink and fall down in front of the Ngola. Now she sat nearby, first looking at him with limpid eyes, then moving her slender neck to show the Ngola her profile and her hair piled high, the way she'd been told hair was worn in Lisbon. She ignored her two daughters, who sat on pillows on the floor. Her son Mbande, who was eight rains old, sat beside her. With two rainy seasons each year, the Portuguese would call him four years old. At Kaningwa's signal, the boy knelt in front of his father, who lifted him up and brought him near.

The Ngola smiled. "Mbande, boy, you have come along. The rains are making you grow as well as the cassava." Mbande smiled shyly. His father said, "You are a prince, my son. You needn't be shy or look away from anyone. You must look straight at them and learn what they are thinking."

•

Mbande later told his mother that he wasn't shy; he simply wasn't interested in what was being discussed. Mbande was never able to concentrate on anything except those things of interest to himself. Nothing held his attention for long.

"My mind runs on other things."

He'd love to ask his father about the big fish he'd seen the fishermen take away from the river, and why it flipped and flashed its silver sides in an effort to escape, and how it caused the men to bleed by puncturing them with its blade-like fins. He also wanted to ask his father about the feeling you get when you swim and feel the buoyancy of water against your body. He knew, however, these weren't the things that interested his father.

Even as his father spoke after returning from the war, Mbande at eight seasons old was thinking of the stool his father sat on, with its beautiful animal skins and how the smooth fur felt against his skin. He liked to see other boys wrestle and sweat. He could wrestle, and several times he'd shown his father that he did it well, but he didn't like to fall and roll in the dirt.

His father was talking, asking one of the court servants to bring something into the room. Mbande hadn't been paying attention but now he heard, " . . . present for Mbande."

"You're going to like this, my son," the Ngola said. A servant brought in a rolled bark-cloth tied into a bundle. At the king's signal, the servant unfurled it on the floor with a flourish.

Several wives and women servants gasped. Mbande cringed, clinging to his father, who laughed.

The king said, "Your mothers may be afraid, but surely the Ngola's son isn't afraid of a crocodile's skin. This is for you. You will have a belt, knife holder, and arrow holder made from it. Just like the ones I have."

"Thank you, sir," Mbande said. He clasped his hands in front of the Ngola.

The Ngola's daughters approached, and he hugged them and allowed them to sit on his knee. The king remarked how they had grown. They told what they'd learned while he was away and showed the baskets they'd woven. The oldest one showed him a beaded gourd. They talked about the animals they'd seen.

"A herd of gazelles dashed by the palace gate. There are still giraffes near here, feeding in the trees. Lions roared late one night, shaking us from our beds."

Kaningwa's servant brought in a drum of solid, shiny brown wood, shaped like an antelope. The children could strike it, but no one seemed to know how to play it. The Ngola gave each child a packet that contained colored beads from Portugal plus the strong bristles from an elephant and a warthog. The girls smiled with pleasure. Their mother and a chorus of servants assured the Ngola that it was the nicest possible present and that the girls would make wonderful things from it.

.

Batayo, the Ngola's younger wife, was tall, timid, and well-shaped. She dressed only in African clothes and wore her hair in a handsome basket-weave, the style of which she changed often. She spoke softly and openly, saying exactly what she thought, but quickly apologizing if she offended.

Batayo waited patiently for the Ngola to turn to her that evening. She truly loved all the royal children and shared in their joy. Many times she told her friend Sufalu, the king's seer, that she wished in her heart for a boy to make the Ngola happy. She'd followed all advice given her. She wished her mother had been there to oversee the birth of the boy she'd lost. Yet she didn't envy Mbande his position as the only male child.

A servant brought in Batayo's new baby daughter, who had just awakened. Newly washed and oiled, the child was a bit thin.

"And who is this one?" asked the Ngola.

"No one until you give it a name," Batayo said. Because the Ngola had been away for more than a year, the child had been given a temporary name that only became official if and when the Ngola sanctioned it.

"What do you wish it to be named?" asked the Ngola.

"She's been called Nzinga."

"A good name."

"I am so sorry, my Ngola, it isn't a boy."

"Are you sure?" asked the king, who already knew, but he turned the naked body of the child to see its sex. "Yes, it is a girl. But what does that matter? She'll be like her mother." He held the child on his knee. She grasped his hand and looked straight at him. "What is this? She seems to understand everything I'm saying."

The Ngola kept talking to the child, telling her where he'd been and how at Luanda he'd seen a whale. He murmured to Nzinga that some people didn't know how to treat her father, like a certain chief who'd betrayed him in battle. But she'd help to show them how to treat her father when she grew up. The child smiled and tried to raise his big hand with hers.

"Did you see that?" said the Ngola. He and Batayo looked at each other and smiled in remembrance of their past joy. "This child is special."

A wild jealousy grew inside Kaningwa, though she had been elated by the attention given her son. She fawned over Mbande and looked sweetly at her husband, keeping his attention as long as possible.

"Listen, husband. Mbande can tell the names of all his forefathers, from the First Ngola, Blacksmith Prince. Go ahead, Mbande, recite them for your father."

Mbande recited them quickly and expertly. His mother nodded approvingly when he was done. Then she passed slowly in front of the king, arching her long beautiful neck, and moistening her lips with a flick of the tongue.

The children, other wife, and servants were dismissed when he retired with Kaningwa to the inner quarters with the iron rings on the door.

. . .

The next day, Kaningwa gossiped that Batayo disappointed the Ngola twice, not yet having given birth to a male child. "The first time she lost her baby and now, the second time," Kaningwa said to Chief Oyimbu's wife, "even though she pestered the royal cook for tender vegetables and the choicest cuts of meat. Even though she rested and thought good thoughts, she only managed to give birth to a little skinny baby girl. Now Batayo too is skinny."

Kaningwa also said to the chief's wife, "And, my cousin and friend, did you see? The Ngola barely glanced at her all evening."

She planted a servant in Batayo's quarters to watch and report. Whenever Kaningwa got the chance, she stole a sidelong look at Batayo. "Wretched woman," she said to friends, but she wasn't sorry for Batayo, who had been the favorite, nearly taking over because she danced so well and played many musical instruments. Batayo was wrong if she thought she'd always get attention.

Kaningwa told Chief Kadu's wife, "After what happened yesterday, I'm sure Mbande will be the Ngola when the Ngola dies . . . I mean, someday. Then let them all watch out. It will be far different." For one, by Ndongo custom, when the new Ngola was anointed, all other male children would be killed. Batayo should consider herself lucky she didn't have a son, who would only die when Mbande became Ngola. Kaningwa remained determined to tie her son close to her by any means possible. *I must teach Mbande to be cunning. If only he was a little less playful.*

Kaningwa gazed proudly at her children, who were playing with their gifts from the king. She looked at the chief's young wife again. "Why did Batayo call this last baby Nzinga? The nerve of her. It is a girl, and yet Batayo gives it part of the name of an ancient king. Well, we shall see."

2.
PALACE WARS

A S NZINGA GREW, SHE ALWAYS found joy in her father's company. For long periods she didn't see him, because he spent time away fighting against the Portuguese or against other chiefs, or in the palace judging disputes. Like many of Nzinga's ancestors, the Ngola was a good hunter, which meant he also spent time away hunting and fishing.

In addition to the wars fought by the king's army, there was a war between his wives and their supporters. Most often it was a quiet, subtle war, unknown to eyes or ears of the king and often unknown to members of the court. The strategies of each wife were often unknown to the other. Eventually Nzinga became aware of the palace wars that had started before she was born and continued for most of her life—that is, as long as her stepmother Kaningwa lived. People told Nzinga about conversations, gossip, judgments, and incidents that were part of the quiet contention between her mother Batayo and Kaningwa.

Fragments drifted into Nzinga's knowing when she was quite young. Snippets passed between her mother and Sufalu, the king's seer, who talked while visiting or working in her mother's rooms. Sufalu had many spies among the servants, people who overheard everything. Because Nzinga's mother had no other ally in the palace, Sufalu repeated to Batayo what she knew.

"*Ngo,* listen to me. There is danger now. Kaningwa isn't just a co-wife. She's a rival to be watched."

The urgency in Sufalu's voice made Nzinga stop twisting her colorful ibis-feather beads onto the long elephant hairs. She left the spot where she sat on the floor with Sufalu's daughter Chatembo and came nearer to the two women, looking into their faces, first one, then the other, and following their voices while the women spoke.

"Ah, sure, my friend, I know," Batayo said, her fingers busily weaving a pattern into a decorative millet-grass mat for the Ngola.

"You always say that, but you never let me help you."

"I don't want him that way. The only help I want is found at Punga a Dongo, from the ancestors that guard my husband and me."

Perhaps before she learned to talk, Nzinga learned that Punga a Dongo was the place of the ancestors.

Sufalu pleaded urgently. "Batayo, *Wo!* Hear me, please."

Batayo's hands paused over her weaving.

"There are things you refuse to hear," Sufalu said. "There are things outside of that of which you speak. Love is one strong thing. Yes. I also know love and have known it." She glanced fondly from her daughter Chatembo back to her friend. "But there is also Evil. Evil things that people use to get their way."

Batayo threw up her hands. "Why can't we trust Suku and the ancestors to watch?"

"It's true that gods and ancestors can watch, but ancestors are selfish and they also want you where they are. We have eyes and ears and must guard against becoming an ancestor while our children need us alive."

Batayo stroked Nzinga's head and face tenderly, then pulled the child to her breast. "Nothing must harm our child." She looked up wistfully. "And oh, Sufalu, I must give him a male child, too."

Nzinga gave her mother a forceful hug, and both women looked at her. Chatembo, who would be a seer and spirit medium like her mother, came over to lean into her mother's lap.

"The children understand us now," Sufalu said. "What you just said is what I want to speak of. You know of the last battle of Shellanga's army in Zaire?"

"Oh, how I hate to think of war. We lose so many people that way." Batayo was patient, but not interested beyond how things affected her children and the Ngola.

Nzinga's eyes never left Sufalu's mouth. Only six rains old, Nzinga tried to make some sense of the women's words. She was nearly three years old by Portuguese time and had one sister, Funzi, who slept in a long, flat basket in a corner. Batayo secretly recorded Nzinga's age on a colored grass platter she'd made for serving the Ngola's fruit. For those six rains since Nzinga was born, Batayo sewed into the platter's edge six dried scales from the giant river fish. They made a sound like the wind when the platter was moved.

"You know the army captured many people after the invaders destroyed their villages, people they took to be sold. Well, those people have been distributed throughout Ndongo. Your co-wife asked her uncle, a commander in Shellanga's army, for some of those people to use as servants here and in her village."

"That's always done. Even I could get a servant that way, but I have what I need."

"Batayo!" Sufalu reproached Nzinga's mother. "You know the proverb says, 'Your enemies may wall you up in a cave, but Suku makes them unwittingly leave a small door for you.' You must always search for the door that your enemies make. It's always there, before your eyes. Why must you always know so much that you leave no space for what you don't yet know?"

"Please don't be angry with me, Sufalu. I get tired of things that don't help the Ngola. He's trying to save our land, and he needs everyone's support. I know you're his right arm. You're always looking out for everyone. It's just that I know he needs us all. Kaningwa and her children are important to him, just as we are. I'm sorry for anything that makes him unhappy."

"I know this, and I wouldn't take sides, except you're too good and trusting to know what's around you. You can't neglect any part without losing it all. Batayo, you must be for everything and yet against everything that does harm."

"What is harm?" Nzinga asked.

Both women looked at the child in surprise. Sufalu laughed her rich, throaty laugh. "I told you they understand."

"Harm, harm," chortled Chatembo, who was a year older than Nzinga.

"To hurt someone or do damage to them. Like falling and scraping your knee," Batayo explained.

"Like the sorcerer in Zaire who sent locusts one year to eat all the grain in Ndongo, so their army could invade us the next year," Sufalu added. "Harm is always sent. It doesn't come of its own." At any other time, she'd have told the children a story to illustrate this, but she was in a hurry to get back to what had occupied them all morning.

"So, Batayo, I came this morning to warn you. You know my spies go along with the army. Some are women and some are women dressed like men, and they learn a lot. At least two of the servants Kaningwa chose are skilled in black magic. What people call *minkisi*. Those women can make things happen. Bad things, good things. They can make women have babies that are already dead or make husbands useless in bed."

"*Choo!*" Batayo gasped, covering her mouth in dismay, because her first child was born dead, a boy taken by the ancestors.

Nzinga watched it all, amused when Chatembo mimicked Batayo, mouthing "*Choo*" and putting her hand to her mouth.

Batayo shook her head in puzzled distress and threw up her hands; the bracelets on her wrists answered in twinkles and jangles. "Sufalu! How can they do that? What do they do? What should I do?"

"They use the things that people touch. Or where they *pika* in the earth. Or the cuttings of toenails or fingernails or hair. Or where you sleep, the impression made by your head on a pillow. They use strings, belts, leaves, or an old discarded tooth. Anything can be used by them: your spit on the ground, your bare footprint on the soil. Just know it. Watch everything and be careful. They will show themselves soon. If they haven't already been busy."

Sufalu looked at Batayo's swelling abdomen, whereupon Batayo drew back and folded her arms over her middle.

.

Nzinga was an escape artist who learned early to watch while not being observed, how to appear and disappear. She was cared for by a servant woman with a penchant for long discussions with other servants. Nzinga drifted away but came back quickly, so the servant got used to trusting the child to be nearby. In this way, Nzinga got to see and hear many things and to learn the palace inside out.

Nzinga and her nurse wandered all over the palace and often outside its gates. Sometimes Chatembo came with them, but most often Chatembo accompanied her mother everywhere, being trained as a medium and learning Sufalu's spy system. Her nurse preferred to wander about where other people worked, talking or helping people do different jobs. Nzinga enjoyed the winnowing and grinding compound. With so many people in the Mbanza, much food had to be prepared: grains, beans, peas, millet, sorghum to be winnowed and ground; maize to husk, that new gift from the Portuguese.

With her nurse, Nzinga watched women put handfuls of ground nuts into a big wooden mortar and strike down with the rounded end of a pole, pounding the nuts into flour. When the women took out the finely ground nuts, Nzinga came near to touch the pole. Often the women gave her a handful to eat. Nzinga took the crushed granules in her small hands and held them to her nose to smell, leaving a smear on her face. She rubbed it in her mouth, her eyes lighting up at the flavor. When millet was being ground, if Nzinga was given a handful, she studied the golden flecks, moving them about on her palm with her fingers. She threw the grain into the air and watched the sunlight play on the golden mix of colors drifting about her.

Nzinga liked to watch this work, because there was always music. The women played games and sang winnowing songs, grinding songs, and stomping, winemaking songs. They beat out husking songs. Often their movement helped the work along, and they did it in fun. When they were husking maize, they rubbed the ears together in a sawing motion that sounded like coarse sand under a wooden shoe. When they made beer or wine, they stomped on fruit, and the juices squirted out while workers danced to a drum. When they winnowed grain, they each had a wide, circular grass-woven winnowing screen. Each woman dipped onto her screen a load of grain with chaff from broken seed pods, then twisted her body and threw the grain into the air. At that moment another person fanned it with a winnowing screen that blew away the chaff, leaving the grain free to fall onto the tray. When it struck, it made a musical sound. They worked rhythmically, with a song that one group sang and another group answered as the grain hit the tray. Baskets and grain bins filled quickly.

The Ngola passed through while people worked. He joined in the winnowing and singing. And sometimes he took a handful of grain and let it fall, playfully sprinkling golden grain by golden grain onto Nzinga's head. They both laughed. When he left, he looked back at her, smiling and waving as he went on to his appointments in the palace.

Nzinga liked best the first part of winnowing any kind of beans or peas. There, they threw dried pods onto wide mats or bark-cloths spread on the hard, level earth and danced on the pods to music, breaking them with the weight of their twisting, dancing bodies, freeing the seeds within. Whenever Nzinga saw this, it was difficult to restrain her. She leaped onto to the heap of pods and danced in a rhythmic frenzy to the beat of the drums. When her nurse picked her up and coaxed her away, Nzinga often wiggled free and ran back again. Then, to the beat of the drums and the clapping of many hands, she danced and twisted her body, hands on hips, looking at them over her shoulders.

But if Chatembo was with Nzinga, the people stopped all work and turned it into a celebration. Nzinga was rhythmic in her movements, but Chatembo was a natural. Different parts of her body waved to the music from all the different instruments; even without music, Chatembo seemed to have instruments in her head. She delighted the women, who laughed and fell over in their work, pushing and pummeling each other and slapping their thighs in glee.

Nzinga didn't always dance. Sometimes she sat and studied the faces of the old women and listened to the musical cadence of their voices. She seemed never to tire of listening to their voices, whether they spoke the language of Ndongo or another language.

She watched their lips, and then afterwards she'd see one of the women and utter some phrase one had used. The women, recognizing the words, laughed. Nzinga was a favorite of these old women, who told her stories and let her sleep on grain sacks or on their laps when they rested. In this way, Nzinga learned many dialects early and also learned to love the music of the country.

3.
VISITORS FROM THE PAST

THE NGOLA'S PALACE AT MBACKA overlooked the Cuanza River. While growing up there, Nzinga and Chatembo often ran through the Mbanza gates to watch countless numbers of people rush to and from the palace. From throughout the kingdom of Ndongo and as far as the Kongo, paramount chiefs and subchiefs appointed by the Ngola came on their business, and these subrulers sent a part of their harvests and bounty to the Ngola.

Long lines formed at the outer gates: people laden with bunches of plantains, baskets of millet, freshly killed antelopes, caged wild boars, coops of chickens, bolts of bark-cloth, rolls of kente cloth, gourds, and pots filled with honey, beer, pepper, salt, wild onions, beans, and yams. Nzinga shied away from racks of crocodile skins or leopard skins.

Just as many people came bringing goods, those in need or those in the Ngola's favor came to get things from the royal stores. Oil and honey, meat and yams were dispensed to the king's soldiers or to the families of soldiers killed in battle.

When the two friends tired of gaping at the people, some in finery and others in old skins from the deep woods or wide valleys of Ndongo, they watched the women in their different modes of dress and their many hair styles. Some plaited their hair tightly around their heads, others with rows sticking out, and still others with hair like colorful, finely woven baskets, some raised high and some concocted into bird cages.

Nzinga and Chatembo at home mimicked the dress and hairdos of women, and they mimicked speech or the way certain women sat, and sometimes they put aromatic tooth-cleaning sticks in their mouths. Once Chatembo practiced half a day how to turn her head sharply and spit decorously through her teeth. They laughed at their own antics, bringing in Kambi and Funzi or girls from the village to watch them.

Once they invited Mbande and his friends Undolu and Mutele, but Mbande wouldn't even smile. Both he and Mutele complained when Undolu asked the girls to do one of their imitations again, calling Undolu silly. They threw their hands up in disgust, leaving the girls to wonder if they really were silly. But behind his friends' backs, Undolu waved and smiled at the girls.

Sufalu taught Chatembo to disappear from a room by simply fading into an ill-lit corner and, in a diversion created by throwing her voice to another corner, gliding out through any entrance. She could enter the same way. Both Chatembo and Sufalu appeared in rooms where people thought themselves alone, or left rooms where people thought Chatembo and Sufalu remained present long after they were gone. Sufalu once told Batayo, "If people think I'm there, to them I am there, although I may not be."

"I don't understand anything you said," Batayo said, a puzzled expression on her innocent face.

"I know it not as they see it."

"Know what?"

"Whatever there is to know."

Nzinga listened to this in the same way she learned and watched everything: the way people sat, the way they spoke to each other, the rising and falling rhythms and timbres of voices that excited her and made her smile with wonder and delight. But most of all, she liked to imitate warriors. She learned early to twirl a fighting stick and to turn somersaults, twist her body, and leap high from the ground, landing close to a person or far away. She loved to run until her chest hurt and her lungs ached. She loved to watch warriors in practice and the intensity of their efforts.

When Nzinga and Chatembo were twelve years old, they each took on a different appearance. Nzinga grew rounder and her skin blacker and smoother; Chatembo was lighter and straighter. Taller now, both girls wore aprons and loincloths, but their breasts marked their feminine growth. Thongs hung around their necks with amulets and medicine to keep away illness and magic. On one thong was a round ingot of iron: the Ngola, a symbol of their birth.

At about this time Chatembo's talents made themselves evident: Chatembo could change her shape and appearance. In a well-lighted room, she'd gradually change in animation and color, becoming one with the furniture, unnoticed. Yet in a darkened room her features were the clearest of anyone around. Sufalu had taught her the power of suggestion, how to change other people's perceptions. Chatembo said people with evil intentions could be made to use that evil on themselves.

When Nzinga asked Chatembo for an example to let her experience it, Chatembo shrugged. "It can happen only when someone does something to make it happen . . . something evil."

"Like what?"

"You will know it when you see it. You will be amazed."

One day, Nzinga and Chatembo went around to the side of the palace and stared out over the river, its dusky water flowing swiftly through the green foliage. They watched the fishermen casting out their nets, saw the silver flipping splashes of fish taken from nets, and listened to the fishermen calling to each other across the water. The river widened below Mbacka and in its flow were islands of green with luscious fruits and many wild animals. Those islands were the favorite hunting places of the Ngola. Nzinga wished she might go there, but before she'd go anywhere, she must get used to another type of life.

•

At an early age, royal children were placed in the care of a patron who had his own land and village and whose duty it was to educate royal children. Because of the wars and the slave catchers, the Ngola wanted his children near him. He arranged for Sechende, the keeper of children, to live near the Mbanza in a new village made especially for children. The Ngola saw the children whenever he desired and took an interest in their upbringing. He appointed special people to visit and report on the education and day-to-day care of the children. The Ngola was at war; the danger in the savannah forced him to guard them more closely.

Nzinga, Chatembo, and other palace children were to go to this village, which lay a bush mango's roll from the Mbanza gate. One morning she and her sisters wrapped their belongings in bark-cloth and bushbuck skins and tied them in neat bundles. With the move of the children to the village, Batayo's soft heart was broken, her chin quivering at the sight of her children preparing to leave the Mbanza. Sufalu, at her side, admonished the girls to obey the keeper but to use their own good sense.

Then they were joined by a grinning Kaningwa.

"I don't know what the bother is," Kaningwa said, with unusual good humor. "My girls have grown up there and left. Now Mbande has been there for nearly four rains. You can see he's doing just fine. You see how tall and handsome he has grown."

"He's a boy . . . and he's pampered," Batayo said quietly.

"Not any more than any of the children, but he deserves it. He's the heir."

Kaningwa acted the part of the dutiful mother to Nzinga, helping her to tie her bundle, but now, having made her point that Batayo might as well not try to have a son, Kaningwa rose to leave.

"Children at the village will be well cared for. Servants will take full care of them." Without a look back or a soft word to the children, she quit the room.

Sufalu and Batayo delayed the children's departure as long as possible.

•

Nzinga and Chatembo played Chatembo's favorite game, disguising themselves and changing voices. Chatembo could sound like a boy or man. They loved to throw bows and quivers over their shoulders, disguising themselves as young warriors. Before they left the Mbanza, they played this game on their mothers. They came in dressed as boys, small capes around their shoulders, their heads wrapped in scarves. They held staffs, like boys who herd cattle. Nzinga remained still, so her movement didn't reveal their identity. Chatembo told a long story about stolen cattle. Batayo became so interested in the story that, at first, she didn't question the identity of the two strange boys, but Sufalu said right away, "Chatembo, you must disguise your big feet. I'd know them anywhere."

Nzinga fell over laughing, pleased because Chatembo always blamed her when they were discovered.

The children formed a line and headed for their new home, accompanied by servants. Nzinga learned long afterwards that some servants were sent by Sufalu to take care of all the children, but that Kaningwa had also sent a spy to protect her son Mbande and to report Nzinga's every move.

The village for royal children was on a small lake fed by the Cuanza River. The river itself was known for hippopotamuses and crocodiles, but the land around the village had been cleared. A fence cut across the stream connected to the Cuanza, with slats that allowed water to flow into the lake but kept the crocodiles out. The village houses and gardens sat above the hillside of this well-guarded lake, where fishermen dug out a large pool surrounded by smooth rocks.

On those rocks Nzinga and the village children bathed, hung clothes to dry, and brought goats, sheep, and cattle to drink. Around this lake they cut reeds and made flutes, sang, played music, and danced. On the hillside above, they hid in the grass, made grass houses, and collected thatch and brought it on their heads to the village women who thatched their huts.

Life was not all play. The children had to help collect yams and cassava from the gardens, and bush mangos and chinguivela from the trees.

And, of course, there was school. Sechende, the royal keeper during Nzinga's time, was an old soldier popular with the children. He was selected by the Ngola according to custom and went through extensive training. His experience and knowledge of the Ndongo people were tested by the trusted chiefs whose sons and daughters grew under his care. He demonstrated a good memory, knew the history of the Ndongo people and their beliefs, and knew the clans, their ancestors, and all taboos, which he taught to the children. He recited the history of the Ngolas, how the tribe and kingdom were started, how new kings were chosen. He hated any enemy of Ndongo, especially the Portuguese, another reason why the Ngola selected him.

"Children must be taught early to recognize their enemies," he often said.

The royal keeper used wisdom, wit, and humor to tell the stories. He also brought along other people at different times to help teach the children. Long after children left the village, they remarked on his goodness and humor, and asked if old Sechende was still the keeper.

In the center of the village was a large house with a huge front door that always stood open. The children ate all meals in this house and met daily during monsoon rains or on extremely hot days. They took a nap there during the middle of the day. In the evening, just before darkness fell, in front of the house a crackling fire with leaping yellow flames flared, and all children came running from their games or sleeping house and sat in a half circle near it, facing two or three elders who told stories.

Nzinga sat on the ground with a bark-cloth or soft gazelle skin over her crossed legs and looked into the fire. When stories were told of the bygone heroes of Ndongo, Nzinga saw the ancestors live again, leaping through the flames. They weren't dead, but were always with the living. While a story was told, she studied the ancestral shrine where the seers kept gourds filled with palm wine for the spirits to drink. She saw her grandmother. She saw that long-ago blacksmith elephant hunter come to the shrine, put down a captured reed-buck from his shoulders, and drink from a gourd.

•

A griot who traveled around the country came to visit the royal children and stayed for what seemed to Nzinga years. Though he was there for only one dry season, so much happened that it seemed much longer.

First, the boys had to learn to play the drums, and girls learned the soft rattle instruments and the flute. Temarku, a chief's son, played many types of instruments; he was especially a wonder on drums. Although girls weren't supposed to play them, it was his sister who taught him. She showed how to strike the drum at different spots to obtain different sounds.

During these sessions, the royal children danced and drummed until it seemed impossible to stop. Nzinga began to think she was back in the palace, with her father and mother at a great feast, and all people who had ever lived came. Everyone was happy and made plans for how to drive out the Portuguese so that they could possess their own country again.

When she awoke the next morning, Nzinga didn't remember going to bed. The children had danced and sung until they were thoroughly tired. The elders, wanting this time of music and play to be forever a part of the children, let them go on to the point of exhaustion, so the children's senses fused memory and music and stories into experience.

One night when the old griot was still there, late after a busy day at games, the children yawned following several stories, many dances, and much laughter. A very old person sat next to Nzinga, a woman who held Nzinga's hand and smiled affectionately. Among the other children were more old people, wrinkled women and men. Two others sat on colorful mats in front of Nzinga. The old ones among the children wore shawls and the finest colored kente cloth, many holding musical instruments, some of regal demeanor. She didn't recognize them, yet they seemed familiar. Drums sounded from across the lake, keeping up a steady rhythm for a time. And then light appeared, like a village of torches that swayed to the beat. The sound of a bushbuck horn shattered the night like a gourd or like a clay pot when it falls full of water on stone.

While the drums were far away, they sounded soft, slow, and sad; as they drew nearer, the drums took on a faster, more hurried beat. Nzinga's heart pounded, and a lump formed in her throat. Her hair rose at the nape of her neck. She was frightened in a way, and then she wasn't. The lights and drums came nearer still. Then dancers emerged from across the lake into the clearing, dancing a furious dance in front of the fire. They were dressed in robes trimmed in raffia ribbons that swung as they danced. They wore masks with both human and animal features.

The music alternated between soft, soothing sounds and loud, urgent sounds, as if the dancers and the drummers were trying desperately to communicate a message. The masked ones danced and leaped up to the children. One poked the mask so close that Nzinga could have touched it, but she didn't dare. Then one of the unmasked ones put a bushbuck horn to his lips and shattered the night again with delicious sounds that tore into Nzinga. Out through the night, over the lake water and into the hills, the sounds echoed, and beams of light and flashing reflections mixed with the sound.

The masked ones called, as if they'd wake the whole kingdom, or indeed, they were the whole kingdom. When another came near Nzinga, he blew on a large reed-buck horn, giving out a deep, haunting sound that changed the tempo, an urgent sound no one dared ignore or disobey. The flames of the village fire leaped about the retreating dancers. While the children watched, the dancers and drummers and the horn blowers circled them and then faded back into the darkness across the night.

Nzinga watched until the last glimmer of light and the last sound faded, riveted to where she'd seen the old ones beside her and sitting among the children. Now the places were vacant where they'd sat in their colorful dress, their wrinkled, warm friendly smiles—all gone, as if it had been a trick of the eye, the ear, and the mind.

The children seemed as puzzled as Nzinga and asked the old griot and Sechende to explain what had happened. The griot said, "Believe what you saw. Your eyes and ears are fresher than my old ones. You saw it with your eyes. What do you think?"

.

Nzinga loved her new home and felt that this part of growing up was important. She never complained, but she felt cut off from her father and the daily life of the country. This village exposed them to danger while making sure they were protected.

Nzinga learned just how dangerous it could be. During the first days at the village, the griot took them to the river's edge to see the fishermen, who were also the king's guard. They prepared nets from reeds and lianas, set their traps, and pulled in the big river perches, flipping silver sides in the sun. While the men worked, crocodiles lurked nearby awaiting a careless moment. Whenever a crocodile boldly came after a worker who seemed to have drifted too far into the water, the fishermen ignored it until the crocodile was almost upon them. Then they surrounded it, stabbing it with spears and sharpened stakes. The captured animal was brought ashore, skinned, cooked, and eaten. The skin was cured and stretched, to be used as a trunk for storage or the seat of a stool.

And the children had been warned of the danger.

4.
A Snake at the Royal Village

DANGER CAME TO NZINGA from an unexpected direction. The boys at the end of the compound practiced with their weapons. Nzinga paused to watch them when she should have selected a water pot and hurried to join Chatembo and the other girls, who already had pots on their heads to fetch water and were near the lake. A servant woman known as Tashana thrust a pot at Nzinga, smiling.

"This is a good one."

Nzinga thanked her and put the circlet of grass buffer on her head, set the pot atop it, and with her hands to her side, swaying, hurried to join the girls. At the lake, the girls put pots on the rocks in the sunshine and went to bathe in the coolness where the stream ran down from the mountains over rocks into a clear pool with a sandy bottom. One side of the stream was shaded by tall tulip trees that lined its banks.

After playing in the water, splashing it on each other, scrubbing their heels with grass, and comparing who had done the best job cleaning herself, they teased one chief's daughter whose breasts were already as full as a woman's. Then they began their usual contest to see who could be held under water longest without waving their arms, frantically asking to be let up. They dried off and lay on the rock in the sun until Tashana came to get them for the noonday meal.

The girls scrambled among the rocks to gather up their pots. Nzinga was surprised that her pot's mouth was sealed off by a twist of matted grass. She pulled the grass plug out, feeling something heavy move inside. She bent to look and then suddenly dropped the pot.

She remained fixed to the spot on the rock while a heavy-bodied creature began to slither out. Its body rose slowly in front of her less than an arm's length away. The snake's head and neck flattened out to form puffed wings on the sides of the head as it wavered from side to side, its tongue flicking.

A dry anticipatory laugh cracked the air. No one could say exactly from where it came, but two girls near Nzinga, dipping their pots in the stream, looked toward Nzinga and saw the snake's scaly head rising from the pot. They ran away screaming.

In a flash, Chatembo appeared in back of the rock with a long stake. If she hit the snake, it would strike Nzinga, so Chatembo tapped the pot that still held the back end of the cobra's body. The snake swiftly turned toward Chatembo, who was already running. Nzinga slid safely into the water. Tashana screamed and kept screaming until men came and killed the snake.

For the first time since the girls had come to the village of royal children, Sechende canceled the afternoon games and the big fireside meeting. The children used the time to search their belongings thoroughly. They brought everything out in the last rays of sunshine and unwrapped the bundles with sticks. Nzinga and Chatembo still puzzled over how the snake came to be in the jar.

"There are people who make pots," Chatembo said.

"And people who catch and sell snakes," Nzinga said.

"These potters and snake catchers all work for Ngola, his chiefs, or their wives," Chatembo said.

"Wives," both girls said in unison.

As a standard rule throughout the kingdom, everything had to be reported to the Ngola immediately. Sechende sent word to the Ngola that his daughter had barely escaped a cobra's bite.

The next morning, Sufalu arrived with several attendants who carried rolled bark-cloths and water pots. They immediately set to work digging trenches around the buildings, replacing roofs, and searching the entire village and everyone's belongings. Sufalu hugged Chatembo and Nzinga and went to sit with them under an ancient rubber tree near the path at the bottom of the hill. From there, she and Sechende directed the work.

She listened as the girls described what had happened at the bathing pool. When they finished, she said, "I thought it was as you say." She then told Sechende and the griot, in front of everyone, "Part of the snake's tail is dead, but its body and head is still alive." Everyone looked puzzled. She said, "If you kill the head of the snake, its tail will also die, but if you kill only the tail of the snake, the snake will grow another tail and go on living."

"You," she pointed to the men who killed the snake, "you killed the tail. The head still lives." The men looked at each other and got up to bring Sufalu the dead snake, but she bade them sit. "A part of the snake's body is here, in this village, among us. I am the *Mukono ya Ngola*—the arm of the king—and I will make it kill itself."

She searched through the crowd. Her eyes fell on the men and women of Ndongo, searching for servants sent by different chiefs and their wives to take care of specific children. She asked Sechende who sent each of the servants. Most had been picked by Sechende and his assistants. Finally, only one servant was left whom a chief hadn't sent.

Sufalu's eyes swept the crowd without seeming to take notice. She watched Tashana, who averted her eyes and tried to shrink and become unnoticed in the crowd. Sufalu said to all the serving women, "Bring me those pots we filled at the Mbanza."

The many pots were heavy and sealed with a twist of matted grass. Tashana went to help, making two trips and bringing four pots. Each time, she brought one pot on her head and one in her arms. She started to go away after setting the pots in front of Sufalu, but Sufalu motioned her to stay.

"I brought simsim seeds. Take them from the pots and put them into these gourd bowls in front of me."

"Please, mistress, don't concern yourself with such a menial task. I'll do the job in the kitchen and bring them to you when they are done," Tashana said.

"No, Tashana, I want it done now, here," Sufalu said. "But perhaps you don't know how I want it done. Watch. I'll show you how. Then you will do it."

Nzinga watched as Sufalu held each pot, one after the other, between her knees. She closed her eyes, and with each pot she touched one of the amulets on her neck and mumbled several incoherent phrases. Then pulling the grass seals from a pot, she violently thrust her hand inside to the elbow, wiggled it around inside, then slowly, while looking directly at Tashana, brought out a handful of simsim seeds and dropped them into the giant gourd bowls. She did the same for the other pots.

Each time Sufalu brought out her hand, Tashana looked closely up and down Sufalu's arms and seemed surprised. She glanced around and bit her bottom lip. She searched the medium's face and each time looked away at the pots, a perplexed expression flitting across her face.

Finally Sufalu resealed the pots with the grass. "Now, Tashana, do as I commanded you."

Tashana knelt. Her hands shook as they reached out for the mouth of a pot. Her knees inched back from the pot. She looked beseechingly at Sufalu, whose expression didn't change. Tashana finally found courage. She lifted the pot, and a dry laugh cracked the air as she stuck her arm into the pot and brought out scoop after scoop of simsim, the small seeds making a *brrrrring* sound like rain on dry banana leaves. She gazed at Nzinga and the rest.

When finished, she went on to the second pot. And now it was evident that the laugh came from Tashana. Nzinga recognized that laugh: Tashana thought she was winning. Nzinga considered Tashana's peril in contesting with one as wise as Sufalu, though she didn't understand the meaning of the contest. She only knew she was glad not to be in Tashana's place. Perhaps Tashana was saying to herself, *"If this is some trick to test my innocence, to see if I fear the contents of the pots, to test whether I put the snake in the pot, this Arm of the King is no match for Tashana from the Kongo. I, too, have seen some things."*

Nzinga and Chatembo sat watching. Tashana reached for the third pot. Nzinga heard again her voice, as when she'd headed for the lake and Tashana had pushed a pot toward her, saying, "This is a good one." She also saw that the pot's mouth was sealed with twisted grass. *But why would Tashana want to kill me with snakebite?*

Tashana gave a dry laugh as she pulled the grass plug from the fourth pot. She bent forward, thrusting her hand into the mouth of the pot. Then Tashana suddenly paused.

Nzinga heard a dry slithering sound and saw a hooded head follow Tashana's hand out of the jar and rise up in front of her. The circle of watchers drew their breath at the same moment, quickly leaning away from the fearsome scene.

Tashana still held the pot. As she let go of the pot and attempted to rise and scoot away, there was a blur and three soft, muffled whiffs as though the snake kissed Tashana three times. Tashana was up on her feet, wild-eyed with terror, pushing through the crowd, heading uphill toward the Mbanza. She dashed without looking back. Nzinga felt her heart race faster, beating at her temples.

Tashana was far uphill, legs flying up and down before becoming limp. She wobbled unsteadily, with flailing arms. One hand caught at her throat. Then she fell heavily to the ground.

Though shocked and fearful, Nzinga and the other children ran to the fallen woman, who twitched, convulsed, and finally lay silent and still.

"Now the snake's body is dead. The head still lives somewhere," Sufalu said.

Nzinga and Chatembo clutched each other, then they ran to Sufalu, expecting her to be hurt, bitten by the snake that had killed Tashana. But Sufalu sat before them. Chatembo said, "I saw you put your hand in all four pots. The snake could have killed you."

"Where is the snake?" Sufalu asked.

The girls looked at the pots. No second snake was killed.

"We all saw the snake that bit Tashana," Nzinga said.

Sufalu sighed. "It was Tashana's snake. She started it. You saw Tashana see the snake. She died from what she believed. She believed it so strongly that she made you see the first snake the second time."

Sufalu held out her arms. "See, no bites."

◈

5.
THE MEETING HALL

THE REST OF THE TIME that Nzinga and Chatembo spent at the royal village was full of adventure and learning. Soon they were spending time around the palace again. While Chatembo was trained by her mother to be a spirit medium, princesses like Nzinga had no definite future. They found a useful job that supported the Ngola and did it. Nzinga learned languages because her father spoke many African languages and knew some Portuguese.

So Nzinga sat in the back of the great meeting house listening to her father, their chiefs, and the army commanders. Her brother Mbande, who needed the training more because he would become Ngola someday, had no interest in or patience with language or extended listening or discussion. He loved to hunt and to wrestle. In the company of his friends, usually Undolu and Mutele, Mbande often passed Nzinga sitting in the back of the meeting hall. He pointed a finger at Nzinga, laughing and wagging his head.

Nzinga kept her habit of sitting in the back of the meeting hall when the Ngola held court, sometimes accompanied by other children, almost always with Chatembo. Now and then Mbande, encouraged by their father, came in with his age mates and friends, but they remained only for a short time. Often they were inattentive and brought playful carvings that showed animals they hunted or miniature wooden disks with different engravings on each side. They flipped the disks and bet each other which side would show. Then they lost interest and went off to wrestle or talk about fishing nets.

Nzinga strained forward from the cramped space to see and hear. She liked it better when she was alone there, because she learned more without distractions. Sessions with the Ngola judging always began slowly. At first he and a group of elders, griots, seers, and priests talked about religious shrines, how the fences could be repaired, how more of them could be opened to the public for viewing and making offerings, how a priest would make the trek to Punga a Dongo to see the footsteps of the ancestral founders of Ndongo. Sufalu was among this group. They didn't think the Ngola made contact with the ancestors often enough. They reminded him that the only battle he'd ever lost was the one he entered without contacting the ancestors before he went.

When they said this, Nzinga leaned forward. The hair on her head bristled at the memory of the royal village and how the ancestors in the form of old people came with light and the sound of the bushbuck horn across the lake. How they sat among the children, blessed them with music and laughter, and then left quickly, the way they'd come.

After that morning session, the Ngola called for his exercise. His selected opponents came in with sticks, and they held a quick moving duel with leaps and sounds of the sticks striking together as they parried and struck, feet hitting the floor rhythmically as they leaped and landed. This fast-paced, spirited exchange left the first opponent winded, but the king was refreshed and ready for the second. After another session, musicians and dancers came while attendants applied towels to wipe away sweat, and the Ngola put on fresh robes and slowly prepared for the next judging session.

While Nzinga watched all of this, Chatembo brought her a packet sent by her mother: taro and yams, still warm, wrapped in leaves by her mother's cook. The odor and warm moisture wafted to Nzinga's nostrils and made her salivate before she unwrapped the green leaves and felt the food with her fingers.

"Come on, Nzinga. Let's go dance."

"Dance?" Nzinga asked, eating while talking. "Where?" She brought the warm packet of food to her nose and smelled it. "There is cassava in this, too! Where is the dance?"

"Out under the big baobab tree. Temarku is on the xylophone. Kintu and the others are on drums. And there are zithers and flutes. You like the flutes." Chatembo swayed and twisted her body, playfully catching Nzinga's free hand and waving her other hand near her ear. "Listen. Can't you hear that?"

Nzinga caught the faint notes of the xylophone and the encouraging call of the drums. Her face broke in a smile. Though tempted, she said, "Thanks for the food, Chatembo." She stayed seated and kept eating.

"Come on." Chatembo pulled on Nzinga's hand.

"You go on. I might come later."

"But what are you doing here alone?"

"I'm not alone."

"I don't see anyone but the old people up there. Listen to that." Outside, the tempo of the drums rose and Chatembo broke into one of her dances, moving gracefully in the small spaces among the benches.

Nzinga caught her by the waist to stop her. "*Sheeee,* we must be quiet or they'll send us away. You go on. I'll come when I can."

"All right. They want you there. I'll watch for you."

■

Nzinga joined her friends. They were all playing and dancing under the baobab, including Mbande, who was a good dancer. However, he and his friends began to joke around and do monkey dances. The older children didn't like that and told Mbande and the boys to sit and watch.

Chatembo was a favorite dancer, and Temarku took over one of the drums. Nzinga played her flute, which she almost always carried. They all danced, but when all music except the drum ceased, Nzinga delighted the children with her animal movement dance. In a frenzy, her body responded to the rhythm, gyrating; her feet shook and lifted and fell while she laughed.

At this moment her father's litter bearers brought him close enough to watch. He gazed down at her amid the circle of children, a smile playing about the corners of his mouth. He didn't say a word, but two adult voices from among his group called, "Mbande, Mbande!"

Mbande left the circle and went over to his father. Nzinga heard her father say, "Get in that small litter there."

"Can I bring my friend Mutele?" Mbande asked.

"Bring your sister only. Someday, you'll need her more than any other friend." The Ngola's answer was curt, impatient.

The servants had been searching for Mbande for some time. They'd looked first among the fishermen down on the banks of the Lugalula River. Then they searched in the hunters' houses near the forest, but found only several dogs penned up in back. They thought Mbande had gone with the hunters and were about to visit a chief's house and *karall* when they happened by the baobab tree.

Nzinga was surprised but thankful that the Ngola asked her to accompany them. The small litter was big enough for two adults, but Mbande crowded against her, allowing her no room. She didn't want to cause any disturbance, so she bore it. She even tried to soothe his anger and disappointment at not being able to bring his friend.

"Mutele can come with you next time, Mbande," she said.

"What do you know?" he hissed quietly so his father wouldn't hear. "He'd have come this time if Father hadn't noticed you. Why don't you just jump out of this litter and run to Chatembo?"

When the Ngola's litter arrived at its destination, Nzinga was curious to learn that they were at the house of the sour-faced minister, Kadu, whom she'd watched many times judging and assisting the Ngola in meetings. Across the path from Kadu's compound, another chief, Oyimbu, waited with a group of women and men with tethered goats, baskets of chickens, and one cow.

It was a bright, sunny day. The compound had been decorated with cut banana trees, and everyone was dressed in an array of beautiful colors. They all fell to the ground at the sight of the Ngola. After long greetings of praise and the sounding of horns and drums, the king called everyone to rise and get on with the judging. Kadu was somber as usual, but he bowed often, smiling, when he addressed the Ngola. Nzinga tried to think what caused this unusual behavior. Finally everyone sat in a circle around the king's stool. Mbande and Nzinga sat at their father's feet.

"Oyimbu, now tell me what is this charge you have brought against Kadu. What is so urgent that I must come here to judge against my two great chiefs?"

Oyimbu said, "Ngola, mine, Rainmaker, the keeper of justice and law for all in Ndongo, my complaint is about stolen property. I have reports that my cows are in that enclosure of Chief Kadu. I can describe them to you. Their markings are like those of no other cows in this kingdom, and they are sleek and fat, while his cows are always scrawny."

The king listened and nodded. "Chief Kadu, what do you say to these accusations?"

"Chief Oyimbu is truly a great chief, but he is misinformed. This enclosure contains only my cows."

"What are the markings on your cows, Chief Kadu?" the Ngola asked.

With his right foot, Kadu drew a shape on the ground, like sticks crossing.

K V

He touched his forehead with his right hand. One of Oyimbu's women companions laughed aloud and then, controlling herself, turned her head. Kadu became brazen.

"They have those two signs cut in their ears. Both ears."

"What markings do you have on your cows, Chief Oyimbu?" the Ngola said.

"Ngola, only one ear of my cows is cut, and that one is cut almost all off," said Oyimbu.

"Then Chief Kadu, have your men open the enclosure for me. My children and I will inspect these cows." He took the hand of Mbande on one side and Nzinga on the other. As they approached the opening of the enclosure, he said softly to them, "Whatever you see or hear, say nothing. Don't let it show in your faces."

Inside, Mbande drew a sharp breath. Both ears of all the cows were cut almost all off, and one side wasn't completely healed. *They are clearly Oyimbu's cows,* Nzinga thought.

But when they rejoined the group outside, the Ngola said, "The cows inside belong to Chief Kadu."

No one spoke or made a sound. A few averted their eyes. Nzinga detected disappointment. But the Ngola had spoken.

He continued. "Chief Oyimbu has been misinformed. But because he lost cows and I'm proud of him as a great chief, I'll give him twice the number of cows that he lost. I have spoken, and this matter should not be talked of again."

Both chiefs shook each other by the hand. Kadu was effusive, trying to be the great host. The Ngola accepted and, at his sign, everyone applauded.

This whole matter puzzled Nzinga. She waited for the chance to catch her father alone so she could ask him to explain. But it took weeks, because he was almost always in a meeting, or away on business, or talking privately with her mother, Batayo. Once after a meal she stepped outside and found Mbande using a mallet and log, striking a gazelle's long bone, trying to get at the marrow. He'd bitten and chewed all the meat off the head of the boiled bone, but he loved to eat the marrow.

"Ho, Mbande." Nzinga greeted him. He sat on his heels, his back to her.

Glancing over his shoulder at her, he gave a perfunctory nod and struck the bone several times until it cracked, showing the gray, congealed prize. He ran a finger through it, capturing a streak of it that he wiped on his tongue. Mbande could have a servant crack the bones, but he loved to do it himself.

"What did you think of the judgment the Ngola gave at Chief Kadu's compound?" Nzinga asked.

"Kadu's a thief, and Father is too good to him. The people of Ndongo should be allowed to eat all of his cows," he said.

"Didn't you ask Father to explain it to you? Remember, he invited you to see it."

"No, I didn't ask Father. And, yes, I saw it. It's tiring to have to talk to people like that. It's a waste of the Ngola's time. Let them settle their own squabbles. I'd rather hunt."

"But Father must—"

"Nzinga, with wild animals all over the place, why do people waste time penning up cattle? Oh, yes, I know milk is good, but . . ." His voice trailed off, and he went back to striking bones with the mallet. Nzinga wanted to argue the point, but Mbande had lost interest in the topic. He kept up his hunt for marrow.

One day Nzinga found her father sitting on his stool in the meeting hall with only a few personal servants fanning him. She came near and waited until he raised his head from something he was contemplating and smiled at her. She sat by him, swelling with pride when she could get his attention, so she was almost too overwhelmed to speak.

"I have a meeting shortly. You look as if you want to talk about something," he said, his gaze encouraging.

"I want to ask," she said, "about the judgment you made at Chief Kadu's that time."

"Aha!" He laughed his deep, bass laugh. He looked around to see if anyone was listening. "I've waited for Mbande to come ask me about that. But it's you who always wants to know it all. Why? Why do you need to know?"

"I . . . I don't know. I don't think it's unusual to want to know answers. I can't say, but it's here," she pointed to her chest, "and here, also," pointing to her head. "I think about things until I know answers. I wonder why you made the judgment you did at Chief Kadu's house, when we all knew that Chief Oyimbu's cows were in his enclosure."

"You're right. But, you see, both of them are my chiefs. I couldn't declare one a thief and make them enemies of each other, or disgrace Kadu in front of his people. Instead, I'll take Kadu's cows and give them to Oyimbu, and let Kadu keep his honor. In that way, I bind both men to me, and they aren't enemies of each other. Kadu made a mistake that he will never make again. Oyimbu, Kadu, and I, all three of us, know that. They are my chiefs, and the people must still honor and respect them."

When he finished explaining and Nzinga had to leave him to his duties, his last words to her were these: "Now if only Mbande will come to ask the same question."

I wish he would, Father. But I doubt he will. As far as Nzinga knew, Mbande never did.

■

The Ngola's spies—men and women in tattered clothes, carrying baskets, mats, and gourds—sat in front of the Ngola. They could be taken for peddlers or servants anywhere in Ndongo. Their hair was unkempt and matted about their heads. They wore kente from other parts of Africa. Some wore fezzes and different colored robes. One appeared to have no teeth. What astounded Nzinga was that they sat in front of the Ngola, and the Ngola laughed and bantered with them, congratulating them. He playfully tapped one on the shoulder with his fly whisk and told her she'd earned the cows she wanted. He said to another man that his family would get additional land and all the grain and chickens they needed.

He called in a seer. It was Sufalu. She put pots all around, poured some liquid in them, and lit small medicinal vines that gave off a sweet, pungent odor. Smoke and fire rose all around them. Then, taking some yellow powder, she inscribed a circle on each of their foreheads. *The ring of the kingdom,* Nzinga thought, *the Ngola's ring of iron.* Sufalu disappeared from the hall. *Why did she leave? She should stay to hear the reports.* Then she reconsidered. Sufalu had picked these people and would know everything they told the Ngola anyway.

They told the Ngola that three Portuguese ships had arrived at Luanda from Brazil. Their captains, all dressed in finery, hats with feathers and swords flashing in the sun, had rushed from the docks to an audience with the governor. They informed him that a rebellion had broken out in Brazil, and he must urgently dispatch soldiers to assist the beleaguered garrisons there.

■

Two days later, most of the soldiers at Massangano and those in Luanda had boarded ships that hoisted anchor, raised sail, and set off for Brazil. This left the Portuguese with no one to make war or even properly guard the town.

It was an ideal moment for the Ngola to crush the Portuguese. But the Ngola had his own problems. His kingdom was neglected during the years of war, and he was always mindful that he must look after it first. Chiefs grew slovenly in duties such as collecting taxes, judging cases, and punishing offenders. No adequate account of the king's wealth in each county was forthcoming. A number of lesser chiefs in the Kongo, who had until recently recognized the Ngola as their sovereign, had begun to act independently. They didn't send delegations, they neglected to pay tribute, and they sent no hides, ivory, copper, grain, nor any part of their harvest of yams. These things required immediate attention.

What followed was not a truce, only a lull in fighting between the people of Ndongo and the Portuguese invaders. The presiding governor was recalled to Lisbon, and a new one had not arrived. It had been five years since Father Gouvieae, the sole priest in Ndongo, last received any message from Lisbon. During those five years, Nzinga had been the priest's student, learning to read and write Portuguese.

The Ngola's informants came to report, and when they finished, the Ngola dismissed them. Nzinga saw him glancing toward the curtained area at the back of the hall as if he wanted to know who might be listening. She'd hidden carefully. No one could see her, but apparently the Ngola thought Mbande was still there, listening and learning at his father's court. He walked a short way in her direction, calling, "*Yewe*, Mbande, come here now."

He called twice. Receiving no answer, he told a servant to see who was there and bring him forward. But Mbande had left long since, so there was only Nzinga, squeezed under a wicker chair. With the Ngola's last request, she came out, bowing as if she were a servant. "Ngola, sir, it is only me, your daughter Nzinga, watching, listening, and learning."

The Ngola had raised his arm in anger, but with her words he paused and dropped it. One of his ministers looked aside and stifled a smile.

"Where is Mbande?" he asked, puzzled. "I wanted to explain to him how to govern this country. Where is he?"

"He's coming back, I think." Nzinga never wanted to anger her father. She couldn't tell him that his only son wasn't interested in how the kingdom was run. She couldn't tell him that Mbande preferred wrestling and hunting to learning. Nzinga had bowed again and turned, on her way out of the hall, when she realized she hadn't yet been dismissed.

"Should I leave, sir?"

He came closer to her then, held out his arms, and hugged her. "Stop so much bowing. You are a princess. One bow every now and then to honor your father is sufficient. And don't go. Stay and learn. Learn everything."

He spoke to his ministers. "Let her learn everything. Let her go anywhere as long as it is no danger to her."

Later, she overheard her father tell Sufalu, "It was just like the night I first held her as a baby, when I came back from that battle near Luanda. She held onto my hand, looking me in the eye. Thinking everything was important. It made me think, 'Child, where did you come from and why on earth aren't you a male?' Suku and the ancestors know. But with her it doesn't matter. It matters only to us."

•••

Kadu, one of the ministers present that day, never smiled because, as he was fond of saying, he never saw anything worth smiling about. Kadu recounted this scene to his cousin Kaningwa, the Ngola's first wife. One of Sufalu's spies overheard and later reported Kaningwa's response.

"You see, that girl is a devil. She's everywhere, making mischief. Well, it will do her no good. Mbande is the only male child, and he will be Ngola. Still, she troubles me, and she bears watching. She wants to learn everything. For what, I wonder?"

◆

6.
FETISHES

WHEN WORD CAME THAT Batayo had given the Ngola a daughter and then died, Sufalu said it was from her disappointment at failing to produce a male heir. Nzinga heard the news and swept out through the palace gates and down the village road. She ran until her chest and body ached. She couldn't breathe for the crying and sadness. These lessened only when her father found her and coaxed her down from the twisted limbs of the baobab tree where she'd hidden, wishing she too could die.

But her father said, "I have lost her, but . . . come to your father, child. You still have me. I'm glad I still have you. Oh, Nzinga . . . we still have that memory of Batayo in you."

Together they returned to the Mbanza.

The Ngola's palace was an enclosure of strong, laced bamboo poles standing on a sloping hillside overlooking the Cuanza River. The inside puzzled visitors, with its many winding passageways laid out to guard the Ngola and the royal family from surprise attack, to confuse intruders while providing the Ngola with many avenues of escape. To one side was the *karall* for the cows, goats, and sheep; to another side were the quarters for the Ngola's soldiers and servants. In the center of this catacomb arrangement was the meeting house where the Ngola and his chiefs met to decide cases or make plans for war. The stores, where spears and knives and shields were kept, stood to the left of the entrance. The house of drums was alongside the blacksmith shop and the treasure shop, where all items of great value were stored: masks, cowrie, salt, sculptures, and Kongo silver and gold.

The living houses of the Ngola and his family were near the back, with a number of secret gates leading to the river. These were guarded by the rapids on the side toward Luanda and by the waterfalls toward Zaire. Outside the palace was an ambling village of people and spread for miles.

To the left of the palace was a road that ran for a short distance along the river bank before it swept out over the savannah and continued on for miles. It travelled first through the high grassland and bush past the hated fort at Massangano, then on to an open stand of baobab trees mixed with palms, until it finally reached Luanda. Nzinga didn't know that road, but she'd heard many tales of it all through her childhood. She hoped to travel it one day.

To the right of the Mbanza was the road that ran through the ambling village with its hillsides and scattering of baobab trees, until it led to a forest of more baobabs nearby. Nzinga knew this place from sad experience: that time when Funzi was born and the Ngola refused to see anyone. The saddest time invaded the palace then and wouldn't go away.

From the time when she was a young child, Nzinga was familiar with the inside walls that surrounded the Mbanza, for she often watched people decorate them with many colorful mats of various patterns. Sometimes she passed and greeted workers who were putting up black, red, yellow, brown, or gold panels on the outside walls of the Ngola's house, the entrance of which bore no door, but was always guarded.

One day, Nzinga passed by the special covered house with no walls where an old man kept constant vigil over the Royal Fire in the great fire pit. To one side of him were large stacks of wood and special flammable sticks and grasses. Nzinga had always known that every fire which burned in Ndongo had to be started from the fire of her father's palace. If by chance the fire were ever permitted to burn out, the keeper would be executed at once. When the king died, the fire would be extinguished and the keeper killed to accompany the king to the next world. The custom was the same with the king's cook. Upon the king's death, the cooking pots were broken and the cook killed. Under those circumstances, Nzinga thought, no one wanted the Ngola to die. Yet she'd seen many times that people were willing to die for their king and seemed to show no fear. Perhaps it was because the Ngola could raise up people and their families with a lift of his hands. He could make rain and make the crops to grow, which amazed Nzinga.

Going on her way, Nzinga went to visit Father Gouvieae, the Portuguese priest her father had captured several years before. At first the Ngola had kept him as a hostage, but later he gave the priest permission to stay in a house and have a small church near the palace. After being there for years, Father Gouvieae had made few converts. Those who accepted the Catholic religion were, like the priest's servants, thought to be spies of Sufalu and the Ngola, who watched the priest, because he often received messages and packages from Luanda. It was known that a few of Father Gouvieae's converts carried messages to Luanda.

Outside the Mbanza, she walked through the village and the short distance to the priest's house. Nzinga went to visit the priest almost daily after she'd been told by her father that she and her brother Mbande should learn Portuguese. Mbande seldom came. Sometimes she sat watching the priest's servants as they laid out his religious vestments. Other times she talked with the servants or listened to the priest speak his language. At each visit he taught her new words and phrases. He had a book called *Cartas* written by a man he knew in Lisbon, called a bishop. It described how the Portuguese went to other worlds in their ships. Over time, he showed her how to read it. Father Gouvieae also was busy with a book called a catechism. It was in another Catholic language that he was translating into Portuguese. He read his pages to Nzinga, asking with each sentence whether she understood the Portuguese words.

Later, she thought deeply about his reasons for talking to her and making an effort to teach her. *He's lonely and taught me so he'd have someone to converse with. Or he wants me to become a convert and then convert my family.* Whatever he wanted from spending time with her, she was an able student who learned quickly and always left him in better spirits than when she arrived. His favorite word was "patience."

"Everything," he was fond of saying, "can be accomplished through patience."

His favorite subject outside the catechism was history. When he was lonely and homesick, he liked to teach her about the history of Spain and Portugal, of the Moors from the north, the Muslims from the east, and the Holy Land. He talked of England and a queen called Elizabeth. Once, after receiving a letter from home, he spoke harshly of the English. It was the only time she remembered him speaking in such bitter tones. He said the English won a great sea battle over the Spaniards, all because of rough seas and an English captain known as Francis Drake. The priest said the English never invented anything themselves, that they were made of words. They could speak and write, but they roamed the world stealing ideas. He spoke of Holland and the Flemish priests such that Nzinga came to understand that he and his countrymen feared the Dutch.

When Nzinga approached the house one day, she saw bundles tied up in bark-cloth lying on the ground beside the entrance. She knocked on the door and called, *"Bom dia."* The priest let her in. His skin was sallow. He shook as if he were cold, then scrunched up his shoulders and fanned himself as if he were hot.

She studied his face. *Malaria, possibly.* She sat on her haunches. "Priest, you aren't feeling well?"

"Bom dia." His voice squeezed over his tongue, scratchy and uneven. "'Reverend,' child. I have told you the proper way to address a priest. Say 'reverend,' or simply 'Father.'"

Nzinga said yes out of politeness. Neither she nor any of the king's family would call him "Father" or address him as if he were a king.

When a servant set refreshments in front of them, Nzinga followed the fellow out of hearing range of the priest and asked quietly, "Excuse me, sir, do you know why this one is sick? Or what he's sick with?"

The servant flipped his wrist. "Do I know? It's a puzzle. But the skin is all yellow. His eyes are gone to greet his ears."

By the flashes of mirth and distaste that alternately illuminated and darkened the servant's face, Nzinga surmised that the servant fought within himself to remain serious. She knew it was degrading to have to serve a disliked foreigner, and it would have been a welcome relief to this soldier, posing as a servant, if his charge grew sick and died. Still, everyone knew that anyone, once given protection by the Ngola, was bound to receive the best treatment possible. Again, the servant flicked his wrists, turning his palms up, open in a questioning gesture.

"My child," he said, his voice rising, "these white ones are like chameleons. They can change their skins daily. Yesterday he was white. This morning he was pale, then blue, and now he's yellow. What can I tell you?"

Nzinga thought it was good that this priest hadn't been in Ndongo long enough to learn the language well. "Is this one getting good food?" she asked.

"He eats," the servant said. He bowed to them and backed from the room.

While the priest was talking, Nzinga sat thinking of the bundles she'd seen outside his house. She heard the word "pope." She'd heard the word before, but had never tried to pronounce it, thinking it was a title higher than that of her father's. She tried the word. "*Poorpe*, what is that?"

"Pope," the priest corrected her. "He is the holy leader of our church, God's representative on this earth. He gets his orders from God."

It was hard to make sense of this, but Nzinga knew some Portuguese. So that's how they conversed.

"Where is God?"

"He's in heaven."

"Is this heaven near Portugal?"

"No, it's up there." The priest looked up into the ceiling. "There, in the sky."

"Near those clouds?" Nzinga asked, following the direction of his eyes out of the small window. "Above Ndongo?"

"No, beyond that. And He sees everything, directs everything, everything we do."

"Did he direct the Portuguese to build a city in Luanda on my grandfather's banks along the bay?"

"He directs everything." The priest went outside and returned with the black cloth-wrapped bundles.

"Priest," Nzinga vied for his attention, "is he Portuguese?"

"Portuguese? Eh . . . no. He is just God, the creator of the entire world."

"But have you been to the house of Suku?" Nzinga asked.

"Suku? I've heard of him. Is he your pagan god?"

"Yes, the greatest of our gods," Nzinga said. "Punga a Dongo is the house of Suku. It's in those mountains, above the waterfalls. It marks the beginning of the land Suku gave my fathers. And my father, the Ngola, is the chosen one of Suku." She said what she'd been taught by her mother and by Sufalu, what she'd heard in stories all of her life, and what she'd seen and learned at the royal village.

"No, child, don't say so, for there is only one God."

"There are many gods, but Suku is the senior god," Nzinga said, "and it is shown in stone footprints at Punga a Dongo that my fathers were given this land by Suku to rule it and its people."

The priest sat in his chair, his brow knitted in thought. This chair, a bed, and one chest to hold his meager belongings were the only furniture in his house. He stared at Nzinga for a long time. Nzinga could tell that she'd said something he'd never heard or thought of before.

"Have you been to the place?" he asked.

"No."

"Then how do you know there is such a place?"

"How do you get to your heaven?"

"You enter it when you leave this world," the priest said.

"You mean you must join your ancestors? You must die to get there?"

"Yes, die, trusting in Jesus."

"But how do you know there is such a place?"

The priest paused. "We must have faith."

Nzinga said, "I don't have to die to see the ancestors. They're here around us. I don't have to die to see Punga a Dongo. My fathers were the ones who put lightning into the earth and made hoes and spears and knives. They knew fire-earth killed elephants. They made rain and thunder, and they came to earth from Punga a Dongo." At the end of this speech, she bowed her head.

While the priest sat in thoughtful contemplation, a question occurred to Nzinga. She hesitated to ask it, for although she felt he was the one needing religious teaching, he was still an elder. But she said it anyway.

"If you are the one God sent, why are you ill? I'm not being quarrelsome. I need to know this."

The priest was busy unwrapping the items that Nzinga had seen at the door.

"I'm in a strange land. I can't travel, and I can't obey my God because I am . . . a prisoner, and I . . . "

Nzinga changed the subject. "What are these things, priest?"

She pointed with her chin, wiggling her nose in the direction of the tied bark-cloth bundles that the priest was unwrapping. There were piles of masks and drums, monkey tails, and statutes of people with different expressions and wistful longing on their faces. Many pieces were from people captured in the latest war. All were things that ordinary people of Ndongo wouldn't touch. Such items, made by African spiritual leaders or artists, were created to cause something to happen.

"Pagan trinkets," he said. "Some of the captured people came to worship and left them. Anyone who comes into the Lord's presence must give up heathen worship. No idols. For the Lord sayeth, 'Thou shalt have no other gods before Me.'"

He went to the pile and, loosening one bundle, he held up a carved mask and a libation sacrifice pot. Then he held some figures with wooden pegs driven through them, and colorful colobus monkey skins with pockets of raffia sewn in that held herbs. Wild-eyed, Nzinga moved quickly away when he brought these things out. Her breath came in short gasps. There were great risks in handling spiritual things.

"No," she said. "Don't bring them near me. You don't know what you're doing." She shook her head from side to side, pulling back. "You should put those down."

Nzinga was near the door and had one hand on the latch.

"Why?" he said, as he placed a monkey skin as a rug beside his chair and put a mask to his face. In a flash, Nzinga saw him change in her imagination from priest to demon, to a dancer in the fertility dance, to an executioner, then to a slave seller, for those masks represented all of these things. Now she had a different view of the priest. And his church. He could be any of these things, at any time, for nothing was sacred to him.

"Aren't you afraid of those things?"

"Why should I be?" the priest said. "The devil cannot harm a servant of God."

Nzinga was still frightened. "Demons can harm anyone. No one but the spirit people who make them should touch them. What will you do with them, anyway?"

"When the Ngola lets me, I'll send some of my new converts to sell them in the marketplace to Portuguese farmers and traders."

"And what will the Portuguese do with them?"

"They'll sell them as curios in my mother country."

"What will you do with the money?" She wanted to know.

"I will use it to make God's Church here, in Ndongo."

Confused, Nzinga left him and went in search of Chatembo and Sufalu to ask questions.

The priest wanted to destroy and sell African religion to make a church. If these things weren't good for Africans to have, why did the Portuguese want them?

◆

7.
AN ELEPHANT HUNT

A S A RULE, ONLY MEN went on an elephant hunt: male trackers, male hunters, male cooks, male skinners. But a herd of elephants came near the palace while the Ngola and his ministers were away judging and meeting in another part of Ndongo.

The elephants made their way into a nearby *karall*, trampled and destroyed gardens, and damaged the villagers' crops of banana, cassava, and maize. After frightening people away from their work and homes, the elephants made for the nearby savannah and disappeared. Young warriors tracked and spotted the herd days before the king returned, and kept watch on their position nearby in a flat valley.

When the Ngola returned, his hunting party prepared to drive the elephants back into the forest. The best way to do this was to kill at least one bull elephant.

When the hunting party left the Mbanza, the Ngola arranged for Mbande to watch with the young warriors at a safe distance but near the actual hunt, as training for his participation as a weapons bearer at the next hunt. Nzinga and Chatembo begged one of the chiefs to let them stand on a hillside with the cooks and skinners. Because there was no danger, they were allowed to go with the cooks. The two girls dressed as herd boys in leather skirts, with colorful kente blouses thrown over their heads and cut short, just below the breast and tied firmly in the back. Each carried a spear.

The hunting site in the nearby valley was hemmed in by a cliff on one side and a forest on the other. From the high hillside, Nzinga had clear view of the entire hunt. Her father, with his general Shellanga and a group of hunters, waited downwind from the elephants. On the valley floor, the grass, taller than the men, moved in the distance. Then a hunter rose within the waving green, stealthy, stalking the herd. He flung into the air a handful of dried grass, then thrust his finger into his mouth and held it up to the air. *He's testing the wind. They don't want the wind to blow their scents toward the herd, or the elephants would smell them and stampede into the forest, then return in a day to do more damage.* She'd learned about that from listening to Mbande and his friends, for that was all they ever talked about.

"What are they waiting for?" Chatembo asked. "If they delay any longer, the elephants may decide to move away."

"Chatembo, look at those clumps of elephant grass." Nzinga pointed with her head toward a clump of shrubs and grass near the herd.

Chatembo stared for a moment, then exclaimed, "Are there other animals?"

"Chatembo, be quiet," Nzinga whispered. "You'll frighten the elephants, and we'll be in trouble. I think those are our warrior-hunters, creeping up on the elephants."

"But they looked like animals. Why do they have skins over their heads?"

"It's to trick the elephants into thinking other animals are near, but no people."

"*Oh, ho,*" Chatembo said.

Nzinga whispered, waving her spear playfully. "Let's sneak away from the cooks and attack that big elephant, the one over there, grazing alone."

"Nzinga! Don't you even say that, because I know you. If you think it, you'll do it."

Nzinga laughed. "Not this time, Chatembo. I'm impetuous, but not fool enough to think I could kill an elephant alone. If Father needs all these people working together, what could we do alone against that big bull?"

By this time, the hunters were so close to the elephants that they likely could hear the animals feeding. The call of an egret filled the air. The girls looked for one of those beautiful birds, perched on an acacia tree or in flight overhead, but there was no sign of one, even after several calls.

Chatembo whispered, "That's a signal. The goatherd boys use that call."

"That's right," one of the nearby cooks said. "The hunters are talking to each other in egret language. They'll start soon."

As if the cook had given the signal, one of the hunters threw off his skin cape, rushed out from the elephant grass into the clearing, and ran up to the bull elephant. With a powerful, fluid motion and a grunting sound that reached the hillside, he threw his spear. It struck the animal's mighty chest just inside the left front leg. Whirling in the same fluid motion, the hunter rushed back as the elephant chased him into the grass.

At this first sign of an attack, the herd ran away, leaving the bull elephant to stand and fight alone. One of the cooks near Nzinga said, "It's that Kajubi. He fears nothing."

Another cook said, "That's right. I've seen him fight a buffalo."

Chased by the elephant, Kajubi was about three elephant lengths ahead. The elephant was gaining on him, even with the spear shaft wobbling in its chest at each giant step. Kajubi grabbed a spear from a waiting spear bearer and turned abruptly as if to attack the elephant again. It would surely have meant Kajubi's death if he had, but at that moment, another hunter ran up and boldly speared the elephant from the side, near its right eye. The animal whirled away instead of crushing Kajubi or lifting him with his trunk, dashing him to the ground, and tearing him limb from limb.

Chatembo said, "That was Shellanga."

As the elephant chased Shellanga out into the clearing, Shellanga grabbed a second spear from the bearer. When he turned as if to attack, a giant figure of a man rocked back on his heels and delivered a spear thrust deep into the chest of the beast.

It was Nzinga's father, the Ngola.

The spear struck near the spot where Kajubi had first speared it. But this spear thrust was deeper. The animal paused and gave out a long, angry, wounded wail.

The Ngola, her father, was an elephant hunter, like his ancestors, whom people sang about on praise days at the shrines all over Ndongo. He continued the family tradition, as had his ancestors before him. This was the same man who sat regally on his stool, deciding cases and making decisions in his quiet, melodic voice. In this dangerous test of physical strength, he matched this powerful animal.

With the elephant chasing him, the Ngola whirled and ran halfway across the clearing to collect his spear. Then Kajubi and two other warriors drew the beast away with their spears. This went on for a long time, repeating and repeating, with the elephant turning and turning as he was speared again and again; now in front, then on the right, now on the left; it was rhythmic war dance with the elephant getting weaker and finally stumbling, yet not going down. The elephant refused to surrender to its attackers. Nzinga watched, entranced. The men looked small against the elephant, more than twice their height. It waved its trunk menacingly over their heads, the ivory-white, pointed tusks threatening to impale them. As the elephant ran, its heavy body destroyed the shrubs underfoot. As it swayed rhythmically from side to side with its attackers, its tail waved straight behind.

Do Father and the others aiming their spears feel the dreadful wail of the trumpeting animal reverberate through them?

Can they see the animal's fierce eyes, hear its fearful breathing?

Can they see the deadly pointed tusks near their chests? See the wrinkled skin of the large, fan-like flapping ears? Do they see the powerful legs and feet that can stamp out a life?

Can they smell the acrid odor of the piles of dung around them?

Are they afraid?

The drum beat was like a dance, with the same rhythm. The hunters, who'd been silent in the attack, took up a chant that encouraged each other and placated the spirit of the dying animal. The cooks, skinners, and butchers waited, also chanting and cheering.

That's when Chatembo began clapping her hands to the rhythm. Nzinga joined in.

"I want to do that." Nzinga waved her spear to the rhythm of the chants. "I want to hunt elephants one day."

"Nzinga," Chatembo said, "the poor animal is dying. Yet all you think about is doing the same things as men."

"Why do men get to do everything, while we can only sit and watch?"

"It's worth it to watch Kajubi," Chatembo said. "He's the only young one among those old men. Don't you think he's beautiful, Nzinga?"

"Oh, yes." She watched the elephant's last, feeble efforts. It had lost so much blood that it couldn't stand much longer. It trumpeted with a last heart-rending call that shook the forest and sent a chilling vibration through Nzinga. It sank down to its front knees before collapsing heavily and rolling onto its side in the clearing. Then all was silent. The hunters didn't approach the fallen elephant immediately. They withdrew a short distance and waited, as though they thought the animal might regain its feet. Nzinga had heard once how an elephant, thought to be dead, suddenly stood and rushed the hunters, caught two of them, stomped one hunter and broke many of his bones, then seized another with its trunk and dashed him against a tree.

The cooks sent down refreshing drinks to the hunters. These were consumed leisurely, while the hunters sat on their heels and talked, before any of them cautiously approached their fallen prey. Kajubi and the Ngola went first, and soon all of the hunters gathered around it.

Shellanga pulled its tail. Its trunk quivered once and after that no part of the animal moved. The warriors signaled the butchers to come down. The cooks and servers brought water to help the hunters wash themselves and poured palm wine to refresh them.

8.

KAJUBI

BEFORE THE NGOLA'S DRUMS were sounded to congratulate him on a successful hunt, Shellanga asked the Ngola to listen to Kajubi's body drum.

Amused, the Ngola asked, "What is this body drum?"

"In the place where Kajubi lived before we found him, they did this body drumming after a hunt to send the spirit of the animal away after it had been killed."

"Let's see this body drum," the Ngola said. Only the king's general, spear bearers, and perhaps the cooks were prepared for what they saw next.

Kajubi was about eighteen years old, a little over six feet tall with a well-proportioned, muscular body. Bare to the waist, his skin coppery and lean, he stood before the Ngola. With one palm open and one fist rolled, he began tapping his body in different places, his chest, his sides, his abdomen, the back of his neck; he opened, then closed his palm over his mouth. Each spot he touched gave off an assortment of notes that Kajubi arranged into a composition. When he struck and breathed out, a different sound rushed out. When he inflated his body with air, the sounds were different. All the while, he danced and leaped in the air, his feet striking the earth and keeping up a drumbeat that underscored his body-beating rhythms. Throughout all this, a long guttural sound issued from his throat.

The sound and rhythm of this body drum floated up the hills and echoed up and down among the people there. Chatembo threw her head back and moved her feet, and soon Nzinga and the entire group on the hillside danced to Kajubi's body drum. The hills rang with it, and animals seemed to pause in their grazing, as if puzzled.

Nzinga and Chatembo, watching from the hillside, sighed in admiration. Nzinga thought it the most disciplined, beautiful thing she'd ever seen. Chatembo reached over and scratched Nzinga on the knee playfully. They smiled at each other. When it was over, everyone but the Ngola applauded.

It wasn't common for a king to applaud, but the Ngola asked for a long stick. He threw it down on the ground in the clearing with great force to signify that he had spoken. He definitely approved of this body drum.

Chatembo said, "What do you think of that one?"

Nzinga said, "He's quite good at drumming."

But Chatembo whispered to her, "Nzinga, we have many drums in Ndongo, but few bodies like that."

That day Kajubi had amazed the royal family, but nothing he did surprised the cooks. They'd known about his talents and his courage since he had first served with them as an assistant.

"You haven't seen anything until you have seen him run and fight," said a thin cook, who seemed to be looking elsewhere when he glanced at a person. "Just ask Chief Shellanga. And you wouldn't believe what Kajubi has lived through, let me tell you."

Nobody knew Kajubi's home village or his people. He'd been captured when he was seven. His first captors found that Kajubi was strong for his age and quick to be of service, so he was kept instead of being sold to slavers. He'd served as a cook and spear bearer for warriors and hunters in many places. He'd traveled for years, through all kinds of climates, sometimes starving for days, always trying to make himself stronger. When others went on cleared paths, he walked in the rough places alongside where the twigs, briars, and thorns punished his feet into toughness. When given a job, Kajubi practiced running while doing the job, not because he was subservient, but because he wanted to keep his body alert and toned. He'd been captured, sold, and traded five times before Shellanga conducted a raid among his most recent captors in the Kongo. The defeated chief wanted to please the Ngola's general. So in dividing the captured people, that chief sent Kajubi to Shellanga, who then sent the young man to work with the cooks. The Ngola didn't know Kajubi's true worth when he first saw him. But Kajubi soon proved he was valuable as a leader of young warriors.

Although it didn't show at first, Nzinga liked Kajubi right away. Kajubi was a warrior and much more, like Nzinga's father. She watched Kajubi for many reasons, but then, she'd always loved to look at warriors: the set of their jaws and the intense, focused manners and gestures that came over them when they fought or when they laced on their weapons and prepared their bodies for battle. She often imitated them when she was alone—jumping high, kicking, presenting a fighting stance.

Kajubi was also like Nzinga, wanting to know everything. He expected life to be a challenge and wanted to be ready for anything. He was kind and thoughtful, and his hard life hadn't destroyed his love of beauty and music.

As Nzinga grew up watching him, she often wondered if he ever laughed. She'd love to make him laugh. She'd love to see that strong, nice, serious face break open into a grin, followed by the full happiness of a complete laugh. She smiled privately, thinking of him.

9.
THE MARKET

B Y SITTING AT THE BACK of the meeting house, listening to the Ngola and his ministers talk, Nzinga learned the Ngola's plans for future months. They would pursue limited wars with tribes in the Kongo in an effort to renew the Ngola's control there. His chiefs, on his orders, would look after their counties, renew the appointment of old subchiefs, or select new ones. The Ndongo people would be told to double their farming efforts, so that they'd have goats and cows to share with the Ngola's army during the war that was sure to come.

The Ngola also ordered the markets be opened. In this way, Portuguese trade goods would become available, including guns and powder the traders had hidden. The Portuguese army usually forbade the sale of arms, but its manpower was now limited. The trade in beads, tobacco, chickens, grain, beans, and the new maize could spread. New cultivation could enrich the country. More people would plant, and storage bins would bulge against a dry season or future poor harvests.

People went once a month to the largest markets, which were held on different days in different parts of the country. During market week people traveled long distances, carrying their trade goods on their heads and shoulders: women swaying with baskets full to the brim with garden vegetables and mint, or with stacks of woven baskets and mats; men carrying carcasses of reed-bucks and wart-hogs, hippo meat, animal horns, ivory tusks, live crocodiles, rats, lizards, grubs, and locusts.

Depending on how far they had to travel, it took several days to reach the market site. Chiefs led caravans of people who carried animal skins, aromatic wood, melons, captured monkeys and other animals, bright red-and-yellow hornbills, and jungle birds. They also hauled smoked fish, Ashanti peppers, coffee, and novelties from the Portuguese: dried tobacco leaves and red peppers. People on the roads often stopped peddlers who carried gourds of all sizes and shapes, some filled with honey, others with beer or palm wine, and still others just empty containers.

The people of Ndongo differed greatly from one another across the kingdom. The many past wars resulted in people moving and tribes intermixing and marrying. Some were tall, like the people of the inland lakes; others were the size of young children, like the people of the Ituri forest; and many others were of average height. All were robust and strong. Their skins glistened in tones from very black to light brown. Along the trade roads, travelers spoke many languages and dialects, yet somehow most of the travelers learned to understand each other.

The market came as near as it was allowed to the Ngola's palace, which was about a day's travel away. Market days always gener-ated sustained excitement, but two days before one market opened, an alarm sounded—the Ndulu, a loud, abrasive sound made by blow-ing through pursed lips while vibrating the hand on and off the mouth. The Ndula was to be made only when something terrible was happening. The Ndulu jarred right through Nzinga where she sat on a papyrus mat, listening to an old woman instructing young married women: never borrow salt from a neighbor after the sun goes down.

Nzinga ran to find the reason for the Ndulu: Temarku had dis-appeared during the night. His zither, xylophone, and small drums remained at his sleeping mat in his parents' house, but no one could remember where they'd last seen him. He was the son of a chief and one of a large group of musicians who played for dances whenever boys and girls met for a nighttime festival. Temarku was a favorite among the children of Nzinga's age set, having grown up with them in the royal village. *Temarku is a great part of the music,* she thought, *the life of Ndongo.* An apprentice to the Ngola's drum makers, Temarku helped select trees to cut and store until the wood was seasoned for drum making. He knew the ritual for driving out a tree's spirit, so it wouldn't inhabit the drum when they finished it. He also selected the skins the drum makers stretched across drum ends and the pebbles that went into the drums.

People arrested for an offense often disappeared in Ndongo, whispered about but never seen again. Sometimes a person who committed a crime was executed on the spot by the king's guards or soldiers, or by everyone who threw stones until the accused fell dead. But Temarku had committed no crime. He was liked and was normally seen every day in the village.

People asked, "Where is Temarku?"

Nilano, a girl who brought goat's milk in gourds from the villages to the Mbanza for cheese making, sat down on the path under a tree. She was soon joined by Nzinga, Chatembo, and some of the other girls. Since Nilano had arrived after the Ndulu had sounded, she knew nothing of the crisis and was surprised at all the attention they paid her. She believed Nzinga was interested in milk or cheese. Her eyes wide and anxious to please, Nilano explained the cheese wasn't ready.

"Nights have been cool. We need steady hot weather to make cheese. But I have cow's butter." She showed them the wooden bowls wrapped in banana leaves. "And I have this big gourd of fresh milk, just taken this morning."

The girls shook their heads. "We're not interested in cheese or milk, Nilano. You go from village to village. Have you seen Temarku?"

Nilano glanced from one to the other, shaking her lovely head and smiling, thinking they accused her of secretly loving the boy. "But I don't even . . . I have never . . . "

Chatembo added, "He's missing. We hoped that since you travel, you might have seen him or heard something."

Nilano was relieved. She sat back down. "He's not anywhere about the palace, then?"

"No, he was in the village. His instruments are still there where he slept. Soldiers searched for him, but came back with no news."

"*Aieee*, what's to be done?" Nilano asked. "I was afraid to travel the road today, for I heard the *pombeiros* are in our parts. You know they steal people and sell them as slaves. But I'm lucky, because I have this." She fingered the smooth rings cut from a goat's horn that hung from a leather thong around her neck. The rings proved she was in the Ngola's service and couldn't be stopped or molested by anyone. "Also, many people are on the roads, going to the market."

They accompanied Nilano back to the Mbanza. The girl, glad she'd made it back safely, repeated a flood of gossip she'd heard in the village where she'd received the milk. "The chief is angry with his servants, especially those captured in the war and given to him by the Ngola. He says they are letting leopards get to the Ngola's cattle and goats. It's also said in the village that the chief traded a servant to the *pombeiros* for beads."

"When did this happen?" asked Chatembo. "It's against the Ngola's orders."

Nilano, who had a full gourd of milk on her head and butter bowls in one hand, could only gesture. She turned her left wrist up and outward. "I don't know."

The more Chatembo and Nzinga talked about Temarku's disappearance and market day, the more they became convinced the two events were connected.

"Chatembo, we must go to the market."

Eyes lit up with excitement, Chatembo said, "I want to go. But we can't go alone. Mother will send someone to help us."

•

The next morning, before the sun cut through the river fog, Nzinga and Chatembo ate bowls of steaming golden millet, wrapped kente shawls over their shoulders, and joined the people on the Ngola's road to market. They traveled with Nilano, three other girls, and Moti and Shimbu, soldiers disguised as servants carrying market baskets.

Nzinga had only ever visited the small local markets, so she was unprepared for this large, crowded market, which extended as far as she could see. This wide area was usually just uncultivated land, with several large buildings owned by the Ngola and used as storehouses when the market was gone. Now people arriving from all over had created a small city laid out in rows with pathways, with tents and makeshift covers against the sun.

The goods were laid out to either side of the endless paths. Trade items were displayed on long papyrus mats, woven grass rugs, animal skins, or layers of bark-cloth. Some craftsmen had built benches or wooden stalls, while others formed small shops covered over with papyrus stalks and bamboo poles. Underneath baobab, willow, eucalyptus, and rubber trees, wares were spread along both sides of the paths so wide that Nzinga's group easily passed other shoppers moving in the opposite direction. It seemed like great fun to search for Temarku while laughing, looking, and hearing different languages. Nzinga enjoyed all the sounds: bells ringing, drums booming, goats bleating, cows lowing, and peddlers yelling loudly to attract attention to their goods.

In former times, the actual goods were passed from hand to hand at these markets, or cowrie shells were used for money. Now, with the Portuguese sitting where cowrie shells were once collected on the Ngola's bank in Luanda, the currency was Portuguese coins and paper money.

People at the stalls bargained for a cheaper price. Stall keepers traded and visited with each other, then smoked or dozed in the shade of trees. They cooked chickens, vegetables, or sauces in pots on open fires, and they greeted long-lost friends and acquaintances.

Big, gray fish, out of water but still alive, lay on banana-leaf mats flipping their bodies sporadically. Flies buzzed and flew up in swarms from recently butchered meat. Nzinga detoured sharply on the path to avoid piles of cow dung, often imprinted with the outline of a bare foot. Spices and cinnamon were measured into little packets for customers. The smells wafting up made Nzinga sneeze.

Excited, not wanting to miss any of sights, sounds, or smells, Nzinga decided to survey all the goods on her right and then give her full attention to the opposite side when they returned. She tried this, but Chatembo, Nilano, or one of the other girls kept catching her arm, forcing her to look at fat, sleeping babies on their mothers' backs. Or to taste a jungle fruit as she passed. Or to notice a display of pots. She recalled her Portuguese priest-teacher when she passed medicine men selling love charms, arm bracelets, mortars and pestles, and grinding stones.

The salt merchants displayed many different kinds of salt: blocks of shiny, glazed salt; brown granular salt with what looked like dirt and sand clinging to it; granular salt, both fine-grained and coarse-grained; some displayed in pots, some in gourd bowls. She walked further and touched and tasted the salt from wooden bowls, wondering about the custom of never asking to borrow salt after sundown. People should never need to borrow it in Ndongo, for there was salt everywhere: salt in gourds, salt in earthenware crocks, and salt wrapped in leaves and tied with palm strings.

Accompanied by the two soldiers, Nzinga and Chatembo passed for miles through these wares. The other girls finally went off by themselves. The two soldiers drifted off once to look at spears, and again to purchase a gourd of palm wine, which they sipped through a reed while they walked. They never went far, however. Whenever Nzinga looked back, at least one of the soldiers was watching her and Chatembo, and they frequently returned to be near the two girls again.

Nzinga and Chatembo paused to watch dancers, to taste roasting fish or grilled ants, to select tooth sticks, and to finger kente or bark-cloth. They stopped often to look at the baskets decorated in many kinds of designs, or to step upon palm and papyrus floor mats to feel the design on their feet, or to run fingers through millet, or to look at simsim, which made them wary, for it always brought back memories of the snake and Tashana.

At last, they came upon the *pombeiros*, whom some thought were slave traders who disguised their trade at the market by offering beads, trinkets, and other goods, which they exchanged for ivory, skins, and Kongo silver and gold. Many *pombeiros* were Portuguese mulattos or Europeans in service to the Portuguese. Unshaven and mostly unwashed, they were feared and shunned by most Africans, but some Africans were in their employ.

These *pombeiros*, some of whom had been fathered by priests in the Kongo and some by Portuguese traders and soldiers in Luanda, had a makeshift storefront of newly cut trees. In back was a tent of coarse brown cloth, the type used to make crude sails for big ships. Inside the tent were open stalls with bolts of colored European cloth, casks of whiskey, guns, wooden casks, and skins filled with oils. Two rough-looking men near the front surveyed any person who came near. Nzinga shuddered; she glanced back to see their two disguised soldiers watching marketers playing *mwoso*. She and Chatembo went into the tent. Midway down an aisle, Nzinga pretended to be interested in long rows of red, green, and yellow beads.

She whispered to Chatembo, "Do you hear these beads rattling in my hand? That's because I'm shaking with fright. I'm afraid to be alone here."

Chatembo didn't answer, seeming preoccupied. In a short time she wandered toward the rear of the shop, pausing to finger bolts of cloth or to gaze at exotic hats with ostrich feathers. Standing in front of two cages, Chatembo beckoned to Nzinga, who ran to see what was in the cages.

"Where did they get these birds?" asked Chatembo.

An unshaven *pombeiro* came nearer. Nzinga backed away, smelling his alien, foul scent.

"I see you like the Andalusian fowl," he said. "It is a cock from Spain."

The fowl had a large, glowing comb atop its head and red body feathers mixed with an iridescent dark color. As the bird bobbed its head, its beak moved up and down with the rhythm, and the color of its feathers changed.

The *pombeiro's* voice was abrasive while trying to be friendly. "It's a chicken, like your yard chickens, only more beautiful. Is it not?"

Nzinga admired the large red comb and shiny red and black feathers, especially the long tail feathers. While the fowl held her attention, the *pombeiro* quietly came closer. He touched the copper and gold bracelets on her wrist. Nzinga, startled, snatched her hand away as if it had been burned. Immediately she and Chatembo ran for the entrance.

The man came after the girls, shouting, "You can have the fowl for five of the gold bracelets."

In the doorway, the two soldiers watched him gravely, capes thrown to the side to reveal their long, sharp knives. One stayed by the door watching the girls while the second, attracted by the guns, went to the display and took note of what was there.

Safe again, out in the bright African sun, the two girls backed away, looking at the ominous tent.

"He wasn't there," Nzinga said, breathing hard. "Temarku was not inside."

"In back," Chatembo nodded. "I heard voices through the cloth walls. We must go with the soldiers and search behind that shop."

The two soldiers were now sitting on their heels. One had begun a game of *mwoso* or *yabarre,* but they came away at once and went with the girls. They walked together down a path beside a stall that displayed baskets woven from palm leaves and goods hanging from poles decorated with colored raffia. They passed another stall selling various peppers, which made Nzinga sneeze again. They soon came up behind the cloth-covered shop of the *pombeiros*.

A bamboo enclosure, its poles so close together that it was difficult to see inside, leaned against the back of the shop. At the top of the enclosure, the slashed, pointed ends of bamboo discouraged Nzinga from attempting to climb over. One of the soldiers took his knife and slit the ropes that bound the poles together, then let the two girls see inside. Two men, a small child, and a woman sat around a small tree. They spoke mournfully to each other while the sun beat down on them.

They were tied by ropes to the tree. Chains clanked when the small child moved. A wave of nausea swept over Nzinga at the sight of chains on the child's leg. In her life in the Mbanza, people had been executed or stoned for crimes, but she'd never seen a baby in chains. She moved to take the soldier's knife to cut her way inside and free them, but the soldiers restrained her.

"No, my princess, these aren't our people. Hear their language. They were caught or bought elsewhere. We'll report and let the Ngola decide."

The other said, "Let's go."

"Yes, let's go," Chatembo said. "Temarku isn't here. Mother will see that these don't leave Ndongo with their human cargo."

Nzinga followed, but she observed a newly made path leading from the bamboo enclosure toward the forest. Before any of the others knew what she was doing, she set out down this new path toward the forest. The grass and bushes were recently trampled. Chatembo and the others followed at a run, calling to her. She admonished them to be quiet, not knowing what they might find. Together they crept into the forest. When their eyes became accustomed to the dim light, one soldier put his arm up to stop them.

"We go back to get help," he said. "This is too dangerous for the Ngola's child. There is smoke." He pointed. "Maybe slavers are here."

"I won't go back," Nzinga said, pushing by him, running on ahead, not knowing what she'd find, but knowing instinctively to go on. Yet with all her haste and defiance, she went quietly.

In a grove of eucalyptus and willows she fell to her knees, staring in disbelief, for a short distance away, in the clearing around a fire, was their beloved Temarku, his hands tied behind his back and the fork of a tree limb affixed to his neck.

A single *pombeiro* guarded Temarku and two other boys restrained in the same way. The guard, his back toward her, bent over the fire, tending some cooking. A gun leaned against a nearby tree.

Nzinga choked back a sob with her hands over her mouth. Chatembo and the two soldiers were soon by her side. The soldiers circled the little camp, came up quietly, subdued the guard, and freed the children.

The soldiers tied up the kidnapper and herded him back to the Ngola's prison, where he'd be soundly beaten. If he wasn't killed, he'd be ransomed back to his associates.

Temarku, though weak and almost delirious, thanked everyone again and again as he rubbed his neck where the forked tree branch had pressed against his throat. He couldn't stop rubbing his neck for a long while. He kept looking back over his shoulder all the way back to the market, saying, "Nzinga, Chatembo, I will make music and a song about you and Suku. I thought I'd never see home or friends again."

Market day had begun with excitement for Nzinga. Now it ended in triumph and sadness. She rejoined Nilano and the other two girls, who had spent the day in frivolous shopping. They had traded three saved *nzimbi* for cinnamon powder and an elephant bracelet with several beads. Nzinga told the sad story of the wretched people and the little child in chains still in the bamboo enclosure to be sold.

Eyes flashing in anger, Nzinga said, "They shouldn't be allowed to steal people."

When they returned to the Mbanza, they ran straight to Sufalu with the story of the captured child in chains at the back of the shop. The soldiers told about the guns.

The Ngola ordered his soldiers to free the captured people, to confiscate all gunpowder, guns, and anything else of value, and to post guards at the shop for as long as the market operated.

And to follow these *pombeiros* all the way out to Massangano.

10.

THATCH

THE LAST DAYS OF THE dry season were long. It was the season for repairing and making new. It was the season for marrying and making new ground for planting.

All around the Mbanza, men and boys worked to build new houses and repair old ones. They cut and carried new poles and mixed the hard cracked earth of anthills into wattle to apply between poles to form walls. Long lines of women moved continuously toward the new houses, carrying on their heads bundles of grass for thatching the roofs.

Although Chatembo and Nzinga weren't expected to work as were common people, they were required to assist newly married couples at this time. Those getting married included people of older age sets who had lingered and found no one to marry before now plus a number of girls in age sets younger than Nzinga. Noting this, Chatembo growled through her teeth.

"Nzinga, I find it hard to stand this. These babies are marrying, yet we are still single. Men, beware!"

When Chatembo talked like this, Nzinga knew she was deeply bothered. Previously unspoken thoughts would soon follow. They joined members of their age set who were in the valley cutting grass.

"Do you girls remember what we did when we inspected a certain girl just over this hill?" Nzinga said.

"Yes," Chatembo said. "The cows had escaped from the enclosure, for the gate was wide open." They all laughed at that joke about the girl's loss of virginity.

"She wouldn't even tell what boy did it," said a tall, slim girl with an open space between her front teeth.

"Yes," Nzinga continued. "So we put pepper in the gate. *Wo!* How she jumped and cried, but she'd already spoiled the sleep of every girl of the age set. We didn't know whom we could trust after that. If you spent the night with a boy, after that you tied your cloth in several knots between the legs and you slept lightly with legs locked together."

"Who was she?" asked a young and curious plump girl. She put down a grass bundle from her head to listen.

Nzinga's and Chatembo's eyes met. They smiled at each other, glancing toward a village beauty with a baby strapped to her back. But they didn't divulge what they knew to the curious girl.

"She's married now. Whoever he is, he knows," Nzinga said.

"If it's not her husband, all three of them know something happened at the enclosure," said the girl with the missing tooth.

Pausing from bending and cutting grass, Chatembo sidled up to Nzinga and whispered, "All of you may inspect me after a week. I hope the cows have escaped, for I'm sure the gate will be open." She burst out laughing, while Nzinga threw grass over her.

Chatembo must be always scheming and thinking of these things, Nzinga thought. There was never a moment when Chatembo didn't have an interesting idea or bit of information to pass on to whomever would listen. Often it was wise, yet funny. She was discreet and choosy and had special things she mentioned only when she was in the company of select people. Nzinga believed Chatembo got this way because of her mother's work. As spy for the Ngola, Sufalu made it her business to know everything that went on in the kingdom. Sufalu had spies as far away, it was said, as Luanda. Some were servants to the governor. And it was known by all that Chatembo would take over for her mother someday.

What will I take over? Nzinga mused.

The long line of women carrying wrapped bundles of grass curved and swayed from the distant hills and valley up to the Mbanza. Some had broken away and trailed from the long line to newly built houses. If the Ngola journeyed to any part of his kingdom at this time of year, his chiefs showed him the progress people were making in building and thatching, like the work underway around the Mbanza.

Some of the very young girls grew tired and sat on their bundles along the way. Nzinga and Chatembo walked side by side. They came upon two young girls sitting on their bundles, having a heated discussion.

"It did move," one of them said, so tired that she lay down on her bundle. She was looking at a distant hill, one that had a big rock balanced at its top.

"I don't know how you can even think that," the second girl said. In the heat of the moment, she got up to illustrate. "Look, now. I am standing on this ground. You can see it's solid. I can stand here until the next dry season, and maybe a few pieces of the dirt will move when the water or wind move them. But this whole valley will be the same, solid place. It has no legs. It can't decide it doesn't like where it is and go someplace else."

The other girl held to her belief. "It moved. My mother and father agreed on that."

"They were wrong," countered the other. "Let's ask these older sisters. That will show you your parents were joking with you."

The one lying down got up quickly. "Yes, let's ask them."

She waved her arms at Nzinga and Chatembo. "Sisters, can you tell us if that big hill with the rock at its top has always been at this same spot where we see it now? My parents say it was once near Massangano, but when the Portuguese came, it didn't like it there any longer. So it moved near to us, deeper into Ndongo."

Chatembo laughed. She and Nzinga exchanged glances. They understood at once what the parents and all of the old people were doing: creating the myth that even mountains and land moved away from the invaders. They'd heard it said and weren't sure whether it moved or not. They sat with the two girls and enjoyed being elders for once.

"Yes," Chatembo said. Nzinga nodded in agreement. "We, too, have been told that long ago that rock and a few of the hills were nearer to Luanda, but when the white birds came, the hills moved here, deeper into Ndongo."

After sitting awhile, talking about the hills and about rivers moving angrily by the fort as they headed to the sea, the two young girls left them. One said, "What if the hill someday decides to go back and push against the fort, and . . . "

Chatembo laughed and waved them away. She had other things on her mind. "Nzinga, we aren't getting younger. We're wasting time. All the good men are getting married."

"Chatembo, what's the use of talking about it? Neither one of us can get married."

"I could," Chatembo said. "I don't care what they say. I know mediums don't have normal lives, but Mother almost did, before my father was sent as chief near Matamba . . . "

"But I thought she was the one who asked the Ngola to post him there."

"She did, because she didn't want him to be sent as a general to Kongo. She didn't know the Kongolese would attack there and that he'd be killed in a stupid little war. But I'm talking about us. We can still have whomever we want. I've been thinking. When that Nabugye comes near me . . . " She shook her head. Then she spoke again. "I like his face. And other parts," she joked, looking quickly at Nzinga and just as quickly away, pulling at the grass growing alongside the trail. "When he looks at me," she fanned her chest with her hand, "I get all flustered and . . . and . . . hot here." She pointed to her chest and head.

Nzinga laughed, but she didn't speak.

"You know, the way you feel when Kajubi is around." She glanced at Nzinga.

Nzinga nodded and caught up her grass bundle. She said a few words in Portuguese. When she was disturbed, she practiced her language. "You're right, Chatembo, but . . . "

"Nzinga, we need to make some decisions soon."

"I know," Nzinga said, "but Father . . . Kajubi . . . I can't hurt anyone."

"Just listen. I used to hear our mothers talking. I learned a lot, and now I listen everywhere. Often, no one knows I'm there, nor when I leave. You know our disguises. I've been in the army barracks with the young warriors. I sat near Nabugye, and he never recognized me. It's scary how you can get that close to someone and he doesn't know. I . . . I wanted to touch him. I thought he'd hear my heart beating. It sounded to me as loud as Temarku's drum. But Nabugye never knew."

Nzinga laughed: their old games of disguises.

"Do you know how Princess Yafia got Shellanga as a lover?" Chatembo asked.

"Chatembo, there you go, insisting that since princesses can't marry, then they must have lovers. Now you're making things up."

"I have enough proof that I never have to make up anything. Let's disguise ourselves and go to Yafia's house when Shellanga has business at the palace. We'll find out if I'm making things up."

Nzinga glanced at her, incredulous. Shellanga was the most trusted general of her father. *He's married and has children in our age set. My aunt Yafia is the sister of the Ngola. She is beautiful and haughty. And she's royal in the way she walks and talks. She is as old as my mother, with the figure and looks of a young girl. She dresses in beautiful, colorful robes with entrancing headscarves. At all royal functions she is at ease, a faint smile crinkling her lips and bright eyes. She never notices men. All the girls admire her.*

"Well, do you?" Chatembo said.

"Do I what?" Nzinga thought how much she loved Yafia.

"Nzinga, you heard. Don't make me repeat names. Someone may hear."

"Chatembo, how do you know all of this?"

"I heard my mother telling your mother things, while you were listening to that silly Jesuit talk about nothing that's going to do anyone any good, because your father will either kill him or sell him if the Portuguese keep building that fort and bringing guns to Massangano."

"*Come, faz favor, por favor,*" Nzinga said.

"What's that? What are you talking about?"

"Oh, I was practicing my Portuguese. I said, 'Excuse me.' All right, I'll listen. Tell me about the princess." But Chatembo didn't answer until Nzinga pleaded. "Please, Chatembo."

"Princess Yafia loved Shellanga for a long time. Since she could not get married, she decided she wanted him as a lover. She changed her outfit, hoping he'd take notice of her shape. At palace functions, she sent servants to serve him. When he didn't notice her, she plotted to put herself in his way. At official occasions, she walked in front of him, but Shellanga never noticed. You know he's married and loyal to the Ngola and involved in his work. Finally she tired of subtle efforts. She disguised herself as a bath girl. When he was in the bath, she lingered and washed his back. And still he didn't recognize her. Maybe he was thinking of his military strategies, how to get men in place, how to overcome an obstacle in a battle, how to take a difficult hill. So he didn't recognize her, but when he came out of the bath, she pulled the string of her robe and it fell at her feet. It was more than the poor man could stand."

"And that's how it started with them?"

Nzinga tried to follow Chatembo's argument, to understand the decisions they had to make.

11.
LOVE AND WAR

NZINGA DRESSED IN HER newest skirt, with hair done in one of the many basket-weaves that she favored, and approached the house that Chatembo had pointed out earlier. She called loudly, "Is anybody there?"

"We're here. You are welcome." The door opened. His eyes smiling, Kajubi invited her in, glad that she'd come.

Two oil lamps burned in the room, which held three stools, a table, and pillows on the floor. The enticing aroma of food filled the close air.

"Come in. Welcome, visitor," Kajubi said again, even after she was in the room, his voice trembling.

It came to her that he was afraid, because she was the king's daughter. No commoner looked directly on the face of the king, because it challenged his authority and ended in death. When one got close to the king without his consent, the people around him acted to protect the entire kingdom. Likewise with the king's relatives. A person didn't have to break rules or taboos to be singled out. You could be sacrificed at a shrine, or be killed because you were on the road when the Ngola decreed that no one should travel.

For example, Kajubi's friend Baraka had been a great dancer, his agility and rhythm highly prized. One man, the medium of the drums, thought Baraka's ability could be transferred to the Ngola.

So the ministers killed Baraka, and now his ligaments and tendons held the skins firmly onto the Ngola's virility drums.

And here Kajubi, another favorite, was entertaining the Ngola's daughter. Nzinga wanted to put him at his ease.

"I came to you, Kajubi, because you are a dear friend and I need you to know it."

"It's good of you to say that. In my travels, I've seen many types of people, but never one like you. My eyes first fell on you that day when you and Chatembo came down from the hills at the elephant hunt."

"I was such a child."

"Excuse me," Kajubi said. "I have never known myself to talk so much."

Nzinga smiled her seldom-seen smile of abandonment. "You were already a great hunter. How could you notice a mere child?"

"I was young in age, too. Since it was unusual to see young ones at a hunt, I noticed you. I was a bit angry."

"Angry? Why?"

"Because it was dangerous, and you might get hurt."

"Do you notice danger? Those elephant tusks seemed to swing right at your chest." She touched his chest. He carried something inside that she'd never seen in anyone else.

"I'm always aware of danger where others can't see it. It's the way that I must live."

"With danger?" she asked.

"It isn't something I chose. Like you, I was born to live with danger."

"Chatembo says you were stolen very young and taken many places."

"We shouldn't waste this important meeting talking of how I grew up."

Nzinga still stood near the door, so interested in Kajubi that she forgot to sit. She didn't believe that her father was stronger because Baraka's ligaments were attached to a drum. *Father was already stronger than three Barakas.* She felt dismay, frustration, and anger when people were disgraced or killed callously, sacrificed to show a chief's power. And why didn't they sacrifice boys at the ancestral shrines instead of young girls? It seemed she was still alive because she was protected by birth. What if she'd been like Kajubi, unprotected and a captive?

She sat and looked at him for a long time, feeling a warmth pass over her. She liked his face. She yearned to touch his hand. She was about to act on that urge when a voice at the door called, "Is there anyone there?"

Kajubi's eyes left Nzinga's face.

They greeted the young men and women who had walked from house to house collecting one another so as to meet at Kajubi's house. It wasn't a prearranged meeting. No one knew at which house they'd all end, except perhaps Chatembo, who was in charge of the meetings. Nzinga knew the tradition was for the girls to all meet to pass a good part of the night together as a group. Later, they'd spend the rest of the night with the boy of their choice.

This first meeting was for the girls to reinforce each other's resolve not to go beyond prescribed bounds, and to give each other moral support and whispered advice. The young men came in, jostling each other and slapping hands, smiling and joking. One of them said in jest, "If you must take honey, you will do well to watch out for bees."

Another said, "Better to build the bee a hive."

All the boys laughed, and a few girls joined in. One girl pretended not to know it was her favorite who spoke lightly. She asked, "Who said that?"

The girls, after hugging and making quick comments, took their places on colorful woven mats they'd brought with them. Boys sat on one side of the room and girls on the other. The girls passed sweet-smelling seeds and powders and combs with ornamental handles. They exchanged these with comments and exclamations of endearment. Nzinga watched the boys' expressions and wondered if they felt left out. She, like the other girls, knew this was a test of their manners. Were they considerate? Did they have patience?

A box of woven black, red, and yellow fibers appeared from among the girls. The girl with the space between her front teeth, without announcement, began to characterize the boys by saying something that happened in their young lives, while handing each of them a small gift, but with no comment on who had made it.

"This boy can outswim crocodiles, for when he was fourteen rains, he fell into the Cuanza and outraced crocodiles to the shore without being rescued."

A shy boy got up after being prodded and took the gift. The girl went on that way about different boys. Then they came to Kajubi. The girl said, "This is the mystery person. He came with a great chief, is a proven warrior, and has always belonged in Ndongo."

Nzinga thought Chatembo told the girl to say that. Kajubi got a pair of wristbands of strong hippo hide that could be laced on to protect his wrists during close combat. He smiled at Nzinga.

The night wore on. After eating, they each told a story. Nzinga told the story of Nakwesi, who went to visit a sister who had married the sun god. To get there, she had to go with a servant to the sky. She could take inside of her anything needed. Then, when she needed something, she simply regurgitated it. Nzinga made the story up on the spot, as surprised as her audience was to find it exciting.

Chatembo had arranged for music, so after stories they all spent time dancing. In the end, couples walked together back to their different houses. The elders were wise in establishing this tradition of sharing together, dancing, visiting, storytelling, and feasting. By the time the young men and women finished these engrossing activities, weariness postponed exploration of each other to another time.

Nzinga lay on a rug for a short time, thinking she'd have an intimate talk with Kajubi, but the next thing she knew, it was morning and a servant brought hot millet and herbal tea. The servant was one of Mbande's mother's personal servants, which Nzinga found curious. She woke Kajubi, who slept nearby.

All that day, Nzinga thought about what had happened. The night had been wonderful. *But could I grow to like him too much? How would that affect his life?* What should she do? With her own mother gone and Sufalu always traveling lately, who to ask? She decided to go to her grandmother, who lived on her mother's land, two days' walk from the Mbanza.

Chatembo and some of the girls tried several times to coax Nzinga to join them and talk about the previous night. They were animated, agreeing that it had to be the best ever, going over every detail. Finally, Nzinga said to Chatembo, "Can you guess who brought our morning meal and woke me?"

When Chatembo couldn't guess, Nzinga told her. Chatembo was indignant. "Nzinga, this is against every tradition. No one distrusts young adults on their together nights."

"No one except those taking part should know who was with whom," said one of the other girls.

"Kaningwa was jealous of your mother when she was alive," Chatembo said. "Now she's jealous because your father loves you very much."

"But he loves her and her children as well. I've seen it in his face. He's so good to us all. And he loves all the people of Ndongo."

"But your stepmother is selfish. She'll cause a disaster, because she can't bear the thought of sharing. She is always plotting something. Mother knows how to handle her. And her servants."

"I'm going to live with Grandmother at my mother's place for a while. I need to think about what to do."

"Why at this great time?"

"Because I need to think and be with Kambi and Funzi."

"Kajubi will be sad."

"He's so good. It's because of him that I must go."

Chatembo's eyes lit up. "Then you do like him."

"Oh, yes, a lot."

"What happened last night?" Chatembo asked, her face near to Nzinga's.

"You were there."

"Nzinga, you're exasperating. I mean after we left."

"Nothing."

Chatembo laughed in disbelief. "Nzinga, we must check you." The other girls giggled.

"No, nothing, by Suku and my mother. It's the truth, we went to sleep." Nzinga raised her hand.

Nzinga did go home, but neither Kambi nor Funzi wanted to go with her. They said she was too serious, and they wanted to be near the palace where their friends were, so they could go to the hills with girls of their age set.

∎

So Nzinga went for a time to visit her old grandmother, to sit and talk about her mother, and to listen to her grandmother judge the villagers' disputes. One woman had lost pots because goats ran among them. The grandmother judged that the goat's owner had to give up a goat to pay for the pots. A palm-tree tapper came to her grandmother, saying he'd tapped trees for a man who had since died, and the sons wouldn't pay. The sons said they had no money. Her grandmother said, "What goods do you have?"

"We have only palm wine."

The grandmother decreed that they must give the tapper palm wine to sell, so he could gain the equivalence of his wages.

Her mother's land had long been the site for training young warriors. The Ngola gave the chief there the job of selecting and training young men of the area to be warriors. Nzinga went in disguise one day to watch the young warriors practice. But then she also went through the spear-throwing exercise. She wrestled, and she ran in competition with the others. But she excelled at stick fighting. The best young warriors grew tired and exasperated with her cartwheels and leaps, and by the way she twirled her stick and parried every attempted blow. At the end, they all puzzled over who this new warrior was, although the chief knew it was Nzinga.

She loved to watch and be with warriors. She loved the way they dressed, with little clothing, since clothing could impede fight or flight or get caught on a bush at a critical moment. She loved their courage and their feeling that the kingdom relied on them. She loved their toughness and their ability to go long periods without water and food. Being a warrior forced one to test the limits of strength and endurance. *So this is one reason I like Kajubi: he is another part of me that is there instead of me. When our warriors fight, he is there instead of me.*

Other women had warrior husbands who came home to their wives and were there as head of the family in peacetime. Women waited for them in time of war. She couldn't marry Kajubi ... but ... Her thoughts stopped there.

She stayed away from the Mbanza for many weeks.

◆

12.
GUNS FOR MASSANGANO

WHEN NZINGA RETURNED TO THE palace, she spent time in the meeting hall, listening to the Ngola and his chiefs discuss and plan: how taxes should be collected; how grain should be stored; how cattle, sheep, and goats should be distributed and traded; how hungry people should be fed; how crops should be planted.

In one sobering moment she understood why the Ngola was needed. He kept the people organized and looked out for the welfare of everyone. *To be Ngola, you had to work and think and make tough decisions every day. You had to try to keep peace, but you had to build an army, and make spears for fighting and hoes for planting.*

With the honor of Ngola came a burdensome responsibility. Everyone had to help, but the Ngola had to make everyone respect each other and live and work together for protection.

That was why people honored him.

One day Sufalu, Shellanga, and the ministers were in the meeting hall with the Ngola. Nzinga sat and listened from her usual place in the back. They were discussing news of a ship that had arrived in Luanda carrying two heavy guns, so big that they had to be drawn on wheels by two horses. One gun was intended for Massangano.

The Ngola said, "The gun will be used to attack this village and the Mbanza. We won't let them through."

Shellanga arrived while Nzinga watched. His tall, coppery frame almost matched the Ngola's size. As always, they shook hands and wrists together. They sat with Sufalu and the ministers and planned how to attack.

The priest had told Nzinga one day long ago how Portugal and Spain used big guns. He gave her detailed descriptions of the guns, how they were transported, and the damage they did. The priest had begun as a soldier in a military school in Spain. Then he got the call to be a priest, to go and save backward "heathens." That, he said, was his reason for being in Ndongo.

She longed to tell her father and Shellanga about the guns, but they wouldn't listen to a girl. They'd say a girl had nothing to do with war. Several women sat with her in back of the screen. She smelled a familiar perfume and heard the jingle of arm bracelets striking each other. Princess Yafia sat further down the line, watching the proceedings intently, but she did not sit forward on her seat. *Was there a soft, satisfied sigh from my aunt every time Shellanga spoke?* Nzinga thought of two ways to get her knowledge to the warriors. She'd tell Sufalu, who would tell Yafia, who would tell Shellanga. Also, because Kajubi would go as one of the lead warriors, Nzinga must see him and tell him everything.

Before she could leave the meeting hall, Mbande and his inseparable friend Mutele came in with several sons of her father's chiefs. They were men of Mbande's age set, one age set above hers. Nzinga smothered jealousy. *Mbande is going to war just because he's the son. I can do everything as well as he can. But there's a war taboo and I cannot I go.*

When she and Mbande were young, they were friends at times, in spite of the rivalry between their mothers. But they grew further and further apart as Mbande increased his love for hunting and began treating Nzinga with disdain. Sufalu said Kaningwa was afraid of Nzinga's strength and her influence with the Ngola, and because of this, Kaningwa fed young Mbande with lies.

In the meeting hall her brother caught sight of her, squeezed in among the palace women.

"Ah, there you are, Nzinga," he said, speaking with unusual intensity. "For once you are among the right group. But the huts to thatch and the garden, goats, and cows aren't here. Wait until you see the leopard skin I'm giving Father. I'm now the man, the hunter." He and his friends laughed. As an after-thought, one said, "But she is beautiful, even if she is a bit fat."

Nzinga could have spat upon him. *Fat or not, I'm not for you.* She said to Mbande, "There's a war. Are you going?"

He looked as if he'd laugh in her face. "Our father's chiefs and generals will take care of that. We're going hunting on the islands for two moons."

She turned her palms down and beckoned him nearer so his friends wouldn't hear. He came reluctantly, and she whispered, "That's selfish. When Father was your age, he'd led men into battle many times."

"And he'll do it again, but it isn't my way. A soldier is a soldier, and a king is a king," he said.

"If a king isn't a soldier, he soon has no country in which to be king," Nzinga said.

"Aha." He threw his hand in the air in salute, as if to say, *"That is your view."*

But it wasn't her view. She'd heard her father say it often. *When it's Mbande's turn, he'll have to learn everything for himself. And he won't manage.* Her father had many generals and warriors he trusted, but it'd warm his heart if he had a son to send.

Mbande rejoined his friends, and they went off without even inquiring about the crisis. She left the hall and found Chatembo at a nearby shrine.

"Listen for just an eye blink," Nzinga said. "The Ngola is going to war. I need to talk with Sufalu and Princess Yafia. I want them to tell the Ngola and Shellanga what to expect. That priest tells me everything when he is teaching me. He's told me a great deal about their big guns."

"Tonight?" Chatembo asked. "And what else? You know the Ngola will soon pick young warriors to go to battle."

"Yes. Who will they pick to destroy that gun?"

"Kajubi and your brother will be among those picked."

"Mbande won't go. He's gone hunting. I need to speak to Kajubi myself. Please help me with that."

"You want to wish Kajubi success?"

"No, I want to make sure he succeeds."

•

"A big gun is being pulled on a carriage from Luanda to Massangano. You must drown that gun in the river."

Just before Kajubi left, Nzinga told him what she knew about how the Portuguese would travel and how he could defeat them.

"When your group receives orders from Shellanga, do everything he says, but to succeed, also do what I tell you. You must run all the way and then rest. Catch the Portuguese at night when they are tired and worried by mosquitoes. Kill them and run off their horses. Don't linger there. Run and hide in the woods until the next night. They'll be tired again, and if you make the right sounds, the African soldiers among them will think you're spirits. You may kill as many as you like. Then push the gun in the river. "

"It will be as you say," said Kajubi, gazing into her eyes.

Earlier, she'd talked to her father, who didn't seem happy. He didn't mention Mbande, but while joking with her, he looked around as if seeking another who should be with them. She'd said, "Everything is going to be all right, Father."

He gripped her hand. "Yes. As always, you lift my spirits."

The Ngola, Shellanga, Kajubi, and the warriors departed, on their way to save the Ngola's kingdom and the Ngola's people.

The days passed without word. Her anxiety grew. She roamed about the palace and several times ran into Kaningwa, who was meeting with Chief Oyimbu's wife to plan Mbande's wedding to a girl from Oyimbu's county. Kaningwa and the wife of Oyimbu described the bride-to-be as a "nice quiet girl who listens."

Nzinga waited impatiently for word of the attack. She longed to strike out on the road to Massangano and go until she met her father and Kajubi returning victorious. Instead, she counted the days and imagined the entire action. She asked a palace soldier how many suns it took to get to Massangano. "Four days," he said. She breathed easier. They were almost there. In her mind, if the battle succeeded, it'd be because of the two ways she'd given help: sending information through Sufalu to Shellanga, and speaking directly to Kajubi. If the effort failed, it might be her fault as a woman for breaking the war taboo.

She left the palace grounds several times to "get outside," going among the herders and cultivators. To keep occupied, she helped mothers with their babies.

Runners, exhausted, finally came with messages, one after another: the Ngola and general were returning. Nzinga wanted to know: "When will they return? How many days away? Did they destroy the guns? Is my father safe? Is Kajubi safe?" But they had no information about the success or failure of the mission, or had been told to say nothing.

The ministers, however, did know something from signs the runners gave, signs Nzinga couldn't read.

Another group of runners raced in with a message: "The Ngola and his warriors are coming. People are preparing shelters and food for the Ngola and his army."

This new unit of runners also carried a rumor: "The Portuguese are dying like lions in a pit." But no one could answer Nzinga's questions. *Why are they dying? Are they being killed by the Ngola's men?*

When the warriors returned, it was a triumphant parade. The Ngola, his general, and the warriors were celebrated and fed. Breathing rapidly, unable to stop smiling, she met Kajubi's eyes. They couldn't look away from each other.

At last their adventures were told. The gun had been on its way to the fort, but nearer to Luanda than they thought. To get to the gun, Kajubi and his crew had to skirt the fort and the Portuguese advance road party. They found the gun crew with their horses, having breakfast. They quickly and silently killed all but one soldier, who had just arrived from Luanda and was still on horseback. He escaped, riding back wildly toward the city. The attack panicked the horses and set them running, pulling the gun after them. The gun's erratic movement and massive weight entangled the horses in their harnesses. They pulled against each other. Then the heavy gun flew over a cliff, taking the horses along. Dead horses and broken gun now lay in a deep river ravine.

The Ngola's forces lay siege to the fort. No food or messages got in or out of the fort. One of the Ngola's spies escaped from it in the night and reported that the Portuguese were dying of malaria and other sicknesses. The Ngola's army stayed for days, allowing a few of the weakest Portuguese to straggle back to Luanda to spread infection.

This was war, the Ngola said. If they wanted to take his kingdom, they'd have to fight his army and everything else he placed in their paths.

13.
LOVERS AT LAST

D URING THE CELEBRATION FOR the victory over the big gun, Nzinga went around to congratulate the returning warriors and their happy wives. Then she spent time talking to Chatembo and Nabugye, a well-respected warrior who'd been selected as one of the Ngola's younger chiefs in the army. He was a few years older, but the great favorite of Chatembo. Nzinga also visited with some girls whose warrior-husbands had been killed or wounded in the battle.

Every chance Chatembo got, she said, "Nzinga, look! Kajubi is looking at you. Why don't you go over to him?"

Nzinga glanced away. "I have mouthed 'Congratulations' to him. But can't you see? I can't go to him."

"And why not?"

"Everyone will see, and I'm not sure how I will act."

"Who cares? Ndongo just won a great victory, so everybody can celebrate any way they like. The ancestors and Suku and the other gods have willed it. I'm going to celebrate." She inclined her head slightly toward Nabugye.

"But look over there," Nzinga pointed with her nose toward Kaningwa, sitting royally near the Ngola. "She watches everything."

"You should give her something to observe. Look at that." She indicated where Princess Yafia was serving Shellanga palm wine and laughing, her free hand all aflutter along her slender neck; her necklaces whirled with her motion; the bracelets jangled on her arms. "She's not worried about what is seen."

Nzinga didn't trust herself to go near Kajubi. But after a while, she couldn't stand to be there and not be with him, so she went to her room and washed, put on sweet scents. When she came back out, instead of rejoining the party, she slipped through a seldom-used opening where guards were drinking and talking and went into Kajubi's house.

People were rarely alone. *Someone is always there who thinks you need a companion or need you to be one.* Nzinga was sure no one needed her at that moment. If they did, she wouldn't be easily found. In the silence, she sat on a pillow and looked at Kajubi's collection of spears. She touched his buffalo-hide shield, used only to fight native armies. It could stop a spear, but not bullets from guns. On his wall was a tanned antelope skin that shone with designs in black, yellow, and red stains down the length of the skin.

One design caught her attention—shaped and crenellated like the point on a spear. It was like the design on Kajubi's face, just to the side of each eye. She put her hand up to trace the design.

There was a voice at the door that she recognized.

Kajubi. With someone. From the sounds and the pause at the door, it was one of the warriors. They were bidding each other good night. She held her breath, waiting, her hands to the sides of her head.

She felt hot, hot all over and breathless. When he came in and closed the door, she threw herself at him. He was caught off guard, startled for a moment, then his face cracked with happiness, and then they were both rolling on the floor, one on top and then the other on top, their legs entwined, and their faces and lips pressed to each other. They couldn't stop kissing and hugging, squeezing tightly. Their hunger, so long pent up, was let loose as they pressed their bodies onto each other, laughing hoarsely. Soon, Nzinga's lithe, shapely body was almost bare and Kajubi's hard, muscled body quivered against her legs and the dip between her legs. Through labored breath, as they kissed and he had his hands on her hips, she murmured, "*Uhumm,* the door. Please kick that table against it."

Kajubi secured the door with his foot, and they continued kissing, entwined and entangled and loving, until their wildest feelings rumbled like the falls at Cambambe. As they moved closer, it was as though they were in the river in a boat moving rhythmically up and down with the rapids, headed for the falls and dangerous rocks on either side, trying to avoid the white spray and waves threatening to engulf them. Then they went near the falls and held the boat there above the falls, and they held onto each other. Then the boat careened down among white spray as they fell down, down into a warm settling pool of sun-splashed water, and their boat whirled slowly in it, until it came to a rocking calm in the shadows of tall, luxuriant trees.

After a long time passed, Nzinga said, "Jubi. I want to call you Jubi. Is that all right with you?"

"*Njoo!*" Kajubi said. "Call me Jubi. Say it again."

"Jubi, please call me Jinga," she said. "Say my name."

"I can't do that," he said.

"Why can't you? Nobody has ever called me Jinga." She held his head between her hands. "You say it. Say it."

"You're a princess. I can't."

"This princess pulled off her clothes for you. Say 'Jinga.'"

"Jinga," he said softly, musically. "Jinga."

"Jubi and Jinga. They are the same. Warrior and princess. Princess and warrior." They fell into each other's arms again.

■

They met afterwards, as often as possible.

Nzinga arranged for them to meet in Chatembo's room, where her friend watched for them. Or they met late at night in Kajubi's room. They made love and laughed, but as always with Nzinga, there were serious moments.

Once she said, "Kajubi, I want to say something to you. It might make no sense. I always think about things that people are not supposed to think about or say, but I want to say it anyway."

Chatembo was there with them, and she waved her hands at Kajubi. She said, "Come on, Kajubi, run. I'm telling you now. Don't listen, just run."

They all laughed.

"I'm saying it anyway." Nzinga looked at him solemnly. "Kajubi, I love the times when I didn't know you and you didn't know me, but you needed someone to love you. I loved you even though I didn't know you. So when you think of those times, don't feel lonesome, because my love goes back to then. I mean, you are here and I love what brought you to what you are now and how you endured, grew, and became something wonderful. But other people don't like that. They are threatened by that and sometimes will try to do you ill because of it. You know us, but what is to become of you if we've done this and someone disapproves? I don't want you to suffer by yourself. If you suffer, I'll suffer, too. Not just in my mind, but physically, all of me. I love everything about you—the warrior you, the hunter you, the musician you, and oh, yes, the lover you."

"You, you, you," Chatembo said from the corner.

"Nzinga, I'm trying to love the talking you," Kajubi said.

.

Once, good fortune came. Shellanga sent Kajubi to train young warriors at Nzinga's grandmother's land. Nzinga wasn't far behind, and Chatembo traveled along. Her grandmother set up a sheltered, quiet room where the lovers could meet nearly every day. They'd have spent entire nights together, but Kajubi had to sleep in the leader's quarters with the warriors.

During that stay at Nzinga's grandmother's, Sufalu learned that Kaningwa had been spying on Nzinga and Kajubi. Sufalu's spy worked as a servant in Chief Oyimbu's house and heard Kaningwa tell the chief's wife, Kaningwa's cousin, "That Nzinga is strong and much prized by the Ngola. And Kajubi is thought to be the best warrior in Shellanga's service. I can't get any news of them since they went away to that place."

"What news are you expecting?" Oyimbu's wife asked.

"Don't tell me you didn't know they were lovers. I don't need them making a baby to give Mbande problems."

"Princesses can't have babies." The chief's wife repeated the taboo everyone knew.

"This girl's father will let her leap the falls at Punga a Dongo, he loves her so," Kaningwa said.

Sufalu passed this information to Nzinga's grandmother, who told Nzinga and Chatembo right away.

"You see what I have been telling you. Kaningwa has to be stopped," Chatembo said.

"But she's my mother now that mine has died. And she's my father's wife. I love him, so I must tolerate her."

"One day she'll make you sad, Nzinga. My mother knows there is only one way to deal with the snake's head. You have let the snake live too long."

Kajubi was called back to the palace not long after this, and sent to make war on a chief in Zaire who had failed to pay a debt owed the Ngola. It was the same troublesome area where Shellanga had fought before and liberated Kajubi. This time, Kajubi returned as commander.

While he was away, Nzinga learned she was pregnant. Kajubi was gone for three months. When he returned, he had to remain outside the village for weeks with his troops, to make sure they were healthy enough to come in among the people. Nzinga saw him only briefly, in the room at her grandmother's. While they were kissing and holding onto each other, a message came from the Ngola ordering Kajubi to report to the ministers about his mission.

Nzinga longed for him every moment of the day and worried, for she didn't know if anyone had learned she was pregnant. She cried over what could happen to him, because she'd be powerless to help. She wanted a little happiness. She wanted time with him, his body against hers. She wanted to spend normal nights with him, to wake up beside him. She wanted as many children as they could have, without taboos.

Then Kajubi came.

Chatembo signaled that he was there. At the same time, his voice came from outside the door.

"How may I stand?"

"Stand inside, Jubi, please. Right now."

When Kajubi came in, his face split in a joyful smile, as did hers. He shook his head. "I have seen many wonders, but Suku did his best work with you."

"And with you. And even better with both of us together." Nzinga rushed into his arms.

"*Ooowoo, oowoo!*" Chatembo said, leaving the room. "I have to help your grandmother do something."

14.
THE MIDWIVES

DURING THE FIRST THREE months of her pregnancy, Nzinga was nauseated daily and had no appetite. The women who looked after Nzinga told Sufalu that the kingdom could very well lose the princess. In private conversation, the Ngola pressed Sufalu about Nzinga's condition and charged Sufalu to take good care of his daughter's health.

Sufalu didn't worry, she acted. One day she brought a mixture of herbs along with Nzinga's food and then sat waiting for her to take them.

"I don't want anything," Nzinga said. She avoided looking at Sufalu.

"What is the real trouble?" Sufalu asked.

"Where is Chatembo?"

"You know she went to spy on one of the chiefs for the Ngola. You mean, where is Kajubi?" Sufalu said.

Nzinga wrinkled her nose but didn't give an answer. She sat with her legs crossed and shook her foot up and down, as she always did when she didn't get her way.

Sufalu took a bite of a steamed plantain from the woven-grass tray and then pointed to the food. "If you eat everything on this tray and take this medicine, I'll tell you where he is."

Nzinga rubbed her abdomen, then pulled at the strap that held an amulet Kajubi had given her. "What's the good of being the Ngola's child when you're a prisoner?"

Sufalu laughed aloud.

Nzinga bristled. "It isn't at all funny."

"It certainly is," Sufalu assured her. "You're pregnant, so it's easy to forgive you. This is unlike you: to be petulant and disagreeable. You know you're not a prisoner." She paused, then went on with a shake of her beautiful head, "This reminds me of when your mother was carrying you. She pestered the Ngola's cook to give her food that would make a growing baby boy strong and healthy. This was after her enemies had made ill-formed dolls and hidden them in a baby's basket to bewitch her and her child. Your mother wouldn't do anything about it."

Nzinga's eyes opened wide. Sufalu said, "You didn't know that, did you?" After a pause, she went on. "I have another problem right now, just as serious—to keep you and your child from harm. So I don't need opposition from you."

Sufalu moved the food toward her. Nzinga caught the older woman's hand. "Sufalu, friend of my dead mother, tell me: where is Kajubi? Does he live?"

Sufalu looked stern. "The food and the medicine."

Nzinga folded her arms over her distending abdomen. "But I don't feel like eating anything."

"It's no wonder you get weaker every day. Here." She pushed the food nearer. "Save yourself. And the child."

"What's the use? I know the law. Even if the child is healthy and beautiful, the royal midwives will not let it breathe once."

"You don't know any such thing." Sufalu looked keenly at Nzinga as she spoke these words. Somehow the words and look gave Nzinga courage she hadn't had since she'd last seen Kajubi.

"I'll eat," she said. From that moment she ate so heartily that after a few days, Sufalu wondered if she should think of a way to keep her from getting too big.

* * *

Sufalu hadn't kept Kajubi away by design. He was busy helping to train the army. With a new governor installed in Luanda, the Portuguese had brought horses to the fort at Massangano. But as she'd promised, she managed to bring him to see Nzinga for brief periods. This revived Nzinga's spirit, and she blossomed and flowered in her pregnancy.

Sufalu secreted Nzinga away to a hiding place where she stayed indoors and was rarely seen. It was known throughout her mother's land that Nzinga carried a child, but no one dared mention it. The Ngola's midwives were ready to do their duty: for if a princess became pregnant, it was their duty to make sure the child did not live. Everyone understood that such child, if a royal male, might contest for the kingship, disturbing the kingdom. The kingship passed down only through the king's sons.

Through her spies, Sufalu knew that Kaningwa had learned of the pregnancy and that Kajubi was the father. Kaningwa had therefore sent along a special midwife of her own to see that the child never breathed. As usual, Sufalu made her own plans and issued orders.

One day, the village women in colorful dresses sat on the floor of a ceremonial house, weaving mats of colorful cured grass. The wind and sun streamed through the open house. While the women compared mat designs, Sufalu noticed Wasema's round abdomen. Wasema was one of the captured people that Shellanga's troops had brought back from a raid. Sufalu smiled at Wasema, admiring the design of her mat, which looked like tiny masks. Sad-faced Wasema wasn't sure who had fathered the child she carried, because she'd been raped by slave drivers. Some women, though, thought Wasema was made pregnant soon after she was captured and began working for the young hunters. Her baby was due at the same time as Nzinga's.

Wasema, a servant girl with no family and no husband, worked daily, carrying on her head full water jugs, baskets of cassava, and bundles of firewood. If she'd been a native of Ndongo and a poor worker, she'd have been banished to a village in disgrace and badly treated; her baby would suffer the same fate intended for Nzinga's child. But Sufalu, seeing ahead, had removed Wasema from her work for the hunters and placed her under the protection of the chief's builder, an old man who served as Wasema's husband. The builder put Wasema to work thatching huts, where women also matted and covered house doors with decorative mats. Wasema was good at it and showed the women how to layer the grass thatch so it ended in level overhangs.

Sufalu moved Wasema and Nzinga into houses beside each other, where a papyrus mat covered a secret door that connected the two houses. With her own midwife, Sufalu intended to confuse the midwives.

The birthing room contained a bed lined with bark-cloth and soft sheepskins with a giant grinding stone in the middle. Cut out of rock and used to grind millet, sorghum, maize, and beans, the stone was marked in its center by an oval depression. Women gave birth by straddling and pressing down while pushing against the grinding stone, finally dropping the child onto sheepskins on the grinding stone.

Nzinga went into labor before Wasema. The house was darkened and the doors closed. Sufalu expected that Wasema would deliver more easily and quickly than Nzinga, so she gave Nzinga herbs to speed her into labor. Sufalu's midwife, sworn to secrecy, brought Wasema through the secret door of Nzinga's room and took Nzinga to Wasema's room.

In the darkened room of Nzinga's house, Wasema gave birth to a boy, which was caught by Kaningwa's midwife as it was born. The deed was done quietly.

When Wasema and Nzinga woke from the potion Sufalu had given them, Nzinga's arms were empty and Wasema's held a baby boy. On the baby's belly, near where the umbilical cord had been cut and tied, was the burned imprint of a spear.

At least for now, one heart is light, Sufalu thought.

But mine aches.

■ ■ ■

Having done their jobs, Kaningwa's midwife and the other women made their way back to Mbacka and reported that Nzinga had had a baby that now rested in the arms of the ancestors.

Kaningwa congratulated herself and breathed a sigh of relief. *If only there was a way to make Kajubi eat a spear before they make more babies. Un Joo! These people keep you busy. This Ngola loves that daughter better than he does his wife. She breaks rules and still lives.*

Later Kaningwa said this and more to Chief Oyimbu's wife, who put her finger to her lips and looked behind her, as if they should worry about spies.

Sufalu's spy, the chief's servant, reported the entire conversation.

15.
YEARS OF LOSS

YEARS MIXED WITH HAPPINESS and sadness passed. Nzinga and Kajubi were accepted lovers now, and no one seemed concerned. They saw each other as often as he could be released from his army training duties. They clung to each other, brushing away sadness while praying to the ancestors not to bring another child.

Nzinga lived alternately at the palace and at her mother's land. She helped Princess Yafia with ceremonial planning. Her sisters Kambi and Funzi were given tasks by their father, the Ngola, to visit other chiefs throughout Ndongo. They collected taxes and sent the best food, skins, salt, and Kongo silver and gold to the Ngola's treasurer.

Then talk of war broke into palace life again. Nzinga sat in the meeting house one day alongside Yafia, listening to the Ngola discuss the Portuguese's new actions. The Ngola had been sick for a few days and didn't react as quickly as normal.

Sufalu said, "They have more horses. They've brought wheels by ship to replace the broken ones for the big gun. They'll use the horses to pull the gun up from the ravine, put it on wheels, and point it at the Mbanza."

"When will this start?" the Ngola asked Kadu, who had contact with spies from the fort.

"In about a month. They are waiting for the ship to be unloaded. Then it will take time to plan."

Mbande sat among them, silent. *This is his time to speak up,* Nzinga thought.

"We must act at once." the Ngola said. "Shellanga, make your army ready. I will accompany you."

For the first time in her life, Nzinga heard Shellanga disagree with his king. "But Rainmaker, king of Ndongo, whose power was granted by Suku, you mustn't do everything yourself. We see you are ill. Let others of us do this work for Ndongo."

The Ngola waited a brief moment. Nzinga wasn't sure if this was planned by the Ngola and Shellanga to force Mbande into combat. If it was planned, it never elicited the desired response, for Mbande didn't rise to the challenge. He sat there looking innocent, as if he didn't hear the grave issues discussed. Nzinga couldn't stand it. She jumped up to volunteer, but Yafia caught her arm and pulled her back.

"I know you can do it, but don't. Mbande will be Ngola. It's his job," she said. Clearly, she and Shellanga had spoken about Mbande's reluctance to take responsibility.

But Mbande didn't have to take any action, because his beautiful mother materialized from a side door.

"I am to be excused for this indiscretion, disturbing you at conference." Seeming concerned, Kaningwa leaned over the chair where the Ngola sat. "I beg you not to go. You are ill. Send Shellanga with your strongest and best warriors, such as Nabugye and Kajubi. Don't go yourself."

"Willing to sacrifice anyone," Yafia whispered.

"Sacrifice? What do you mean sacrifice?" Nzinga asked, glancing at Yafia.

"Everyone is needed. They need the keen analytical ability of the Ngola. Shellanga says he knows how to fight the horse-soldiers. They wear armor spears can't pierce, and they ride into our foot-soldiers and cut them down with swords."

"What does Kaningwa mean, saying, 'Send Kabugye and Kajubi?' They're not here."

"Nzinga, you know what it means. They are already near there with a number of soldiers, and they cannot be warned."

"Yafia, please tell Shellanga to warn them. Nothing must happen to either of them."

Nzinga found her father after the conference, resting in his rooms. Kaningwa, the dutiful wife, was moving his pillows. Before she entered, Nzinga heard Kaningwa's voice.

"He's still young. He's strong and won't disappoint you."

The Ngola said, "When I was his age, I commanded an army and fought against these same kinds of horse-soldiers in Kongo."

When Nzinga came in, Kaningwa left the room, perhaps because Kaningwa preferred to listen to their conversation behind a secret door screen. Nzinga smiled at her father. He returned it.

"I'm concerned about you, Father. I need to prepare special food for you."

"Nzinga, since you were a child you have worried about me. I'll be all right. It's just a fever from those days I didn't eat or sleep well when I was with the army."

"Kaningwa is right. You shouldn't go, but you should send someone you trust."

"I'm sending Shellanga."

Nzinga took a deep breath. "Father, let me go with Shellanga. I know more than you think."

The Ngola's face changed. "Nzinga, don't ever ask that. How about the taboos? And oh, your mother Batayo. I couldn't bear losing you. Don't think of it."

"But, Father, even though I wasn't there, I helped stop the guns before. I know the Portuguese, too, with all I've learned from the priest and the traders and you. I do."

He said, "You helped Kajubi to destroy that gun? I bet you did." He sat up, called her to him, and squeezed her hand. "It's true. I'm sick, but I'm not sick enough to allow you to go."

He called guards and told them not to let Nzinga leave the palace. Nzinga was now her father's prisoner. She got word to Chatembo, hoping her friend might find a way to warn Nabugye and Kajubi about the horse-soldiers. Although Chatembo and Sufalu sent messages, no answers came back. This meant that Shellanga's army was between the fort and Luanda, and those Portuguese at the fort were preventing any travel between the Mbanza and Shellanga.

•

Nzinga never held her child and endured sad moments seeing any mother carrying a beautiful fat baby on her back. Wasema, from her mother's village, had a boy that Nzinga saw taking its first steps and running about the palace. Nzinga often stopped to play with the boy. At times, in a certain light, it seemed the child moved in the same way as Kajubi. She imagined hints of her father in the child's face. *The ways of Suku are beyond understanding. I wanted my child so badly that I imagine Wasema's child looks like Kajubi.*

Even Chatembo, who now had a little girl named Chiambo after her great-great-grandmother, commented how the child had nothing of Wasema, but looked like Kajubi. She shook a finger. "Did Kajubi do something here?"

Nzinga laughed. "Kajubi did something here," she said, pointing to where her heart beat in her own chest.

"Anyway," Chatembo said, "it's strange. I wouldn't want anybody's child to favor Nabugye as much as this one favors Kajubi."

•

Months later, the news trickled in ahead of Shellanga's victorious but much-depleted army. They had lost many warriors. Kajubi and Nabugye had killed many Portuguese at night and sent another team of horses with wheels over a cliff, this time into the river. Horses and soldiers were dead. They did this at night, but one day while traveling back, the two young commanders and about twenty men were found by Portuguese horse-soldiers on an open plain.

With no place to run or hide, Kajubi speared horses and used his strong bow, shooting arrows into the foreheads of the horse-soldiers, knocking them from their saddles. His arrows all gone, Kajubi stood with his spear-bearers as he had at the elephant hunt: throwing spear after spear onto the armor of the advancing horse-soldiers. A horseman cut down Nabugye, who fought beside him.

Kajubi thrust his last spear up through a horse-soldier, who cut through Kajubi's neck and shoulder.

Nzinga, weeping, never forgot the name of the beheader: Cordero. *I am going to get him someday, Kajubi. I'll show you I meant the vow I made to you.*

Chatembo placed her anger elsewhere. She said over and over that Kaningwa had caused this, and she swore to get her someday. "It's because of her that Chiambo has no father. And why you, Nzinga, have no child."

16.
FIRES OF THE NGOLA

RELEASED FROM HER FATHER'S palace, Nzinga went to her grandmother's and began to train daily with the young warriors. Once more, she dressed like them. She ate their food, went into the field with them, and went through the same exercises, believing a time would come when she'd need a mind and body as firm as iron.

She loved to see the young men train. She loved the coppery shine of their bodies in battle practice. She loved the way they carried their weapons and their assured manner. She loved the way they used fighting sticks and long knives. She now had nothing to do but train and practice.

While she did this, she learned from each of them and she practiced daily, twirling the fighting sticks, throwing the spear, and using a long knife like a sword. Entering combat was a distant wish that could never be true. Yet she and Chatembo knew that many men could never measure up to Nzinga's knowledge and skills.

Years passed with this "useless practice," as her grandmother called it. "No one is ever going to let the daughter of the Ngola go into battle."

"Then what are we good for? We can't do anything else."

"People like Yafia are useful. They support the Ngola."

"By doing the same work as servants? No, thanks. If a son can't go to war, then a daughter can. I'm not going to sit and watch the Portuguese occupy my ancestors' land, Grandmother. I will fight them. They have no right to come here and treat us like their vassals. In Europe, they must honor other countries."

"Only when they are powerful," Sufalu said. She stood at the door with Ntongu and Chiambo, Wasema's and Chatembo's children.

"Then we must be powerful. Actually, we are. Why do you think the Portuguese wait instead of coming directly in and capturing this whole country?" Nzinga asked.

"Because they fear us. They know if we came with all our strength at once, we could drive them into the sea," Sufalu said. "If they came as you suggest, the people would flee elsewhere, and the Portuguese would have only empty land. They want trade. They want slaves."

"We will be strong."

"What's this?" her grandmother asked. She'd been playing with the twisting, turning Ntongu and now studied what appeared to be a spear print on his abdomen.

Sufalu took the child quickly. "Probably a birth print."

"No," Chatembo said. She'd brought in roasted groundnuts for snacks. "It's one of those that are burned in."

"When did Wasema have this done?" Nzinga asked. She took the child from Sufalu, who released him reluctantly.

"She didn't do it. I asked her. She didn't know anything about it," Chatembo said.

"It looks like the markings on Kajubi's temples. He had those—" Nzinga looked up into Sufalu's wide eyes, pleading. "Is it? Could it be?"

Finally Sufalu nodded.

"Oh, Suku, how can this miracle be?" Nzinga pulled the boy to her and squeezed him so tightly he began to cry. "Oh, you," she kissed him, "I'm more than sorry, and happy. Happy!"

Sufalu said, "It would be useless to deny it now that you suspect. He is your child's and Kajubi's, but you can't show it. It would mean the child's life if your enemies knew."

Chatembo was surprised. "Mother, it's the best work you and Suku ever did."

Kajubi had once said something like that to Nzinga.

.

The Ngola recovered from his illness, but after the death of his two young commanders, he wasn't the same. It was true he was getting older, but Nzinga thought it was his disappointment in Mbande that caused him to lose the energy and eagerness for life that he'd always shown.

The Ngola went around the kingdom visiting chiefs, judging cases, and celebrating. He was a much-loved Ngola. Everywhere he went, people cheered and fell to the ground before him. Every time he sat or drank or ate, gongs and bells sounded. Whenever he decreed anything, even if it was a single statement, the drums sounded and dancers underscored his words. He kept the people happy and working while keeping his interest in his army, making sure that the Portuguese were kept off balance, and seeing that they progressed no further than the fort at Massangano. He periodically took the army and laid siege to the fort for months, and he made night incursions with a few warriors into the farming areas the Portuguese kept trying to expand.

Through the years, the Ngola continued to influence those around him to do their best work for Ndongo. From time to time he opened the palace stores and treasury and distributed among the villagers what he'd collected from taxes and wars, using the products of their own labor to reward them.

Nzinga believed there were no bounds to what she could gain from watching him work. When in his presence, she found him watching her. Once he called her to him.

"About Mbande. He is good, but he doesn't have your mind or heart. I'm afraid his mother indulged him in his weakness."

Nzinga waited for him to say more. Kaningwa approached. He said quickly, "He'll need a lot of help."

Kaningwa, beside them, looked from one to the other. "Father and daughter having a private chat?"

"Not private," he said, squeezing Nzinga's hand. "I don't get enough time to value this good child."

"But you do," Kaningwa said. "You let her do everything any daughter of an Ngola could possibly do." She alluded to Nzinga's loving Kajubi, whether the Ngola noticed or not.

.

That was the last time Nzinga and her father ever came close to talking about things that might affect Ndongo. A problem arose with chiefs in the Kongo. Since the Ngola hadn't been there for many years, he told Shellanga to stay home and watch the fort at Massangano while he, the king, went to the Kongo. Those chiefs needed to see his face and know he was still to be respected. He took along a small army which swept aside anyone who opposed him.

He was away for only two months, but when he came back, he was slumped in his litter, too sick to sit up. For days after the Ngola returned, he lay desperately ill. Nzinga paced up and down outside his rooms, trying to learn news of his possible recovery.

Doctors and medicine men came and went, trying to think of a remedy. They couldn't stop the rattle in his throat and the terrible fever that wracked his body. The medicine men whispered about how hot his body was to the touch. The ancestors were consulted. The medicine men divined a white chicken's bones and intestines, but no evidence of any offense to the ancestors was detected.

Once, when Nzinga peeped in past his doctors, her big, wonderful father was hard to recognize in the wasted figure lying so quiet and still on the bed, his breath labored and arrhythmic. His eyes were sunken into his skull and his skin sallow. Sweat formed like great globes on his forehead, and then coursed in rivulets down his face and onto his chest. His lips, parched and shriveled, seldom moved. His hand clutched his flywhisk as if it were a source of strength. He seemed to recognize no one.

Nzinga stayed around just outside the Ngola's room. Surprisingly, Kaningwa wasn't at his sick bed often. Where was Mbande? Her brother appeared near their father's door only once, briefly, in four days. He spent time whispering with his mother. While passing near Kaningwa's room to leave the building, Nzinga caught a glimpse of Mbande and his mother sitting together in quiet conversation. She passed near them, but neither acknowledged her.

When Nzinga entered her sisters' room, Kambi asked, "How is he?"

Nzinga shook her head. "Worse, I think. Whatever this sickness is, it's slowly eating him. Where is Funzi?"

"She went to pour libations at Mother's shrine. She hopes Mother will intercede with the ancestors." Kambi seemed doubtful that it would help.

"It's too bad Father sent both Chatembo and Sufalu away to Matamba. Sufalu would find who did this to him, and then find a way to cure him."

Sufalu and Chatembo had gone to Matamba to be the eyes and ears of the Ngola, since he was sick. By unfortunate chance, they were absent when both were most needed at Mbacka. And of all places to go to: that Suku-forsaken Matamba, not easy to reach by messenger. Nzinga's grandfathers had ruled Matamba years ago, a place of lush forest and leaping rivers, of deep grass-covered valleys, with many wild animals and venomous snakes. Her grandfathers had left Matamba in the hands of a chief who drove the elephants back into the forest. Now the chief's great-granddaughter, Fanvu, ruled Matamba and considered all the trees as her own. But who cared about Matamba? Certainly not Mbande and his mother. They were too busy thinking about him becoming Ngola if her father died.

Without Sufalu there to help, the other spirit mediums and doctors gave up hope, helplessly watching. The whole palace seemed to hold its breath. No sounds were heard from the pots and gourds in the kitchen. The fire in the royal pit had a high, crackling blaze, as if the keeper thought more fuel would infuse the Ngola with the energy to recover. People even walked slowly and quietly.

Nzinga believed that if she took care of him, if she bathed his hot forehead and made him herbal tea, she could make his fever go away. But he was not only a father, he was king; he was the father of many, and he was the husband of someone. So the chiefs held her back, and the doctors took him away from her. She watched from a distance as he sank further and further.

Three days later, the Ngola suddenly opened his eyes.

Nzinga flashed into the room from where she was watching at his door. The Ngola was looking straight overhead, speaking to a spirit, taking the blame for not driving out the Portuguese. After words she didn't understand, he said, "Will it fall to another to drive them out?" Then he was quiet again.

The next day, while Nzinga was in the room, her father strived to make a comeback. As Chief Oyimbu told everyone later, the Ngola reached over and caught his arm, saying, "Shellanga, Shellanga, there he is. Let's take that big elephant." He rose up as if to throw a spear. This time, Nzinga caught his hand and held it firmly. He looked at her, as if he'd say what he had many times before: "I knew it would be you. It was always you, supporting your old father."

That night she kept vigil outside his door. She caught her breath as he rose up from his bed, as if he'd bring that once-mighty body upright and take charge once more. But that powerful effort sapped his final strength. He fell back. The chiefs attended him, touching his face and neck, shaking their heads with each gesture.

Finally they announced to everyone: "The Ngola's fires are out. He has joined the ancestors."

◆

PART II
THE NEXT NGOLA

1615 – 1621

◆

17.
THE FIRST SACRIFICES

A CHORUS OF MOURNING CRIES rose up first from the palace and quickly spread throughout the kingdom. People threw themselves on the ground in sorrow for the much-loved old Ngola, elephant hunter, rainmaker, judge, protector of Ndongo.

The next day, with people gathered outside the palace as far as the horizon, the builders raised a stage for where the chiefs and ministers could sit. As Kaningwa smiled with pride and triumph in her eyes, the ministers led in all the sons of the Ngola's brothers, and, with loud drumming and exhortations, they put their hands on Mbande and declared him the new Ngola. Mbande was forty-two years old. Nzinga was thirty-five.

Mbande had to prepare for his father's burial and oversee the mourning period, with the assistance of ministers and mediums. First came the executions by Mbande of many people, including the traditional killings of the Ngola's cooks, guards, and keepers of the fire, and human sacrifices at the ancestral shrines. But the deaths of family members proceeded at the same time: all princes who could be regarded as future Ngolas were killed, with the exception of Mbande's own son.

No child of a princess had ever been known to become Ngola, so Nzinga didn't think there was any danger to her son Ntongu. Her child, along with Chatembo's daughter, was at the royal village. But

Kaningwa wanted to know how a child of Wasema, a captured servant, could go to the royal village. She bribed and questioned. The old midwives had finally gossiped, and the true identity of Ntongu became known.

Wasema brought Nzinga the news: Mbande's soldiers and Kaningwa's spies had taken the children from the griot at night. She'd seen both children afterward, poisoned and drowned, their young bodies floating in the lake near the royal village. When Nzinga heard, she felt she should have known from Kaningwa's whispering while her father lay dying. She held on to Wasema, her son's other mother. They cried and comforted each other.

How she hated Mbande. And Kaningwa.

Mbande was giving orders to safeguard his rule, and his mother was at the back of it. After all these years scheming and waiting, Kaningwa was in power.

And Nzinga had lost most everything dear to her.

Her own mother died trying to give the Ngola a son. There had been twins, Funzi and a little brother, and both mother and that baby brother died.

Kajubi died because Kaningwa had orchestrated his fate at the hands of Cordero, a swordsman who rode a horse.

And now, her father and her son were dead.

•

Nzinga had nothing left to love except Chatembo and Sufalu—and she had her father's love for Ndongo and its people. She'd heard her father's last words—*"Will it fall to another to drive them out?"* It would pass to someone else to drive out the Portuguese. Now that was Mbande.

Nzinga went to her mother's land, ruled over by her old grandmother, and welcomed the return of Sufalu and Chatembo, who had been summoned back from Matamba.

Without stopping to rest, Chatembo made the two days' journey to the royal village and demanded the griot show her where the children had been killed. Grabbing a heavy stone, saying she didn't want to live without those babies, Chatembo threw herself into the lake, where she sank. The griot made the workers dive in, saving her from drowning. They forced her out of the lake, kicking, screaming, and splashing water, and then guarded her until Chatembo's sadness turned to hatred for Mbande and his mother.

The death of the Ngola and then the two children also shocked and disoriented Sufalu. When she heard the news, Sufalu collapsed on the floor in Nzinga's grandmother's house and didn't move for a week. When she arose, she'd lost her visionary powers. She spoke continually of finding the children and wanting to go to Punga a Dongo, near the falls, to find Ntongu and Chiambo.

When Chatembo returned and saw Sufalu's condition, she did what she usually detested: she drank herself into a stupor with palm wine. The next morning, Nzinga and Wasema found Chatembo and pulled her from a granary where she'd made love with a warrior, the son of a nearby chief.

"My mouth is bitter," Chatembo said as they walked.

"From the palm wine?" Wasema asked.

Chatembo hung onto Wasema's arm. "From everything. Look, why aren't you bitter?" She studied Wasema's face. Her speech was slurred, still a bit drunk.

Wasema patted Chatembo on the back.

Chatembo shrugged off her hand, saying, *"Njoo! Njoo!* That's too good! Unacceptable. Shouldn't be too good, too quiet, like Nzinga there. Both of you." She almost stumbled, but got control and, with an effort, walked straight.

Nzinga came closer to her, almost touching her, but believed Chatembo needed to stand alone, without their help.

"Both of you," Chatembo pointed unsteadily toward first one and then the other. "Don't you know Mbande is nothing? Nothing! It's Kaningwa. Poison. She is poison. Always has been poison." Pointing to Nzinga, she said, "Tried to kill your mother for years. Tried to make your father infertile. Didn't want you to be born. Mother thinks she killed your mother and baby brother. Mbande isn't monkey poop on the ground. And you." She pointed to Wasema. "Poor captured child. You still don't know what hit you." She pointed back at Nzinga. "You have got to make up your mind. Get drunk and have sex, or get mad and kill her. Somebody has to kill her. Kaningwa will give Ndongo to the Portuguese with her jealousy and control of her son."

Nzinga let Chatembo talk until she described Kaningwa's control of Mbande as endangering the kingdom. Now Nzinga listened carefully, for she sometimes had the same thoughts.

Chatembo said, "Wasema, you were a captured girl. You'd have been banished if Mother hadn't protected you. Your baby wouldn't have grown up anyway. Who sent spies to make sure Nzinga's baby died? Kaningwa! Wasema, why didn't you tell who the baby's father was?"

"Everyone thought it was one of the chiefs," Nzinga said.

"No, it is Mutele," Chatembo said. "Mother knew. And you are still lovers."

"He told me he'd be a chief and have power next to Mbande," Wasema said. "Then we will marry."

"He won't marry you, Wasema. Kaningwa loves him."

Wasema's eyes moved from one woman to the other. "He said we'd have more children. I believe him."

"But Mutele is a snake. A snake is a snake. Now that the old Ngola is dead, just watch."

They went home in silence.

When they came in, Sufalu said, "Chatembo, where have you been? Don't you know? We have to go and find the children!" Sufalu tried to rise from her pillows, but Chatembo sank down by her, holding her.

"Dead, Mother. They're both dead."

.

During the time of mourning for the dead Ngola, no one worked the crops. No one went to market. No one dressed well. People wept often, and the dirge drums sounded night and day. Mbande had to visit the ancestral shrines, the beautiful bamboo-and-papyrus structures where the Ngola's fires always burned. But Mbande cut these duties as short as possible and spent time instead hunting and fishing on the islands in the river.

Nzinga had no time to grieve. She helped care for Sufalu and watched Chatembo closely. She kept them at her mother's village, where the Ngola had long ago given her land. She supervised the preparation of food, talking softly to them, making mats and baskets to pass time over the mourning period. When that period was finished, the rains soaked the sun-scorched earth, as if to bring soothing forgetfulness; the land burst forth with green.

Chatembo's spirits returned when they walked along the paths among fields of millet, sorghum, tubers, and the new maize high above their shoulders, and when they heard the chirp of insects and the melodious calls of songbirds. Chatembo seemed to awaken at the calls of fishermen along the Cuanza River and the flute of the boys herding goats.

She said, "Nzinga, let's call people in to dance."

Gradually, though shadows still hung over their days, Nzinga and Chatembo returned to laughter and dancing. But Sufalu remained lost. She'd aged. Her hair grew scraggly, and she had no interest in regaining her powers. She wandered from village to village seeking the dead children for years after. In the middle of a celebration, her hair in unkempt ropes, she'd seek out Chatembo and Nzinga, grasp their hands, and shout, "Let's go find Chiambo and Ntongu."

They hugged Sufalu then, kissing her old wrinkled face, whispering softly, "They are dead, Mama. They're both dead."

Sufalu usually sank down wherever she happened to be, head lowered, chin sunken into her chest. But later she'd disappear for days. Chatembo and Nzinga searched for her, only to find her in a village, well cared for but always saying, "I must find the children before the snake comes from the pot." She'd hold onto Nzinga and Chatembo then. She'd shake her head and say, "Oh, no, Kaningwa. No!"

Nzinga assigned two caretakers to follow, watch, and feed Sufalu wherever she went. Whenever Chatembo found her mother in this condition, she drank palm wine. Her favorite drink had always been light, sweet beer made from sorghum. But now, palm wine made Chatembo forget. Then, longing for Nabugye, she'd take a strong, young favorite and disappear into a grain bin.

But Nzinga kept busy, judging small querulous disputes among the nearby villagers, and organizing and improving the farmers. She sent young men who'd make good soldiers to Mbande, along with food, hides, and anything she had to strengthen the kingdom. People recognized her wisdom, knew her sorrow, and were proud to have a royal one so near.

Nzinga had Sufalu's spy system, which still reported to her; but without Sufalu's knowledge and Chatembo's attention, she couldn't use it as effectively as Sufalu had. She tried to keep informed about the movement of Portuguese troops. From time to time she received messages from sources in Luanda itself, reporting how many Portuguese were there, and warning them to be alert. Closer to home, she learned that her brother was ruling well, but he left too much to his chiefs and went hunting on the islands in the river.

·

One season supplanted another. Years passed. Crops were planted and harvested, trees and children grew taller and taller, rainy seasons came and went, and event melted into event. Nzinga gloried in the busy business of people and their problems. Being a long way from Mbanza and still further inland from Luanda, she heard only incomplete accounts of battles, either with other tribes or with the Portuguese. But it was common knowledge that the Portuguese were unhappy that Mbande failed to pay attention to trade. Nzinga heard often from traders who came by that the Portuguese wanted silver. Then news came trickling in to her that horse-soldiers were seen in great numbers around Massangano. She sent this information to Mbande. Her message was delivered, but she got no answer.

Then some soldiers fleeing Ndongo crossed her land. She arrested them at once and drew their story from them. The Portuguese horse-soldiers had won a great battle. They had a cruel captain who rode his horse among foot-soldiers, and no spears or arrows could kill him. It sounded like the same man who had killed Kajubi years before.

With each breath, the soldiers gave worse news: these horse-soldiers with swords, matchlocks, and noisy blunderbusses had won a great victory, capturing all of Mbanza. The Ngola's wife and mother were taken to Luanda.

Nzinga showed such wild anger at this that the soldier who spoke cowed in fear, as if she might kill him.

"If they are all taken, what are you doing alive? You come running here when the kingdom is . . . lost . . . "

The soldier, already on his knees, fell to the floor face down, begging for his life.

"All taken to Luanda," he began again.

Chatembo, tipsy at the start, sobered on hearing the story. Sufalu, who'd sat in a corner as if indifferent to the inquisition, now came forward.

"His mother?" Sufalu asked.

"And the Ngola's sisters," the soldier answered.

"All the Ngola's sisters?" asked Nzinga.

"All. Yes, all of the sisters."

Nzinga, animated, moved around the room thinking. All the sisters. That meant Kambi and Funzi had been taken.

"And what about the Ngola? Captured too?" She knew this was unlikely since there were so many avenues of escape from the palace, and there were people whose only job was to take care of the Ngola.

Chatembo burst out: "I hope they kill him."

The soldier said, "No, not the Ngola. He wasn't captured. He wasn't in the Mbanza. He was on an island, hunting."

▪

Nzinga silently cursed Mbande for not planning, not fighting, and for letting their ancestors' kingdom be overrun by outsiders. Now even the shrines of Ndongo were in the hands of the Portuguese. She sat for a long time alone, in darkness, wondering what she should do. She finally rose with the conviction that they must be ready to fight.

She communicated this to the surrounding chiefs, who all agreed, but one asked, "What can we do about the horses?"

Nzinga said, "We'll ask the ancestors."

The kingdom was in disarray by that time, the roads crowded with fleeing people. Nzinga went out to the people and told them, "Don't run away. We are going to fight for Ndongo."

But what to do? Ndongo had an Ngola. Action should start with him. It was all confusion, with people lost or running about trying to escape, so that the usual seers weren't to be found.

Nzinga sat with her grandmother, Chatembo, and Sufalu. Hoping to find out how best to get answers, she said to Sufalu, "What is to be done?"

Sufalu, not comprehending the situation, said nothing.

Chatembo sat with a hollow reed stuck in a gourd full of palm wine, and Nzinga became angry. She snatched the gourd from Chatembo's hand and dashed it to the floor, breaking the gourd and spilling liquid over everything. Nzinga charged at her, waved her arms angrily.

"This country is being taken away from us because of people like you, feeling sorry for yourself, wallowing in self-pity. The next thing you know, we'll all be roped and sold to Brazil."

Nzinga went on unleashing a verbal fury that her friend Chatembo had never known she harbored.

"Look at you! Your child is dead, your mother is out of her mind, and you, groomed all your life to take her place, can't do any better than suck on a piece of grass and jump into a grain bin with anyone who has a dinger. I've looked after you, your poor mother, and everyone else. Now I need help to save Ndongo, to save our people. Do I have to nurse you, who should be helping?"

Chatembo fell on her knees before Nzinga. "Oh, forgive me. Forgive me, my dear friend. Everything you say is true." She cried long and loud, until Nzinga lifted her up, begged her not to cry, and said that everything would work out.

All that day Chatembo sat with Sufalu, talking with her, begging her to try to help remember something. That evening she came to Nzinga.

"She's no better. Yet she did say that Musungu the Ironworker can see the children. He is the one closer to the Ngola."

Nzinga didn't know what that meant. Of course, she'd heard of Musungu. Everyone had, but he and his work were shrouded in mystery. He was a priest, a medium of fire and Ngola, fire and iron.

18.

MUSUNGU

U P THE RIVER FROM THE Mbanza, a well-worn path ran along the banks toward the great waterfalls at Cambambe. Further along, nearer the falls, a wispy spray rose up from the waterfalls and fed a dense forest of ancient trees. The trees were festooned with mosses and other hanging plants with leaf-like hands that trapped water and dropped it as a constant, nourishing rain on the ancestral growth that reached from the falls and Punga a Dongo straight up to Suku in the low clouds.

A little way into the forest the road forked, forming two paths, one along the river into the spray, another veering deeper into the green vegetation and away from the riverbank. In the center of this fork sat an ancestral shrine. All wet, misty, and mute, it held sculptures, pots for offerings of libations, and garlands made from human skin, and it was decorated with branches whose leaves mysteriously remained forever green.

These paths forced the traveler to make a choice: was it to be the falls or the forest? Through this canopy, the path to the falls ran along the banks, beaten by seers, mediums, and pilgrims of Ndongo who periodically made the trek to the monolithic sandstone hills that featured the footprints and the knife- and spear-prints of the Ndongo people's ancestors. The forest was an unknown place, its path nearly overgrown with plants, evidence of fewer travelers. To all of Ndongo, this place was sacred. It was Punga a Dongo, the place where the Ndongo god Suku and their ancestors met to give the elephant hunters a kingdom, which they had since held by earth, water, wind, and fire.

Nzinga, Chatembo, and Sufalu came with their servants to this shrine at the fork in the path when the sun was high in the sky. Nzinga and Chatembo offered food and poured millet beer, milk, and palm wine as an offering to the spirits and ancestors. They spent some time there praying and meditating. When they started along the path to visit the medium Musungu, Chatembo looked around nervously.

"What's wrong?" Nzinga asked.

"I don't see Mother. Where is she?"

"Maybe she went on ahead. She knows this place."

Chatembo shook her head. Aggravation and dread colored her features. "No," she said. "I was standing on the path to Musungu's, and she did not go by me."

"I also know she didn't go back." Then Nzinga said, "Oh," and ran down the path toward the falls. "She must have gone off looking for the children again. Let's find her."

They hadn't gone far before the path became straight. Nzinga saw Sufalu ahead, running, stumbling on the path, falling in the wet vegetation along the way, then getting up and running on.

"Wait, Sufalu," Nzinga called. "Wait for us."

But Sufalu didn't stop. Nzinga ran faster to catch her. Chatembo was also running and calling, "No, Mama. You're going the wrong way. Wait!"

But nothing slowed Sufalu. Nzinga was surprised at her speed and her determination. While Nzinga ran behind her, Sufalu must have fallen on the path or in the weeds beside it three or four times. Every time, she rose to her feet quickly and shakily and then raced on. When Nzinga came nearer, she heard Sufalu mumbling: "The children . . . at Punga a Dongo . . . with the ancestors."

Nzinga caught Sufalu by the waist. They both fell on the path. Then Chatembo, unable to stop fast enough, fell on top of them. They all lay there, holding, hugging, and cooing to each other.

Sufalu said, "Want children . . . "

Chatembo murmured, "They're all right, Mother. We're here now, Mama. I love you."

Nzinga said, "Sufalu, Chatembo . . . It's going to be all right. We're together. Oh, Suku, look where we are . . . so near to you."

They sat holding each other, rocking back and forth.

A tall, ebony, muscular man suddenly appeared nearby, gazing over the ledge into the falls with a somber, faraway expression.

Sufalu stretched out her hand. "Musungu, Musungu, son of the ancestors. We need you. The kingdom is lost. We need you. Ndongo is lost. The children are lost."

Musungu towered over them. He put out his hand and lifted them up one by one. He said, "Come," pointing the way back along the path into the forest.

Musungu was the medium through whom Suku and the ancestors worked to keep the pact made with the people of Ndongo. He was seldom seen, but he and his people were always working. Without them, there'd be no crops growing, no maize, plantains, simsim, sorghum, or groundnuts. Without him, no battles would be won, and without him no animals would be killed. But only the king and his messengers usually took the path into the forest that led to the medium and blacksmith, Musungu.

As they walked, Nzinga thought about Sufalu. Even in her delirium, Sufalu knew more than most people; she'd said it years before: "If the children are lost, Ndongo is lost, and the kingdom is lost. After that, there is nothing left. If you want anything, you must keep everything. It starts with your belief in the past. The ancestors. They are then, and they are now. If you lose the connection, there is nothing. You can't think only of hunting and keep a kingdom."

Nzinga's father had hunted, fished, wrestled, and ruled. He loved, he judged, he fought, and he danced to music. He worshiped, and he made rain. He kept it all.

While Nzinga thought about this, they trudged into the forest, passing a place where the pungent smoke of unburned wood assailed their nostrils. Then they saw people busily making fires in symmetrically stacked piles of logs. Once the fires burned, they covered them with green leafy branches and piles of dirt, so that they smoldered beneath. These workers made many of these piles, and the ash piles in the forest told of many such fires made in the past. When she was a child, Nzinga had seen the night ritual in which a visitor spread this ash in gardens of the royal village. A worker said it was something to do with rain and growth, but he didn't know the details. She knew now that this was the process of making charcoal.

They passed through the forest into a dry land dotted with many anthills. Workers bent among the anthills while smoke issued through vents cut in the tops. When Nzinga came near, she saw that these anthills had been transported from where the ants had made them. Their hard, rock-like structures were being used for a new purpose.

Musungu did what he would not have done for anyone but an emissary of the Ngola. He showed how the workers knelt by a slit cut in the bottom of one of those hills, pumping air with an animal-hide bellows. Kneeling before the hearth of the anthill, Nzinga looked into the flame, which was first yellow, then blue, fed by charcoal. A hot yellow liquid dropped downward.

Musungu took them to another anthill that had been cooled. The workmen raked out ash and debris with forked sticks. Small, hard rings showed among the ash. They were still hot, but cooling. A workman took a stick, lifted the rings, and dropped them into a pot of water, which sizzled and sputtered. Steam rose from its surface. The workman put one into another pot of water and then reached in and handed it to Musungu. He passed it to Sufalu, who shook her head and looked wistfully at him.

Then it was Nzinga's turn to hold it.

"It's an Ngola," said Musungu.

"Yes. 'Ngola' describes this ring I'm holding," Nzinga said. "It means ring of iron." The meaning about her country and her father was right there in her hand. *Does Mbande understand what he is and what he has to do? He can't just spend his time hunting with his friends.*

Chatembo said, "I've been here before with Mother. With your father the Ngola. And with Mbande. Yet I don't know what any of it means."

Nzinga said, "It means many things. First, this is a ring of iron." She held up the piece of ashy metal. "But it means we can make tools from it: hoes, knives, spear points, and swords. This," she held the ring higher, "puts a ring of iron around the people of Ndongo. And their leader is named after that ring. He is strong like the ring of iron, and he uses that ring to protect and govern Ndongo. He is himself the Ngola, ring of iron."

She stopped, out of breath, her eyes flashing with the excitement of discovery. The more she talked, the more she understood.

"Here, let me show you," Musungu said.

They went with him toward a small building with a bamboo enclosure that contained a fire pit and a metal bench. Musungu threw some powders from a gourd onto the fire, which answered with flashes and sputters. Then he threw the ring of iron onto the hot coals and waited until it glowed red. Using tongs, he brought it to an anvil and, with a fierce rhythm, he struck it with a hammer, beating music from it, flattening it with every note, then reheating it and shaping it, until it formed into a knife. He cooled it in water and deftly wetted a piece of warthog skin that lay nearby. Attaching a wooden handle to the knife, he covered the handle with warthog skin and handed it to Nzinga.

"When the skin dries," he said, "it will fit tightly on the handle. You will need this one day."

She and Chatembo walked together behind Musungu, who strolled in front alongside Sufalu. He asked her over and over: "Sufalu, are the swans coming to Luanda?" as if he were trying to understand something from her answer.

But each time he asked, she answered by throwing up her hands and saying, "Oh, Musungu, what an aggravation. The children can't be found anywhere."

While looking at her intently, he countered by asking, "Was it an ancestor who told your great-grandmother of the swans?"

"You know. You see everything, Musungu. Can you see the children?"

"What's he doing? Why is he talking about swans now, Chatembo?" Nzinga asked.

"I think he's trying to make Mother remember and get her powers back."

"With swans?" Nzinga said.

"Nzinga, have you forgotten Mother's history? Have you forgotten how she came to be your father's spiritual seer?"

"No. We first heard that story from the griot at the royal village. Your great-great-grandmother had a dream that the Portuguese were coming on the backs of swans."

"Not a dream, a vision! My great-great-grandmother had a vision!" Chatembo became excited, the way Nzinga had been while holding the iron ring. Words poured like water. "She was a diver at Luanda along the bay, what we call the Ngola's bank. The bottom was rich in *nzimbi*, cowrie shells, our trade money. But one day my great-great-grandmother stayed down too long. She remained in a deep sleep for a month. After that, she could see things happening far away. Or she'd have a vision. And later that thing happened."

"I remember it all, Chatembo," Nzinga said. In that ancient vision, two giant swans in the sea proved to be ships. One split open and threw smoke and fire through the palm trees. Men came who wore shiny head plates and long knives fastened to their hips, and they carried sticks that belched fire. They took all of Luanda and remained there.

Chatembo said, "That's my great-great-grandmother's vision. She told everyone, including the old Ngola. And it happened just as she'd envisioned. She became the arm of the Ngola, and so have all her female offspring, down to Sufalu. And me. Someday."

Nzinga caught up to Musungu. She said, "Do those anthill furnaces create all the iron Ndongo needs to make spears and knives for war? And all the hoes for farming?"

"No," he said. "Those furnaces are only for practice. For training young ironworkers. Look, the work of Ndongo goes on over there."

He pointed to a hillside far beyond the clearing. Along its border stood row after row of furnaces made of plaster-covered clay, twice as tall as a man, reinforced outside by large wooden poles roped together with pliable saplings. The fires blazed. Men worked busily around the bottom of each furnace. Behind the furnaces, people on the hillsides dug into the earth.

Musungu said, "They're digging the iron rock for the furnaces." He looked at Nzinga the way her father did, and he seemed to be thinking the way her father had: *"She wants to know everything. I thought so. That is why I gave her the knife. Ndongo needs her now. The Portuguese have come too close to this shrine. If they aren't stopped, soon they will be here. These people will disappear back across the falls, deep into Africa, or into Matamba."*

As they passed the rows of furnaces, Nzinga spoke with men working there, asking if she might see one unlit so she might know how it worked. The men didn't answer until Musungu told them that she was the daughter of the old Ngola, the sister of the present one. Then they laughed and talked with her. They hoisted her up so she could see inside. One told how it was loaded with alternate layers of charcoal and iron rock, how the air was pumped in by bellows, producing a high temperature that melted the iron ore so it flowed out at the bottom.

Musungu nodded, but said nothing about the pot below, which held the magical vines and powders that made the whole process successful.

They passed on to the potters' sheds where women were firing pots, and then on to areas where pots of different sizes and designs lay in the sun. Sufalu sat down here, rubbing her hands over a smooth pot with lizard designs.

"Tashana. Tashana. Which one is it? Sufalu, you saw so much. Why then didn't you see the snake before it went to the royal village? Why didn't you see what was happening all around us?" She started to cry.

One of the working women brought her water. Sufalu poured it from the gourd onto her head, holding some in her hand and trying to suck it into her nose, until she coughed and sneezed, strangled by her efforts. Then she jumped up and ran to Musungu, shouting, *"Minkisi, minkisi, minkisi!"*

Musungu was smiling, but silent.

"Everything you do here is for a purpose," Sufalu said. "That's *minkisi*. It served me well. My great-great-grandmother saw the swans, saw the ships bringing the first Portuguese."

"You remembered!" Chatembo shouted. She ran to Sufalu, hugging her. Then Nzinga came, and they were all crying, while Musungu stood above them, smiling.

To Nzinga, this was a place of wonder. They sat now, having cool fruit drinks in one of the potters' shops. Religious masks hung along the walls. Tables held finished and unfinished sculptures and other works. They sat among pots, bowls, and baskets of many shapes and patterns. What went on here created the base for the whole of Ndongo. *How good it was that the Catholic priests never found out about this place. It's the first thing they take away: whatever you believe in. I want to know more about how they think. How they use their religion to control people.*

Chatembo, regarding her mother lovingly, said, "We came here to find out what to do next. The Mbanza is captured and Hyena Face—I mean, the Ngola's mother—and sisters are captured. What should we do?"

"Should we go into your cave and beseech the ancestors?" Sufalu looked at Musungu. "Perhaps we can get direction from the old Ngola about what to do."

"Ngola Mbande came here one day after the loss of the palace," Musungu said, his voice lowered. "He was sad. We went into the caves. As an offering, he killed fifteen warriors and six girls, barely twelve rains old. Their bodies are still there. He put skin-covered garlands of human flesh at the shrines to appease Suku. We tried to call your father, Nzinga, but he sent a lesser spirit as emissary. He's angry with your brother. His message was, 'Never give up. Use everyone and everything. Do what needs to be done. Don't let the kingdom slip away. Fight. Fight. Never give in. Never give up. No matter how hopeless.' We tried to get the spirit back several times, but it was no use. He said he wouldn't come into a kingdom inhabited by Portuguese soldiers."

Nzinga was on her feet. "Where is the cave, Musungu? My father will talk to me. He'll give me directions."

Musungu got up to lead her out, but Sufalu said, "No. You can't go to see the ancestors at this time. Do not bother them when they are angry. They will cause calamity, unmindful of who they are hurting. They are no longer alive and don't think as we do. They belong to another world, another time."

Nzinga hesitated, not yet convinced.

Chatembo spoke with conviction. "I don't need to see any bodies of those killed by Mbande. We should wait."

"What else happened while Mbande was here? What are his plans?" Nzinga asked.

"He's coming to see you, Nzinga."

Chatembo and Sufalu frowned, puzzled.

"He'd better bring his soldiers with him," Nzinga said.

◈

19.
THE FIRST JOURNEY

THREE DAYS LATER A LONE runner dashed up the shore, laboring for breath. He dropped at the door of Nzinga's house.

"The Ngola is coming."

Nzinga, Chatembo, and Wasema looked down the bank, shading their eyes. The man needed to catch his breath. *Even the messengers are poorly conditioned*, Nzinga thought. She asked the runner for more information, but he knew nothing, just pointed toward the old Mbanza.

"What will you do if he comes?" Chatembo asked.

"I'll help him."

"Yes, I know, for Kambi and Funzi, but I wish . . . "

"That's not the only reason I must help."

"Hyena and Hippo have got their way again."

"Chatembo, we have lost our lovers and our children. We can't let him throw away Ndongo. I know how you feel. I think you should go help Sufalu when he comes, because you know how much power he has now. He may do you ill if you forget and say something."

"I won't say anything. My hate is deeper than words. I might do something."

"Please, Chatembo. We've had enough sorrow."

Three more runners arrived at intervals that morning, shouting the message: "The Ngola is near."

Nzinga gave up waiting and went back in the house. "When he comes, we'll know it."

Soon after, Wasema ran into the house waving her arms. Muffled sounds of drums and xylophones came through the opened door. When Nzinga went outside, a crowd of people on the river-bank pointed and waved over the water. In the middle of the river, the Ngola's large boat glided swiftly toward them, propelled by strong oarsmen, with deep chest sounds and music loud enough to carry over the roar of the falls. Small boats were making shore and then dislodging runners who made their way straight up the bank to Nzinga's house. Falling on their knees at her feet, they shouted, "The Ngola is near."

The Ngola didn't alight from his boat immediately, but sent up a litter containing Kadu, the old minister who had served her father. *A wise move,* Nzinga thought. *Kadu will help keep the kingdom together for a while.*

"Why is he sending Kadu instead of coming himself?" whispered her grandmother.

"Because Mbande killed my child, and he's afraid of me. He wants Kadu to soften me up."

They stayed on the riverbank while people bowed and worshiped their new Ngola, who sat on a cushion in his boat as it rocked with the moving water. He raised his hands several times to acknowledge people.

Wasema had gone down to the water's edge with a few other people, who bowed and called out praise names for the Ngola: "Rainmaker, Child of the Sun, Keeper of the Flame." Away from the crowd, Wasema studied the boat, but neither the Ngola nor Mutele took notice of her. Chatembo watched the boat, shaking her head.

"I'm pleased to see you, Minister Kadu."

While talking to him, Nzinga remembered when he stole Oyimbu's cows. *Like Father said, he's a good man who made a mistake. Now he's serving Ndongo because of my father's good judgment.*

Kadu was respectful, according Nzinga great honor and describing this meeting as auspicious. He said, "The old Ngola was experienced. This disaster would never have happened in his day."

He even smiled once. "You know Mbande is doing well for someone of his experience. True, he's made mistakes in judgment, but whatever he has done has been for the good of Ndongo. And Ngolas can cover up their mistakes, making them less noticeable."

"What does the Ngola want of me?" Nzinga asked.

"Well, *eh, humph.* We had a conference. The Ngola is very sad that his mother and his wife are . . . and . . . well, your sisters are held in Luanda. At the conference, they said you were the only one who could get them back. He's come to ask your help."

"Who else was at this conference?"

"Who else? The Ngola, Oyimbu, and Shellanga, a few of the Ngola's hunting friends. Some of the princesses . . . Princess Yafia especially was invited to sit in. She'd have been taken, but she was quick to take the escape route down to the river."

"What did Princess Yafia say?"

"They first asked her to go to Luanda, but both she and Shellanga were against it. She doesn't speak Portuguese. She said it was a lot to ask of you, but if anyone could do it, it would be you."

"Is he coming to talk to me?"

"He sent me to invite you to join him."

"All right." Nzinga started down the bank, her bare feet sliding in the mud.

"Princess," Kadu called. "Take my litter. Ride down."

Nzinga didn't stop until she reached the boat, where she paused and bowed, showing the people how a princess displayed respect to her brother who was the Ngola.

Mbande nodded in her direction. "Help the princess in," he said to the boatmen. His friend Mutele, who seemed to accompany him everywhere, was there.

Nzinga shrugged off their outstretched hands. Throwing her leg over the side of the boat, she climbed in and then sat facing her brother.

"Nzinga, I think you are still angry with me," Mbande said. "But I did what is usual and right. The ancestors decreed it, not me."

"He was a baby. How could a baby be a danger to you?" she asked, her anger controlled. "And what could Chatembo's baby do? She wasn't your father's daughter, just a little girl."

"I have my own son, Nzinga, who will be Ngola. I did what all Ngolas do. Even Father did it."

She put her hands on her hips and looked sternly at him. "That wasn't the story the old griot told."

He said, "His ministers did it, because he refused. It's still his doing—Mother told me so. Anyway, the ancestors, including the father you loved so, need you to rescue or ransom your mother—my mother, wife, and sisters. Will you help make a treaty with the Portuguese?"

"How would I do that?"

"Go to Luanda. Get my mother, wife, and sisters released first, and then negotiate the treaty while you're there."

"You're asking me to put my head into a crocodile's mouth. Why don't you go?"

"You know why," Mbande said. "If they have me, they have Ndongo. I cannot go. The ancestors depend on you."

"They were depending on you until you let the Portuguese take the palace."

"I won't argue or get mad. Give me an answer."

Nzinga sat before him on the polished seat of the boat. Nets, knives, one matchlock gun, hunting spears, and bows and arrows ranged to the side behind her. *As soon as this discussion is over, he's going hunting.*

Not one word of warmth or glimpse of kinship passed between them. She was ready to work with him. Clearly, he was not. This was merely a business arrangement to get his mother and wife back. Nzinga wanted him to express love for his family and his people, wanted to provoke him, to make him declare that the kingdom mattered. "What will you do if you get everything back again?"

"That is only to be answered when it happens," he said. "You can make it happen. I'll put the whole of Ndongo at your command to prepare you to be my ambassador."

He doesn't fathom the greater issues that drive a leader.

"Father went as far as Kongo to be seen by the people. By living on the islands, you're disconnected from the people. They can't see you there."

"The Ngola must be safe. In the river I'm safe from the horse-soldiers."

She gazed up the embankment at her house for a moment, thinking how to answer. Glancing back, she caught an eye signal and a smile that passed between Mbande and Mutele. Wasema stayed by the boat gazing at Mutele, who never looked her way.

"I'll do it, but I must have Princess Yafia help me prepare. And Minister Kadu must accompany me to Luanda." Nzinga jumped out of the boat.

"It is as you say. Just hurry," he said.

Kadu entered the boat, and Mbande nodded to the people in the boat. The drums started up again, and the boat moved off. Neither Mbande nor Mutele looked back. Wasema remained where she'd been. The people standing with her waved at the departing boat. She did not.

When Wasema finally came up the hill, Chatembo put an arm around her shoulder. Nzinga saw Wasema shaking, tears glazing her eyes.

Mbande had no idea of the power he'd just granted to the sister that both he and his mother had scorned. Ndongo was large and wealthy. It stretched from the coast to the mountains many miles inland, and on one side it embraced some tribes in the Kongo. Even the old Ngola didn't know the extent of his wealth. Now Nzinga could know. Every part of the country produced valuable products. Fruits, grain, and wild animals abounded. Ivory in large quantities, skins and cloth, salt, cattle, goats, sheep, and copper. Every chief in Ndongo owed his chieftainship to the Ngola and yearly sent part of whatever was produced to the Ngola, along with the best cooks, drum makers, musicians, potters, sculptors, and craftsmen of every kind.

Nzinga ordered it announced by drum, runners, tax collectors, and word of mouth that she was going to Luanda to bring back the Ngola's family and win back the country. Every chief wanted to be the one that did the most. Princess Yafia, who was a great organizer, talked with people who were rebuilding the Mbanza and its shrines without the knowledge of the Ngola. They felt cut off from him, because he lived on the island. Yafia collected everything and sent it to Nzinga.

The chiefs sent their best soldiers. Nzinga sent them on to Shellanga and then asked for their best dancers and musicians. They sent her spears and shields. She said, "Send me fine cloth, salt, colorful mats, and animal skins. Send me ivory tusks, ingots of Kongo silver, and copper bracelets." And they came. In bundles. A steady procession of people came and went, delivering the goods of Ndongo. So much came that Nzinga built extra storage houses in the forest near Musungu.

The whole kingdom was busy night and day with selecting, fashioning, and finishing. The process was the same with people as with material goods. Yafia and Chatembo helped Nzinga select the people who would accompany her, the ones who could help make the greatest impression of wealth, beauty, and discipline. These people were as disciplined as they had been under her father.

.

Nzinga set out for Luanda a month later, on her way to win back the Ngola's mother, his wife, and Nzinga's sisters. From the ruins of Mbanza as far as the eye could see, there was a silent, flowing mass of people that stretched out toward the sea. In the forefront of this body was a large contingent of the Ngola's army. Shellanga, the king's general, commanded it.

Most of the women, plus Minister Kadu and his helpers, were carried in litters. Like a chair but with a pole attached to each side, a litter wasn't a comfortable way to travel. With the rough forward motion, Nzinga rose up and down with each step depending on the levelness of the earth. Nzinga often got out of the litter and walked, giving her bearers a rest. She sent carpenters along to build her a dwelling wherever she stopped.

She'd never been this far away from home. As they neared Luanda, Kadu sent runners to notify the governor that the Ngola's sister was coming. Kadu's assistant minister met them to report that he'd requested an audience with the governor, but the governor kept him waiting for two days and treated him worse than a vassal.

The Portuguese settlers continued to urge the governor to pursue the war while he held the hostages.

"They want to attack the Ngola while he is routed. They want to hold the Ngola's family until he pays with slaves and silver."

Kadu was apprehensive. "We are all unarmed and have no chance if the governor decides to make us hostages also."

Nzinga, however, detected in the governor's posturing the signs of her future success. "Shellanga can take care of any attack at home. They have no right to hold the Ngola's wife and family as hostages. Let's go on to Luanda."

.

Shellanga accompanied Nzinga as far as the fort. When he halted his army and the people after a long day's march, he and Nzinga went into conference with Kadu. Nzinga was dressed as a warrior, but he was well aware of who she was. Everyone there knew her and her habits.

Shellanga said, "Tomorrow we reach the fort by noon. There, I'll bid you and your entourage goodbye."

"But I hope you will consider what Father would do," Nzinga said, "and stay to assist us a little longer."

"Princess," he spoke sternly, "the Ngola gave me strict orders to turn back when we reached the fort."

"I'm not asking you to disobey him. But I know the importance of what I ask. I can't go to Luanda powerless and expect them to give me back the Ngola's people. We have to make the governor respect us."

"You want me to attack the fort."

"No, I'm asking you to lay siege for three days."

"How do I do that without attacking it?"

"Don't let any messages get to the fort's commander or any messages get out from him."

"Princess, daughter of the old king, what will you do?"

"This is our country. They have no right to invade."

Shellanga paused. "You sound almost like your father."

"You know they have spies out watching us, reporting to the fort and to the governor. I want them to be uncertain. I need them to fear the people of Ndongo. That's the only way we can win back what is ours."

"But, Princess Nzinga, how will we change that?"

"These people are our enemies. I'll do what my father would. I'll take ten warriors and steal inside the fort tonight and slit some throats. Then I'll come out. They can't follow me while you and your army are still here. I'll change into my ambassador's clothes and go on to Luanda. They will know that we have power here at home backing us."

"They have always been afraid of us, Princess."

"You're right, they were afraid of us. But when an enemy can take your palace, enter your house, and molest your family, he no longer has that fear. We must put that fear back into them."

When they neared the hated fort of Massangano later that day, Nzinga and Shellanga's army split off from her entourage. She warned her people to go with Chief Kadu no farther than the baobab trees and to wait for her there. Restless, the people wanted to go on to Luanda, but Chief Kadu talked long about the wishes of their Ngola. They decided not to travel into the edge of the savannah where Portuguese raiders often ventured.

Shellanga set up his army around the fort. Nzinga and her band waited in the nearby vegetation down near the river until nightfall. One of her soldiers spotted an African servant from the fort, possibly a cook, who had come out to draw water. She gave him a warning: keep all of the Ngola's spies in the fort's kitchen where they wouldn't be harmed.

Nzinga and ten men entered through a door left open for them and swept through the fort, killing many sleeping soldiers. She found the fort's commandant sleeping and didn't awaken him until he was securely tied, naked, in his bed. When he yelled out, she stuffed banana fibers into his mouth and slit his face and his arm muscles. At her command, one of her men shouted, "This is for the horse-soldiers who defiled our palace and ancestral shrines." Then she left the commandant lying there; he never knew it was a woman who led the attack.

Nzinga met Shellanga at daybreak and reported their success. She then bade him goodbye and turned toward Luanda, dressed again as the Ngola's ambassador, riding in a litter beside her father's old chief, Kadu.

◆

PART III
A PRINCESS IN LUANDA

1622

20.
NZINGA ARRIVES

I N NZINGA'S GRANDFATHER'S TIME, the Portuguese had taken land near the ocean and held it by force, but until now they hadn't been able to proceed inland beyond the hated fort at Massangano, about two days' distance from Luanda.

Nzinga and a royal entourage of one hundred people neared Luanda in western Africa during the dry season of August 1622 by European reckoning. The landscape around Luanda differed from the lush, rich green of Ndongo. Few trees, bushes, or tall grasses grew here. When Nzinga left her litter to walk, she felt hot sand underfoot, and the fiercely intense sun shimmered in the branches of the giant, ghost-like baobab trees that dotted the land. Clumps of palms waved their fronds in the languid breeze.

Nzinga had lived through seventy-eight rainy season—thirty-eight years. She was weary from months of preparation and two weeks of travel to reach a hostile area in her own land. Her mission was the most perilous and yet the most important ever undertaken by any of her people, for its outcome would determine the future of the entire country.

Chief Kadu rode in a litter beside her, each of them carried by four men. Whenever his bearers brought his litter near Nzinga, he said the same thing.

"This never would have happened with the old Ngola."

Nzinga looked at him sternly. "Father is dead." She couldn't utter that without sadness, but she had to be firm. "You're a trusted minister, but you can't speak that way about my brother. He is now the Ngola."

"Princess, I know I could be killed for it, but it is the truth. We, the ministers and the council, tried to warn him. He wouldn't listen. Look how he left the palace unguarded. If your brother had paid attention to the army and not spent his time hunting and wrestling with his friends, this wouldn't have happened."

"It has happened, Chief Kadu. What do you think Father would do if he were in my place?"

"*Njoo!* You are a woman! Your father would never have been in your place." As an afterthought, he said, "Nor would he have been in your brother's place. Your father was ever watchful. He planned and trained his army. He left trusted generals in charge all of the time. That's why the Portuguese haven't conquered our people until now." His voice trailed off.

There it is again, that business of being a woman. But maybe he has something valuable to say, so let me hear it.

He brought his litter even closer and looked at her with steely eyes, imitating the manner and demeanor of her father. "He'd have brought every soldier in Ndongo with him and driven the Portuguese into the sea."

"Yes, you're right," she said. "Father would have done that. But the Portuguese have guns and we have spears. They have members of the royal family as hostages. If we tried that now, what would happen to my sisters? And Mbande's wife and mother? That's why Mbande didn't try to force their release."

"If not for the ancestors and the gods, and for the possible rescue of your sisters, you wouldn't have helped him. He sent you because you know the Portuguese language. But he had the chance to learn it himself. Your father brought him an African tutor who'd been to Lisbon."

"One who was brought back to Ndongo by the Portuguese to entice my father to trade in slaves." Nzinga had also learned under that African tutor. Then she'd studied the language for years under that priest her father had held captive, Father Gouvieae. When the horse-soldiers captured the royal family, they took the priest back to Luanda. Would she see him there?

"Enough of this, Kadu. As you say, I'm here because of the ancestors. I'll use what I know about the Portuguese to free the hostages."

"These Portuguese don't give up anything. They believe in force." Kadu's face, in his old age, was as wrinkled as a dried palm date and his manner as sour as an unripe bush mango.

"We'll see," she said. "Let's camp here. How far is Luanda now? There's all this sand underfoot. I've heard stories from Sufalu about how sandy and barren the coast is. But I like the palm trees and how the wind talks to them, how beautifully they move. There," she pointed. "Let's camp somewhere in that grove."

The Ndongo people traditionally built a temporary dwelling wherever the king or any member of his family stayed for a night. While the people constructed a house for Nzinga, Kadu—who had traveled to Luanda several times before—pointed out sights to Nzinga.

"The main road is just beyond that biggest baobab tree." The tree's trunk was disproportionately slim; with its short branches, the tree looked like it was upside down, its roots in the air. "Look carefully. See people moving on the road there? That's the path to Luanda. When we go nearer to the tree, we can see the fort and town buildings."

As Kadu and Nzinga approached the baobab tree, people passing stopped to speak to their guards. These were the Ngola's people who traveled back and forth to Luanda to trade. When they were told Nzinga was the old Ngola's daughter, and when they recognized the Ngola's iron and copper circlets on spears and on the amulets around the warriors' necks, the people fell on the ground in greeting.

At the baobab tree, she saw the town's tallest structures, which seemed only a short distance away. Most of the buildings were enclosed by a wall. The fort at Luanda was spread over a much wider area and had stronger, higher walls than the fort at Massangano, which was a stark, gray eyesore with a reinforced gate and gun turrets. The fort at Luanda was built in the shape of a cross, as the priest, Father Gouvieae, had told her. Nzinga compared it to the

Ngola's palace, which was also built for strength and protection, but in another way, with lots of mazes and secret passages. Building a fort like this, firm and strong on the edge of a foreign country, meant that its builders were unsure of their power and fearful of their surroundings. Nzinga intended to use that fear to gain the freedom of the Ngola's family and his kingdom.

They made camp and spent the rest of the day and night getting ready for their entrance into Luanda. Nzinga and Kadu arranged all their people to present the greatest effect. Before the sun was up, every member of her entourage was washed, scrubbed, and dressed according to her directions. They arrived at the gates early, just as the sun streamed across the fort's turrets. The palm trees stirred in the breeze, and the white ocean surf rumbled in the background.

• • •

A new Portuguese governor, João Correia de Sousa, had arrived in Luanda not long after the Ngola's palace was taken. Although the governor had been informed months before of Nzinga's mission, no outward show or preparation was made to receive Nzinga. The Ngola's minister announced that she was coming to Luanda; after that, daily reports came to him on the progress of her entourage.

Then news came that the Ngola's sister was just outside Luanda. The next morning, the governor was still at breakfast when he heard the bells signaling her arrival at the gates. He'd heard reports about her intelligence, charm, and regal bearing from Father Gouvieae, who had been rescued when the royal hostages were taken. The governor hurried to the curtained room, where he intended to watch the procession unobserved. Surrounded by his own African servants, he was unprepared for what he witnessed.

First, drummers pranced in to herald the entrance of the Ngola's sister. Then came her warriors, unarmed but with bodies molded and muscular, each step speaking of power and discipline. The onlookers stood opened-mouthed in awe.

Fifty strong men marched behind the first group, laden with wrapped packages, furs, skins, caged animals, monkeys, birds, and a cheetah. Her women followed, of all sizes and hues, dressed in finery.

Some wore local dress while others were dressed in European clothes bartered or captured during the century of trade between the Ndongo and the Portuguese. People at the front faced forward, while a group among the exotic birds and caged animals turned backward, bowing and pointing to a giant litter borne on the shoulders of eight men.

Atop the litter sat Nzinga in regal dress. Two attendants on either side constantly circulated the air with large papyrus fans. Three drummers marched on each side of the litter, beating a marching cadence. Two men in masks blew intermittently on large bushbuck horns. After them came more women and marching men.

The men and women in the fort all watched in awe: African, mulatto, Portuguese, and a few Englishmen and Dutchmen whose ships had been captured. Stable men paused in currying the horses they tended. People with water buckets paused. Soldiers atop the parapet along the fort's wall rested their matchlock gun butts and leaned over to gaze upon Nzinga.

An unarmed Portuguese attendant ran ahead to direct the parade to the meeting room, a giant hall on one side of the fort. The governor watched from behind a curtain until he lost sight of her, then he shifted his view so he could see her in the meeting room.

Inside, her many servants attended Nzinga as she alighted from her litter. She wore a crown of feathers and brocaded robes studded with Kongo silver and gold. She was tall, agile, and well-proportioned, with an ample bust, a slim waist, and curving hips. Her smooth skin and eyes were black, her manner calm and assured. She moved with deliberate, unstudied regality, barely turning her head, apparently seeking her family.

Then she waited to receive a chair.

The governor's ministers, the old priest, and several servants watched her enter, but no one offered a chair. Kadu, the Ngola's minister, requested one. The governor's counsel, having heard it was the custom for African women to sit on the floor, pointed and offered the rug, to place her below the governor's chair.

Kadu clapped his hands.

Three men came forward, fell on all fours, and together formed into chairs. Nzinga's ladies assisted her in sitting upon one of them.

While she waited, she changed places from time to time to give them relief. Each time she rose, bells and gongs sounded among her servants, who came quickly and put out their hands to assist her movements.

The governor could hide no longer. He was captivated. He had to see this woman up close. He hurried into the room, bowed to her, gave a nod, and raised an eyebrow to his courtiers—a grand name for planters and government servants who administered the town and were responsible for trade. He took his place on the throne-like governor's chair, wondering how to begin. He raised his puffed, lacy sleeves and finally addressed her in Portuguese:

"Are you comfortable, madam ambassador?"

She answered him in Portuguese. "Not as yet, but I shall be when I have accomplished the king's mission, securing his family and his kingdom to him."

From the looks on the courtiers' faces, they were aghast at such audacity. Several approached the governor's chair, but he stopped them with a raised hand.

"Senhors and senhoritas, we are in the presence of royalty. Whether in Europe or Africa, we comport ourselves accordingly."

Governor de Sousa knew the history of his country's attempt to dominate the Ngola and Ndongo, and he was aware of his country's failure to do so. He knew how Ndongo, the whole of it, had been granted to a Portuguese nobleman almost a hundred years before. He knew how every attempt to conquer it had failed. He'd also heard stories of the mountains of silver in the interior, though he personally doubted these were true. Perhaps with this encounter with the Ngola's sister he could embark on a new relationship with these people. For now, the governor chose to proceed slowly, listen carefully, and take advantage of any new opportunities.

His courtiers seemed amazed by this woman, appearing from the African interior, speaking their language, comporting herself with dignity. Her brother was weak, but Nzinga appeared in the meeting room with the kind of force for which her uncompromising father was famous.

The silence in the hall grew thick with expectation, as if everyone waited to see what might happen next. Yet the princess Nzinga seemed to be in no hurry.

·

She chose to give them time to become accustomed to her presence. For the moment, Nzinga was only mindful of her discomfort with the heat. She signaled for water by fluttering her hands at the sides of her face. Her servants brought it quickly. An attendant poured a cupful and drank from it before offering a cup to Nzinga. When Nzinga drank, they blew horns, sounded bells, and fell down in front of her.

The governor conversed with her in his language.

"I hear this is your first time coming to Luanda. You are welcome. I hope you like it as well as your home."

She answered in his language.

"This land where we sit is my home," she said, regarding all around as if surveying the country. "But I prefer the inner Ndongo, the rivers, lakes, and green mountains. I don't like sand, and the ocean holds drifting debris and strange birds."

That priest, Father Gouvieae, joined them. He greeted her, but then spoke with the governor to express approval of "his student" and to take credit for her knowledge of the Portuguese language. She spoke with the priest about the weather, and the priest asked about her journey to the coast.

"Was it difficult?"

She answered as her father had when she asked him about traveling for a long time.

"One does not think of difficulty when undertaking a task of monumental importance."

"We should allow you time to relax," the governor said.

"I shall relax when I've seen the Ngola's wife, my mother, and my sisters."

The governor struck a grave pose. Looking straight at Nzinga, he said, "Your family members are hostages taken in a protracted military venture. I can let you see them, but that is all I can agree to."

He leaned over and whispered to one of his courtiers, who left the room through a side exit. Nzinga had expected all that had happened so far in the course of the morning, rising from reports by African servants who were the Ngola's spies. Her people were prepared as well as she was. When her relatives were escorted in, Nzinga's entourage jumped up, sounded drums, clapped hands, and threw themselves face down on the floor in honor of seeing them alive and well.

Kaningwa, her stepmother, led the others. Nzinga kept her decorous manner, but received them all warmly, hugging each of them and greeting them affectionately. She poured out her heart to Kambi and Funzi, her two birth-sisters. She expressed her brother's concern and confirmed that her mission included obtaining their safe return to their people.

All their heartfelt affection and emotions were expressed while the governor and his court watched the reunion. The priest moved among them, as if taking credit for the reunion. Nzinga's people expressed joy through incessant drumming, dancing, and singing, putting on an impromptu performance for the royal family.

The governor could be heard commenting to his courtiers, "It is as though we were back in Lisbon, eh?"

• • •

When Nzinga's entourage entered Luanda, Kaningwa watched from a window. African servants and peddlers stood with their mouths open wide in admiration and wonder. The men slapped their thighs. The women clamped their right hands over their mouths. Their voices echoed up to where Kaningwa watched.

"Nzinga. It's really that child."

"Nzinga, daughter of the great, old Ngola."

In the meeting room, Kaningwa couldn't take her eyes off Nzinga. She nodded, as if she'd been right all along to fear this one. Nzinga had the look, bearing, and manner of her dead father. *Look at what she's done so quickly. Yesterday we felt so alone and afraid. She comes and changes all that in a flip of a bird's wing.*

A chill passed through her, and she felt fear for the future of her son Mbande.

"Nzinga is so strong and smart." She spoke with her son's wife, Chala, later that night. "She has such power and presence. She got it all from her father."

We're lucky she isn't a male child.

21.
THE DOCK

NZINGA UNDERSTOOD, AS DAYS passed, that the release of Ngola Mbande's wife and mother was tied to the governor's plan to court, convert, and conquer Ndongo through Nzinga and her sisters. The governor's manner changed from stern officialdom to overt congeniality. She'd seen such changes and intrigues while sitting in the Ngola's meeting hall, watching her father meet Ndongo people or traders and visitors to his kingdom.

She practiced listening and then analyzing entire conversations. Little phrases the governor uttered came to her mind, especially the governor's words when he turned to the priest in the heat of debating with Nzinga: "You know what I have decided."

Their strategy changed: let the Ngola's mother and wife go, but retain the sisters in Luanda, convert them, and then send them back with different ideas, to convert others and to oppose the brother.

The governor's spies undoubtedly knew about Mbande's cruel act against Nzinga's child. While she lay sleepless in bed, it came to Nzinga that the governor would seek to use that knowledge to divide the kingdom. That notion took hold when Nzinga was instructing the first messenger about what to tell her brother, that he could expect the release of his mother and wife and that, for now, Nzinga and her sisters had to remain guests of the governor.

She spoke with Kadu, who was accompanying the freed hostages on their journey home. "My goal is to win back everything that was lost. I'll never waver in my resolve." She hoped Kadu's report would ensure that Mbande supported her efforts.

The next day Nzinga, Kambi, and Funzi went along with the released hostages, traveling part of the way to the old baobab tree on Luanda's outskirts. Most of her entourage would return home. A few of Sufalu's trusted people remained with Nzinga and her sisters as guards and spies.

When they reached the old tree, the parting was tearful. Chala, Mbande's wife, cried. "We can't leave you here while saving ourselves. You, Nzinga, have done so much for us."

At this moment Nzinga almost liked her, but Kaningwa spoiled it. She pulled Chala away, patting her hand and putting a firm arm about her, abandoning Nzinga coldly, as she'd done often in Nzinga's childhood.

"Come on, Chala. Let Nzinga take care of things," Kaningwa said. "She's so brave . . . and strong."

Kambi glanced around. "They didn't send soldiers along. Now that we are out of their sight, we can run."

Kadu said, "It may seem we are unguarded, but they have horses. The fort at Massangano is between the Ngola's army and us. They would catch us."

He didn't want to leave Nzinga and her sisters, but acknowledged it was the diplomatic and practical thing to do. Nzinga remained steadfast in her decision to accept the governor's proposal.

"We'll stay here," she said, standing close to her sisters. "This is a game I can play. I need to learn more about the Portuguese. Now go to Ndongo. Tell Mbande we support him and that the gods of Ndongo, Suku, and the ancestors at Punga a Dongo are with him."

Several moments after she turned toward Luanda, she glanced back and saw Kadu. He waved and then gave an order. The litters moved away, taking home Kadu, Kaningwa, and Mbande's wife.

▪

At the next meeting with Governor de Sousa and Father Gouvieae, they decided that Nzinga would meet with the governor twice a week to work out details of a treaty between Luanda and Ndongo. She'd represent her brother the Ngola, and the governor would represent Portugal and Luanda. At first he said some planters and merchants would be present.

But Nzinga answered firmly. "These people have nothing to do with Ndongo. They are your responsibility. They came from Portugal and don't even belong on this shore."

The governor hesitated a moment, then said, "Quite right. As you wish."

He never mentioned it again. From that time on, the governor was hospitable and agreeable. They also agreed that she and her sisters would take religious instruction from the priest, and they'd accompany him when he visited African converts. The rest of their time each day, Nzinga and her sisters were free to roam where they desired in Luanda.

"You were introduced to Senhora Adelita Alacantara, were you not?" the governor asked.

"Yes, a pleasant and agreeable person," Nzinga said.

"I've secured her services. If it pleases you, she'll guide you in Luanda whenever needed."

The treaty sessions progressed in proportion to the progress of the sisters' religious instruction. Nzinga believed that the priest and the governor compared and discussed their guests' dispositions and enthusiasm for that enterprise, because whenever she and her sisters missed a catechism lesson, the governor canceled the next treaty session.

Nzinga soon tired of the attempts to control her. She and her sisters feigned illness, remaining indoors for a week. The priest heard of their illness and came to visit but was denied entry. They refused all food. Finally, Adelita came with a special message from Governor de Sousa, entreating them to attend a luncheon with him. Nzinga refused but sent a message that she'd recovered from her recent illness and would attend the next treaty session and the next religious lessons. After that, the governor never canceled a working session.

One day, while reading the scribe's notes of the previous day's treaty session, Nzinga found the record differed from what they'd discussed and agreed upon. Penciled into a space above their signature was, "'Governor or his envoy is welcome to visit anywhere in Ndongo, and any of the Ngola's emissaries are free to visit anywhere on the coast of Luanda by simply providing the planters with written notice prior to their visit."

She made a scene the next day, accusing the governor.

"This is called bad faith, isn't it? You intend to deceive the Ngola's ambassador?"

He denied her accusations and upbraided the scribe in her presence. He dismissed the scribe and replaced him, and then gave the new scribe explicit orders to never alter any of the proceedings.

"The princess knows our language and has been trained in observation and negotiation at her father's court. Her teacher was our own priest. You will adhere to the record as we agree and sign it."

Nzinga redoubled her efforts to read and understand each point, especially anything to do with the fort at Massangano and supplying it with provisions.

.

While Nzinga worked on the treaty with the governor, Kambi and Funzi roamed the small town, visiting the two shops that offered trade items from Portugal. Funzi was eager to see women's fashions, but since there weren't many Portuguese women in Luanda, there were few choices.

Adelita's house proved to be a treasure; they came back raving about her dresses and shoes. Funzi wore a pair Adelita had given to her. Kambi was more interested in the African clothing and African workers. She talked to them in doorways and on the streets. They brought her foods prepared the way they knew in Mbacka. The workers sat in the courtyard and sang and danced for her until late evening.

Except for people brought in from other coastal ports of Africa, the Africans of Luanda were the Ngola's subjects. They were a close-knit group who protected each other and were constantly alert to the peril of being kidnapped and taken as slaves. The Portuguese raided villages along the coast and took people away, but they operated with extreme caution when dealing with subjects of the Ngola. That's why it had been a surprise when the palace at Mbacka was attacked.

Many times Nzinga accompanied the priest alone on his rounds. That's how she came to visit the dock. All cargo that entered or left Luanda passed over this flimsy structure, which consisted of tall tree trunks sticking out of the water, with logs secured near their tops, and row upon row of rough boards screwed and nailed to the logs, forming a flat surface that jutted a distance out into the ocean. Several small sailboats and a medium-sized African fishing boat were anchored near the shore. A big ship of the caravel type, its sails furled, swayed alongside the dock, its hull rubbing against soft logs placed there to prevent damage from the rough vertical logs of the dock.

The hot sand invaded her sandals when Nzinga went to visit the dock. She waited with the priest under a shelter on the shore, watching African men load big casks and barrels of water, ivory tusks, bananas, cassava, yams, sheets of copper and Kongo silver, and skins from lions, leopards, and sable antelopes. The workmen's conversation indicated that they weren't from Ndongo but were apparently imported by the Portuguese. Armed white men and mulattos stood over them, directing the work. The workmen didn't sing, chant, or seem to take joy in their work; their faces were sullen, their eyes watchful, as if in anticipation of an impending catastrophe. Nzinga felt a terrible foreboding about this place.

"Why are we waiting here?" she asked Father Gouvieae. She felt wary of this big ship.

"We're waiting for Father Alvares, who is to bless the ship. He sits there." The priest pointed to a spot along the dock, with a railing on each side and wide wharf planks that led up to the deck of the ship. There was a large chair with a huge wooden cask beside it. The cask gaped open skyward.

Six African men carrying a litter came racing, their bare feet beating rhythmically against the earth as they ran. In the litter was a huge man in a dingy white cassock. His face, ruddy as if he drank palm wine often or spent time in the sun, was shaded by a brown hat with an enormous brim. He climbed down from the litter cumbersomely and made his way to the big chair on the wharf.

Father Gouvieae motioned for Nzinga to come with him, to stand beside the huge priest's chair. A small African boy slept on the deck near the chair, previously hidden from view by the cask. The priest belched while acknowledging their greeting, the sweetish sour odor hitting Nzinga in the face. *Yes, it's palm wine that makes his skin red.*

"This one is the Princess Nzinga?" Father Alvares asked. His mouth twisted slightly to the right when he spoke.

"She's my charge. I taught her the language."

"That so? If she's as smart as the governor says, she didn't need much teaching. Married yet, Princess?" he asked.

"She can't marry," said Father Gouvieae. "But ... "

Nzinga said, "That's not of any consequence."

"Did you not teach her about the sacrament of marriage?" Clearly, Father Alvares was having fun with the priest.

"Some things have to be shown, and I did not."

"Shown, eh?" The large priest arched his brow, smiling. Father Gouvieae hastened to explain but was cut short by a commotion at the far end of the dock.

Near the shore, a line of ragged African captives, hands and feet bound, were being pushed and pummeled, forced to move toward the priest's chair. On either side of the captives, Portuguese sailors and African dockworkers herded the captives, shoving and cursing them. Several captives who refused to move forward invited the ire of a tall, sturdy, beet-red man wearing a three-cornered hat and bearing a twisted mustache. He came with a truncheon, flailing and striking solidly at the offenders all along the line. He struck at men, women, and children alike, and wherever his weapon struck, blood oozed from the contact. He frowned menacingly, gritting his teeth, and his muscular arm came down with the force of his immense weight. He grunted as he delivered the blows.

Nzinga stepped forward, wishing to ward off blows aimed at a woman with a child, but stopped, helpless. The desolate throng dragged slowly up to the enormous priest, who now set to work sprinkling each of the passing African captives with water that he called holy. Father Alvares mumbled to himself in Latin, which Nzinga had heard from Father Gouvieae in their private studies. He used his boot liberally to urge into action the small African boy with a censer, who roused with fear in his eyes. The boy shook as he moved quickly among the slaves, wielding his scented, smoke-filled cylinder to drive off evil spirits that might enter the caravel with the slaves.

"If they aren't saved, they will at least smell better." Father Alvares joked with his friend.

Nzinga remained a distance from the enormous-hatted priest Alvares, who was busy sprinkling the Africans moving into the hold of the ship. This was their baptism. From this moment on they were blessed, saved.

At a moment when Nzinga glanced from the ship to the water, two slaves chained together hand and foot broke out of the line and rushed toward shore. When the huge guard pushed them back, they fought fiercely. He wasn't able to subdue them. The force of their movement and their weight split the ramp's railing, and the two men together with a woman and her baby tumbled through the gap, falling between the ship and the dock pilings.

Their screams tore into Nzinga's head and heart.

The two slaves were carried down by the weight of the chains, their heads bashing the sides of the ship several times until they sank from sight.

The woman and the baby landed on the logs between the pilings and the ship. The woman was on a lower log, but the baby landed above her in the soft pulp of a beaten log that guarded the ship's hull from striking against the pilings. She grasped the baby with one hand, the other holding onto the log beneath her.

The ship, riding up and down with the rhythmic waves, seemed intent on pushing them under. The woman's leg was astraddle the log, but she held on to the baby, who was caught above her head. The ship lurched with the waves, pushing against the pilings, catching the woman's leg in a vise-like press. She screamed until her head went under. Large bubbles burst from the water. When the ship rocked away, the woman resurfaced and didn't move, but her hand held onto the baby on the cork. It was clear the woman was dead. The baby cried, fighting for breath in the spray that dashed in its face with every movement of the ship.

The big guard reached down with a long pole and swept the child off the cork into the sea. While Nzinga' watched, neither priest looked over the ship's side. The large priest instructed another guard to remove the bangles from the wrists and legs of the slaves and deposit them into the barrel near the chair. Nzinga heard a part of what he uttered: " . . . devil worship."

Shaken, Nzinga left the dock and waited for the priest ashore. With glazed eyes, she watched the white birds whirling in the air above the ship. Then she gazed at the trees and rocks along the shore and waited. Her eyes fell on two men who sat on upturned casks, looking her way. One wore a fez and a vest with gold filigree. She couldn't tell where he was from. His skin was olive-tan, his hair straight and black, and his teeth stained brown with betel nut juice. He studied her through greyish-brown eyes.

By his manner, he seemed to think he was important, apparently having provided the cargo being taken onto the ship. He kept commenting and pointing as though he could account for every captive being loaded. The other man, thin and white, wore a helmet. He spoke with a different accent. When the priest came off the boat, they caught his attention and insisted on being introduced to the Black Queen, as they called her.

"She's a princess," the priest said. He prepared to lead Nzinga away.

But Nzinga said, "Let them speak."

The black-haired one in the fez said at once, "I'm Mafunga. I sold the cargo that was just loaded." He referred to the thin white man. "That's a captured slave, name of Batelle, Andrew."

Batelle quickly corrected him. "Not slave, indentured man. And you have no right to hold me. Portugal and England have a pact. I was captured by these bloody Portuguese on the high seas. For a debt I don't rightly owe, I was indentured to this," he pointed his thumb at Mafunga. "I'm a sailor and adventurer, and slave to no one. You saw for yourself a few moments ago. A man is born to be free and he'd rather die than be a slave. You saw those men refusing to go quietly. Why, they committed suicide. And that poor woman and child. It's horrible."

"Me," Mafunga said. "I'm not a sailor or sea captain or anything. I sell slaves. It's what I do."

The priest nodded. "You have a reputation for helping to make these people Christian."

"Christian?" Mafunga said. "I'm a Muslim. I sell slaves. You see, priest, my religion isn't like yours. You convert them and keep them as slaves all their lives. In that way, you sin. If one of my captives or slaves professed conversion to Islam, he would become my brother at once. I would strike off his chains immediately. That's why I'm not a missionary. It's bad for business. I sell slaves."

Father Gouvieae moved nervously from one foot to the other, begging Nzinga to come with him, but she was rooted to the spot.

Batelle, the thin white man, spoke up. "It's a dirty, unholy business by any man's religion. Bound and degraded women and children. I've seen women raped, then chained, dragged, and dumped into the sea. I've seen despicable conditions in sugar cane fields. I've seen a whole ship sink with a full cargo of screaming humanity in its hold. I've seen all kinds of hunger. And I say it's all wrong. Dead wrong. And one day you'll all answer to God for it."

"It may be wrong, but it's business. It's competition. It's a race to see who will live and profit and who will die," said Mafunga. "All I say is, I sell slaves. I do it well. I can sell anyone as a slave."

Nzinga sighed nervously. She was frightened now and ready to go. She took a few steps away, the hot cushion of sand burning through her sandals. The sun blazed. Mafunga's words seemed to bring out beads of sweat on her neck that ran under her short blouse. She moved away.

But Mafunga wasn't done. He rose from his seat and halted Nzinga and Father Gouvieae.

"Let me tell you," he said, throwing up his right hand with a finger pointing up as if seeking a past experience. "I once had a feud with a white man like him," he said, pointing to Batelle by his side. "We were in the African interior, not a civilized soul around. And we became enemies, though I can't remember what caused it. He didn't matter to me. I'm Muslim, he's Christian. I found him sleeping and tied him up. I immediately got my sharpest knife and cut out his tongue."

He made a laborious sawing motion with his right hand while he pretended to hold something with his left hand.

Then he continued his story. "And I left him tied to a pole in the sun for days. He became as black as that one." He pointed to an African cargo handler. "When I delivered him to the ship's captain, he was delirious, using his hands, trying to communicate something. I used my hand like this." He twirled a finger next to his ear. "You know, to let the captain know the man was mad. But black and mute. The most desirable slave. He fetched a good price."

Mafunga paused a moment, then went on. "In a way, though, Andrew is right. That cargo I sold today is going to be trouble for someone. They love freedom. It's hard to load them. They won't go peacefully. That's why we're building this small tunnel. We'll send them from that house straight to the ship. They won't know where they are until they're loaded."

A crude way to make a slave without protest.

◆

22.
WHITE WINGED BIRDS

MORE THAN A WEEK PASSED after Kadu, Kaningwa, and Chala began their journey back to Ndongo. One evening, Nzinga returned from a treaty session with the governor, weary after a strange thing happened.

All during the session, the governor's scribe, Jacinto, had been lax in his notetaking. Nzinga, who'd been concentrating on the governor's words, noticed the scribe, his head bent to the side, staring at her instead of marking his scroll.

The governor also noticed this odd behavior. Livid, he flung his arms up.

"Jacinto, it's no wonder you find yourself making corrections long into the night . . . "

He called a short break and had a servant serve Nzinga an herbal tea while he held a private meeting with the scribe in a corner of the room. At a side table, Nzinga drank her tea and talked to the serving woman while also listening to the governor's animated discussion with the scribe. When the governor reconvened the session, he studied Nzinga, his eyes coming to rest on her colorful robes and her hands, quietly folded in her lap.

"Princess, you must excuse this dolt of a scribe," he glanced at Jacinto, "for staring at you and neglecting his work."

"It's the treaty that should keep our attention," Nzinga said, her shoulders raised in indifference.

"It's the treaty that causes the distraction," the governor said.

Nzinga arched her eyebrows and shifted in her chair, glancing sidewise at both men. "Then why doesn't he give his attention to what we've decided?"

The governor reached for her hand. "May I?"

She nodded, yielding. He lifted it, exposing her arms and the Kongo silver and gold bracelets that jingled and flashed in the light. Gifts from the Ngola to her dead mother, bought from traders at great cost. Princess Yafia, her aunt, urged Nzinga to wear them on the trip to Luanda.

The governor seemed serious, yet he smiled as he explained. "Jacinto heard the stories and now he is seeing evidence. He's reacting to what all of us have heard."

Nzinga still didn't understand. Her failure to comprehend must have shown on her face, although the governor still didn't explain. Instead, he seemed puzzled.

"The precious metals, Princess Nzinga. Jacinto cannot understand why, with all of this evidence of gold and silver, those aren't included in the treaty?"

"Precious metals . . . evidence. What evidence?"

"Here, on your arm." He shook her hand lightly. The jangle filled the hall. "Look. You can see the effect these bangles have on him. Jacinto's eyes nearly popped out when he saw these. You're wearing a fortune on each arm. Those who first came to Luanda wrote that there are 'mountains of silver in Ndongo.'"

A soft gong of memory sounded in Nzinga's mind, returning her to this very room on her first day of arrival. The entire family had gathered. Kaningwa sat near the window. The curtains behind her caught the sea breeze, billowing like the sails of a ship with big black crosses, as if Kaningwa were on the deck of that ship.

"Princess Nzinga . . . Princess!"

Nzinga came back to the moment. The governor and Jacinto waited for her to answer a question she'd missed.

"I was asking if we should make mention of silver and add the Ngola's permission for us to explore and mine for precious metals in Ndongo."

Nzinga shook her head. "Silver? Mountains of silver? It's not there. That's a story made up by your sailors. There is no silver. My father was a great elephant hunter. He traveled, ruled, and traded all over. The Kongo is rich in gold and silver. Go and make a treaty with them."

"But the story is about silver and precious metals in Ndongo, where—"

"That's all it is, a story. Governor, we agreed to make a treaty that returns the sovereignty of Ndongo to its people. And to grant you the right to live in Luanda and trade along this coast—"

"But we must pursue any interest that would ensure that the treaty is agreeable to both parties."

"As the Ngola's ambassador, I was empowered to perform one task. Any other, such as a discussion of precious metals, is for another time."

"But you have your brother's power—"

"I have none. Let us not discuss it further!"

·

With a firmness that the governor called stubbornness, Nzinga cut off all conversation concerning precious metals, refusing to answer any questions on the subject. At last, vanquished, the governor agreed that they should resume working on the treaty when they met again the next day.

This incident was still in Nzinga's mind when she climbed the stairs to their living space and found Funzi and Kambi excitedly conversing with each other, stopping when Nzinga entered the room.

Still thinking of her experience with the governor, Nzinga said, "I have just witnessed a strange—"

Funzi interrupted. "We have something to show you."

They spoke over one another, so neither sister could be understood. Then they stopped talking and laughed.

"Nzinga, you go ahead with what you were going to say, because we have plans and you'll have to wait to know them." Kambi playfully shook her lovely head with its beautiful basket-weave hair style. She wasn't her usual quiet self. She kept moving about the room, straightening pillows on the bed, looking out the window several times, and laughing nervously.

Nzinga told them about her session with the governor and what had caused them to mention mountains of silver. Funzi took Nzinga's arm and held it up, admiring her bracelets with a mischievous smile.

Kambi said to Funzi, "You see! The ancestors brought us here. Nzinga, you will soon see. What happened with the governor is connected to what happened to us today."

Nzinga sat down on the Portuguese rug in the middle of the floor and began fiddling with the cowrie shells on her elephant-hair bracelets. Funzi laughed happily, further puzzling Nzinga.

"This place, Luanda, is different," Funzi said. "Nzinga, I can feel it." She closed her hands into tiny fists, brought them close to each other, and pumped them up and down. "The ancestors sent the three of us here for a purpose. I know it."

"Kambi, Funzi, will one of you tell me what's going on?"

Funzi said, "You will know in the evening, after we eat. It's better to know the whole thing at once. But you already know. All of us do, but none of us has seen it. Not like this."

Had Kambi met someone? Had she fallen in love again? *I know she's done it before, like that warrior killed in battle with horse-soldiers.* Cut down by the Portuguese, along with three favorite warriors from their age set, years before the attack on the palace. Killed like the father of Chatembo's child was; like Kajubi, her own brave lover. *We lost many men in war with the Portuguese. It's time they paid for it.*

Another more disturbing thought arose. *Oh, no. Maybe she's fallen in love with a Portuguese soldier. It's possible. My sisters are young and beautiful, and for months they've been exposed daily to lonely men.* And what of that Portuguese woman who escorted them around the town?

Nzinga said, "Where's Adelita?"

"She had to do something with one of the farm wives," Kambi said. "We haven't seen her all day."

"But we had a wonderful time," Funzi said, her eyes gleaming, showing the beauty that was like that of her mother, Batayo.

"We've been making discoveries all day," Funzi said, teasing Nzinga.

Kambi waved out the window toward the shops and African dwellings. "I must go meet someone."

When the door closed behind Kambi, Nzinga looked out that window. In the sandy street near the shops, Kambi stood barefooted, her colorful skirts moving with the wind. She engaged in excited conversation with two Ndongo women in native attire, with long cloths wrapped around their bodies and colorful shawls around their shoulders. Waving her arms, Kambi first started back toward the building, but returned to talk with them again. The two women then hurried away.

When Kambi came back upstairs, Funzi was still seated, humming a Kimbundu song, imitating the beat of drums, and moving her arms in the air as though she were dancing. Nzinga laughed, wrinkling her nose. She couldn't figure this one out. The dress of those women indicated that some kind of celebration was planned. Although evenings were cooler here near the ocean, people dressed scantily unless there was a celebration.

"You've been working too hard on treaties," Funzi said. "Tonight will relax you, Nzinga, and help you to remember important things."

"We can go to eat now," Kambi announced. The two sisters led Nzinga down the stairs and out into the street instead of into the hall where they usually had their meals. They escorted Nzinga past a shop to a large building that housed the Africans who served the governor. Inside, Kambi introduced the two women Nzinga had seen through the window. Nsobia, the short dark one, was quick on her feet and reminded Nzinga of her grandmother. Shanulu, slender and bronzed, swayed like the palms as if there were music and mystery in her.

The two women bowed, greeted the princesses, and begged to be told what they could do to make the sisters comfortable. They rambled on in Kimbundu and threw out phrases in other African dialects, as if the doors of a prison had been suddenly thrown open and they were birds trying the lost power of seldom used wings.

They were chambermaids and assistants to the governor's cook, a thin Portuguese woman named Dalantia Gonzalez, who often took palm wine with the big priest who blessed the captives at the dock. This Dalantia, they said, spent long evenings in the priest's house. That was why they were free of her now.

Shanulu said, "That's not just idle gossip. It is all important to know, because we are Ndongo's eyes and ears."

Nzinga smiled, taking them both warmly into her arms.

They seated the princesses at a table spread with Ndongo food. It had been months since Nzinga smelled steaming yams, roasted wild guinea, beans, cassava, and rice with sauce. There were yellow bananas and passion fruit. To the side were Portuguese bread and a small decorated pot of honey.

"The men sent that," Funzi said. "We'll meet them later."

Pleased and smiling, Nzinga said, "I love this food, but I wish I knew what this is about."

Nsobia raised her hand toward Funzi in a playful scolding gesture. Kambi moved quickly to ensure the curtain was closed and then listened at the door. Smiling, Nsobia said, "They didn't tell you. But Shanulu did just tell you. We're the old Ngola's spies."

Nzinga's eyes lit with pleasure. "Oh, I have been so involved with the treaty that I didn't think properly."

Shanulu said, "As soon as we eat, we'll go there."

Although Nzinga was anxious to know what was meant by "go there" and what would happen, she didn't rush through the meal. She proceeded to enjoy every stage of eating and talking. Nsobia and Shanulu had troves of information. Nzinga had heard their reports from Luanda before—while sitting in the back of her father's judging hall. These two women knew enough Portuguese to understand what they overheard at meals and in the shops. They knew of happenings in Brazil and the news of ships arriving from Portugal.

They knew when horse-soldiers moved to and from Massangano. While serving the governor, his courtiers, and the old priest, they heard talk of England, Spain, and Holland. The Portuguese were afraid of the Dutch. These two women had informants among local Africans and explained to Nzinga how they guarded their sources carefully while being outwardly loyal to their employers.

Nsobia got up from the table to peep out the small window and glance out the front door. She came back to the table with one hand raised. "Shanulu," she said, "is a relative of Sufalu."

Nzinga went to hug Shanulu. She whispered, "Sufalu was my father's right arm. I'm sure you know that. She isn't well now, but she'll be better when I return."

As they were finishing the meal, soft music sounded outside. Nzinga caught the sound of a stringed lyre, flute notes, and drums. The women rushed outside.

Leading the musicians was a tall, old man with a white beard, his back bent over the lyre as he strummed. He wore a soft red-and-black fez. His hoarse bass voice delivered a rhythmic chanting tune that needed no other instrument. Near him, a young, shirtless man beat softly on a drum. His muscles glistened and pulsated as he worked, reminding Nzinga of Kajubi. The flutist accompanying them was also young and agile, like the goatherd boys Nzinga knew in her youth. The years rolled back as she watched the flute at his mouth and his foot moving up and down to keep time. While she clapped to the music, she felt as though she were a child among the goatherd boys on the hills near the Mbanza in Ndongo years ago.

They left the fort and town behind and marched to the music up the shoreline, where the ocean curved around a rocky shore and came closer inland to a spacious beach of white sand. On the land beyond the rocks and behind them, palm trees formed a grove. Beyond that was grassland.

The sun danced on the water as it slowly descended toward its night's sleep in the ocean. The gulls wheeling and calling in plaintive voices charged the air with natural beauty and mystery. Now and then Nzinga looked up the path.

"The farms are that way," the old man said, catching the direction Nzinga gazed. "But this is where it all began." He pointed to the sea with his nose and mouth.

The roar of ocean waves and the flying wisps of spray captured Nzinga's imagination as she remembered Sufalu's stories about this place and Ndongo's past. Her chest raised, Nzinga breathed deeply. Each step was light as they walked until they reached a circular lake near the ocean. A narrow strip ran from the pool. In this depression, the ocean rushed in during high tide, but at low tide the pool was an entity alone with its circle of living things. The connecting channel was filled now with limp green seaweed, which lined the beach as well, revealing the highest point the water climbed at high tide. Sea-salt-bleached logs, barnacle-covered rocks, holdfasts of seaweed, and small pools of quivering animals dotted the beach and lined the opening where water flowed into the pool. Great herons, sandpipers, and gulls stalked along the sands, inspecting the deposits with cursory pecks of their beaks.

The constant sound that Nzinga had heard since she first set foot beyond the big baobab trees was a loud hum here. Then, as she came closer, it proved to be the rhythmic beat of incoming waves crashing on the shore.

Kambi halted them with outstretched arms and spoke with great seriousness. Her firm voice rose above the ocean's thunder.

"Shanulu will now tell you why we came here," she said.

Nzinga now knew why they visited this pool. It was owned by her great-grandfather. All Ngolas told the story of the ancestor from far back in tribal memory: an elephant hunter from the interior who first broke from the forest to the wide savannah to witness the majesty and immensity of the ocean and the world beyond.

"Is this where Sufalu's great-grandmother . . . ?"

"Yes," said Shanulu, "this is where Chiambo, the great-grandmother of Sufalu, labored beside the Ngola's bank when the ancestors made it all happen to her. This old father," she said, pointing to the old musician, "has lived near here all his life. He knew Chiambo's daughter, Sufalu's grandmother. He is the griot nearest to the time of the story."

They played music again. With the ocean's rumble, the cadenced voice of the old musician, and the evening sun flashing on the water, Nzinga felt as if she were being lifted up, transported back to another time.

"This place is called the Ngola's bank," the griot said, pointing to the circular pool and the shallow ocean beyond it. "And there—" he pointed to the curve of beach, "that's where the fishermen's boats pulled up on shore. Each and every day the ocean's pounding bids them to ride the waves and fish, fish, fish. Ride the waves and hear the cry of the gulls and fish, fish, fish. And for Chiambo, the ocean's hum is *nzimbi, nzimbi, nzimbi*: the cowrie shells, the little shells. The king's money, the money of Africa."

He fingered the shell necklace around his neck.

"And here you see the beauty of the divers. You see them dive and swim, their skill rivaling the springing flight of the gulls and sandpipers. You see the lovely bronze bodies of women divers, who wear only a cloth around their middle, a tiny frond of palm tree or bark-cloth on their bodies, so beautiful and brown, so warmed by the fires of the sun, and glistening as if rubbed with palm oil.

"And you see the baskets of *nzimbi* are with them, always with them, shining with the glaze of water. Those on the banks pull up basketsful of them. The divers tie ropes onto the baskets and rope stones to their legs, and they dive down and fill the baskets with *nzimbi*.

"You see how clear and blue is this pool? Can you imagine Chiambo there, putting her leg through a loop in a rope tied to a stone to make her sink? First you see her preparing for the long dive. She doesn't know it will be long, but she is drawing into her body a deep, full breath of air, puffing life in, becoming filled with it, elevating her chest . . . then taking a dive, and sending up a dash of spray . . . "

The griot sang and drummed Chiambo's story, the story of a Chiambo from long ago.

·

Chiambo sank down, down into that deep pool where it is cool. She picked *nzimbi* there, *nzimbi* after *nzimbi* from the many *nzimbi* on the bottom of this pool. The bubbles rose from her until the air in her was no longer sustaining. She should come up then. Those around the pool watched for her. They knew of her exploits. She was a champion diver and swimmer. But perhaps this time she'd stayed too long. Perhaps the stone was too heavy.

It wasn't safe to stay long in the cool, deep pool that steals thoughts from the mind. The body cries, struggles to come up for air. It is hard to fight against the body. But the ancestors whispered to her in a different language, to keep her under the water to give her a message for Ndongo. They changed her eyes, gave her a sharper, more penetrating vision. When they finished, she emerged glistening, as though propelled to the surface. She was no longer a diver, but a seer.

Her head was cold. She wanted to speak but had no voice yet to utter it. Then she drifted off to sleep and couldn't be awakened.

From that day, Ndongo had a savior.

∙

"They always send a savior, though we don't always recognize the savior. She came up and sat right there." The griot pointed to a spot on the sandy beach as if he'd been with Chiambo when she emerged from that pool so many rains ago. "The ancestors sent her."

The music of the drums and flutes played like soft, concerned voices while he spoke. Nzinga, Kambi, Funzi, and Nsobia swayed, and Shanulu chanted and clapped, as if they were back there in time looking at Chiambo.

The griot said, "She sat on the grass right there, not feeling well. My grandfather took her to his house in the village. My grandmother cared for Chiambo until she awoke many days later, a changed person. She called out: 'Oh, no! Suku, please help Ndongo.' And so my grandfather journeyed to the Ngola and told him, 'There is a woman with me who can see Ndongo's future.'"

The griot paused, as if remembering. "That Chiambo! She was never one to show fear. She was the Ngola's best diver. She picked more *nzimbi* than two women did together. She could even go down into the pool at night. But when she came in to see the Ngola, she was ashen and shaking from her trance. Her body was thin and frail and vibrated with every word she spoke."

Then he sang the story that Chiambo told the Ngola.

.

One day the divers and the fishermen at Luanda will see giant white birds far out to sea. I have seen it as if they were there now. As the birds swim closer, the divers and fishermen behold wind moving their wings. The birds' wings rise high in the sky and spread around the birds, waving in the wind there in the sky, all white and gleaming. As they speed closer, the white birds break open, sending flashes of lightning and thunder that vibrate up the beach and break the hearing of those nearby, tearing palms and throwing coconuts down to the fishermen's boats.

The thunderclaps break the coconut trees and kill fishermen as they sit in their boats or repair their nets on the shore. The women divers run, carrying baskets of *nzimbi* on their heads with many of the shells falling in a confused jumble onto the ground. The sand burns their feet. The divers and fishermen see the birds now as big boats, ships, firing giant logs and sticks.

And men come out of the ships, wearing strange clothes that cover their bodies head to foot. The fishermen of Ndongo flee, but the divers in the lagoon, the women, are captured. When the strangers see that the divers are bringing up cowrie shells, they take everything aboard ship and sail away. They leave a few armed soldiers, who set up a trading post that grows into a giant market and then a city of many different peoples. In this market, the seeds of war are sown. I saw it all in a vision.

.

"Chiambo fell exhausted onto the floor," the griot said, "too tired to go on. People who gathered around the Ngola heard it and scoffed.

What a story! Everybody knew the arms of the Ngola were powerful and far reaching. His power stretched into the Kongo, inland as far as the lakes, and down the coast to Cassange. Their elephant-hunter ancestor had ranged over most of the land. And by his choice and that of Ndongo, they had settled near the ancestors at Punga a Dongo, the great falls on the river. The people went away, voices raised in laughter and making fun of Chiambo: 'She's just a crazy woman with wild dreams.'

"Then, as now, people who brought false stories to the Ngola were publicly punished by the chiefs, but Chiambo wasn't harmed. The Ngola listened. He'd heard stories of invaders along the Kongo coast. Was there truth here?

"Chiambo's story was told in the villages and discussed in the Mbanza. But everyone went back to tending their cattle and harvesting simsim and cassava and winnowing millet and thatching roofs. Slowly people began to forget what Chiambo had said.

"Ten days later, Chiambo returned to tell the Ngola more of her story. She'd been too weak to tell it before, or maybe the ancestors had held her back. After waiting for days at the Mbanza gate, she was given a second audience with the Ngola. This is the vision that Chiambo told."

.

You, my Ngola, must beware of silver seekers, for that time isn't far off. There will come stories that endanger the whole of Ndongo, in that same market I described to you. Now there are only your bank and palm trees and waves and the bare land. But as the town grows, people come from miles around on foot and in boats along the shore. People from far beyond Punga a Dongo will come to trade. And among them will be a woman bringing on her head baskets and mats, decorated gourds and amulets.

This woman comes to trade for Portuguese beads and cloth, but she wears bangles, bracelets, and necklaces far more valuable than any bead or cloth, many of which were given by her husband at marriage.

In that market, while placing her wares, she is jostled by a soldier. His sword hilt grazes one of her arm bracelets, scraping away the dull coating and revealing its shiny luster beneath. It casts a glint with a brilliance that is like looking into the face of the Ngola. The light blinds the soldier to all else.

Upon recovering his vision, he sees light from her bracelet dancing around the market with her every movement. He lays hold of the woman and, in spite of her protest, she is whisked away by many soldiers.

The woman is taken aboard a ship, her arms stretched to show the captain what she is wearing. Frightened, she thinks they will take her away or kill her. Instead, the captain orders a pillow and seats her on the floor. He orders food for her, tries to question her. Failing with the language, he sends for an interpreter.

．

Nzinga heard many parallels between the old griot's song and her dealings with the governor. *When these people think you have something of value, they feed you and make you comfortable to win you over, or to gain what they want by capturing your mind.*

When the governor and his scribe questioned Nzinga about precious metals, the twitch of the scribe's facial muscles and his intense grip on the treaty papers as he stared at the bracelets on her arm showed greed over the minerals. That greed had brought them away from their own country, friends, and families—to take the goods of Ndongo. Nzinga vowed to the ancestors that the Portuguese would never steal her mind nor her resolve.

The old griot said, "Perhaps Suku and the ancestors sent me as a witness, to sing that old story to the princesses of the dead Ngola. For these are different times and who can say which of you will be called to save Ndongo from its enemies? Here is more of the vision Chiambo told to the Ngola."

．

The woman is too frightened to eat or drink. She pretends to take a sip of the wine but the bitter taste frightens her more. Is it poison? Her eyes dart around, seeking a sympathetic face among the curious men. There is none. A man who speaks her language comes. She is pelted with questions.

"Where did you get the bracelet?"

"It's mine," she answers.

"Yes. But where did you get it?"

"From my husband."

"Where is he?"

"Dead. He's long dead."

"Where do you come from?"

The woman is silent. In a flash, she jumps up from the floor, dodging among soldiers who try to catch her. She makes her way to the deck and throws herself over the side of the vessel. Hands seize her and bring her wet, screaming, and kicking, before the captain again.

The man who speaks her language motions with his hands and says quietly, "They only want the bracelets."

She asks, "Will they take me away on this boat?"

"They won't harm you. Tell them about the bracelets."

"Will they give me presents if I tell them?"

The man relays this question to the captain, who piles before her beads and cloth. She says, "I have more bracelets. On my arms, see? On my legs, there are several." The bracelets have been worn a long time, for her flesh has grown over them. "I've had them so long, they no longer slip over the ankle. In my tribe you do not pull off bangles given by your husband. My husband was a great hunter, and—"

Suddenly frightened that they might cut her to get the silver bracelets, she falls to the floor, begging them not to cut off her arms or legs. The man who speaks her language reassures her.

They bring cutters and remove the first bracelet. She sits up, rubbing the flesh of her arm. They are quite generous then. They pile more beads and cloth in front of her as they take her precious silver marriage dowry. A soldier polishes their find, while men nod to each other and smile happily.

The questions again. They give her a gift for each answer.

"Where do you come from?"

"There." She points with her nose, as is the custom in Ndongo.

"Is there more silver there?" They point to the bracelets.

"Yes. My husband was a hunter in the mountains. He dug it from the hills." She speaks to please them, to get away.

"Do many women wear silver bracelets?"

"All of them."

"So there are mountains of silver in Ndongo."

And then the captain sends her back to the market.

That, my Ngola, is the message from the ancestors. When all of this comes to pass, the men from those ships will come to conquer Ndongo.

·

"When it did come to pass," the griot said, "do you think how the Portuguese laughed after they sent the woman back to the market? That is how it came to be known by every Portuguese sailor and immigrant that Ndongo has 'mountains of silver.'"

The griot's drum-like voice ceased. Flute notes brought Nzinga back to the endless sound of waves crashing against the shore.

"We know it all happened just the way Chiambo saw in her vision," Nsobia said. "The Portuguese came in their caravels, killed many fishermen, and captured the women divers and the Ngola's bank. They are still trying to conquer us and find the mountain of silver."

"A mountain that doesn't exist," Nzinga said.

Kambi said, "Do you see? The ancestors sent us here for a purpose."

Nzinga agreed. "I wish my brother Mbande could have heard this story."

She congratulated the old musician for telling such an important part of Ndongo's history. She asked if he'd walk with her out to the rocks by the ocean where the fishermen and divers first sighted the Portuguese white birds.

Tucking his instruments under his arm, the old man guided her around the pool that was her father's ancestral bank. He pointed out the position of the fishermen's boats and the divers. Nzinga absorbed the scene. In this bay the silvery water was quiet, sighing as it flowed with the tide over the small connection between the pool and the sea. A few shore birds picked among the seaweed.

The racing, foaming water seemed furious. As they left the inlet, the thundering sound of the breakers made it impossible for her to hear the old griot's words. In front of them, angry waves gathered into tall, threatening walls, moving swiftly toward the beach. The wild ocean flung its heavy, formless body skyward, forming predatory crests that curved like the beaks of attacking birds of prey. Then, breaking high, the waves cascaded down to the white sand and fell back, gurgling and hissing, to form again the monstrous, predatory crests that dove onto the immobile shoreline. Along the shore, sandpipers flew up from feeding, taking the spray in their faces, and then landing again, running to escape the receding water that pulled at their long legs.

Gulls flew low over the crests of waves, their white wings just above the spray. Each time the waves struck, the gulls cried in loud, haunting voices that carried past the shore toward the interior of Ndongo.

◈

23.
MESSAGES

IN THE SIX MONTHS NZINGA had been in Luanda, she'd received only two messages from Mbande.

The messages congratulated her on doing the ancestors' will in freeing the royal family and instructed her to speed the completion of a treaty between Portugal and Ndongo. Mbande said he'd have sent Kadu back to Luanda to help, but the business of protecting Ndongo from tribes in the Kongo and administering the kingdom prevented that. He also said that Chatembo wanted to join Nzinga in Luanda, but because Sufalu wasn't at the height of her powers, Chatembo must stay to assist him and Princess Yafia in restoring the ancestral shrines destroyed by the Portuguese invaders. If she needed extra assistance he'd be glad to send his new second in command, Mutele.

When Kambi and Funzi heard this correspondence, they stood beside Nzinga's chair, both talking at once. Kambi won. "We are in terrible condition with those two irresponsible babies in charge of the kingdom," she said. "All they ever did was wrestle, hunt wild animals, and tell jokes."

"They were silly boys, never serious. And now that they're men, I don't see any difference," Funzi added.

"Our father hunted elephants and wrestled," Nzinga said. "But he could lead an army, judge a case, make rain, and be a husband and father." Nzinga shook her head. "I like Mutele, but he isn't wise enough to be minister to the Ngola. He wouldn't be useful to us here."

"What if Shellanga could only hunt and wrestle? Would Father have picked him as a general just because they were friends?" Funzi went on to answer her own question. "Father was tough and demanding. He picked only the best. And don't forget, he knew what anyone from Ndongo would face here in Luanda."

"Let me tell you, Nzinga." Funzi sat down, but then got up from her pillow again. "Father, like all Ngolas before him, could be hard and cruel. Yet people around the Ngola have forever protected him and the kingdom. If you didn't support the Ngola and his effort, people secretly killed you. If the kingdom and our way of life were challenged, Father would be harder than a giant ant hill."

"We could ask Mbande to send Temarku," Funzi said. "We know he's loyal."

"But too gentle," Kambi said. "After what happened to him at the market that time, he'd never come near Luanda. He was nearly sold as a slave.

Funzi said, "But Temarku is also good, all music through and through. They need his music at home."

"We can do by ourselves whatever is required, together with people here in Luanda who work for Sufalu," Kambi said. "Shanulu, Nsobia, and the old musician are here. They have struggled against domination always. No matter what the Portuguese do, we have people all the way to the old Mbanza. You saw the ones we met on the outskirts of Luanda at the big baobab tree."

"Nsobia says more people everywhere just wait to be contacted," said Kambi. Then she added, "Some look after the barracks and take care of the horses."

But Funzi had moved on to another topic. "I see jealousy and fear all through this message. He needs your help, Nzinga, in spite of the evil he did to your child. Yet he makes it difficult for you to succeed by not sending Kadu to help. And he deprives you of Chatembo, your age-mate."

"But he can't see that this hinders his rule of Ndongo," Nzinga said. "Mbande needs to surround himself with age and wisdom.

Even if his young assistants offer useful ideas, he needs loyal people, not people who merely seek power."

Kambi said, "Mbande and his mother are afraid of you, Nzinga. She has always been afraid that you would outshine her Mbande. Even though you aren't a male."

.

The second message from Mbande was much more alarming. It was brought by one of his hunter friends, a short, stocky, muscular man named Topi, whose bare upper torso shone coppery in the sun. In winter, he wore a cape made of gazelle skin, but at all other times his upper body and legs were bare. He always wore shoes made of tough crocodile skin. He moved quietly, even silently, but when roused he chattered like a colobus monkey. Kambi sent him to eat with the Ndongo people who dwelt in a small house behind the Catholic church.

Mbande's message was all about the treaty this time—brief, with only one demand. He asked Nzinga to add to the treaty that the Portuguese would honor the sovereignty of Ndongo and trade without restrictions, and that the Portuguese would regard any enemy of Ndongo as an enemy of Portugal. He wanted this because a fierce marauding band, the Jagas, had attacked two counties and carried off all the livestock. The messages bore no warmth or greeting to connect Nzinga with the Ndongo people, the ancestors, or the gods back home.

The sisters again discussed the message in their room, sitting on pillows on the rug.

"This is even worse than the first message. How can the Ngola be sovereign when begging our enemy to protect us?" Nzinga said. "I'm glad it is only a verbal message."

"You know the governor will have Topi detained on the way back and learn what message he brought," Kambi said.

"Perhaps not," Nzinga said. "But perhaps Mbande sent Topi to create a new contact with the governor because he doesn't trust me to follow his directives."

"Let's find out more from this Topi," Kambi said.

Nzinga said, "You and Funzi take him out near the dock and question him. It's dark, and there's no ship there now. I'll listen but not get involved, because whatever I say will be reported to Mbande."

Although the dock was quiet and a warm breeze blew, Nzinga couldn't forget her past experiences there. On the rough boards near the priest's chair, she shivered as she gazed over the side of the wharf where the woman and baby fell and were swept away by the loader's pole. She heard again Mafunga's boisterous voice: *"I sell slaves. It's what I do. I can sell anyone."*

Light from the starry sky caught the wrinkle of waves intermittently. Kambi, Topi, and Funzi sat on stools, leaning against casks of palm oil and palm wine that waited to be loaded and shipped along with crates of coconuts and copra bound for Brazil or Lisbon.

They knew Topi as a hunter who often accompanied their brother on gazelle hunts, a favorite of Mbande because of his skill in tracking gazelles. Topi seemed happy to have attention lavished on him by the Ngola's sisters. At first he sat quietly, one arm on his left knee. His eyes moved from side to side, but his head and body stayed still.

Kambi asked, "Are there elephants around at home?"

"Too dry. They've gone to the forest to graze." His answers were brief.

"You had a wife and child. How are they?"

"Good. The boy grows big and strong."

"Is the weather good for crops?"

"Everyone is digging, preparing to plant."

"What do you know about the old palace, the Mbanza?"

"Totally destroyed. But Shellanga's soldiers stand with spears night and day to keep away large animals and birds."

Throughout these questions, Topi hadn't moved once. His position on the cask remained exactly as it had been. Nzinga was getting tired for him. How could he sit that quietly, sit that still, for so long?

Kambi had asked all the questions, while Funzi watched. Suddenly Funzi let out a squeak and a snort, like a warthog's, so authentic that the others looked around quickly, expecting to see an animal. Topi dropped his arm and gazed all around.

"Are you still hunting warthogs?" Funzi asked him.

"*Wo!*" said Topi. "I could use you on the hunt. How did you do that? How did you know I hunted warthogs?"

"We lived in Ndongo, remember? Do you still hunt them?"

"I do, but I got a big kudu two days before I set out for here. It took ten porters to carry the meat. I'm going to have Portuguese coins in my pouch when I sell the skin."

Topi didn't stop to think that Funzi only had to look at his neckpiece—three boar's tusks hanging by a leather thong—to know his chief occupation. But with that, he started to talk.

"Things aren't like they used to be. The people are on the mainland, and the Ngola built a big palace and meeting hall on an island in the Lugalula River. Now all business is done on the island. The people want to see him, but they cannot. They gather on the riverbank daily, in large numbers, and look out to the island. Few people are permitted on the island. They can't get close to their Ngola like they did with your father." He paused for an instant, as if thinking how what he said was being judged. Then he went on, amending his previous stance. "But your brother, the Ngola, is doing fine. The big meeting house serves everyone well, and he has the people bring cases to judge from the land to the island."

At first, Topi seemed nervous around the princesses. But Kambi had brought along a bottle of palm wine. She said, "We gave orders for you to have food and everything you needed when you came. Did you get enough? Are you comfortable where you're staying?"

"Yes." He thanked them and then went on talking. "Chief Kadu and Chief Mutele do what they can on the land, but those Jagas are troublesome warts on the skin of Ndongo. Once I was hunting in the deep forest, quiet and alone. Mutele and the others who used to hunt with me are too busy advising Ngola Mbande now. I saw through a clump of vines and trees what made me sick enough to die. Why, I was right there on the edge of their camp. I could hear them snoring. If I'd made a sound, I might have died. The camp was huge, more like a big village that stretched for miles. That's the kind of army we need to fight the Portuguese. They love to fight. And they take no prisoners. They kill you and eat you. All around them, nothing remained alive. Plants were trampled and cut down. When they come near, animals flee. We need the horse-soldiers to attack them. Mbande's army will just be food for their tables if they don't train better."

Topi put his hand over his mouth as if he'd said too much, and then he was silent for a long while.

"How are the Ngola's wife and mother?" Funzi asked.

He took more swallows of the palm wine. "They are well. But you know the Ngola's wife, Queen Chala, loves to dress up and make mats and visit markets in search of fine clothes from Portugal. She is a beautiful queen. She sits with ladies and visits shrines. But things are different now. The Ngola's mother, she helps with ruling, always there, always helping the Ngola and his ministers. She helped him pick Mutele when the Ngola needed another minister. Some people complained to Chief Kadu and Chief Oyimbu that Mutele was too young and didn't understand enough about ruling. But I heard her tell Mbande that he needed a loyal friend, that it didn't matter how much Mutele knew. And that no matter what, Minister Oyimbu would have to support the Ngola. A certain woman who works in the palace told my wife that Mbande's mother is quite fond of Mutele. She calls them both her sons. She has meetings with them into the night. You know how much Mbande likes Mutele. Well, this lady told my wife that the Ngola's mother fawns over and hugs Mutele and tells them both how to judge cases. Chief Oyimbu, who was trusted in your father's day, refuses to come to the island. He trains warriors for Shellanga's army and looks after his lands. He and his people are helping Seer Chatembo restore the ancestral shrines."

Nzinga listened silently to all of this, agitated, but not interfering with her sisters.

"Ndongo needs young warrior-hunters like you," Funzi said. "You must have rested to prepare for your journey here. You're a hunter in good shape, but the journey is long and arduous. Yet you seem so rested, even though you just arrived."

"I was carried all the way, right up to a giant baobab tree."

"Carried?"

"You know, by litter."

The princesses were aghast. Messengers for the Ngola were always warriors and runners, not hunters treated like royalty. To Nzinga, this was another indication of the decay that set in when Mbande became Ngola.

"Oh, and who granted you the litter?" Kambi asked.

"We were sitting in the meeting house talking about the Jagas. I told what I'd seen in the forest, and Mutele said we should ask the Portuguese to help against them. That's how the message was made. Mutele said, 'Let Topi take it. Topi will do it quickly. We need it done before Nzinga finishes the treaty.' The Ngola and his mother agreed, and she said I should have a litter. And that's how I came."

With that, Nzinga signaled to her sisters that they should let him go to rest. Kambi gave him the palm wine bottle and said goodnight. But this encounter couldn't be terminated so easily. The palm wine was fueling his tongue. Topi went on.

"Everything is right for me." He was unsteady on his feet now. One foot scraped against a crate of copra. He righted himself. "I'll sleep just fine. But I want to say how much you princesses are missed back there." He inclined his head toward Ndongo. "Mbande is concerned. He said to me as I was leaving, 'Topi, see what they need me to do. Anything.' He's willing to support you in any way."

Nzinga felt that this last statement was all Topi's effort to fill a gap that he knew to be missing in the message, a warmth that should exist between an Ngola and his sisters.

Topi reluctantly left them, alternately ambling and lurching up the sandy street, finally disappearing behind the white Catholic church. Nzinga joined her sisters.

"Home is worse than I thought." Her voice was grave. "The hunters are now ministers and advisers to the Ngola. They make decisions that affect the entire kingdom. They no longer go on foot. They ride in litters and spend evenings with the Ngola and his mother. Soon they will have the power of the Ngola. Gone are the respect and order that our father maintained."

Kambi fumed. "Let's cut out his tongue and sell him to Mafunga."

"Yes, Nzinga," Funzi said. "He'll likely talk to the governor's spies. All they need do is ply him with palm wine. Like we did."

Nzinga said, "What could the governor do with the information if he had it? I won't sign a treaty that takes away our rights as a kingdom. So Topi has served our purpose, not that of Mbande. He brought us news we needed. You said it the other evening, Kambi. The gods and ancestors are working with us even though we aren't near the shrines."

Funzi said, "I don't see that at all. This hunter comes to Luanda riding in a litter with a message that we should give Ndongo to the Portuguese. How is that a message from the ancestors?"

"If he hadn't come, we wouldn't have known how the Ngola's decisions are being made until it was too late. At any time, Mbande could send Mutele or Kadu to negotiate a treaty surrendering to the Portuguese. We wouldn't matter. He could sell us here. Now that we know, we can act first."

"How can we act, so many miles away?"

"We have Topi. You can tell from his talk, he's not a part of it. They're using him. He hunts alone, he came alone. They thought of using him as a courier at the last moment. I think he is his own person. He's strong, and he has a wife and son. You heard his last statement. It was a condemnation of Mbande's treatment of his sisters. We can use him as an ally, but we must send him back to do it."

"He won't agree to help us against Mbande."

"I'm not against Mbande, he's the Ngola. He's surrounded by snakes. Topi will help us to get rid of the snakes without agreeing to do so. Chatembo and I are age mates. When we lived in the royal village of children, I was almost killed, but Chatembo and her mother's magic saved me."

"What?" Funzi said, confused.

"Oh, you'll understand it later. Anyway, Chatembo and I have our own language. We can send each other messages. Right now Mutele is the problem. He's at the Mbanza, the palace, but I'll send Chatembo a message that will kill him."

Kambi was confused. "*Njoo!* Nzinga, have you been eating sour berries? You sound sick."

Nzinga laughed, thinking how happy Chatembo would be to receive the message. "Here is what I'll tell Topi tomorrow when we send him back."

"By litter?" Kambi asked.

"Yes, by litter. I'll ask him to tell Mbande we will do as he asked. And we hope to finish our work in a few months. He should send for help if the Jagas cause any more trouble."

"I thought you were tired of catechism study and wanted to go home," Funzi said.

"I am tired, and I do need to go. But that message is for Mbande. When Topi is leaving, we'll say, 'And oh, Topi, see Chatembo and say I need a message from her soon. Tell her I see Mutele is a minister, and I'm so happy. I wish he'd gone to the royal village with us when Tashana was there.'"

Kambi said, "Oh, Tashana is the woman . . . I remember."

"Chatembo will, too," Nzinga said. "We shall learn results soon. Our next job is to hurry the treaty work. And for Father Gouvieae to baptize us. Then we can go home."

"Will the governor let all three of us go home?" Kambi said as they walked back from the dock.

"Of course he will," Nzinga said. "I won't go without you."

"Nzinga, I've been thinking. I'm growing to love this life in Luanda. You know, fancy shops, beautiful dresses, handsome Portuguese officers." Kambi smiled.

Both sisters caught Kambi in a punishing hug.

"I've never seen you look at a Portuguese man. You want to be a spy like Shanulu, that's all it is." Funzi pulled her sister's hair. "Isn't that it? Isn't it? Say it or you will be a bald, unattractive spy."

"Sure, I admit it. I don't want to go back home where I can do nothing. Mbande shuts us out."

Although there was danger involved in the path Kambi wanted to take, Nzinga admitted to benefits for Ndongo.

"Do what you want to do," she said. "But I have to know more about horses. And you have to help me."

24.
TUSCANY FOUND

EARLY ONE MORNING, NZINGA rolled over in bed and lay wide awake. She worried. Nearly three weeks had passed since they sent Topi back home by litter. No word had come from Chatembo. Nzinga began to doubt that Topi had delivered the message. Maybe Chatembo was too busy at the shrines, or perhaps she was taking care of Sufalu. Or didn't understand what should be done. Yet there was nothing Nzinga could do but wait.

Nzinga had always been an early riser. Even as a small girl she'd felt the need to know what the world was like without people moving in it. Mornings were quiet, as clean as though Suku had washed them with wet chinguivela leaves. And at home, this early in the morning it was soundless with a silence so big that it challenged you to create something important enough to break it.

She lay for a time listening to Luanda's sounds. Here it was never silent. Surf beat incessantly against the shore. Gulls wheeled and cried, or came and sat on the masts of ships, the steeple on the church, or the top of the flagpoles. Birds sang in the date palms. When she first came, she learned to sleep with the violent pulse of nature that came with being near the ocean. It reminded her of the rhythmic movement and pains of birth. She felt tense here, as though something was always about to happen, as if she were swept with the sea into a foreign force. It was frightening, and yet to be here was necessary to the survival of her people and Ndongo. She must learn as much as possible. That is the way life had always been for her.

Yet there were benefits to living on this edge of turmoil and change. The meeting with Shanulu, Nsobia, and the musicians let her know that others quietly pursued the path to freedom. The arrival of Topi with news about what was going on at home told her she was doing the right things. Being able to talk and joke with her sisters was part of the great feeling of living and striving, the three of them together for the first time in years. Even now, she was fully awake while Kambi and Funzi slept in a bed nearby.

When they awoke later, there would be time to plan, but there'd also be moments of frivolous ambling, not all business. There'd be breakfast in the governor's dining room as usual. She and her sisters would bathe and dress. Then they'd spend a while in their rooms, Funzi and Kambi trying on dresses, seeing if they needed corsets, though they already had the slim waists and wide hips that European styles made foundation garments to accomplish.

They'd join Adelita, their assigned companion, to look at hats and feathers and pieces of jewelry. They'd view themselves in full-length mirrors, all the while talking of Mbacka—home, people there, past dances, and childhood acts. Now, lying here in the quiet, Nzinga again thought of a horse ridden by the cruel armored Portuguese soldier who slew her lover with a sword.

She must see horses.

People here tried to distract her, to tempt and corrupt her and her sisters. Even the governor, after their first treaty session, had sent one of his traders to her. He was a slender man with prickly, shedding skin wherever it was exposed to the sun and grey wherever it was protected. His restless, cat-like eyes were always roving. He licked his lips constantly, as if an appetizing meal had been set before him. And while he talked, his right thumb ranged back and forth over his other fingers. He carried the usual white straw hat, which he placed on the table before leaning toward Nzinga as if he were about to speak in a hushed confidence. He began nervously.

"Queen, eh, Princess." A cat-like smile passed in his eyes, but not showing on his lips, for he busily licked them. "The governor said I might speak with you about investment opportunities. There are many. For example, we could talk about yams, casks of palm wine, coffee, copper, silver. All of these could return enough to make your life and those of your family members most comfortable."

At that point, Nzinga almost stopped him. She and her family members were already comfortable. She was the daughter of a king and now the sister of a king. Ndongo was rich. If that weren't so, why did the Portuguese come? It was clear they came to share the riches of Ndongo. But she listened, settling her anger and frustration by patting the soft rows of the basket-weave design of her hair.

He went on. "The governor has told everyone how much you love your sisters and your family, and how you came all this distance to rescue them." He paused for confirmation from Nzinga. She nodded. Her hand still rested on the table, on the papers she and the governor had been working with. He slid his thumb over the tips of his fingers again. "Maybe, you might be thinking of something that would bring you greater returns, something that might enable you to take even greater care of them."

At this moment, Nzinga wished that her sisters, her brother, all the people of Ndongo, and even all of Africa, could hear what she was hearing. It took a lot of restraint to listen to this invader lead up to propositioning her, to sell herself and to sell others.

"I don't think you realize your position," he said. "Why, you could have the riches of Europe. Fine clothes, linen, beds, jewelry, even horses, sugar—all these could be yours."

The phrase, "realize your position" sounded dangerous gongs in Nzinga's mind. *What a thing to say to the daughter of a king!* Were he in the interior, were her father alive, one gesture and this man's head would lay on the table where his hat now rested. She presented a false face of innocence. His thin face strained with an ardor from the possibility of profit making. He sweated slightly with the effort. A few wisps of hair escaped and ran undisciplined down, continuous with the lines and small fissures on the sides of his head.

"What would I have to do for that?" she asked.

He smiled. His eyes darted around. He touched his face briefly and elbowed his hat. After moistening his lips, he said, "You have the means. You can do it without much effort on your part. I've been to Brazil, and the market is there," he announced, stretching his hands wide apart. "Cane fields, fertile lands. No-o-o restrictions! Why, we could supply plantations from here." He wandered, then came back to the point. "You have wars all the time. You capture people in wars, don't you?"

"Yes," Nzinga said. *Go ahead, say it. Ask me to sell people from this soil away from their ancestors and family, while telling me I am taking care of my family. They are all my family. What kind of thinking is this?*

"Invest with us in a few captured people from other tribes. Say a hundred or so. You will see wealth greater than you have ever dreamt of."

Nzinga got up from the table. "I'm afraid you and the governor misunderstand my position and my power. I am neither the Ngola nor am I his queen. I am his sister, a mere ambassador. I cannot make decisions such as you suggest."

Shadows of disappointment marched across the man's sun-burned face. His thumb moved more slowly across his fingers, but he didn't at once give up.

"Then how about silver?" he said. "Surely your brother would not object to selling some of the silver from his mines. We've heard that there is so much."

"I don't know of any silver mines. Good day, sir." She'd swept from the room.

That was only one of the many propositions she was offered in Luanda. The planters tried to negotiate a market agreement that also included the selling of slaves. They said she could send them salt, bananas, cassava, and skins to the market on the backs of cap-tured people. They'd keep everything, including the people, and pay her well. Nzinga knew that all the goods they named, with the exception of slaves, could be obtained from the African markets.

She pretended not to understand their proposal. Servants brought notes in the night from some captain or lieutenant, asking for a private audience with Nzinga or her sisters. Several offers of marriage followed. Crude offers. These soldiers and planters had no manners or respect. And the priests alluded to messages sent to the pope about the grand work they were doing, of reaching out with the arm of God to take in princesses from Africa. Then came invitations from the governor, and even the Portuguese king and queen, to come to Portugal.

Nzinga and her sisters compared the offers and messages in their room at night and laughed at them. They learned early to play the game by giving answers that held out hope to the pursuers and didn't offend them. To them she was a prize to be won, for she represented the entire country, the people, the silver mines that didn't exist, and the entire interior of Ndongo that they had tried to capture for so long.

Nzinga answered, saying she was bound by love to her people and to the Church, that she couldn't leave her country. She couldn't marry, for she was contemplating marriage to the Church.

And Nzinga pressured Father Gouvieae to hurry along her baptismal studies.

.

With her sisters present and the huge priest presiding, she stood in the Catholic church and faced the small congregation of African parishioners, with several white planters standing in the back. Nzinga and the governor, dressed in his official robes, stood on a raised stage, with the big priest on a level slightly lower. The priest was so close to her, she smelled palm wine through the mint of his breath. He recited a litany of rules, requiring an answer from Nzinga after each of them. Most of them, as she'd been taught, required a simple "I will."

Peering around the bulk of the big priest, she caught sight of Shanulu, Nsobia, and the old musician sitting near Funzi and Kambi. Nsobia put her hands together in front of her face, and Shanulu nodded in approval. During the singing that followed, Nzinga picked out the hoarse, bass voice of the old musician. The big priest took water in his big hands and baptized Nzinga, saying in the name of the Trinity that she was now a servant of God, free of sin, and named

Anna De Sousa from this time on. He further committed her to God's service by drawing the sign of the Cross on her forehead with his hand. He did the same sign on her chest.

Then it was over.

The governor seemed to regard her even more favorably after that. He smiled whenever he looked her way.

.

At breakfast one day, the governor said they'd visit a nearby farm in the afternoon. Then, before noon, he sent a letter of apology.

Out the window, Nzinga saw him being carried in a litter to the docks, where he boarded a small sailboat. One of the women who attended the sisters, the wife of a lieutenant, said that the governor had been called away to a trading area down the coast. Nzinga suggested that they walk around the town with their companion Adelita, try on hats and dresses, and later see the stables and horses.

The sun was half way up the sky when Nzinga, Kambi, Funzi, and Adelita finished browsing the shops and started their walk. A servant girl followed with a basket of boiled eggs, cheese, bread, oranges, and bottles of water.

Nzinga liked the palm trees waving everywhere. She was used to the baobabs. The sand got into her sandals. It was hot and burned her feet. She was used to moving forward with every step, but the sand pulled her back. Kambi laughed at her irritation. She and Funzi kept telling Nzinga to relax.

"The three of us could marry and go to Lisbon," Funzi said.

"What? Not that again," Nzinga said.

"It's such a carefree life." Kambi tried to draw Adelita into conversation. "Everything is easier."

"Oh, Kambi," Funzi said. "Are you so blind so quickly?"

"I see there can be a different life, a better life. Fine clothes, no cares—and the men, they are so different."

Adelita asked what they said, since they were speaking Kimbundu to avoid her attention.

Nzinga said, "How your men are different. Better than ours."

Adelita let out a burst of feeling. "Better than yours? I doubt that. I envy you. You're so carefree and sure of yourselves. Women in Lisbon would never speak to a governor the way you spoke the first day you came here."

"That was all talk about people and country. It had nothing to do with feelings," Funzi said. "I'm interested in how men feel about women."

"Men are the same everywhere, I suppose," Adelita said. "They only think of rough, mean things: horses, swords, ships, and wars. They only come to us women when they want to be babies."

"I like them to be babies," Funzi said, a mischievous glint in her eye. They all laughed. Nzinga thought she sounded like Chatembo, who always had a ready joke with sexual overtones.

Kambi looked straight ahead, her jaw set. "Like Funzi, I feel this is all different and interesting. But I love my own country, my own people. I'd hate to give birth to a mestizo, a half caste who won't be accepted by my people and will be hated by the Portuguese."

Her sisters played their game to draw Adelita out, to learn her true feelings and more of the men in Luanda.

Adelita said, "Lisbon is . . . well, it's difficult. I wasn't happy at home. This is better than there. For a long time, I longed to leave and just go, go somewhere and make a new life. Jorge and I are doing that. Before I came here I used to get letters from a friend, Consulita Cordero, who came here and then went to Brazil. She said that for women like us the colonies are fabulous. We can have servants, fine clothes, and be highly regarded. It's true."

When Adelita mentioned Consulita Cordero, Nzinga grew silent. Cordero . . . Cordero . . . Cordero. The name caused blood to pound at her temples. When Kajubi, her child's father, was killed in the battle with the Portuguese at Massangano, the soldiers straggled back to Mbacka, disheartened, telling stories of terror. A cruel captain from Brazil named Roderigo Cordero, a horse-soldier, ran his horse among the African foot-soldiers, smiling as he killed with his sword. He wore a breastplate of metal that spears and arrows didn't pierce. Even his horse was fitted with a leather harness so spears and arrows couldn't easily enter. He laughed and yelled as he ran the Africans through with his sword and cut off their heads, all the while yelling the Kimbundu word for beheading: "*Zenga! Zenga!*"

This same Cordero had stormed the palace and captured her sisters. He'd tried to frighten Kambi by putting his sword to her chest. Every time his name was mentioned, Kambi spat. Now Cordero was in Brazil. Nzinga had promised Kajubi's spirit that she'd get to see and know horses. Every chance she got, she'd gain more information about horses. And this Cordero.

They stopped under a baobab tree to get sand out of their sandals. Adelita, new to Luanda and not yet hardened to colonial life, pointed further down the path where someone approached at a slow pace.

"I hate the sight."

Nzinga couldn't tell what she meant at first. But she did see a group of people approaching in the distance. As they came nearer, another group of captives appeared, reminding her of the horrific deaths of the woman and baby in the water between the ship and the dock. *Yes, life is good here for you women from Portugal. But how about the captives who are taken to the cane fields? Or who are your servants for life?*

First came the men, strong African men with forked tree limbs pressed and bound against their necks. Leg irons and chains joined one man to another. Then came women and children, their necks twisted and contorted by the ropes and branches that bound them. All were driven by two Africans, three mestizos, and one white. Each driver tapped the prisoners with a thorny branch to keep them in line and moving. These were captured or kidnapped people who would pass through Luanda's dock, like the ones several weeks ago.

Each driver tried to catch the eyes of the women, the Portuguese man bowing to Adelita. But all three sisters shrank from them. Nzinga made herself look into the people's eyes, include the pleading, pitiful eyes of a tall captured woman who walked with shoulders square and head up. *What a pity. But this one will stay alive.*

Few words passed between the women until they neared the stables and heard the hooves of running horses.

·

Adelita ran ahead to the front of several low stable buildings where uniformed Portuguese soldiers moved to and fro. One officer with a scrolled sheet and a pen made notations as men mounted and rode off. There were eight horses and one colt, which stayed near its mother. African servants led horses about or rubbed and curried them. In the distance, across the rough poles and ropes of the paddock, other Africans bent over work in the gardens.

Adelita's husband, Jorge, who was known to Kambi and Funzi, came over with the officer who had sent off the riders. Young and smiling, Adelita had her arm interlocked through her husband's. Both men smiled and bowed to Nzinga at the same time. An African servant, leading a horse past, saw Nzinga and her sisters. He threw himself on the ground, then rose and bowed, speaking rapidly in honor of them. Then he went off smiling.

Jorge still held the reins of a horse, which Nzinga inspected by passing around its great flanks and hindquarters and then back again to its head. The animal was massive, muscular, and strong. A person riding this animal would have great advantage over a person on foot. She tried to look into the horse's eyes. The animal's ears moved erect and alert.

"Tuscany," Jorge said. The horse shifted its attention. Its neck muscles tightened. All four feet flattened on the ground.

"That's his name," Jorge said. He rubbed the horse's muzzle. "He came from Lisbon, but his Italian trainer named him after his home region. We don't care much for the name, but this is a superior horse."

With a smile, as though joking, Adelita said, "Nzinga wants to ride him."

Jorge smiled in derision, shaking his head. "No, it's impossible."

"She does," Adelita insisted. "She told me. I told her how at Coimbra women ride side-saddle."

Actually, Nzinga had planned for this day weeks ago. Nzinga and Chatembo, as children of a king and a seer, realized they could go places where other children couldn't and do things other children couldn't do. This idea carried over into Nzinga's adult life. Like the work to rescue the Ngola's wife and mother, everything depended on Nzinga being prepared and ready to do anything. She intended to be familiar with everything that the enemy used, especially horses. She'd mentioned her desire one day, weeks before, to the priest.

"Is it possible, Father, that I could ride a horse?"

"Ride a horse? Have you ridden a horse before?" He seemed quizzical. Then he answered his own question with a question. "Of course not. How could you? These are the only horses about here."

"No," she said, and she used one of their common expressions. "But, God willing, I could do it."

"God willing?" He didn't give her an answer, only studied her as she thumbed through her catechism, the handwritten pages in Portuguese that Father Gouvieae gave her. "God willing." He repeated the phrase, nodding. She watched and listened to the priest without appearing to do so.

A few days later, she put the proposition to Governor de Sousa when they rode together in a wagon to a farm. He was skeptical at first, but she reminded him of her diligence in studying her catechism. He said, "These aren't ordinary horses that any person may ride for pleasure. They are heavy, war-trained animals. If they fall on you, they could crush you." He studied her with a rakish smile. "We certainly wouldn't want that to happen to you."

Nzinga closed both her hands together in front of her face, to make the governor believe that this was a wish for which she'd prayed, not planned.

"Father Gouvieae is pleased with the way you include God in your plans and how you acknowledge His control over our lives." He looked intently at her. "We'll think how this can be done."

So Nzinga had already laid the groundwork for this day. If it didn't happen now, it would later. But she believed in seizing the opportunity. She'd do it now.

She called to Jorge and Adelita. "This Cordero of whom you speak. Is he a good rider?" She already knew the answer, but she was searching for more. "As good as Adelita thinks?"

"He's in Brazil," Adelita answered. "Remember I told you about his wife, my friend Consulita."

"Everybody knows Cordero," Jorge said. "What a fighter, I hear. He went to Brazil before we arrived. This horse was assigned to him while he was here."

Nzinga's eyes widened. Perhaps this was the same horse that he'd ridden when Kajubi was . . .

"How old is this horse?"

"About four years old," Jorge answered.

About eight rainy seasons. No, it can't be the same horse. Yet, I will ride him.

Jorge laughed. "That Cordero. Everyone here praises him as the best soldier in the army. The most knowledgeable, the most experienced. He's coming back."

"You are also a good soldier, but you said you wouldn't want to be like him," Adelita said.

Jorge, glancing at Nzinga, said quickly, "I can't criticize fighters. I'm an engineer. I now train horses, but my real work is to build bridges and forts. I couldn't kill people in battle. That's what I know."

"I was referring to what you said about Cordero's treatment of prisoners and slaves," Adelita said.

"I heard he's cruel. He even killed a fellow-soldier who looked at Consulita. Not spoke to her or insulted her, but simply looked at her," Jorge said.

"But could he have ridden Tuscany?" Adelita said.

"Oh, no, I see what you mean. Tuscany only arrived here from Portugal last month. The horse that Cordero used to ride was called Muerte. Cordero named that horse himself. That horse is in Brazil with Cordero now. But if Cordero comes back, he'll ride Tuscany."

When Nzinga heard him say that, she was not so afraid of riding Tuscany.

Nzinga was always alert to the thinking and actions of people around her, such as how the Portuguese officers looked at her sisters. Like most Portuguese here, they had no wives in Ndongo. And there were few white women here. So soldiers, settlers, and even priests fathered children by African women. Nzinga considered ways to use the soldiers' attraction to her sisters in order to learn more about horses and to ride one.

Her glance fell then on Kambi and Funzi, standing near the lieutenant who held the scroll and whose eyes kept darting from his work to Funzi. His eyes swept up and down the length of her body, now pausing briefly at her waist, then her breasts, before moving again to her face.

Nzinga spoke to Adelita. "He'll let me ride Tuscany."

"Impossible! Only Lieutenant Pedrone rides Tuscany these days. When the men go to the practice and firing range, he rides Tuscany. That's part of his job to make sure the horses get exercise and stay battle ready. Tuscany isn't a pleasure horse for people to ride. He's a horse of war. He's the only one to ride him, you'll see."

.

The women sat on logs smoothed by the nearly one hundred years of wear from Portuguese soldiers sitting to eat their lunch in the shade of palm-wine trees. The soldiers moved off in columns to drill on a different practice range several miles away in the bush. The African soldiers kept looking with downcast eyes over at Nzinga and her sisters as they passed by. Their faces showed interest and wonder at the presence of the old Ngola's daughters here in Luanda. Their eyes questioned: *Why? Wasn't it dangerous for them? Couldn't they be sent on those ships to Brazil?* Nzinga saw their looks and their veiled concern.

Kambi caught the eye of the African stablemen who was feeding the horses. She beckoned him to her with a turn of her head. He came, bowing, and she met him a short distance away. He fell to his knees. She told him quietly to rise, then greeted him and found out where he came from in Ndongo. He told her, saying he hadn't been home for years. He belonged to one of the generals now.

Kambi said, "You belong to no one person. You belong only to Ndongo. And so do all of those." She pointed with her nose in the direction of the departing African soldiers. "Tell them there is land and wives for all of them if they come home. Do it quietly."

Nzinga laughed. *That Kambi is dangerous.*

When all the soldiers were gone, and even Jorge had followed them to the range, only Senhor Lieutenant Pedrone was left. He appeared to be busy with his scroll until finally, he touched his mustached lip, glanced over toward the palms, and went into a near-by building.

Soon he reemerged, leading the horse Tuscany. With an expert military movement, he approached the side of the horse, threw his foot into a stirrup, and, as the horse leaped into motion, swung his body into the saddle. He glanced over his shoulder at the group in the palms. While appearing not to notice them, he made a few practice runs with the horse. He rode swiftly away and stopped abruptly, and then, turning his mount quickly and smoothly, he jumped it over the high bars of the paddock. He galloped back and brought the horse sharply to a halt in front of the women. Pulling the reins while applying force with his spurred boot, he made the horse rear on its hind legs. Its front legs were another horse's height above Nzinga's head. The other women caught up their skirts and retreated. But Nzinga, though seeing the danger and feeling the fear, didn't move.

Sure of the impression he was making, Pedrone spurred the animal and set off again at a brisk pace, leaping high shrubs and disappearing in an instant into the woods. Then, reappearing from another direction, he raced toward them, halted, and dismounted in an easy, graceful motion.

Nzinga was all attention. She could see why a foot-soldier with a spear and ax or bow and arrow was at a frightening disadvantage in battle against this animal and its rider armed with a two-edged sword. *Poor Kajubi, you never had a chance.*

While seeing the challenge, she'd never let fear daunt her. When Pedrone brought the animal to rest, Nzinga rose.

"Now I'll ride him."

"Jorge said he wouldn't let you," said Adelita.

"But he will," she said. *I am princess, the governor's favorite. My sisters, the princesses, are very beautiful.* She spoke to Funzi. "Go tell him what a great soldier he is and how he has mastered this horse Tuscany."

From the distance, they watched Funzi approach this man from another culture, her long Portuguese skirts flowing, her basket-plaited hair on her well-shaped, small head, her slim waist, her rhythmic steps. He stopped feeding the horse small cylinders of sugar cane, patted it once, and gave full, adoring attention to this princess.

Nzinga gave them a moment together before joining them, followed by Adelita and Kambi.

"Now can I sit on him?"

Pedrone was dismayed. He glanced from the horse to Nzinga, then to Funzi and around again. His mouth opened, but he didn't speak. He fumbled with the reins, rubbed the saddle, and then looked at Funzi, who smiled, her eyes never leaving his face. Finally, he spoke to Nzinga.

"You can sit on Tuscany." To the horse he said, "Hold still, Tuscany. Still now."

Tuscany tipped its head to watch as Pedrone attempted to lift Nzinga onto its back. But Nzinga backed away.

"No, senhor, I want to do it as a man. I'll straddle the horse. You may assist me."

She hitched up her dress, put a foot in the stirrup, and threw her leg over the horse. Pedrone held the reins. Adelita put her hands to either side of her head. Both Funzi and Kambi watched, used to Nzinga never conforming, but always surprised at what turns her actions took.

"This is the way men ride," Nzinga said sitting astride the horse, erect in the saddle.

Pedrone led the horse around the paddock, telling her all the while how she'd use the reins and bit to control Tuscany if she were riding it alone. He seemed nervous and talked because he didn't know what else to do.

When Nzinga dismounted, Pedrone still held the reins and walked with them back to Luanda. Adelita didn't say three words on the return trip, seeming thoughtful and detached. Kambi couldn't stop talking.

Funzi kept saying, "Amazing!"

Nzinga laughed.

25.
RETURN

NZINGA COULD FINALLY REST, in spite of a stirring deep within warning that a decision would have to be made soon. She'd need all her energy and resolve for that.

One morning she slept late. Who needed to get up? The weariness of the past weeks was over. Kambi had been baptized the day before, and at the same meeting Nzinga was confirmed. Funzi was indifferent to her lessons and so had fallen at least three weeks behind, disappointing the priest but pleasing the governor and officers. They delighted in her presence, for Funzi was beautiful and funny and the most easy-going of the three sisters.

To Nzinga's certain knowledge the governor believed that the longer it took Funzi to complete her studies, the longer the three sister would remain in Luanda. He spent more time riding to nearby farms with Nzinga, introducing her to farmers. Nzinga sensed from the farmers' talk and the way they received her that he'd sold them on his idea of using religion instead of force. This was also evident in the number of farmers who had attended Kambi's baptism.

But a browned, ham-fisted farmer named Delvin Santos, who protested the governor's gentle handling of Nzinga on the day of her arrival, mustered opposition to the governor's plan. Although it was a small body of dissenters, Nzinga believed that it would take only one season of failed crops before they'd need another source of income. And they'd again think of the rich slave trade and the myth of silver mines. Then the farmers would force the governor to go to war against Ndongo.

More Portuguese farmers arrived every month. The governor let slip that even more would arrive but for the threat of the Dutch, who challenged the Portuguese on the seas.

·

Kambi shook her sister awake.

"Nzinga, Nzinga, come look. Someone's here. Hurry."

"Who is it? Why must I hurry?" Nzinga tied a scarf around her hair, folding it at the front and throwing it back over her head. She folded and twisted a cloth around her body quickly to form a dress.

"Shanulu is here. She's brought someone you've waited for."

But when Nzinga went out into the living area, she found Shanulu with a boy of about fourteen years.

Shanulu began nervously. "I've tried to stay away so that the governor's people don't realize we work together, but I had to bring this child." Shanulu was near to tears. "He came all the way from Mbacka to see you, Nzinga. One of the African soldiers Kambi spoke to at the stables found him. He kept saying your name. The Portuguese officers tried to sell him, but he kept crying out your name: 'Nzinga, Luanda,' is all he'd say."

She started to cry. Funzi held her. Shanulu said, "Let him tell you, Nzinga. I can't . . ."

The boy, who reminded Nzinga of someone, was on his knees, wild-eyed with fear. "It's you, Princess, just as my father described you." He bowed, chanted, looked all around. "Suku and the ancestors today witness my joy to look upon these faces."

Kambi pulled him into a sitting position. They saw a boar's tooth hanging from a leather throng around his neck and near it a small ring of iron. Funzi pointed. "Look, he belongs to the Ngola."

"Or from someone near to him," Kambi said. "It's the ring of iron, but a small one that someone didn't want to be seen."

"He's from Chatembo. He's our answer," Nzinga said.

"Luanda? Luanda?" The boy held out his open arms in question, as if he wanted to be sure.

"Yes," they answered in unison.

"And this one?" He opened his arms in the direction of Nzinga. "And is this one Nzinga? Nzinga?"

"Yes, I'm Nzinga." She put her hands to her chest.

Joy flowed over his youthful face. He fell on the floor again in front of Nzinga and then raised himself. "Every day for so many days, with the sun at my face, I hurried to seek you as my father and Chatembo told me, but for so many days the sun hid on the savannah or went behind trees, and I didn't see Luanda. Sometimes I travelled with people, but I always lost them. They left the path and went home or to a village far away. Sometimes they fed me. They told me to be careful, because people might sell me. Again with the sun in my face I sought Luanda. Then some people tied my hands and took me away. They kept me for five suns. Then I was given to other people. I ran away, but then others caught me while I slept and tied me up. For days we went with the sun at our faces. This time I didn't worry so much because I was coming to Luanda. But they sold me again at a place with many soldiers and a big fort. Massangano. The Africans there said the Portuguese would sell me to a ship to help make sugar in another place, but I kept saying, 'Luanda, Nzinga,' as Chatembo and my father had told me. And now they have brought me here."

Her friend Chatembo had often amazed her, but it took Nzinga several moments to recognize who he was. His hands pulled at the leather thong.

"Chatembo, daughter of the most wonderful Sufalu, gave me this." He held out the little ring of iron. "She said she went to the royal village and saw Tashana. She told me to say to you, 'Everyone in the Ngola's palace is sad because Minister Mutele was bitten by a cobra that came from a pot near his sleeping mat. He died. The Ngola's mother is searching for a Tashana in the palace, wild with fear.'"

They jumped up to hug the little boy, shouting, "Thank you, Suku!"

Funzi said, "That's not the prayer of a confirmed Catholic."

Nzinga did make the sign of the Cross. When they looked at her, she said simply, "We need every God we can find."

Funzi looked at the boy's necklace again. She caught up the ivory boar's tooth. "You're lucky they didn't steal this from you. Hey, who is your father?"

"Topi, the hunter," the boy said. "At first he didn't want me to come here. Very dangerous, he said. He told my mother he would not like to lose me, but he also wouldn't like to lose Ndongo. She agreed to let me to go, but she cried very much."

Funzi asked, "Nzinga, did you know who he was all along?"

"Not at first, but soon after I saw him. He looks like Topi. And it's the kind of thing Chatembo and I do. Answer a problem with part of the question."

The son of Topi was handed over to Shanulu's care. He praised Suku for letting him see Nzinga and the princesses his father had described, and Luanda as well.

·

The treaty signed by the governor and Nzinga recognized the sovereignty of Ndongo. It stated that all the land in and around Luanda was the property of the Portuguese, including the port and the land occupied by the farmers. It forbade the Portuguese from encroaching any farther inland than the fort at Massangano, but it didn't specifically grant ownership of the land where the fort stood. Free trade between Ndongo and Luanda would be allowed as long as no slaves were taken from Ndongo.

She knew Governor de Sousa was satisfied with the treaty, but the planters and slave traders were gaining power. At any moment they could effect a change of governor. It was time for Nzinga to go back, acquaint Mbande with the articles of the treaty, and help as much as possible to enforce it. She prepared to leave.

Kambi said she'd stay with Funzi and they'd both come when their religious instruction was completed, but Nzinga believed that Kambi had decided to stay longer to help Shanulu and Nsobia. Nzinga would need a line of communication to and from Luanda, and Kambi could help maintain that. Some of their people would stay with the two sisters to act as servants and couriers, and Nzinga would take the rest home with her.

The night before she was to leave, Nzinga took a tearful parting from Shanulu, Nsobia, the musicians, and many African people. They gathered on the beach where the old musician had told the story of the first coming of the Portuguese. They made a big fire and ate. Then they danced, drummed, and sang into the night. In their hearts they called the ancestors and gods to come back to Luanda.

The governor prepared a ceremony in front of Government House where Nzinga had come the first day. He made a speech announcing that they had concluded a treaty to usher in a new era of cooperation and respect. He promised to send the results to Lisbon by the first ship.

Nzinga made a short farewell speech, congratulating the governor and the people of Luanda, and paying respects to the two priests who had taught her and her sisters the Catholic doctrine.

She'd never forget them, she said.

The governor sent an honor guard of uniformed soldiers to accompany her party as far as the giant baobab tree outside Luanda. That's where Kambi and Funzi almost changed their minds, but once a decision was made, Nzinga believed it brought ill fortune to change it. So she hugged them and said, "I'm going to Ndongo, and you are going back to Luanda."

She and Topi's son walked past the giant baobab tree, where she stepped into a litter and headed for home.

·

Drumming, dancing, and general celebration delayed Nzinga's return to the Mbanza. The way at every village was lined with cut palm trees mounted erect in the earth to form a path through which Nzinga was carried for miles. All over Ndongo and stretching even to Matamba, people waited for days to greet her and to celebrate.

They said she was the son of the old Ngola, with his fire and fight. She'd conquered the Portuguese and restored Ndongo's birthright. Before her trip to Luanda, the people were downcast because they had lost their palace and their shrines. Now, all along the way people were proud of their villages and farms, and they showed a new spirit that Nzinga swore to preserve. She felt that the past losses should be a lesson to Mbande, warning him of what might happen if he didn't pay attention to running the kingdom.

When Nzinga came to the hated fort at Massangano, she camped outside of it. The thousands who accompanied her swarmed around it, occupying the area on each side from riverbank to riverbank. The soldiers and commander tried to be friendly. He invited Nzinga in and she went, happy at the chance to see its internal layout in daylight. No part of it was put off limits to her. She, after all, was Anna de Sousa, protégé and convert of the governor himself. The commander prepared a meal for her, which she graciously refused, but she said she'd inspect the parapet of the fort with his permission. The walls were made of stone and reinforced with wood girders inside. Slanted gun turrets let the Portuguese soldiers fire upon attackers without exposing themselves to enemy weapons.

Back outside, she and her party camped for over a week. During the time she was there, her people prevented messages were from passing between Luanda and the fort. Even traffic on the river was shut off. The commander of the fort grew nervous. All communication from Luanda regarding this princess had been favorable. Why was she now attempting to provoke him?

Every day he came to stand with his aide on the parapet above the fort walls, seeking a glimpse of Nzinga and any opportunity to discover her plans. He sent out envoys who were not received but were instead sent back without any message except "return to the fort." Every day it ended the same way: the commander stood on the parapet conversing with officers. Nzinga watched him from a small window in the house the local people had made for her among the trees, using a spyglass the governor had given her. Daily, the commander threw up his hands in frustration and then left his place on the parapet. One day she waved gaily to him as she'd seen the Portuguese ladies do to people from a distance, a friendly wave. He hesitated, not knowing what to make of it, then he waved in return.

Nzinga laughed gleefully. None of her family had ever liked the Massangano fort, and now she was making sure the Portuguese knew it. Nzinga and her entourage packed up their equipment and left late one night. She imagined the commander's face when he came to the top of the fortress the next morning. *He'll look puzzled when he sees no one. Not a single spirit. I'd like to see him send a hasty dispatch to Luanda.* Her imagination raced on. He'd probably write, "Are you sure that the Ndongo princess can be trusted?"

In her litter, bouncing happily homeward, Nzinga completed the imaginary exchange: *"Well, even she isn't sure."*

She now knew the hated fort inside and out, information she might have to use someday.

▪

Nzinga's entourage on her return consisted of all the people who'd followed after her along the way. Sometimes full villages, hearing of the treaty, had joined her. These people spread out for miles behind her, reaching over the savannah and past Massangano.

Her party included some of her father's old soldiers who had gone back to their villages. They complained that the present Ngola had deserted the mainland for an island in the river. They had nowhere to go and no work to look forward to as warriors. So they drifted back to their villages to farm and to sit and talk about what they had done in the past. They had no worthwhile work to give them pride. What could they say or do at the shrines when they went to show Suku and the ancestors that they had secured the ring of iron and served the one chosen?

But now word of the treaty and the return of the old Ngola's daughter brought them new hope, and they said it loudly. They came to Nzinga and told her their stories along the way. They came in crowds, awaiting her orders and ready to be led. Their officers formed their old warrior groups, enclosing her in the mass of people, heading toward Mbacka. They marched, they drummed, and they danced in celebration.

Nzinga felt the power of the people flocking around her. It was power she could transfer to Mbande. Properly used, it could ensure the future of Ndongo. But would he use it?

Nzinga, coming home now as her father had years before, swayed in a litter and heard the chants and the rushing footfalls of the soldiers, imagining what it was like then. She'd been one and a half years old, so all she could know had been told by her family and by the griots. The old Ngola's procession after a battle had also started on this savannah. Unlike the battle of wits and words Nzinga had been engaged in at Luanda, her father's war had been a bloody war of weapons and betrayal, and he had lost. Trusted chiefs deserted him, sold their alliance to the Portuguese. She'd won her war in Luanda and prevailed back at home, for the moment.

Slowly the stories told over the years came back as she crossed the savannah. Her father came here to fight a war, and a chief named Kassa betrayed him and sold out to the Portuguese for guns, wealth from slaves, and cloth. If her father were killed, the Portuguese promised to use their army to crush Ndongo and make Kassa the Ngola. Kassa would have killed the Ngola, except Sufalu's spies warned her father in time. Sufalu cautioned him that he'd be attacked from either side at night by a massive army of Portuguese soldiers with guns and African soldiers bought in the Kongo. Her father's army used only spears—they would have been defeated. But, warned in advance, her father attacked one great part of the army before they were ready, defeated them, and escaped in the night back over the very savannah where Nzinga traveled now. Her father had won that battle, but in the end his plans were defeated and the kingdom was left weaker, for he lost a trusted chief and he couldn't pursue the battle he'd originally set out to win.

As Nzinga swung along in the litter, she imagined how it was for her father returning home back in that time, crossing the savannah, swaying in a litter.

◆

PART IV
THE NEW NGOLA

1621–1663

26.
HOMECOMING

PEOPLE AROUND NZINGA MARCHED in cadence, collecting more at every village on the way to the Mbanza, the crowd stretching for miles. She came to the palace in triumph, with drums overwhelming the rumble of the falls.

During the trip home from Luanda, Nzinga did two things: retraced her father's return across the savannah, where he saw her for the first time; and retraced her life, which was joined to her father's and his fathers', the long line of elephant hunters. Her success in Luanda was equal to an elephant hunt.

Now she must see that the kingdom was secure. The treaty was the key. *Father! Kajubi! I am back. Now, let us rebuild what you left us.*

Chatembo, Kadu, and Yafia were at the old Mbanza, but not Mbande or Kaningwa. Messengers reported that people waited for days at the new Mbanza, gazing out at the island in the river, trying to see their Ngola, but only a few were allowed on the island.

Kadu came to her. "The Ngola told me to welcome you back. He'll have a feast on the island in honor of your return."

"He should be here," she said. "The people should see their leader. They know what we did in Luanda. We won back our country. He should be here to make them understand."

The people shouted her name.

"Nzinga, Nzinga, Child of the Flame!"

"Nzinga, Daughter of the Old Ngola, Savior of Ndongo!"

Out of their great love for her father, the people had restored the whole structure of the old palace and, with the help of Yafia, refurnished it. The people had placed the chair of honor for her, and they danced up and down the hillside where the old Mbanza stood, reclaiming their kingdom.

She honored Mbande as the Ngola. She wanted to see him occupy the Mbanza of her fathers. Mbande did not yet understand that Ndongo belonged to the people, and they were the ones who cherished him as the center of their unity and strength. She couldn't enter the new Mbanza without his presence.

And yet she felt certain Mbande and his mother had a troubled sleep that night.

After the next day passed without seeing Mbande, Nzinga went to her own house. In Nzinga's absence, Chatembo had done wonders. Workers were cultivating the land, and several small decorated houses had been built like the ones at the Mbanza. Sufalu, well cared for, slipped in and out of her regular self. Nzinga's grandmother sat with Sufalu often, making baskets and mats or weaving Chatembo's lovely hair. The grandmother wove Sufalu's hair and dressed her in finery collected from Nzinga's trip to Luanda.

Chatembo also trained warriors.

During the first days back, Nzinga went back into training. At first she wasn't pleased with her reactions in combat. Her fierce, decisive moves and quick reactions were absent. She was slow and tentative.

"You aren't your regular self, Nzinga," Chatembo said. "You're still thinking about things as you did in Luanda.

Her friend was right: in battle you didn't have time to think. You acted, you did what you already knew how to do. Nzinga let her body be free and ready to expect the moves of her opponents. Gradually the old fast-flowing motions returned, and the lightning speed of the leaps and twirling, causing the new recruits to marvel at her skills with the fighting sticks and her agility and strength.

Chatembo whispered, "I took this job, to train these young warriors, so I could pick the best ones for the granary." She laughed it off as a joke, but however much of it might be true, Nzinga was happy that Chatembo no longer drank palm wine.

For part of each day they sat with Sufalu and Nzinga's grandmother to talk about what had happened while they were apart. One day the talk centered on Wasema, the captured woman who'd had a child at the same time as Nzinga. Wasema was a useful member of the household, and Chatembo put her in charge of all the servants, a job she did well. But Wasema was silent unless someone asked a direct question, which Chatembo often did.

"Wasema, what are the cooks preparing today?"

Brooding and unhappy, Wasema seemed to be trying to figure something out. Chatembo let fall a hint that explained it. "Wasema received a message soon after you left. She's been like this ever since."

"Who was the message from?" Nzinga asked.

"From him or her," the grandmother put in.

"We don't know, Grandmother," Chatembo said.

"Will someone tell me the whole thing?" Nzinga asked.

Chatembo said, "A small polished boat came from the island with only an oarsman and a woman from Wasema's tribe who was a captured servant. She waited in the boat with a message for Wasema. It was, 'Don't ever stare into the Ngola's boat again. Never come near him.' Then the woman was rowed back to the island."

Nzinga called to Wasema, "Who sent you that message?"

At first, Wasema shook her head. "I can't say."

"We care about you and would never let anyone harm you, unless they did the same to us all," Nzinga said. "Who sent it?"

"Only a woman sends a woman with such a message," Wasema said. "I could tell how the woman who delivered it talked. It came from a woman with great power."

"Kaningwa," Chatembo said. "The hyena was eating once again."

"I thought he had a great heart," Wasema said. "He said it would be all right. Even then, I thought he sent the boat to bring me to him. Yet he never even looked at me that day. Why? Why?" She shook her head, not understanding. "Then the cobra bit him, and he died."

Chatembo said, "Mutele had his eye on power. He didn't care for you." She glanced at Nzinga, nodding.

■

It was fourteen days until Nzinga woke one morning to find a boat waiting for her. Mbande wanted her at a conference, and he was having a feast the next night in honor of her success in Luanda. She hadn't been notified and so was unprepared. She made the boat wait most of the day while she got ready.

When she finally arrived at the island, Mbande had canceled the conference and gone hunting. It was late the next day before they met.

Nzinga gave a full account of what had transpired with the treaty and the release of Mbande's mother and wife.

"Why are Kambi and Funzi not here?" he asked.

"They're kept there to make sure we maintain the terms of the treaty," she said. *Why wasn't he concerned about his sisters the day I arrived home?*

After she explained that the markets had to be opened and trade goods exchanged again, he asked about the mutual protection he'd requested. She hid her surprise that he still depended on their enemy for protection.

"It can't all be done at once." The governor, she assured him, was a man they could deal with—if they kept the treaty, the one Mbande had originally authorized her to negotiate. "When will the markets open?"

"Oyimbu will appoint someone to take care of it."

She then asked about the old Mbanza and whether he'd come to meet with the people there on certain days.

"It will be considered. I'll appoint one of my generals to look after it." Mbande smiled often, outwardly pleased. "I hope you'll enjoy the celebration tonight."

Although they were with only Kadu and Oyimbu at the conference, there was an open door and a servant came in frequently. Certain the proceedings were being watched, Nzinga felt Kaningwa's presence although she didn't appear until the conference was finished.

Kaningwa greeted Nzinga warmly, smiling and holding her away to examine what Nzinga wore.

"You are much more stylish and royal since you were in Luanda. You must tell me about the dresses. Thank you for the ones you sent to me."

The Ngola's little wife Chala was playing music and helping Yafia make everything beautiful. She was quick to change any opinion that didn't match her mother-in-law's ideas. Yafia threw sidelong glances of disapproval at Chala. In any discussion, such as moving a wall ornament from one place to another, Chala invariably deferred to Kaningwa, while Yafia often said, "Chala, make up your own mind."

Then Kaningwa sat to chat, more talkative than Nzinga had ever known her to be, perhaps because she felt she'd secured power and no longer needed to be cautious.

"I like it in the river," Kaningwa said. "I feel much safer here. Imagine the night we woke up and those Portuguese horse-soldiers were all over the palace." She shook her aging-but-beautiful body as though chilled by the memory. "But, you know, Nzinga, something odd happened here." She moved her chair closer to Nzinga and leaned forward with a conspiratorial tone, touching Nzinga's arm. "Sometimes I feel we have enemies here. Before I heard what happened to poor Sufalu, I thought she was doing mischief here, but it's not her. Nzinga, I know, because I changed all the servants. It may be that we have many snakes here, but a cobra in a basket appeared near his sleeping mat. I mean, poor Mutele. Doesn't it sound suspicious? I was absolutely wild with fright. I couldn't sleep. I had servants throw out all the baskets and look under every mat. Mbande had his own suspicions. He killed many servants and a few of his hunter friends, those who were good snake catchers. We knew them . . . from a long time back."

Nzinga showed her interest by nodding.

"What will you do, Nzinga, now that you are home?"

"Anything I can do to help Mbande. I still train and send him warriors."

"I envy you that, Nzinga. You are so strong and command such respect. It's a great asset. Do you have a male favorite?"

"None."

"Yes, that's the way it's been for me since your father passed. There's no one to compare."

Nzinga wanted to say, "How about Mutele?" But she remained silent. Listening is a virtue, especially where virtue is at a premium.

"But," Kaningwa went on, "there's always food. If one has no mate, one can eat. That gives satisfaction." Looking at Nzinga's well-proportioned body, she said. "I see you keep a nice figure, Nzinga. Is it because of exercise? I know you like sweet fruits just as I do. I tell Mbande he shouldn't eat so much meat. That's why he's getting thicker."

"Meat makes you thicker, then?" Nzinga kept the conversation going.

"Absolutely, though it's not the only thing, but it also spoils your stomach." Kaningwa paused. "And Mbande, let me tell you, Nzinga, ever since he was a child, he likes that stuff inside of the big bones. He'd rather crack a bone than eat a spoonful of honey. I can't understand that craving."

"All of us have our preferences," Nzinga said. "I'm fond of yams and cassava."

After that, the topic was clothing. Mbande's wife joined them, along with Yafia.

"I'd love to know how you've kept your figure all this time, even with having children," Yafia said to Kaningwa.

"I had only three children. They were the right ones, so I didn't have to repeat. But I would say control is the answer. You have to control things that matter. That's what I do. I control things." She seemed to search for another topic. "It's lovely on this island. I can't see why people beg Mbande to allow them to work on the mainland. I advise him to deny permission. As I said, I live in the palace, but I have my own house out there." She pointed to a brightly colored cottage on the grounds. "It's decorated the way I want it. When I don't want to be involved, I go there to rest and think."

"I go there with her some days," Chala said.

"Mbande protects us, too. He says, 'Mother, don't worry. Everyone knows that if anything happens to you, this Ndongo is going to be a dead place.'"

"What does that mean?" Nzinga had to ask.

"Just that." Kaningwa seemed to know, at that moment, she'd been too talkative. Yafia's face showed shock and discomfort. Kaningwa had just made known a threat to the lives of all of Ndongo, even members of the royal family.

The celebration in Nzinga's honor was staged beautifully, but only a few people were permitted to come over to the island. Nzinga attributed this to Kaningwa's control.

Mbande made a speech, crediting Nzinga with gaining the release of his mother and wife and negotiating a treaty that ensured the sovereignty of Ndongo. Though only a few heard it, Nzinga was satisfied that the crowds who greeted her on her return home had already spread her accomplishments throughout Ndongo.

The food was in huge quantities and delicious. The Ngola demonstrated his love for gazelle leg bones and palm wine. He still ordered a mallet to his table and personally cracked the bones to extract the marrow. He extolled it as healthful and, unlike his mother's, his appetite knew no bounds. He had no control.

The drummers and dancers were people she'd gathered from throughout the kingdom when she was preparing her trip to Luanda. Often in the feasting, Mbande danced with the dancers, or challenged one of his age-mates to wrestle. Unlike his father, Mbande became petulant and sullen when thrown. Therefore, many thought better of wrestling with him. When they did, they let him win, for when he was displeased, he'd order a servant killed or a chief demoted without reason.

Nzinga had only one audience with Mbande after that night. He avoided being seen with her. Soon after, Yafia left the island and moved to her land near Shellanga.

As Nzinga stayed on the island, she found no happiness there. The palace atmosphere was uncomfortable. The smiles and happiness weren't real. Laughter wasn't open or sustained. People were frightened and tense. She was ignored by Mbande, who made no attempt to carry out the treaty. No attempt was made to open the main markets or, with the exception of Shellanga's army, build up protective forces. The soldiers were drifting away from their units, going home.

Chatembo came to visit Nzinga one day. Kaningwa watched them all day. The two childhood friends sat under an ancient tree that had grown there from before the river spread, taking part of the land and placing it into the center of the meandering river. Nearby was a fence that kept out hippos and crocodiles. Now and again, they saw the snouts of hippos rise in the water and big crocodiles swim or walk outside the fence near the river.

Nzinga told Chatembo about Mbande ignoring the treaty and refusing to take care of his army or discuss the kingdom with her.

Chatembo said, "It's jealousy. The hyena and the hippo are talking. The hippo says, 'She swims too easily in the water.' The hyena says, 'She could ride on the back of a rhino and fly away. There's no catching her if you let her fly.'"

In this way, as they had for years, Chatembo spoke of Kaningwa as the hyena and Mbande as the hippo that ruled the waters. The servant Kaningwa sent to work near them and spy couldn't make out what the two friends said. Nzinga, laughing, asked how the hippo and hyena could forget so soon after they escaped the crocodiles. Crocodiles were the armor-plated horse-soldiers.

They talked about the feast, and the wrestling and dancing. "Why does he have to crack the bones? They already have little holes in them," Chatembo said.

"But the holes aren't big enough to get the marrow out," Nzinga said.

Chatembo laughed. "I just had a thought."

"I'll bet it's about warriors. And the granary."

"It is about a man."

•

After this, Nzinga went to her own home to wait. More than a year passed, and Mbande did nothing to keep the treaty. She requested an audience, and found him playing a hand organ and laughing with a few of the small people called the Twa, who had been brought back years earlier from Kongo.

She bowed and talked about the news of the day. Mbande was cordial until she mentioned the market and the treaty. Kaningwa came to the door and called them to look at the hill where the old Mbanza had stood. Mbande didn't move, but Nzinga followed his mother out, where they saw high billows of smoke and flames rising there.

Nzinga ran to tell Mbande there'd been a new attack. But before she could speak, he said, "My soldiers are burning it down. All the goods have been transferred here. Yafia allowed the rebuilding without my permission. Nothing moves in Ndongo without the word of the Ngola."

"The Portuguese are taking more and more land without having your word."

"Nzinga, my ministers are doing what I order them to do. Leave it to me." He went back to playing his hand organ and watching the little people dance.

When Nzinga told Chatembo and Wasema that night, she asked, "What reason could Mbande have to turn his back on everything?"

"The reason was the hyena in the doorway. Mbande and Kaningwa will understand only when they hurt in the way they have made others hurt."

Nzinga crossed her arms, looking stern.

"Someone has to kill her," Chatembo said.

Wasema clamped her hand over her mouth and refused to speak. Like a child, she placed a finger first on Chatembo's lips and then Nzinga's. Then she went out of the house. No one could make anything of her act.

Except the old grandmother said, "That child is tired of hearing, 'Kill this, and kill that.' She doesn't want to hear it again."

• • •

A few days later, Wasema came to Chatembo. She needed to see the old man who'd once been her protector, who was now keeper of the royal fire and lived on the island in the river. Chatembo helped disguise Wasema to get past the guards and then went along. Nzinga remained behind because there was a feast that night.

Wasema was talkative on the boat. She spoke of her old benefactor. "He knows so much about fire. He used to be just a farmer. Did you know that once during the dry season, the whole savannah was ablaze, and the Ngola came to his house to get him to teach people how to control the fire? When I was pregnant and we sat at night in his house, he told me how you can carry fire a long ways without anyone knowing it. You carry it just like a little bird, giving it just enough air to breathe, but not enough to make smoke."

Chatembo laughed at the bird analogy. "A little bird? I doubt that can be done." Then she told Wasema the boat would go back soon after the feast started. "Be at the dock when the feast begins."

Two things happened on the island that night. The first began during the feast. Mbande, while drinking and cracking gazelle bones, fell down sick. At the same time, his mother, in her house resting, woke up to find her house on fire. Her screams rang through the river palace as she tried to escape the building. Her thatched roof burst into flames, burning bright yellow in the dark night, and then fell into the circular house.

Wasema and Chatembo were in a boat out on the river, headed back home. They saw the wild yellow-and-red flames lighting up and reflecting eerily on the river water. Chatembo wrapped a shawl closer around her shoulders.

On the island, would-be rescuers found a wooden pole blocking Kaningwa's door from the outside.

Mbande died during the night. Rumors circulated later that it was poison.

Now Ndongo had no Ngola.

．

At their house late that night, after messengers brought the terrible news, Chatembo told Nzinga how Wasema spoke in the boat about carrying a flame as if it were a little bird. Wasema swore it was possible, but that she'd never do such a thing. When Nzinga doubted the possibility, Wasema was anxious to show them.

"We did it often, the old man and me, when he was a builder. We took fire home from the royal fire." Wasema searched outside for banana fibers and, coming inside, twisted them several times in her hands and held them up. "See this." She produced a piece of smoking banana fiber from beneath her shawl. "You light this new one like this, at this fire. Let it burn like this blaze a while." A bright flame lit up the new fiber. "Now, snuff it out like this." She held it up. No sign of fire. "Watch." She blew softly on the fiber, and it burst into flames. "The old carpenter told me. You can attach a fiber like this to a thatch and be miles away before the wind blows it into a flame."

"Oh, my Suku," Chatembo exclaimed. "Wasema, you are a wonder. Ancestor, mine. Just look at her."

Wasema held up her hands, shaking her head in denial.

"I could never do that," she said.

After a moment, Nzinga asked, "And how did poison get in Mbande's food when royal tasters always taste food before the Ngola?" Nzinga asked the old grandmother.

"The messengers say it was inside the bones," the old grandmother said. "How could that be?"

27.
NZINGA BECOMES NGOLA

THE CHIEFS AND GENERALS met and declared Mbande's twelve-year-old son to be Ngola, but until he was old enough, Nzinga was to be regent. She'd act instead of the young Ngola, with all her decisions subject to the approval of the chiefs and generals. They put the young Ngola under the protection of the youngest chief-general.

The young Ngola disappeared without a trace.

Soon, Nzinga appeared before crowds of chanting people who supported her, who urged her to take over the army and make herself Ngola.

Chants rang out all over, and people ran to her.

"Nzinga! Nzinga! Ngola, Rainmaker!"

"Nzinga, Daughter of the Old Ngola!"

Nzinga stood on the banks of the river near the ashes of the old Mbanza. People flowed to her from throughout the kingdom, shouting her name.

"Nzinga! Nzinga! Ngola! Ngola! Rainmaker!"

"Nzinga, Savior of Ndongo, Daughter of the old Ngola!"

Nzinga wisely rebuilt the old Mbanza, so the people would know that Ndongo wasn't giving up any lands. She placed her army there and rebuilt the great meeting hall. For a time, she put Chatembo and Sufalu in charge of it. Meanwhile, Nzinga built an army post between the Mbanza and the fort, and her soldiers set traps and cut trees to delay any attack by horse-soldiers.

At first Nzinga wouldn't go near the island palace. Instead, she built a temporary palace close to Musungu's forest, with a great meeting hall like the one her father had occupied. She visited all the shrines and waited for her brother's chiefs, ministers, and generals to come to her.

Kadu, knowing what a great leader she was, endorsed Nzinga at once. Oyimbu, Shellanga, and some of the other chiefs, however, had never served under a woman. They searched for a male heir to put in her place. But Mbande had killed all of the males. Still, they wouldn't recognize her.

She went to the meeting house daily, expecting the chiefs to recognize and support her. When this didn't happen, she went after Oyimbu first—Oyimbu, who loved his wife and his cows. She didn't harm his people. But her army was large and spread over the kingdom—they needed to be fed. She set them on Oyimbu's herds and flocks. She sent out an order: *My generals and soldiers can kill and eat Oyimbu's cows.* By the late afternoon, herds milled around bellowing as army cooks and skinners slaughtered choice cows. Smoke and the aroma of cooking rose from their open campfires.

On the second day, Chief Oyimbu came with his wife. His people carried chickens, goats, baskets, and Kongo silver and gold bracelets that had been presents from Kaningwa. They fell down in front of her. Oyimbu's wife addressed Nzinga.

"Princess Nzinga . . . "

Nzinga held up her hand. "Who are you to address me here? I'll talk woman-gossip in the market, or if I'm ever weak enough to pay a visit to your home. Here, you have no right to speak unless I order it. Now, Chief Oyimbu, do you wish to address me?"

Oyimbu's wife clamped her mouth shut and slid further down on the floor. Chief Oyimbu had always spoken with ease and flamboyancy, but this time he said, "Nzinga, Daughter of the Ngola—"

She held up her hand again. "I am Ngola of Ndongo. I don't want crying chiefs who cannot make up their minds."

"Ngola Nzinga," Oyimbu said, strong and loud enough for people to hear outside the meeting hall. "Ngola Nzinga, I want to serve you as I did your father and brother."

He was about to go on, but Nzinga gave him a list of things to do: taxes to collect, and soldiers and other chiefs to bring before her. She assigned soldiers to help carry out those tasks. "Now if your wife is willing to help, I have a job for her. There is a job for everyone to help rebuild Ndongo."

Getting Kadu and Oyimbu to accept her would go a long way in convincing other chiefs. But she regarded Shellanga as the key person. Because Shellanga was known throughout the kingdom as a trusted military leader, he could command an army. And he had the respect of the people, even in Matamba and the Kongo. She couldn't understand why he didn't support her.

Nzinga sent for her aunt Yafia, but the message came back that she was in Matamba.

Nzinga left everything at home to Wasema and her grandmother. She told Chatembo to rebuild Sufalu's spy organization and to administer the palace on the island. Nzinga planned to deal with Shellanga.

28.
CALL ME KING

ON THE FIRST DAY AT the temporary palace, the big ceremonial drums hadn't yet been set up in the meeting hall. Smiling with satisfaction, Nzinga listened to the music and the chanting, and then saw the surprise and dismay on the faces of the common chiefs as well as the disapproval of the whispering elders.

They won't like the idea of a woman as a king. They think, "A woman Ngola! I don't know what that kind of Ngola is about."

However, she didn't think of herself as different from the men and wasn't prepared to tolerate prolonged disapproval and opposition. They might not like it, but for the sake of her father, she believed that they'd finally accept it. The common people were with her.

So during these times, Nzinga rose and dressed before dawn. She wore full armor, with a leather shirt laced up at the back and wristbands of thick rhino skin, the ones she'd given Kajubi. A long, sheathed knife hung from her slim waist. The small knife Musungu had made for her was in her waistband. Her hair was braided and tied back. When she left her house, she picked up the shield and double-bladed spear that were always propped against a wall. Then, still before sunrise, Nzinga hurried into the big meeting hall of the temporary palace to sit in the king's chair.

Thousands of people waited daily to see her and ask favors. They wanted, among other things, to offer a son or daughter up for service, but she wasn't ready to see people yet. She told Ndowe, a son of Topi, who was now one of her ministers, to inform them to go and serve the king in any way they could, promising that their deeds would be brought to Nzinga's attention and rewarded later.

For weeks she waited for Shellanga to acknowledge her as king. But he didn't come. She sent him messages, but answers to her messages never arrived. It was time now to teach him a lesson. She regretted doing this to her father's old friend and supporter, but her father was dead and she was the ruler now. She must act. She'd learned this from her father. And she chose to do what he'd be proud of, if he could see it.

One day Chatembo, once again disguised as a man, rushed into the room and fell to the floor with arms aflutter, as a bird preening in a bath. Casting her eyes first at Nzinga and then at the floor, she chanted in a high-pitched voice.

"Oh, keeper of the fire, she whose face puts the sun to shame.

"Oh, she who makes rain to fall and the simsim grow.

"Oh, ruler of the wind . . . "

With this, Chatembo endeavored to show Nzinga that everything was working out well.

Nzinga smiled in spite of her troubling thoughts. Rising from the throne, she cuffed Chatembo on the head. "Get up, Chatembo. Stop acting like Mbande's court fools. Tell me your news!"

"Shellanga has lost his princess. Yafia has returned to her lands, angry that he doesn't move to support you. She sends a servant begging you to kill his wives so he'll serve you. Do it, Nzinga. You have waited long enough."

"No, Chatembo. I will do nothing out of spite. Yafia might say that today, but then she'd hate me. I will do as my father would have done. Shellanga is a friend and servant of Ndongo. I will remind him of that. I won't harm his people. I will take his cows."

She sent for Ndowe, her minister, and prepared to go by litter to Shellanga's land, a three-day trip. Chatembo was left behind with most of the army to guard the palace. A large troop of soldiers attended Nzinga, and they rested every night after setting up camp with a house constructed just for Nzinga.

The once mighty Shellanga no longer had command, because his soldiers now were a part of Nzinga's army. She arrived at one of Shellanga's compounds with her army just at the highest point of the sun, while the cattle were still grazing. The crowd of people who had followed Nzinga's troops pointed at the Ngola, shouting her praises. At once she set the soldiers to cut the heels of Shellanga's cows. Disabled, the cows tried to run but keeled over, and the huge animals were bellowing on the apron of the grassland. Then Nzinga gave the order for them to slay the cattle and take meat as they desired.

Soon, cows lay butchered and skinned. Basketful after basketful of beef was rushed away. The news carried quickly to other villages. As one group of people left, another hurried to appear.

Frightened herd boys ran for miles to inform Shellanga of Nzinga's visit. He arrived to see the butchered cows, with carrion birds flying over his land. Stunned, he struck his forehead in disbelief and sat dejectedly upon the earth.

By this time, Nzinga rested in a newly constructed temporary palace. Her cooks were preparing choice chunks of Shellanga's cows for a feast. The drums and dancers celebrated around a giant fire of wood cut from Shellanga's land. His grain bins stood empty. Fires burned in several of his houses.

That night Nzinga waited for her father's favorite general and chief to come, but she was disappointed. At noon the next day she told Ndowe, "Tomorrow we'll move to his other compound. Go to the villages near his house, and tell people to come to get meat. This time, kill all cows, spare the calves. Slaughter the goats and sheep. Harvest the gardens. If he doesn't come, we'll cut down every standing tree. But don't touch his wife or children."

All afternoon cows bellowed, sheep and goats bleated, and grasslands lay bloodstained. Bloated blue flies buzzed up beneath the feet of soldiers as they walked along the carnage. In the trees, scavenger birds waited. And trees fell. Many feet trampled over Shellanga's land, but no member of his family was seen. They'd run into hiding, fearing the Ngola's wrath would fall on them after the cattle were all killed.

The feast continued for six days. Drums sounded. Runners bearing gourds of wine and honey arrived. Chatembo couldn't stay away from the celebration.

"Nzinga, you should have done this from the beginning," she said.

Nzinga held court and judged local cases. People brought their children to see and serve the Ngola. One day a group of Nzinga's soldiers brought in a tall, slumped, unshaved man whose skin was blotched with mosquito bites. He was dressed in a ragged cape.

"This old man has been begging to see the queen."

Nzinga, who was in another part of the house, peered unobserved at the man standing bowed before the guards. She ordered her servants to give him food and send him on his way. Then she returned to her duties, but the next day, the same old man requested to see her.

"Did you feed him and send him away before?"

This time she'd give the beggar a job. Everyone in Ndongo was valuable and could be of service. When she saw him this time, he'd cleaned his face and stood straighter and taller. His bearing reminded her of someone. Then she knew. This thin, dirty, disheveled shell of a man was once the tall and stately Shellanga.

"Have him washed and fed. Then bring him to the meeting hall," she ordered.

•

Nzinga made Shellanga wait for a day so he could witness how far he had fallen. She took her time dressing in her robe of royal white bark-cloth with a colorful sash around her waist and a headband of leopard skin. She carried a flywhisk of elephant bristles and hairs from a zebra's mane mounted on a smooth ebony wood handle. As she entered the hall, the drums sounded, the flutes and harps joined in, and dancers pranced up and down the way they had in her father's time.

She sat in her father's chair. Chatembo sat nearby; her anger for anyone who defied Nzinga was like the protective feelings Sufalu had for Batayo. Now Chatembo's ire for Shellanga rose. She whispered to Nzinga over the drum and flute notes, "Why did you send him to wash and to eat? These people should have seen him as he was."

"Chatembo, I must do it this way. It's best."

"Best? He didn't think of what was best for you when he deserted you, leaving you to defend yourself against enemies. Why even talk to him? You don't need him."

"Chatembo, be patient. You will see. I don't want to dishonor him. He was my father's friend, and he'll be mine. He'll help me defeat the Portuguese."

A signal from Ndowe caused a flurry of action at the back of the meeting hall. Two soldiers roughly ushered Shellanga before the Ngola's chair. Even now he was too proud to avert his eyes. He bent only slightly and looked into Nzinga's face. With a smile, Nzinga nodded as the soldiers forced him into a prostrate position in front of Nzinga's throne.

She motioned for a stool and allowed him to rise to a sitting position. She said, "Shellanga, my father's friend. How are your days?"

"Sometimes good. But lately the days are as sour as cow's piss."

"And, Shellanga, how are your people? Your wife, your children, and servants?"

"I cannot tell. They are scattered like ash in a dry-season fire." His hands moved restlessly over his face and head, and his body weaved unsteadily.

"You should take better care of them, Shellanga."

"I do what I can. These days I'm weak."

Nzinga thought the light caught a glaze in his eye. *Was it a tear?*

"You never wanted for strength in the old days. You wrestled with my father, the Ngola, and beat him. Once you saved his life at an elephant hunt."

Shellanga raised his head at that. For a moment there was the flit of memory and even the hint of a smile.

"Ah! Your father saved my life when I fell into an elephant trap. Nobody knew where I lay for three days, with spears piercing me. Leading the search, he hunted and hunted, and wouldn't give up until he found me and saw that my wounds were healed. I had a king as a friend."

"You were a friend to my father. You served my brother."

"I served your brother because I loved your father."

Shellanga passed his hands over his eyes as if to wipe away a mist of ignorance.

. . .

Shellanga searched around the room and saw the soldiers, the masks, the Ngola's drums, and the shields of royalty all arranged. Signs that Nzinga truly had the power.

"You, you have plundered and killed many of our people. Will you kill more?" he asked.

"I have done what my ancestors have done. I needed to do it. I have held back my hand many times when I should have slain."

"Oh, my queen—" Shellanga began.

But Nzinga cut him short.

"Call me Ngola," she said. "Call me 'King.' A queen has limitations. I have none. I am Ngola. The same as my ancestors, my father, and my brother. Shellanga, call me Ngola."

Shellanga heard the resolve in the voice he'd admired since she was a child. He saw her royal carriage and her face, which was so like her father's. He bowed.

"You are the Ngola. Oh Ngola, let me help you rule your people."

"You shall. Now take your place among the chiefs."

She signaled for the drums to sound as servants escorted Shellanga to a seat designated for a minister or a chief.

29.
THE SOLDIER

KAMBI AND FUNZI SENT messages from Luanda: Governor de Sousa had been replaced and was leaving for Lisbon. He invited Nzinga to go with him to Lisbon. If she wanted to go, she must come to Luanda at once. The sisters also reported that the planters and traders were angry because the markets weren't opened, which had been promised in the treaty. Father Gouvieae had gone to Brazil, so they were left with only Father Alvares. The message ended with the note that all of Sufalu's family was doing fine—which told Nzinga that Shanulu, Nsobia, and the musicians all still worked for Ndongo.

By the time Nzinga received this message, the new governor had arrived. Kambi and Funzi sent an urgent message: "Cordero is coming, Nzinga. Be ready for horses!"

Two weeks later, Nzinga's army met the Portuguese on the Ndongo side of Massangano. They fought for days on the hills around the fort until the horse-soldiers arrived. Then they pulled back at night to a place that Nzinga, Shellanga, and another general, Kabangana, had decided was better for defeating the horse-soldiers. They heard taunts daily from any Portuguese they captured, some even dying while they said it:

"Wait until Cordero comes!"

Nzinga didn't know how she might defeat Cordero, but she resolved to find a way, even if she personally had to attack his camp

in the middle of the night. The troops under Shellanga and Kabangana had shown that they could beat the Portuguese army fighting
on the hills, where the Portuguese could not stand as an army to
shoot at Nzinga's troops from a distance. In close combat, the Portuguese were out-classed. Only the horse-soldiers could change the
battle's outcome.

Then the horse-soldiers came, two of them.

They rode at the head of the army, but as they went forward, the
lead horse-soldier pulled back on the reins. The horse reared, giving
time to let the warriors from Nzinga's army and the African soldiers
from the Portuguese side surge toward each other. Some used throwing spears, others used long knives for close combat. From the hillside
above them, Nzinga saw Shellanga's warriors slicing into the ranks
of the Portuguese. He made little progress, but Shellanga didn't signal Kabangana to sweep down from the hills in support.

Then the Portuguese horns sounded, and the horseman took
action, racing toward Shellanga's forces. Nzinga was finally witnessing what Kajubi must have experienced. They were an awesome
sight, riding unimpeded into the ranks of Shellanga's men. The
spears and arrows of Shellanga's archers bounced off the horses'
leather armor, clattering against the breast-plates and metal helmets
of the riders. One horseman's sword sang through the air, slicing
shoulders, necks, and skulls as his horse reared and neighed—a
frightening beast, forcing even the bravest warrior to pause. The cries
of the trampled and dying rose from beneath the horses' hooves.

It must be Cordero.

Then Kabangana's troops swept down from the hill, engulfed,
and surrounded the Portuguese. The charge had little effect, however, because Cordero, seeing the danger, ordered a retreat. His
men quickly pulled back, though several small units still contended
in the bush and on the hillside. Kabangana's and Shellanga's troops
beat them into submission, capturing many and driving them into
the surrounding hillside.

Nzinga's generals did not pursue the retreat. For now, they
satisfied themselves with the fifty African soldiers they'd captured
and forced to join Shellanga's troops.

On their side, the Portuguese did not seem worried and did not hurry back to the attack. They seemed satisfied, as if they knew the outcome this time. Their attitude was revealed by some of the captured African soldiers. They'd joined because the Portuguese had the guns and the swords, and they'd win.

Both armies encamped on a hillside, making a surprise attack unlikely. They set up guards around the perimeter.

Among the soldiers captured by Shellanga's forces was a *pombeiro* named Boca Epejo. Nzinga had heard about him from Kambi and Funzi. He'd been with Cordero when he invaded the Mbanza. She glanced at his hand, delighted to see that Kambi's bite had done lasting damage, since Epejo seemed unable to close that hand.

They questioned Boca Epejo about Cordero's plans and about the horse-soldiers. Instead of giving information, Epejo seemed assured that the Portuguese would win. He offered advice.

"You should all give up, or Cordero will kill you," he said. He gestured, running a bony, ill-bandaged hand across his throat and pointing against his chest, as if he showed the placement of sword wounds Nzinga's men would suffer.

"Every one of you should give up," Epejo said. "I know you're scared. The way Cordero and Penote use their swords is enough to frighten St. Gabriel." He rose to his feet and made a few simulated slashes in the air with his closed hand, as though it held a sword. Looking around at the generals and orderlies who questioned him, Epejo wanted everyone's attention, including Nzinga's, who was busy nearby in conference with Shellanga and Kabangana. She heard his every word but didn't raise her head from the discussion with her generals.

Epejo's coarse voice rose and his large head of hair flipped around his pudgy face as he turned from side to side, spraying his adversaries with whiffs of saliva that escaped in bursts with the staccato force of his speech. He laughed and brought his wounded right hand against the palm of his left hand and acted with abandon, overstepping the bounds of civility among enemies.

"Even the queen, there," Epejo said, nodding toward Nzinga, "she wouldn't blame you if you gave up."

When he made this gesture toward the queen, the captured Africans rose up, mumbling angrily, and moved to kill him. With a small inclination of her head, Nzinga warned them away. She wanted to hear all he might say.

For his part, Epejo had no hint of his peril and ran on. It was all Cordero: Cordero this, Cordero that.

"Their horses are fearless and will chase you Africans everywhere. They'll leap shrubs and even tall trees."

Epejo continued on: how he had seen Cordero's horse leap fences and small trees, and that they shouldn't misunderstand Cordero, because they had seen him only in war, where he was a terror, slicing through skulls or riding enemies down into the dust with his war horses. That was expected in war, Epejo claimed, but once you surrendered, "Why, then, Cordero is a different person. He is generous and courteous, and a true Portuguese gentleman." Why, he'd treated Epejo to ale in a cantina in Luanda.

As if with the mention of drink, Epejo became thirsty. He rubbed his lips and beard. "And palm wine . . . Do you have any? Cordero is fond of palm wine. It's crazy to fight a war when we could be sitting under a tree drinking palm wine. Just think of the danger you're in if you don't surrender." He paused for only an instant and was off again. "I have some influence with Captain Cordero and I could—" He stopped in mid-sentence.

Epejo's eyes fell on an African artisan sitting nearby, busily carving a wooden statue. He was one of many artisans whose religious duties included following the army and complementing the efforts of soldiers by making objects that helped them win battles. This artist sat working with an adze, chisels, and wooden hammer. Boca Epejo pointed a twisted finger at the statue.

"What in the name of the Holy Virgin is that?" he asked, with derision.

"Can't you see what it is?" an orderly asked. He'd recognized that the queen wanted to keep Epejo talking.

"It appears to be a wooden statue of a horse and rider with a sword . . . Oh, I see it's meant to be one of us, say even Cordero, but hey, ha ha, this worker is no good. He can't sculpt, see. The thing won't stand up straight. It's tottering and the rider's body is all distorted. It's all wrong. Where did he learn? He should come to Luanda. Cordero has pictures in his quarters . . . "

Nzinga listened to him until she tasted bitterness in her mouth. It galled her to hear him praise the man who had killed Kajubi. She knew Cordero fought on orders. He took pride in being a soldier. He needed to be given a passion to blind his judgment. She believed she knew how to do it. It was clear that this *pombeiro* was his chosen lackey—one whom Cordero had picked to spread fear through fame.

Nzinga wanted Cordero angry and frightened. Boca Epejo would try to escape and give Cordero information about Nzinga's camp. And Cordero wouldn't expect her to attack in the night. She now had a plan, and the *pombeiro* had helped her with it himself. The *pomberio's* death would greatly anger Cordero. To start, she ordered Epejo beheaded and then had her spies sneak into the Portuguese camp and hang him upside down from a tree, with his head swinging nearby. She counted on Cordero feeling personally offended and needing to seek revenge. Then, not disclosing her plan to even Shellanga, Nzinga took a large number of men armed with axes and knives and went off into the night.

It was near daybreak when she returned, tired and weary, but even then she did not rest. She consulted with Shellanga and Kabangana, explaining that they could beat the horse-soldiers by leading them through the narrow gorge she'd selected.

"The battle must be fought there, not on an open plain."

They agreed to move the camp back toward the new Mbanza, to make it appear they were retreating. This would make the Portuguese eager to follow. Cordero's scouts could be fooled into thinking their army had an advantage, making them eager to pursue Nzinga.

After breakfast, Nzinga's troops hurried across the plain and took up positions in a narrow gap between two hills. This spot would seem to Cordero a golden opportunity to win the battle through his famous slaughter of fleeing men, thus instilling fear into the retreating army. Nzinga remembered the careless abandon Cordero and his fellow horse-soldiers had shown in the first skirmish, when they dispatched warriors with swords.

But when Cordero chased, he'd have to move through this narrow gap—where a surprise waited.

Nzinga was busy giving her troops instructions when Shellanga's orderlies ran in with a message: the Portuguese were already in the camp that Shellanga's troops had occupied the night before. Nzinga's final instruction before moving to a distant hill was that neither Cordero nor his horse was to be killed. Shellanga sent her Benege and Nsubuga to spring her trap—the fastest, most athletic, and bravest men.

They heard the Portuguese horns before they saw the troops moving cautiously towards them. The Portuguese were only a hundred yards from Shellanga's well-hidden troops, crack spear-men who also carried knives belted at their waist. The Portuguese spotted Kabangana's army on the hill. For an instant, the Portuguese foot-soldiers and horse-soldiers came forward, then they waited. The horses reared, pranced, and capered.

Like the wind, Shellanga's fleet men broke from cover, swept over the short distance, and were among the surprised Portuguese troops—stabbing with knives, slashing with spears, releasing arrows.

A drum sounded from the hills, and the attacking army fled, lost in the surrounding bush. The attack had been so swift and effective that the Portuguese had no time to respond. Nine Portuguese soldiers and seventeen African soldiers lay dead, plus many wounded. Not a single man was killed on Nzinga's side.

From her vantage point on the hill, Nzinga watched Cordero rise high in his stirrups, unsheathe his sword, and wave it above his head, exhorting his men to give chase. *He's vowed to not let us get away with this. Now, here it comes!*

Cordero ran his horse forward into the bushes, pursuing the warriors. His blade flashed down, slicing through the neck of the first runner he met. Blood gushed, spraying Cordero's leg and horse. The fearful act gave time for the others to disappear into the short shrub of the narrowing plain.

The fleeing warriors seemed light-footed now, almost as if they ran on air, but Nzinga knew they fled over logs placed at intervals across a large hole her men had dug the night before. Cordero chased close behind, the reins with his left hand, his sword ready in his right hand, all the while urging his horse on. Now his horse leaped high in the air over the small trees that had been unearthed and left to trap the Portuguese captain. Cordero and his horse went over the logs, crashing through the collapsing trees, and disappearing into a mammoth hole.

Another Portuguese horse-soldier followed behind Cordero. He pulled back furiously on his reins, managing to turn his horse, and then rode hurriedly back through the ranks of his foot-soldiers.

Kabangana's warriors swarmed down from the hills, crushing the Portuguese from both sides while Shellanga attacked from the front. A chant sprang up from the field, marked by drumbeats.

"Cordero is dead! Cordero is dead!"

"Zing, zenga, zenga!"

With confusion everywhere in the Portuguese ranks, gunners had no room to fire heavy matchlocks. Ndongo shields blocked their guns and spears. On a far-off hill, a captain paused. It was the one who'd stopped himself from following Cordero into the trap. He seemed to recognize that the battle was lost. He rode swiftly toward Massangano.

Nzinga wanted to learn whether her strategy had worked. *Where's Captain Cordero? What's happened to his horse?* Excited, she ran toward the bush, where she heard jeering voices and found her soldiers around the hole, pointing and laughing.

"Come on," one said in accented Portuguese. "Get up and kill us now."

Cordero lay under his horse, unconscious, his upper body twisted between two logs that had plunged into the hole with him. The horse, snorting with great effort, struggled to rise from its entanglement with the brush. It was not badly injured. Nzinga slapped her leg with joy, remembering the wind in her face when she rode the horse Tuscany in Luanda.

Her men dug a ramp and led the horse out. It had a slight limp but no broken bones. Cordero wasn't so lucky; his pelvis was twisted and broken. By the angles his arms formed, they were broken in several places. The men took care not to move him. They didn't question their ruler's order not to kill him, but clearly, without her interference Cordero would not have lived one more moment. When he regained consciousness, he studied his arms and legs, twisting his neck to do so. Finally he stared up into the hostile faces of his captors and found an amused one: Nzinga, who brandished his sword.

"Give me that!" he demanded.

She laughed, waved the sword, and shook her head.

"Then kill me. Kill me. In the name of the Holy Virgin, kill me now," he said.

She shook her head again. "You won't have any further use for this sword."

Nzinga waved it in the air. Nzinga's soldiers were silent. Her glances told them not to taunt him.

Cordero begged her again to kill him. She towered over him, pleased. *Here he is, Kajubi.*

Cordero gazed along his broken body, his face filled with pain. He spat at her before he began to shake. She signaled for her medicine men to wrap him in the blanket from his horse and care for him. If he recovered, she'd use him to strike fear into the hearts of other horse-soldiers.

She donned Cordero's belt and sword and mounted the horse. With the sword raised she rode up and down the valley. The soldiers in her army, both women and men, cheered.

At first it seemed Cordero would not live. Nzinga's doctors tried to dissuade her from intervening on his behalf. They sent gloomy predictions of his imminent demise. Keeping Cordero alive went against the popular but unvoiced opinions of the people, but Nzinga warned the doctors to do their utmost to save him. She had plans for him to help her secure her kingdom, and she'd deal harshly with anyone who tried to circumvent her order.

30.
CORDERO, BROKEN

ALTHOUGH HER SOLDIERS SAW Nzinga's ride on Tuscany as triumphant, it was also awkward, because she'd mounted a horse only once before, that time in Luanda. But while Cordero's recovery was in doubt, and later while his broken bones healed, she practiced every day, riding up and down in front of the makeshift infirmary where Cordero was held.

"The captain's anger is enormous." A mestizo who'd been sent to clean the infirmary and spy on Cordero reported what occurred when she first rode by.

Cordero tried to get up out of bed, but was barely able to rise on a pillow to glimpse her through the open door. "She's riding with her legs over the saddle. What kind of woman is this? She must be sent by the devil, eh?"

The mestizo servant, who had been baptized by a Portuguese priest, said, "Or the angels. She rides the horse as if she were born on its back."

"No." The captain remained angry. "She killed poor Boca Epejo, a good man. She cut off his head. I liked Boca."

"Are your soldiers more fearful of fighting her now?"

Cordero spat on the floor. It took great effort for his twisted body to perform the feat, and he didn't do it with the correct aim and force. The aim fell short and spattered on the servant's foot.

"I wish I were dead," Cordero said. "I'm a servant of Portugal and the Almighty. Why has God left me here?" He tried to lift his broken arms, but only shuddered in pain.

"Who knows the ways of God?" the servant asked.

"When I lay in that trap, with horse and logs crushing the life out of me, I begged her to kill me. She laughed. Laughed at me. Me, Cordero!"

Cordero repeated it three times, angrier each time.

"With my sword in her hand, she laughed. If God makes me whole again . . ."

When the mestizo servant reported this to Nzinga, he imitated the captain: how he clenched his jaw and shook his head—and then how the pain had caused him to howl.

.

Nzinga came to visit Cordero in the infirmary, greeting him in Portuguese.

"Como vai, Capitão?"

He refused to answer or look at her, but she kept talking in a pleasant manner, and soon her beautiful voice and infectious laughter brought his eyes up from the floor.

"What can I do for you, Captain?" She smiled.

He bared his teeth. "Give me back my horse and sword."

"Ah, no, Captain. Neither will ever be of use to you."

The captain gritted his teeth, shuddered. His bandaged arms rose and he tried to move his body, but it wouldn't answer his demands.

"Are you comfortable, Captain Cordero?"

"I have never been comfortable out of the saddle. It is all I know. I cannot be useful otherwise."

"You'll be useful again, Captain."

He seemed surprised.

"You'll be useful to me, to my people, to Ndongo."

Cordero shook his head in protest, then grimaced in pain. "Never. Impossible," he said. "I'll never help you."

Nzinga, courteous and quiet-spoken, said, "Helping us isn't a request you can deny, Captain Cordero. You can't stop it. Look at you. It is a condition of your existence. Everyone from Ndongo to Portugal knows of your terrible defeat. The news is talked about in Luanda. You see, we let some of the captured soldiers go, after they looked at you through the window. While you were unable to move. Horse-soldiers and others hear of you, and now they fear to fight in Ndongo. *Adeus, Capitão.*"

She swept from the room, her riding pants singing with each step.

Cordero's misshapen body healed. Six weeks later he hobbled from the makeshift infirmary to find Nzinga on horseback, watching him. His one leg was arched where it never set properly. His hips were twisted. His balance was awkward, because one arm pointed backwards while the other vibrated up and down when he hobbled toward the four-man litter that would take him toward Luanda. He'd be passed from village to village. Nzinga's orders were to see that Cordero came to no harm and then to leave him, in the dark of night, at the gate of the Massangano fort.

Supported on the litter, he craned his neck, regarding Nzinga with clenched teeth and with hatred in his eyes. His hand gripped the crutch he used for balance.

A smile dancing on her face, Nzinga said to Shellanga, "Other soldiers will see him and then shake when they think of fighting in Ndongo."

Shellanga said, "Then they will want revenge."

"That will cause them to make mistakes," she said.

Shellanga glanced at her. "It's as if your father were here. The same wisdom flows from you as did from the old Ngola."

Nzinga saluted Cordero and his bearers and then rode toward the palace, feeling Cordero's eyes boring into her back as he swayed on the litter on his way out of Ndongo.

31.

TUSCANY LOST

WHENEVER POSSIBLE, NZINGA LED her entire army against the Portuguese, but she commanded small units of warriors in attacks against them, also.

Her sisters kept her informed of enemy strength in Luanda with messages about troop movements and when the Portuguese had only a small number of soldiers in Luanda and thus were unable to reinforce the fort. When this happened, bands of Nzinga's soldiers lay siege to the fort, allowing no food to get in. They captured all guns sent to the fort. A few brave warriors would slip over the walls at night to set fires, slit several sleeping throats, and then scamper out before dawn.

Her raids and incursions caused rumblings among the African soldiers inside the fort, whom Nzinga constantly urged to desert. She promised them wives, land, and honor while all they could expect from the Portuguese, according to Nzinga, was to be killed, sold, or eaten at any moment. She burned the land bare around the fort. And she attacked all slave caravans that passed through her land, freeing captives and killing *pombeiros*. She avoided the mistakes her brother had made: her palace was wherever she was, and she moved the ancestral shrines inland, beyond Punga a Dongo.

For the Portuguese, it was a terrible, sleepless time.

When she didn't attack the fort, Nzinga camped in view outside, as if contemplating—waiting, as if she planned to attack. This was especially galling to the Portuguese, because it was their horse that she rode, captured from their captain, whom she'd maimed beyond total recovery.

The Portuguese announced a reward for whoever could deliver Nzinga's head. However, with the fate of Cordero so well known, no one stepped forward with a desire to earn that reward. When the Portuguese devised a plan to capture Nzinga, she retreated, and the soldiers who'd been sent to capture her were instead captured or killed by her army.

These skirmishes and battles went on for years, until Nzinga's horse wasn't as fast or sure-footed as it had been. Then Nzinga lost her horse, and the Portuguese almost won the kingdom. This is the way it happened.

·

The Portuguese bought the chiefs between Massangano and the coast with small gifts and fear. Those chiefs even had their own Ngola, who wasn't related to any royal Ngola but a commoner who couldn't make rain, predict the future, nor command the movement of fire, and whose drums didn't call all people together throughout Ndongo. He was a puppet, like a scarecrow propped up in a grain field, but with no power unless the wind or his Portuguese owners were present.

In Luanda, a new and craftier governor arrived and, wielding his military power, closed off Luanda from the rest of the country. He ordered his soldiers to prevent the movement of Africans. Nzinga's sisters were closely watched. No news came into or went out of Luanda. They shipped in many fresh soldiers with faster horses, unloaded ships at night, and came without warning to engage Nzinga in battle.

"Capture the Ngola!" was the governor's order. The soldiers were to ignore every other objective. "Capture her at any cost!"

The Portuguese came swiftly and furiously, foot-soldiers and horse-soldiers, sweeping upon Nzinga's unprepared camp near

Massangano and almost surrounding it. Nzinga mounted her horse and dashed across the savannah. Her soldiers followed, as many as could escape into the tall elephant grass.

In the distance through the trees, the Portuguese horse-soldiers caught glimpses of her fleeing party and pursued, exhorting the men not to lose this chance to capture her. They paid no heed to her army retreating in disarray, knowing that if they captured Nzinga, they captured all of Ndongo. The chase went on through grassland and bush, dust flying, until late evening, when they reached the place where the land turned from savannah to hills, shrub to high plateaus, then to valleys and canyons.

.

Up, down, and over went Nzinga and the remnants of her army. In the late afternoon, they looked back into the last valley to see the Portuguese horse-soldiers and foot-soldiers trailing after. Coming nearer.

All about them, gazelles sprang and bushbucks leaped across their path. Warthogs raised their snouts in query, then ran off into the bush. An elephant herd moved rhythmically to their left. Big piles of elephant droppings, brownish oval-shaped pans, gave off their pungent, grass-fermenting odor. The dust made both Tuscany and Nzinga sneeze. Long-necked giraffes flowed by in their fluid way. Zebra bolted across her path.

Nzinga sought to get lost in any wild herd, to confuse her pursuers. These encounters did delay and confuse them, but their intent was singular. Since she was the only target this time, they always regained whatever distance they had lost.

Once, winding up a hill where the trail up doubled back onto itself, the two groups passed dangerously close to each other. Ill-placed shots from a harquebus tore into the shrubs near Nzinga's horse. The charge from that cumbersome gun rang along the rocky hillside, echoing eerily, ricocheting, and breaking off lethal fragments of rocks and branches from low-growing trees, but missing Nzinga and her band.

Tuscany, her old horse, was tiring, and the young, fresh, horses were winning the race. Sharp rocks underfoot further worried and slowed Tuscany, who was lathered, breathing hard, and snorting with fatigue and frustration from the turning and twisting among the boulders.

Then the land flattened, with grass underfoot and low shrubs and high hills to either side. The dusky hand of evening brushed at the shadows of the valley. A cool, sobering wind blew in Nzinga's face. *Those sheer cliffs will break and show a rock pathway through.*

But the cliffs rose on both sides, towering, menacing, and steep. A cluster of green trees stood to her left, near the cliffs. She reined in her horse. Fifty of her ragtag, disheveled soldiers trailed behind, armed with only spears and long knives. She couldn't see beyond them but knew they were trapped in a canyon. It was impossible to get out and equally impossible to go back, because that meant humiliation and the loss of the kingdom forever. *Why, in the growing darkness, haven't the Portuguese closed in?* They'd surely recognized her plight. They'd be making a plan to seal her in the canyon and capture her come morning light.

Before darkness set in completely, Nzinga sent several exhausted soldiers back to locate the Portuguese. With the others, she searched for water among the green grove. The soldiers fanned out. A night-bird call from one of them directed all to a small lake within the stand of trees below the cliff. Even in the darkness, the soft mud revealed the footprints of animals that watered there. A soldier produced a bamboo cup for the queen, and they all drank.

The cold mountain water sent a chill to her head as Nzinga drank. On her knees, she immersed her head in the water, wishing there were time to jump naked into this mountain lake.

In silence, the soldiers gave her dried meat from their pouches. While she finished eating, they set about making a shelter for her. The only sounds came from their knives cutting trees, Tuscany grazing on leaves, and the constant music of locusts and other night creatures.

Then answers to night-bird calls brought the scouting soldiers to the lake. They came in, arguing heatedly, but grew silent in front of the queen. She ordered food and drink for them and then heard from the tall older soldier who led the scouting party how they'd crept close to the Portuguese camp until they smelled roasting meat and spices and saw their soldiers sloshing wine into metal drinking cups. Their horses were being fed, and people were sitting down to eat.

"Then I saw these officers, the ones who ride the horses. They sat on logs, and their African orderlies pulled off their boots. They talked in Portuguese. One said, 'No use to chase them in the dark. They can't get out. We'll round them up at first light.' Once, perhaps, they heard me, because one stopped talking and raised his hand for silence, but their soldiers were making much noise moving their gear, and the horses stamped and snorted. They laughed and went on talking. They will sleep now."

Then the scouts' leader peered into the darkness. He asked, "Are they right? Is there no way out?"

No one answered.

A young soldier, who'd been arguing when the scouts returned, said with heated emotion, "The queen can escape. She can ride Tuscany right through them while they sleep."

"But there are so many of them, and they are spread out," the older one said.

Nzinga listened for a while, tempted to try the younger one's suggestion. The younger, impetuous Nzinga would do it, but now the whole kingdom depended on her. Seeking solitude, she walked to the steep canyon wall. Sounds drifted in the night air: the munching horse, night insects, and splashes of her soldiers bathing in the lake. She touched the bulges and crevices of the wall. Trees leaned against its rocky face. A small tree provided support when she put her foot into a crevice and hoisted herself up.

One foot gained a protruding rock out and the other foot found a limb higher in the wavering tree as it wiggled and swayed. She pushed up, reaching out, not knowing what she might touch, but daring to hope. The outcropping was wide enough to hold a human foot. And where a foot could go, a person could follow. She grasped the sharp rocks for a handhold. They cut her fingers.

The old soldier, who had never let the queen out of his sight, watched her in the moonlight. He called softly to the others to come help. The top of the tree where she stood bent under her weight. Below her, they begged her to come down and let them climb, but she wouldn't yield. Just one more limb might get her high enough to . . . In her grasp, one rock came away and went hurtling downward, eliciting a painful yell when it landed below. Feeling around, she found the space from which it fell offered no immediate advantage. The weight of the rocks above had wedged the gap closed. Her feet cramped, squeezed between the angles formed by the limb and the main trunk, so she rested a bit, looking up into the steep blackness. With a great effort, she raised one foot and fixed it upon the outcropping, and then, tottering, she stood upon the ledge with support of the tree.

Her men again begged Nzinga to take hold of the tree, but she said, "I have climbed this far, so we can go farther. Cut more trees. Tie them with strips of bark until we have enough to climb out of here."

They set to work. The moon rose high while Nzinga remained on the ledge until the men climbed by her and wedged short trees between rocks. Little by little they all climbed. It became easier as they came toward the top, where water had cascaded over rocks during rainstorms and hot sun had cracked them, leaving space for a foot and hand and a whole body. Nzinga's crew passed out of the canyon.

Except for Tuscany.

The young, boisterous soldier repeated that the horse shouldn't be left behind, because he could ride him through the sleeping Portuguese camp. Although no one in the group believed there might be any chance of success, Nzinga told him to lead the horse quietly to the camp, mount it then, and ride as fast as Tuscany could run. She warned that if other horses smelled Tuscany, they'd wake the Portuguese. And she gave him a copper pendant, so that Ndongo people wouldn't harm him if they found him riding the queen's horse.

They left him to climb down, and then they drew up their tree steps. Nzinga's final glimpse of Tuscany and the young soldier was in the moonlight as horse and rider disappeared into the deep darkness of the canyon.

Nzinga never learned the fate of that brave young warrior. She sometimes imagined him riding through the sleeping enemy camp, escaping free into the African night, the wind in his face and the great power of the animal beneath him, fleeing into the center of Africa away from these live white ghosts that haunted the land, stealing its strength and beauty. At other times, just before a raid, she'd picture him riding into the Portuguese camp, where traps were set that cut down horse and rider, and the warrior tortured to tell where she could be found. Imagining his terror, she hardened her resolve, determined never to give up or be captured alive.

32.
NZINGA, MATAMBA AND JAGAS

AFTER NZINGA'S ESCAPE FROM the canyons, the enraged Portuguese took advantage of her absence, sweeping through Ndongo, threatening, buying, and coercing chiefs to join them. They brought with them the commoner that they'd put on the throne of the Ngola, their puppet who didn't command the respect of the people. He couldn't judge, he couldn't make rain, and no one came to his meeting house. But in this way, the Portuguese decreed an end to Nzinga's leadership.

The people, however, moved and left the land vacant, following Nzinga toward Matamba. Musungu had already moved from his forest past the falls. Chatembo, Sufalu, and Nzinga's old grandmother lived there with him.

Nzinga took time to regroup, living in the hills and mountains. Her loyal followers escaped the Portuguese and came to her. She raided the enemy camps and added their slaves to her army. Once she captured an entire caravan of slaves that had been bought and collected from all over Africa. When she freed them, they made their own village. When they celebrated their freedom at night, with all the diverse knowledge and culture they brought, it was as though the divergent tribes of Africa met in one place, in peace. Nzinga walked among them, witnessing their drumming and dancing, meeting faces of every shape and hue, and bodies of every size and shape.

She was living well and safe, but she wanted Ndongo to be free. Her ancestors were there. Their shrines were unattended. She couldn't forget her father's spirit. She said to her people, "I will not come into a place inhabited by the Portuguese. Fight! Fight for Ndongo. Never give up!"

Word came that a powerful Jaga army had clashed with the Portuguese in the Kongo. This huge army of Africans swept like a horde of locusts through the Kongo, destroying villages and taking women and children as prisoners. They'd come into Ndongo briefly during Mbande's time and took many cows while she was in Luanda. Like locusts, they came during rainy seasons and after a famine. Sometimes they caused famine. People made use of locusts, roasting and eating them, and Nzinga wished to make use of these Jagas. Old people talked of them every day, reminding young people that they, too, were once a roaming band, led by a blacksmith elephant hunter who settled down and became the Ngola. Without an Ngola, they'd become homeless wanderers again.

Nzinga needed these fierce, fast-moving warriors against the Portuguese, if only she could make them allies. But to do that, she had to make her own army strong again.

As Nzinga moved about the countryside, attacking chiefs and showing that she, as the true Ngola, made rain and made the crops grow, more and more people rejoined her. She daily trained new soldiers. She was always armed, often disguised as a male soldier. Other times she dressed to seem a common peasant with a market basket, a pot, a pack, or a baby hidden by a shawl that in fact hid weapons. And nearby watching were her fighters, spearmen, archers, and drummers, all the best she could find.

.

In Nzinga's wandering, her growing army passed the Cambambe falls, ran over the savannah beyond Punga a Dongo, and came to the inland high plains backed by massive forests where the people were hidden and safe from war, except for a few intrusions by *pombeiro* slave seekers. This was Matamba.

The day Nzinga arrived, an envoy of Fanvu, the queen of Matamba, visited her camp to invite Nzinga to a feast. Along with the food, Fanvu provided drummers and dancers that entertained Nzinga's people. During a pause, the queen joked with Nzinga. "Why do you, Nzinga, want to be called king?"

"Because that is what I am," Nzinga said. With that, she joined in a dance, much to the delight of the people. Displeasure creased Fanvu's aged face. She later asked Nzinga, "Why do you say you are a king, but you act like a common person?"

"My father used to do it. We are all human, and no one is more important than another is. And it makes people happy."

"How long do you and your soldiers intend to stay here?"

"Long enough to train an army. I intend to regain Ndongo. I need your help," Nzinga said.

"I can't help you do that," Fanvu said.

"But you must help."

"You can stay a short time and rest. You can have food and clothing, but you must go back," Fanvu said. "Matamba is at peace, and I want it to stay that way. You can't win your fight, and I don't want you to lead them to us."

"Fanvu, don't you know your own history? All our ancestors, yours and those of all the people here in Matamba, are at Punga a Dongo. Do you think the Portuguese will let Matamba stand if Ndongo is lost? No, you'll be next. They think you have silver mines here. You haven't seen the ships at Luanda, waiting like open mouths, eating our people. Fanvu, I'm only one leader against them, but I must do what I can."

"Don't do it here," the old queen said. "I will do as the ancestors direct me." They parted then, since Fanvu had no more words for Nzinga.

In the following weeks, Nzinga stopped all food festivals and celebrations. She took no action to enforce discipline, and consequently encouraged disagreement and then fighting to break out between her soldiers and the poorly prepared army of Matamba.

Then she ordered the queen arrested and taken to a distant part of the kingdom. In an elaborate ceremony Nzinga brought back the ancestral shrines from Ndongo to Matamba, to join those that had been left there. She declared herself Ngola and promised to oppose the Portuguese invaders wherever they were.

Two days later, leaving a trusted chief and several women in charge in Matamba, Nzinga crossed into Ndongo to attack the Portuguese army.

•

From her frequent experiences escaping capture, Nzinga had learned to take the higher elevations in order not to be trapped in canyons. Looking down into one canyon, she saw many fires glowing in army encampments. Because of the random arrangement, she knew it wasn't a Portuguese camp. And it was too large for any *pombeiros'* slave-raiding band.

Her scouts, with obvious fear, reported that they should retreat at once because it was the *imbangala*. The Jagas. Nothing was sacred to Jagas except their word. They ate human flesh, strangled their babies at birth, fought like demons, and raped at will.

Yet nothing is ever exactly as you hear it. It is either more terrible or less. *This horde could be useful.* She still had the glass for seeing in the distance, the one given her by Governor de Sousa. Using the glass, she learned the entire layout of the camp, seeing that one part of the camp was used for cooking and was mostly inhabited by women. This part of the camp was beside a small lake where men were bathing. She waited until nightfall, then placed her archers and spearmen in the rocks just above the camp. In the early morning, she went boldly into the camp. Immediately, the Ndulu went up from the women and children, and they ran through the camp screaming. Armed men came hurriedly from the bush, surrounding Nzinga and her small party.

Nzinga wore a woman's clothes: beads and amulets around her neck, a leather skirt and blouse, her hair short and loose. She was armed with a long knife, a dagger, and a fighting stick. When she moved forward, a group of still-wet, half-dressed bathers emerged on the path. One fighter tried to detain her, but she gave a warning look and moved quickly to the side as he gasped for air.

Meanwhile her wrist was actively turning the fighting stick so fast it made singing music about them. Fighters surged toward her at once, but she singled out the nearest one and, with continuous quick motions, struck the calf of his leg.

Before he could bend over in that direction, sharp, cracking raps struck his left arm, leaving it dangling. Then the stick raked the right side of his head, leaving the ear cut and hanging, blood oozing from the temple. The camp fighters fell back, then all surged forward again, rushing her and arresting the small party that accompanied her, some raising knives. But a huge, muscular man with a glistening body spoke in a bass voice that sounded like a drum.

"*Woo hoooo! Njoo!* What's this?"

He pulled a spear from the hand of a fighter near him. "Stand back!" he ordered. "This man will fight me."

The people fell back, making a wide circle with Nzinga in the middle, between the water's edge and the cooking fires. She stood, ready for battle, her stick in one hand, knife in another, arms crossed away from her body in a fighting stance, prepared to whirl among them. She took a determined step toward the huge, bearded man.

He lowered his weapon, surprised. "A woman?"

Nzinga moved closer, twirling her stick, waiting for his first move. He circled around her. Then a woman recognized her and yelled, "It's that daughter of the king."

"The Ngola!" Several people cried out, kneeling in her honor.

The big man handed his club and knife to a bystander.

"You . . . You're that one? Nzinga?"

She didn't answer.

"You're a fighter. So quick, I thought you were a man."

"No difference. I am Ngola. I cause rain to fall, fire to burn, crops to grow, drums to sound. Just like my fathers before me. Nothing moves without my command."

"There's no difference?" He gave her a man's look, slowly up and down her body. "No difference at all?"

"Ah, yes, there's that difference, but it doesn't matter."

"It matters," he said, nodding.

This leader was called Kallandula. At his invitation, Nzinga sat with him.

The people moved again about the camp. These people seemed happy and content. She'd heard so much about their savage acts: how they ate people and killed their babies, and how their ways of killing struck terror in their enemies. This last part excited her. She needed the Portuguese to be fearful again, as they had been after she sent a broken Cordero to them. Now they had new governors, new officers, and different soldiers. These new Portuguese had forgotten how fearsome fighting a battle could be in Ndongo. She needed the Jagas to help her remind them.

The men were muscular and strong. The women well dressed, jubilantly going about cooking, washing, plaiting hair, and grooming behind the makeshift houses. Nzinga recognized a few captives: they either stood aside or were extra quick to respond to any command.

Nzinga asked Kallandula to join her in fighting and chasing the Portuguese from her land

He asked, "Why should I do that? What do I gain?"

"I'll give you a part of Ndongo. You can live there and carry out trade."

Kallandula laughed heartily. He threw his hands out toward some of his people. "Did you hear that?" To Nzinga, he said, "We're Jagas, not traders. We take what we want."

"How about wives? Do your men want wives?"

"Yes, and we take them, too." He moved toward Nzinga and caught her arm. "And I have an urge to take the queen."

Nzinga didn't flinch. "Ngola. I am Ngola, King. No one takes me or mine. He who tries that dies."

It was clear Kallandula wasn't afraid of her: he was puzzled. He removed his hand. "Africa is changing. A woman-king. A good-looking woman."

His musing gave Nzinga time to think what might appeal to a marauder who had seen and taken everything on the continent. She said. "I know what you want."

"No, you don't," he said.

She smiled. "You're anxious to get your hands on more Portuguese goods. I know the inside of the fort at Massangano. I've been to Luanda, and I know how everything is stored. I have spies who can send us information on their strength and when it is best to attack them."

Before she finished that statement, Kallandula was grinning. She had him. His eyes flashed. The flat of his hand struck the tabletop. "Woooo!"

Interested only in driving out the Portuguese, Nzinga said, "Whenever we raid, you can have everything taken except the guns. We divide them half and half."

His eyes flashed again, and his huge hands closed greedily. "Whatever our armies capture, I take all."

"All except the guns." She paused. "And the horses."

"I thought you had forgotten those." His laughter echoed in the hills among Nzinga's waiting army camped there.

To seal the bargain, Nzinga threw a feast and gave the Jaga chief some captured gunpowder, two swords, knives, and spears from her own blacksmith.

Kallandula still wasn't satisfied. He shook his head as if he doubted her. "I have two challenges for you. I don't know if you can meet them."

"Challenges? There are no challenges I can't meet. I am Ngola." As she boasted in this way, Nzinga wondered if she'd forgotten anything or hadn't been told something about this marauding band.

"These challenges are beyond what kings do. One is to make my people trust you, and the second is to make me trust you."

"Just state it." Nzinga needed Kallandula as an ally.

The feast had begun, and a big pot of steaming meat and vegetables was set before them.

Nzinga was accustomed to eating only after a servant tasted her food. One approached and put food before her and tasted it, then bowed and left. Nzinga at once began eating along with the Jaga chief. "This meat has a strange flavor," she said. "Perhaps it is the herbs. What is it?"

Kallandula looked straight at her. "A kind of goat."

When they finished their meal, Nzinga demanded to know the two challenges.

"You have just met one challenge. The people will now trust you."

"What challenge did I satisfy?"

"You ate our special goat meat."

Nzinga knew then that the Jaga chief had tricked her into eating human flesh. Angry, she leaped from her stool upon him and clawed at his face. He held her and laughed and kissed her. She became quiet and lay there with him until, with his massive strength, he lifted her and carried her into his tent. That night she fulfilled the second challenge.

The next morning, Kallandula said, "All challenges are more than met."

Hearing this, she laughed with him.

▪

After that, the two armies laid siege to Massangano and then captured a small garrison near Luanda, freeing a number of slaves who promptly joined Nzinga's army.

On one of these raids, Nzinga and a small band from her army came through the farmlands into Luanda and had a brief, dangerous meeting with her sister Kambi and the spies Shanulu and Nsobia. They related sad news: the young drummer who had accompanied the old griot in telling the story of the white birds had been caught passing messages. He'd been tortured but wouldn't talk and had been sold and shipped to Brazil.

With only a short time to talk, Nzinga begged Kambi to come away with her. "It's too dangerous in Luanda now. You must come with me."

"At home, I'm of no use to anybody. But here, I can do something. You go to Ndongo. I'll send you messages." Kambi repeated words Nzinga had said years before when freeing hostages. In the end Nzinga had to leave her.

"I'll be back for you."

They squeezed hands and hugged, and then Nzinga ran out into the African night.

·

No inland Portuguese venture was spared. Any African chief who supported the Portuguese was raided. His wife and children were taken. His goats, sheep, cattle, and grain went to feed the Jagas and Nzinga's army.

Among Nzinga's prized possessions were two captured horses. One was a pregnant mare taken in a raid on the paddock where she'd first seen Tuscany. Back in Matamba it gave birth to a colt.

That raid had been made because Nsobia sent a message to say the paddock wasn't guarded. However, when returning from Nzinga, her messenger was captured. He led the Portuguese to Nsobia, who was tortured and questioned, yet she wouldn't give up Shanulu and Kambi. The torturers drowned Nsobia in the ocean. When Nzinga got the news, she cried for days and sent a message to Matamba, asking Chatembo to treat mourning for Nsobia like that for royalty or a warrior deserving high honor.

Nzinga and the Jagas often struck at the same time in different parts of Ndongo and where the Portuguese had a port in the Kongo. These small, quick raids kept the Portuguese off balance. During these years, Nzinga moved between Matamba and Ndongo quickly because she had a swift horse beneath her. She avoided traps with the aid of spies who informed her of the Portuguese's movements and plans. Wherever she went, she had an army waiting to form and, after a raid, to disperse quickly. She was loved as the Ngola, obeyed, and worshiped. People mentioned her name with reverence alongside Suku and the ancestors.

The idea spread among the people that Nzinga was everywhere. She might be in this very village, in those hills there waiting for the Portuguese, or on the island in that river. Nzinga often appeared among her people in Ndongo when they thought she was in Matamba. Her cadre of strong men ran miles carrying her on a litter, or she arrived on horseback or along the river in a boat. She believed, as her father had, that the people needed to see their Ngola. She appeared smiling, resolute, vibrant, and confident.

One evening Nzinga was camped on a hill near the old Mbanza, preparing a night raid on Portuguese who were coming down the river in boats to take over Mbande's old island palace. A group of her soldiers brought her the message that some people had come with important news all the way from Matamba. They awaited her at the old shrine in the forest on the path to Punga a Dongo. Nzinga's runners went along with soldiers to secure the place and to say, "The Ngola is coming."

When Nzinga arrived, she was surprised to find Wasema and Musungu waiting for her in the abandoned iron-making village. They sat in the old pottery shop, Wasema with a long, sad face and Musungu with a grave expression, looking about as if he didn't know what to do. Wasema greeted her by bursting out crying, holding a finger over her lips and shaking her head sadly.

"Oh, Nzinga, Nzinga, the news has almost killed your old grandmother." Her tears flowed again. "She said I must come at once and tell you, since it all happened near here. That is, part of it." She put her arms around Nzinga. "Nzinga, you have suffered so much. You know how much we loved them."

Nzinga looked over Wasema's head, her eyes pleading with Musungu to explain.

Pain showed in his aging face. He said, "It's Sufalu. She went looking for the children at the falls"—he inclined his head toward the falls—"at Punga a Dongo. She climbed to the top where the footprints of the ancestors are spread, along with prints of their tools, spears, and bows and arrows. Chatembo caught up with her there. Sufalu was hanging over the roaring falls, calling for the children, Chiambo and Ntongu. Chatembo begged her to come back, that Sufalu might fall, that she'd help search if Sufalu would come back. Chatembo believed she'd persuaded her. But Sufalu slipped, even as Chatembo reached for her. Like that"—he threw up a despairing arm—"Sufalu went over the falls. She's gone to the ancestors."

In battle once, Nzinga had been struck by a solid blow to the side of the head, a blow she never expected from another soldier's opponent. It dazed and disoriented her, the same way the news of

Sufalu's death dazed her then. She should be hearing this from her old friend and age-mate Chatembo.

"Where's Chatembo?" When they didn't answer at once, Nzinga cried out, "Musungu, Chatembo? Where is Chatembo? Over the falls, too? Why isn't she with you?"

Wasema shook her head and hugged Nzinga tightly, squeezing and rubbing her back. "You see, Chatembo didn't know about grain pits. She didn't grow up in a village where they scoop the dirt out of the ground and make grain pits on the hillsides, like underground pots. Where they line the pits with clay and fire the same as any pot, making them air proof and animal proof. Sometimes they make little underground lanes that people can climb through from one grain pit to another. But grain can grow old and give off bad air."

Nzinga put her hands over her mouth, shaking with sobs as she sensed what was coming.

"People who know this," said Wasema, "let chickens down in the pits to make sure there is no bad air before they go into them. But when Chatembo was sad because of Sufalu, she drank palm wine again and didn't think when she went to sleep there and . . . and they . . . well, they found them, she and a young warrior, and they couldn't wake them, Nzinga." Her wail reached up to Punga a Dongo. "Nzinga, Chatembo is dead, too. Oh, Suku, everybody is dead!"

They cried, leaning on each other. Then Nzinga said, "We must all do what we have to do. Musungu, shall we go into the cave to roll the bones and ask the ancestors what to do next."

"We already know what to do. Your father told Mbande what to do. Keep on fighting and never give up."

"But why did the ancestors let Sufalu go over the falls? And let Chatembo sleep in the grain pit? We still need them."

"They are still here. You see, Nzinga, a long time ago the ancestors took Chiambo below the water and told her about the coming of the white birds. The ancestor knew then that the world was changing."

"What's the best we can do? Delay being conquered and scattered over the world? To Brazil and other places?"

"They are with us here, and they will be with us wherever we go. They are with slaves aboard those ships, and they are in the cane fields or wherever we go in Ndongo. Even if we leave Ndongo, Kongo, or any part of Africa."

"And if they forget?"

"Some, for a time, will forget to know and honor the ancestors. But the ancestors will wait. As time goes on, the ancestors will again come to us with their music and their dances. They will sit among us and teach us and laugh with us, and we'll reach out to each other and to them, wherever we are. They will let us know that we are all, everyone in this world, children of the sun god Suku."

"So we must keep fighting for what is ours and never give up."

"Yes, for now, Nzinga, go on fighting this war. And I will go on making rings of iron."

"I know you are right, Musungu. We will fight on."

∎

After years of Nzinga's raiding, Portuguese goods became scarce, so Kallandula and his Jagas saw less to gain. They sent scouting parties down the coast into places called Cassange and Bie.

"There are more people to raid there, Nzinga. Come with us," Kallandula said, laughing. "I know you won't. But we Jagas, we need more space."

"You can spread out here, all the way to Ndongo. We can share this land." She'd do anything to save and keep Ndongo.

"No, we can't do that. We're not like you. You're an Ngola with people here who love you and wait for you. We're like ants, always moving and stinging those in our path. That's our way of living."

"But you could change that."

"Nzinga, you understand many things, but you don't know that people were not all made the same, nor have lived like you from birth. One day we'll break camp and be gone, like the *harmattan* wind that blows hot for a short time, then gathers its force and passes over the land."

As Kallandula had predicted, one morning Nzinga rode up the hill and looked down at the wide expanse where the Jagas camped to find it barren. Fires still burned, but there was nothing else. They had taken everything: horses, women, food. Like locusts, they had cleared the land of every single useful thing. Nzinga was left with only her people and what she'd stored in Matamba.

33.
THE DUTCH

MANY YEARS OF FIGHTING did not lessen Nzinga's zeal to win back Ndongo. With the deaths of Nsobia and Chatembo, Nzinga became more determined to defeat her enemies. In her prosecution of the war, she became more uncaring toward those captured and more hostile toward the enemy.

One night two of her spies from inside the fort at Massangano came out to buy food from nearby villages. Soon they were in a small house, reporting to Nzinga.

"The Portuguese are sick. Many are dying," one said.

"Why are they dying?" Nzinga asked.

"I don't know. Their skin turns redder and spots come out on their bodies. They say the water is bad. There is only one well. They say the water from the well is killing them."

"Why aren't you two dead from the water, then?"

The men laughed. One said, "We drink from the river and eat fruit that has lots of water. They say there are bugs in the river water. They say Portuguese have died from river water all over Africa. They're afraid of it."

Nzinga smiled with them.

"Now some of them get water from the river," he said. "But they don't like the taste. The well water is sweeter."

"Who buries these dead Portuguese soldiers?"

"Some African soldiers," one man answered.

"Then join those who bury the dead. When the soldiers aren't aware, drop a few of the bodies into the well."

"But, Ngola, they will all get sick and die."

"Just so!" Nzinga said, a grim look on her face.

"But, Ngola, must we go back there? We're sick of the sight and smell. The African soldiers are slipping away."

"Yes, you must go back. The ancestors will smile on you. We are all sick of it, but we can't stop. Tell the African soldiers they will have wives and land in Matamba if they join me."

They bowed as she left them.

•

Nzinga attacked the Portuguese anywhere she found them. No one knew where she might appear. She burned crops on a farm near Luanda while she attacked one of their outposts near the Kongo, and she harassed pombeiros traveling to the interior seeking silver and slaves. She appeared where no one expected her to be bold enough to show herself. Once she burned a ship at anchor, and her men stole a longboat to get away. Down the coast, she ran into a camp of Jagas, Kallandula's camp.

In her honor they had a feast. Nzinga made Kallandula laugh by asking him to show her the skin of the goats they were eating, because the other kind of meat they ate didn't agree with her stomach.

"But you ate human flesh before."

"Yes, but you tricked me when I was desperate. I'd have eaten hyena if it would have convinced you join me."

Kallandula hinted at news he had, then laughed at Nzinga and kept it from her until the dancing and drumming. Then he said, "You're wise, but I'm wiser."

Nzinga was amused but puzzled. He had his men bring in a box. He took out a new kind of gun, held it up, and shot dead one of the male dancers. Nzinga looked from Kallandula's weapon to the dead dancer, who had been so animated an instant before but now lay in a crumpled, lifeless heap, bespattered with blood. She was never indifferent to suffering or wanton disregard for human life. But she long ago realized on the dock in Luanda that some things shouldn't be protested, because they are over. Feeling this, she concentrated on an opportunity to save a country and the lives of many.

She'd seen guns before, guns that broke legs, blew gaping holes in stomachs, and even tore off heads, but she'd never seen such damage done by a weapon that produced less noise and explosive impact on the person firing it. She wanted guns like it.

"How do I get such guns, Kallandula?"

"What will you give me for this gun?" he teased.

"What would I give . . . ?" What did she have to exchange?

"How about a horse?" he said. "I lost mine."

"Ah, *Njoo!* The Portuguese no longer send horses in battle against me."

Kallandula still laughed as though he enjoyed a private joke. "I got that gun from the White Monkey. There are other white men who hate the Portuguese."

Nzinga remembered the captured Englishman who worked for Mafunga, the slave trader. Once, long ago, the Portuguese held another such a man prisoner, made him fight for them, and raid for slaves with the *pombeiros*.

"They are one day from here. You will meet the White Monkey. I'm wearing his shoes."

The shoes were made completely of wood. She laughed. "Of what use are these? You can never run in them."

"On a ship, there is nowhere to run. On land, they use these only for trade."

"They are fools, then," Nzinga said. "Africans need their land, not wooden shoes."

At the coast, Nzinga waited to join the captain known as the White Monkey until her soldiers were positioned along the shore, ready to cut off any movement of the longboats to the ships if these men tried any deception.

The captain proved to be a short, gnarled, muscular man, as thick as a baobab tree. He had scraggly, unkempt blond hair and blue eyes. He spoke with Nzinga in Portuguese, but to his tall, stiff soldier-aides, he spoke in another language Nzinga had never heard before. He said his name was Peter Haims. He called the Portuguese cockroaches.

"And I will rid the seas and Africa of the cockroaches."

He offered Nzinga a stately chair under his colorful canopy, saying graciously, "Do sit here, if you will." He poured wine for her in a tall glass, which he offered with dry wheat bread and cheese on a white linen tablecloth. "Is this the amazing, magical queen of whom I've heard so much?"

When the aides and the bowing servant announced that indeed she was Nzinga, he rose from his seat, approached her chair, clicked his broad boot heels together, and nodded in genuine admiration.

From the beginning they agreed they had a common enemy — the Portuguese. He made it clear all he wanted was Luanda, and he'd take it, keep it, and then be off to take Brazil next. Nzinga and he could be allies because he didn't want her land, he said, but he needed Luanda as a port. So it was settled. Nzinga was amazed it went so quickly.

By the next rainy season, the Dutch had driven the Portuguese out of Luanda. The Portuguese fled to Brazil and the Kongo, leaving a scraggly group of *pombeiros* and farmers who eked out a living by supplying the white man's vegetables to ships that came through.

This state of affairs went on for a dozen years, with Nzinga again controlling Ndongo and trading hides, horns, and elephant tusks with the Dutch for guns and cloth, while harassing the *pombeiros* and chasing the Portuguese from Massangano to the Kongo.

Though she had control of Ndongo again, all those she dearly loved were dead, gone to join Suku. She often visited the shrines, and went to spend days at Punga a Dongo. But all the wars had made people flee their homes and shift around, and now Ndongo had a population of *pombeiros,* Portuguese, and people running to escape the Jagas and other raiding tribes.

▪

Nzinga was growing older. During the campaigns against her enemies, she left the fighting and planning to her generals more often. She preferred to watch from the hill or stay in her camp miles away from the fighting, to receive reports and issue orders, or to retreat to Matamba and rule her people.

She had seen the White Monkey only once in all these years. Rumors were that he'd attained a high military honor and settled at a place called the Cape. But Nzinga dealt with a series of Dutch captains, much as her father had dealt with governors, priests, and soldiers who came and went, or died there. There were growing graveyards at Luanda and Massangano, littered with their dead, who by dying managed to claim a part of Nzinga's heritage. It rankled her to think of the patch each dead invader claimed.

Then, in a conference with a Dutch captain, there was mention of compromise and a treaty by the Dutch with Portugal. For a year she heard of these dealings, which would lead to some kind of agreement. She surmised from the conference that if Dutch made a treaty, then they'd end their relationship with Nzinga. She had to prepare for when the Dutch would pack, board, and sail away from Luanda.

Her soldiers disguised among the farmers, Nzinga retreated to Matamba to wait. In about a year the Portuguese drifted back slowly, settling in Luanda, securing and restoring it, then taking Massangano once more.

Nzinga, though well informed by spies, did nothing in Ndongo. But in Matamba, life bloomed. She visited and watched the army training daily, and she added to its number by gathering recruits from every village and from people captured in wars, both women and men. She made speeches, asking the people, "Would you rather fight for your soil and your ancestors, or be eaten by the birds with white wings and taken to die beyond the reach of the ancestors?"

This brought fierce determination and zest to the competitive training of her soldiers. Farmers produced more cassava, taro, maize, and bananas. Salt was stored. Drums and chanting reverberated through the night. Nzinga waited for the Portuguese to take one step past Massangano toward Matamba. The country was rested now, battle scars healing.

Matamba was ready for battle again, and this time Nzinga wanted it to be decisive.

34.
FIGHTS ALONE

AFTER KALLANDULA AND HIS army of Jagas left to raid cattle in Cassange and the area far south of Ndongo, Nzinga knew she must fight on alone. She made use of her network of spies to keep her informed of the plans and movements of the Portuguese. Chief among her spies were her sisters Kambi and Funzi, who had remained in Luanda, only coming back to Matamba once in all the years Nzinga had ruled.

Kambi, who formed a liaison with an African interpreter and had two children, was the greatest source of information because she still lived near the governor's mansion. Her husband worked with a lieutenant who was indispensable to the governor. Soldiers visited her husband daily, and from their quarters by the bay, Kambi could see the ships arriving and departing, loading and unloading, and soldiers marching, as well as fishermen in their boats and women diving for cowrie shells. Anything that passed under her eye was told to Funzi, who had three children with her husband, a ship's captain. Funzi's servants passed news through the lands of puppet chiefs and on to Nzinga.

The messengers were trained from childhood to memorize full particulars at one hearing and to repeat on demand the minutest detail. This enabled Nzinga to communicate with Portuguese officers by name in the field of battle.

In one such exchange, Nzinga sent a message to one officer, Captain de Lusia: "Why do you come to fight your sister Anna de Sousa? Am I not of the same Holy Father as you?"

He sent a message back: "That is why we called a truce, so you can come home with me. You have strayed too far from your family. We'll take good care of you."

Nzinga mocked him in her return message. "I know you would adorn me with gold chains on my neck, wrists, and feet and send me on a nice boat ride to Brazil, the way your baptizing white priest did to countless Africans. You would probably take me with you, since you have been assigned there. Just send me some colored beads and a nice lacy linen tablecloth to show affection for your sister."

The captain answered this message indirectly. Nzinga had let slip details that only someone in the military fortress at Luanda could have known. For the first time, Kambi and Funzi were suspected of sending information to Nzinga. How else could Nzinga know so quickly that Captain de Lusia was posted to Brazil? Both women were questioned, but because Funzi had three children by another captain, she was cleared. However, Kambi was treated harshly, since she'd long treated the Portuguese with disdain, openly censuring Funzi's cohabitation.

Now Kambi taunted and cursed them and admitted to spying. She had the fire of Nzinga, but not the guile or patience. In the end, they wanted to ransom her to Nzinga, but decided it was too dangerous. Kambi knew too many secrets. They kept her in prison for a while, but when she showed she had the power to bribe people for her release with royal promises, they had a *pombeiro*, on the pretext of taking her home, take Kambi far from Luanda where she drowned in a river. Accidentally.

Runners brought Kambi's body to Nzinga the same day, still wet, unscarred, wrapped in bright cloth. Nzinga wept bitterly when she learned that an idle remark in her playful message had precipitated Kambi's death. In her anger she raided more Portuguese outposts. She feared now for Funzi's safety and sent her messages to flee. But her messages went unheeded.

◈

35.
NZINGA AT HOME

A NEW GOVERNOR ARRIVED IN LUANDA with new orders from Lisbon. Nzinga prepared for war.

But instead of immediate war, the Portuguese sent an envoy to Nzinga to make peace. They no longer wanted to fight her, they said. A treaty was what they sought, they claimed. Letters from the king of Portugal praised her, invited her back to the Catholic Church, and offered to send priests. They no longer had any interest in war. They no longer wanted to take Ndongo. They'd discovered that no mountain of silver existed. They'd retain possession of Luanda and Massangano and hoped that Nzinga would keep the markets open and no longer attack. The bulk of their army was sent to Brazil.

Nzinga didn't respond at once. She left the markets open and waited to see what the Portuguese would do. After two years, the Portuguese were still using Luanda as a port for trading goods that they secured in the south at Cassange. A few Portuguese farmers and traders migrated out near Massangano, but none beyond that.

A Jesuit priest arrived at Matamba by donkey. He brought an invitation for Nzinga to come to Luanda to meet the new governor and sign a treaty. Nzinga sent a firm no. She'd signed treaties before, and they were not honored.

"Didn't you like Luanda?" the priest asked.

"My sister was assassinated there. She's buried here."

The Portuguese were not to be trusted. In the years her father had dealt with them, the Portuguese had seldom been true to their word. Nzinga, white-haired and old by now, was still strong-willed and commanded a firm voice. She said, "If a treaty is made, it will be signed here in Matamba. If it isn't kept, there will be war!"

For eighty rains (forty years, to the Portuguese) she had out-maneuvered and out-fought them, and now it seemed she had out-lasted them. They were never able to penetrate beyond the places where they'd come during her father's time. Had they finally given up? The ever-cautious Nzinga doubted it. In her resolve, she felt she had the approval of the ancestors.

The priest said, "I shall deliver that message to the governor, Queen Nzinga."

"Ngola!" Nzinga corrected him: *King!* "All during my reign people have tried to tell me that I'm queen. They say I'm a queen, because I'm a woman who rules. But all who think that way are wrong. Yes, I'm a woman. But I'm not limited in action by my sex. In my country I can order anything, even to kill you or anyone here. I am Ngola, king. You call me 'Ngola Nzinga'."

The people at court heard this exchange. All around her, the people began to chant.

"Ngola, Nzinga, Ngola Nzinga!"

Drums sounded. Dancers came, also shouting.

"Ngola Nzinga!"

That's how it was in Matamba and Ndongo. Even the puppets the governors put in place honored Nzinga and paid her tribute in salt, animal skins, and servants. The priest's mouth moved as his eyes witnessed this display of loyalty, service, honor, and organization. In awe, he joined in the chant.

"Ngola Nzinga!"

Nzinga, sitting in her royal seat, nodded her approval.

After years of watching, after small skirmishes, attacks on cara-vans, and detention of farmers, *pombeiros,* and soldiers, Nzinga received priests and ministers to negotiate a peace treaty. On the day of its signing, Nzinga made a surprising promise.

"I shall return to the Catholic Church."

She promised to remain a Catholic as long as the Portuguese respected her rule and left her country and people alone. At her reconfirmation ceremony, she left immediately when the new priest began a detailed chronicle of her transgressions in war against Portugal and the Cross. Everyone followed her, leaving the priest with only two mestizos and an empty church.

Afterward, she explained to him that he was fortunate she was a good Catholic. No one had any right to judge her in her own country, and if it happened again, he would not be permitted to remain. The breach was mended, and the ceremony finished two days later—with dancing and drumming, although the Church forbade it.

．

Nzinga's chiefs and soldiers spent their days watching and displaying their strength along Matamba's border or exacting tribute from neighboring tribes.

Now Nzinga truly became Ngola. As she was released from constantly planning for war, she could now look after her country. She spent days appointing chiefs, judging disputes, making rain, honoring dead kings, celebrating the harvest, and feasting and dancing with her subjects.

She traveled throughout the country at leisure to view crops, wild animals, and waterfalls. She was often dressed in the finest bark-cloth and leopard skin, or fine silk and linen—though she still loved to disguise herself as a soldier, fully armed and appearing where no one expected her. People in a province or village might go to bed without any thought of Nzinga being near, only to awake the next morning to find her neat, temporary palace set among them, decorated in different designs with bright colors and palm raffia streamers all around. This uncertainty kept chiefs alert, diligent, and fair.

The people smiled and danced often and worked harder. Everywhere Nzinga went, her people showed love and admiration for her. She'd long since restored the old queen of Matamba to rule over a large chieftainship.

Her sister Funzi came to live in Matamba. Nzinga was very old now, but she still loved to work. She'd often spend all day traveling in a litter and walking. She wanted to be tired at night to sleep well, so she had her personal drummer and favorite dancers with her. Even so, she had dreams and saw images of Chatembo, Kajubi, Sufalu, Batayo, and her father. All beckoned to her with smiles. Her father nodded approval.

Nzinga rose often to go to the shrines to honor the ancestors, to pray in the Catholic church, or to make a pilgrimage to Punga a Dongo to honor Suku. She took as many people as wished to go. Upon her return, there was always a celebration. After a day thus spent followed by a night of drumming, she slept. She slipped away in the night to watch Kajubi, her father, and Shellanga kill an elephant. She sat on a hillside with Chatembo and the royal cooks and moved her head in step with the hunters, rhythmically, as they killed the elephant. Then she heard the young Chatembo say, as Kajubi made music on his body, *"Nzinga, what do you think of that one?"*

She didn't return from the hunt.

The next morning, her attendants found she'd died in her sleep. She was one hundred seventy-two rains old, eighty-six years by the Catholic calendar.

. . .

◆

CHARACTERS

THE KING OF NDONGO AND HIS FAMILY

Ngola Kilijua *(ki li' jua)* – King of Ndongo; Nzinga's father.

Batayo *(ba ta' yo)* – Ngola Kilijua's second wife; Nzinga's mother.

Chala – Wife of Mbande; Nzinga's sister-in-law.

Kaningwa *(ka ning' wa)* – Ngola Kilijua's first wife; Mbande's mother.

Kikambi *(ki kam' bi)* – Second daughter of Ngola Kilijua and Batayo; nicknamed Kambi.

Kifunzi *(ki fun' zi)* – Third daughter of Ngola Kilijua and Batayo; nicknamed Funzi.

Mbande *(mm ban' da)* – Son of Ngola Kilijua and Kaningwa; Ngola after his father's death.

Ntongu *(nn ton' gu)* – Son of Nzinga and Kajubi.

Nzinga *(nn zing')* – First daughter of Ngola Kilijua and Batayo. Born 1582; ascended to Ngola 1621; died 1663.

Yafia — A princess; sister of the old Ngola; Nzinga's aunt.

NGOLA'S CHIEFS, WARRIORS, AND THEIR FAMILIES

Chatembo *(cha tem' bo)* – Daughter of Sufalu; age mate and friend of Nzinga.

Chiambo *(chi om' bo)* – Daughter of Chatembo and Nabugye. Named for Sufalu's great-grandmother.

Kadu *(ka' du)* – A senior chief of the Ngola.

Kajubi *(ka ju' bi)* – Elephant hunter-warrior, lover of Nzinga.

Kabangana – One of Nzinga's generals.

Kassa – A betraying chief.

Musungu *(mu sun' gu)* – Spiritual medium and master of iron making and weapons.

Mutele *(mu te' le)* – Power-seeking hunter friend of Mbande.

Nabugye *(na bu' gye)* – Junior chief-warrior; lover of Chatembo, father of Chiambo.

Ndowe – One of Nzinga's ministers; Topi's son.

Nsobia – Nzinga's spy in Luanda.

Oyimbu *(oo yim' bu)* – A senior chief of the Ngola.

Shanulu – Nzinga's spy in Luanda.

Shellanga *(shel lan' ga)* – Chief and general of the Ngola's army.

Sufalu *(su fa' lu)* – Seer; great-granddaughter of Chiambo, "arm of the Ngola."

Tashana – A betraying servant woman.

Temarku – A musician in the king's court.

Topi – Patriotic hunter who brought a message to Nzinga in Luanda.

Wasema *(wa se' ma)* – Lover of Mutele.

AMONG NEIGHBORING BANDS

Fanvu – Old queen of Matamba.

Kallandula *(ka lan' du la)* – Chief of the Jagas.

AMONG THE PORTUGUESE AND SLAVE TRADERS

Adelita – A Portuguese senhora; escort for Nzinga and her sisters in Luanda.

Andrew Batelle – A captured indentured Englishman.

Captain Cordero – Cruel Portuguese captain; a horseman.

Dalantia Gonzalez – The governor's cook.

Epejo – Captain Cordero's orderly.

Father Alvares – A Portuguese priest in Luanda.

Father Gouvieae – A priest held captive by the old Ngola.

Governor de Sousa – Governor of Luanda, a devout Catholic.

Mafunga – A Muslim slave seller.

Place Names

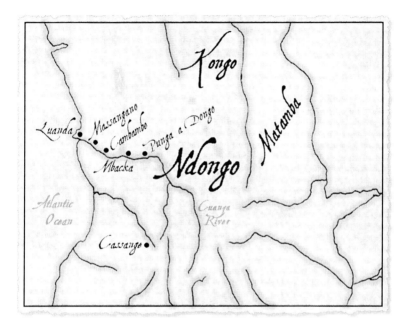

Cambambe – A town near waterfalls on the Cuanza River.

Cassange – A historic region in Portuguese Angola.

Cuanza River – A river that empties into the Atlantic Ocean; spelled "Kwanza" on many modern maps.

Kongo – The countryside and major river in central Africa; spelled "Congo" on many modern maps.

Luanda – A West African seaport town founded by Portuguese explorers; capital of Angola in modern times.

Lugalula River – A tributary of the Cuanza River; spelled "Lucala" on many modern maps.

Massangano – Location of a Portuguese fort on the Lugalula River, near the confluence with the Cuanza River.

Matamba – Country bordering Ndongo; part of modern-day Angola.

Mbacka *(mm bac' ca)* – Location of the Ngola's palace.

Mbanza *(mm ban' za)* – The Ngola's palace.

Ndongo *(nn don' go)* – The most powerful of early-modern African states; modern-day Angola.

Punga a Dongo – Place of the ancestors.

GLOSSARY

dik-dik – A small antelope.

griot – Member of the hereditary caste who keep the people's oral history.

imbangala – Nomad raiders from south of the Cuanza River.

Jagas – A Portuguese label for bands of African warriors from east and south of Ndongo.

Kimbundu *(kim bun' du)* – The language of the Ndongo people.

mestizo – Person of mixed African and white ancestry.

minkisi (min ki' si) – Art form that is designed to help get something done, either good or evil.

mwoso – A game.

Ndulu – A blowing sound made when tragedy occurs.

Ngola *(nn go' la)* – Ring of iron, symbol of power.

nzimbi (nn zim' bi) – Cowrie shells, used for trade-money.

pombeiros – European or mulatto trader-soldiers, suspected of being slave traders.

senhors, senhoritas – Gentlemen, ladies.

simsim – Sesame.

Suku – The name of a god of Ndongo.

yabarre – A game.

zenga – Kimbundu word for beheading.

About the Author

MOSES LEON HOWARD, an American writer and educator, has written for children and adults for fifty years. A retired dean of a community college, he has worked as a biology teacher, assistant high school principal, and mentor and counselor for students at risk. He lives in Tacoma, Washington. In addition to his long career as an educator in the U.S.,  Mr. Howard served as a Fulbright Fellow in Africa and spent ten years training medical technologists and preparing secondary school teachers in Kampala, Uganda.

Mr. Howard has also published children's books such as *The Human Mandolin* and other titles under the pen name Musa Nagenda, including *Dogs of Fear* and *The Ostrich Egg Shell Canteen*.

Find more publications by Mr. Howard at
www.jugumpress.com/MosesHoward/

◈

Acknowledgments

I want to own and confess my debt to the many people who assisted and otherwise encouraged me in the writing of this biography. I owe this debt to students, researchers, librarians, old people, and trees. In Africa, most living things have short lifespans, all except trees: trees live long naturally. If trees live past the bush and small tree stage, they can go on for hundreds and even a thousand years, just living as trees. Trees can also live on as part of a ship, a stool, or a drum, on to hundreds of years. But a tree can live on even longer as a book made from a tree. Books can keep stories, and they can be told with a drum or while sitting on a stool.

The students who took my class in Explorations, in which I taught about the explorers who expanded our knowledge of the globe starting in the fifteenth century, were excited about explorers like Ferdinand Magellan, Sir Francis Drake, and Vasco da Gama. That included Prince Henry the Navigator and his building of ships at Sagres. Christopher Columbus and Sir James Cook were always exciting them. During my classes in Explorations, my students always pushed me further and further, always wanting to know more. They were always laughing and asking, demanding more.

Their queries sent me searching during summer vacations in Rome, Spain, and Portugal, where two librarians at the Biblioteche at the University in Lisbon shared information.

Their queries also forced me to visit Ghana, Nigeria, Senegal, and other parts of Africa. Because of my students, I have awakened to different smells, strange tastes, the frenzied sound of alien drums, and the solaces of measured tapping rhythms in unknown villages. I once got off a bus in Ejebo-Odee and spent several days there sampling the food, because I thought it was a good place to stop over. I was not disappointed.

This book has been further enriched by assistance of the following:

Deborah Cherry, my longtime writing partner, who was a constant reader of the manuscript at various stages of its development.

Annie Pearson, author, editor, and publisher of the Jugum Press, who does the work of a publishing house, with editorial support from Laurie Cropp and Cindy Rinaman Marsch.

Eight co-researchers participated in a phenomenological study presented as a part of my contextual essay on the biography of Nzinga. Their names follow:

Elspeth Alexander, a lover of words and a professional corrector of manuscripts in the graduate department at the university, who wrote, "Before I had read very far in *Nzinga* ... I began to notice how absolutely, intensely real everything is. Somehow there's an instant connection between the words on the page and the image in the mind."

Rachel Kelebu, a master teacher from Uganda.

Natalie Lessigner, a musician and performer.

Lee Ang, Carlton, Tia, Merylee, Letha, Benjamin.

My Union Institute Graduate Committee Members were constant readers and helpers:

Dr. Henry Raymond gave line-by-line criticism of the proposals.

Dr. Phyllis Sloan encouraged me at challenging times.

With the help of many people, a writer wills a story or a life story into being. He sees a piece of it or envisions it whole, and when it is done, it completes some missing part in the writer's life, and hopefully it produces a part that was missing in the lives of those who read it. Some stories and especially lives of people who are no longer alive require a bit of audacity and boldness at the outset to attempt the realization of a believable story or life.

Nzinga was such a life story. When one considers the time in which she lived, the place, and the surrounding conditions, and, too, being a female with boundless restrictions, it is almost impossible to realize a person who could surmount all the difficulties facing her and yet attain the successful life she lived, and who could to such an extent affecte those living around her.

And yet, there is something about character: if it is known, it drives forward on its own and seldom deviates from its arc. With Nzinga, there was just sufficient quantity and quality of the arc of her personality still available around her name and acts that once the thread of life and action were attached, it led the writer through without a necessity of invention.

— Moses L. Howard
Tacoma, 2016

◆

Author's Notes

This project began as a personal overriding need to know what life was like for Nzinga, a woman at that time, with so many barriers set in front of her, even before her birth. How did she dare? What motivated her to persevere in the face of overwhelming odds? What sustained her over the long years that she pursued the goals of freedom for herself, for her people, and for her country?

As far as I know, Africa is my place of origin. Africa is an immense and varied continent with many countries and many different peoples. I have no idea owhere in this vast continent my ancestors belonged or from what part they were taken. I do feel and have always felt, as far back as I can remember, that I belong somewhere in Africa. When I was selected as a Fulbright Scholar and Teacher, I came to Uganda, then a Protectorate under British rule, not a colony. Some months after I arrived, I was walking along a road with two of my students who had invited me to visit their homes and meet their parents, which began for me a journey of discovery of self. In our travel to their homes, as the road wound through verdant farms of bananas, cassava, pineapples, and maize, we passed many villagers. Some places were uncultivated bush, some long swaths of high elephant grass, and now and again ancient trees lined the way. People moved along on this road, some carrying loads, others standing, talking, or working in their fields and gardens.

As we came nearer to the village where the students lived, more and more people greeted them in passing. One group of three women, after inquiring after their families and their progress in school, spoke directly to me, wanting to know why I refused to speak or communicate with them. I did not understand the language, and so I was unaware of the content of the query or that it was directed to me until one of the students, smiling, turned to me and said, "This old mother wants to know why do you not speak? Are you so proud of your life in the city and your European clothes that you no longer remember that you are an African?"

The school boys laughed as I spoke to the women in English. But the women, all three, stepped backwards in surprise, their hands flying up to cover their mouths as they said to the boys, in their language, "You see what pride education can bring. I hope you boys don't grow up to despise your people and your language as this man does."

The boys explained this complaint to me, and then they told the women that I didn't know the language. This surprised the women even more. They came nearer, wanting to know why I did not know the language.

"Then who is he?" the women queried.

The school boys explained, "He is a Negro, you know, one of those people who was stolen years ago and taken to America."

They wanted to know where was America, and one of them, a very old woman, was quiet for a time during the discussion, watching me, moving around me, looking at me curiously as if I interested her immensely. Then she pointed at me with her nose and turned her head toward a giant tree some distance from the road. And she said, in a flood of words, that she knew about people like me because she lived in a village near that tree where very many years ago sellers of people used to chain people to the tree to be sold and taken away. It was long, long before she was born and before her parents and their parents were born, but people still knew it and talked about it and told stories about it to children when they were bad. They told children that if they wandered away from their homes they would be taken and sold. There were stories about it, and there were signs on the tree left by those people sellers, she said.

We went to the tree. It was tall and very old. Its trunk was thick and the bark was healthy and smooth except in places where the tree's trunk was scarred and gnarled with knots. There, jutting from one was the rusted end of an iron ring, its last visible flakes of rust crumbling against the bark. I stood for a time staring in amazement, then, instinctively, I turned my back to it, measuring myself against the tree. I held my hands behind my back as if they were tied there.

I stood on the soil covering the tree's roots, and I lifted my hands behind my back, touching the last of the rusted iron ring.

More people had gathered about us now, talking with the women and uttering phrases that showed surprise. The people were very excited, and as more people came, speeches were made. I did not understand much of what was said. People begged me to stay, and we ate goat's meat, plantains, and cassava. And amid drumming and celebration, we drank pineapple and passion fruit juices, and my students interpreted my conversations with African villagers.

It was as though I myself was a stolen one who had been taken three hundred years before, and now that same one, me, had returned home. I felt accepted, but I did not deserve all of the attention. I was not worthy when there had been so many African-Americans before me who had done so much, and so many over the past three centuries who had begun the journey in their hearts and minds and yet were not fortunate enough to arrive. Besides, who knew if any of my ancestors had ever in the history of time passed this way?

I set to discovering Africa. I explored the roads, the forests, the animals, the trees, the rivers, the villages, and the people. Everywhere I went, I studied the people and their problems. I discovered that the ones who had remained in Africa had something that the children of slaves did not have. I saw it in the people everywhere. They had a sense of belonging and they had a great sense of self. You felt it in their talking, in the complacent way they worked and knew that every day belonged to them. You heard it in their unrestrained talk and their laughter of abandonment, and in the way both men and women related to each other. I taught in school, but I learned from the students and their families much more than I taught.

I went from one country to another, feeling the heat of the land and basking in the glow of the sun and greenness of the land, the fresh air, and the large bright moons and dark nights with torrents of rain and yellow streaks of lightning on dark stormy nights. I studied history. I caught again the words from my anthropology class where it was noted that to become acculturated, you had to know the language, you had to see how people were born, how they grew, how they passed through stages of life (rites of passage) from child to adult, to middle age to old age, how they ate, how they married, how they grew old, and how they died. I went into villages and went through life as an African experiences it. I went through a courtship, paid a bride's price, married there, and fathered children. I remained in Africa eleven years. And my wife and children are all in America with me now.

I came to the study of Nzinga through a course I taught in a Seattle school in Great Explorers and Their Explorations. Working with my students on the study of such leaders led me to the intense study of the first contact the Portuguese explorers made with the people of Angola, and finally to Nzinga, a great leader of her country that was then called Ndongo. I was again drawn back to Africa through the study of these ships and their travels along the west coast of Africa, from which many Africans forcibly embarked for lives of slavery.

I had been in some West Africa countries. On school holidays, I made study visits to Senegal and the island of Goree. I spent time in Accra and Ghana, with longer stays in Nigeria. However, Senegal was under French influence, and Nigeria and Ghana were former colonies of England. I had seen a bit of English Africa in Uganda and Kenya, and had seen a little of the past of Portuguese influence when I viewed Fort Jesus at Mombasa. But I had never been to the land of the *Black Mother*, which I took to allude mostly to Angola, as described in the work of that name by Basil Davidson.

I renewed my study of Africa, paying particular attention to Angola. A brief history mentioned Nzinga and how she had disrupted Portuguese attempts at domination of Angola. Jan Vasinna's *Kingdoms of the Savanna* had a more insightful perspective of Nzinga and Angola. James Duffy's *Portuguese Africa* showed that she was a force difficult for the Portuguese to conquer. Then, by chance, in a bookstore one day, I opened a volume called *Africa: History of a Continent*. In the index, I found "Nzinga" and the page number. Searching the designated pages, I found a drawing that depicted her sitting on the back of a servant at the court of the governor of Luanda after being refused a chair. I sensed two things at once: here apparently was a great leader, and also, this woman was one of the vital missing links in the history of Africans everywhere.

In 1982, I started a card file and a notebook with a list of references. Then I tried to get a visa to Angola, but it was not allowed, because a civil war was raging in that country. Cuban soldiers were supporting one faction while the United States and South Africa were supporting the insurgents. I reasoned that if I went to Portugal, I might have a better chance to get a visa. I travelled to Portugal in 1984 but was denied a visa by the Angolan Embassy there, because they determined it unsafe for travelers. Being in Portugal, though, was a huge opportunity to research Angola and Nzinga in Lisbon. For two weeks, with the assistance of two Portuguese librarians who spoke English, during the day I went to the libraries and museums. During the evenings, I walked the broad avenues and observed the architecture and the people. I met a number of Angolans who were students at the university in Lisbon. Sadly, they could not tell me much about Nzinga, only that she was a Jaga. One said she was Kimbundu, but he was from a tribe in Cassange, a part of Angola separate from the old Ndongo where Nzinga's family of Ngolas ruled.

In 1996, when I worked as an assistant principal in the Seattle School District, I joined the Union Institute. There I made a decision to immerse myself in studying Nzinga to understand and write about her as a leader. I set to work in earnest: I reread everything I'd accumulated about Nzinga, finding new trails of information. I came across a biography of Nzinga written by a Jesuit priest who travelled to Angola shortly after her time. The biography, though it presented many bits of information, did not agree totally with other sources. It had many gaps, and there were parts that showed the priest either was not familiar with African philosophy or preferred not to honor it or report it accurately. It was published in Flemish. Since I do not read Flemish, I searched the universities until I reached one department of languages that had a student who agreed to translate it into English. He read the translations onto cassette tapes. Although the book gave much information, it had many errors and numerous assertions that did not conform to other historical documents. Also, it lacked basic information, such as the definite tribe to which Nzinga belonged, details about her birth order and her mother, details about her trip to Luanda, and her exact relationship with the governor.

I wanted to write a biography, but the information for a definitive rendering was absent. I had a choice. I could write a shallow biography or use the information I had to construct a biographical novel. I had uncovered information about her childhood, how her father taught her by example, how she had contact with a Jesuit priest and learned the Portuguese language from him. There was information about her brothers and sisters, and the seer whose vision of white birds on the water foretold the coming of the Portuguese. I could study the European mindset of the times and the African response from other regions such as Congo and Nigeria. And since this was a time of upheaval and roaming, and since the people of Ndongo were roamers also, I could make use of things they learned and taught as they hunted elephants. Information is on record about the gods, the ancestors, and their secret place. I had only to think of day-to-day happenings. I had to listen to the Bantu languages that I know and that would tell me how to phrase dialogue. To start, I wrote a personal abbreviated biographical outline for Nzinga based on what I knew.

There is also evidence of development in Nzinga's early life as well as the adult years, and I have made use of this information in writing her psychobiography. Nzinga's personality and her beliefs came through clearly from her early years as well as the later ones. From evidence given, I could almost tell from who Nzinga was what actions she would take, and what she would do in certain circumstances. I was confident that when I didn't know, I could just "ask her" and let her and the evidence of her life point the direction. I let her do that in the writing.

While I was working, I was reading African philosophy. At odd times that later contributed to writing the mystical parts about Musungu and iron making and about Sufalu the seer who was the "arm of the Ngola," I was building a clear understanding of how seers and mediums work, especially in this setting. I began to understand their functions in Ndongo.

From my research, there was much more material and evidence than I could possibly use for one book. It was impossible to record every battle she fought with the Portuguese, or use every bit of evidence about her mother, the markets, her uses of weapons, or how she looked or dressed on most days.

As a final note: the most difficult part for readers in English is, of course, the names. Many research sources showed names that mixed Angolan and Spanish from the Portuguese habit of baptizing people near the coast and giving them Spanish names. If I used Portuguese or Spanish names, the reader would not discern the nationality of the character. So I have used Bantu names, but I did not want to mix local tribal names.

• • •

Some References

Benedict, Ruth (1934), *Patterns of Culture*. Houghton Mifflin, New York.

Cuvelier, Jean (1919), *Knongin Nzinga van Matamba*. Brugge, Desclée, De Brouwer, Brussels.

Davidson, Basil (1966), *Africa: History of a Continent*. Weidenfeld & Nicolson, London.

Davidson, Basil (1961), *Black Mother*. Little, Brown and Co., Boston.

Kerlinger, Fred N. (1973), *Foundations of Behavioral Research, 2nd ed.* Holt, Rinehart and Winston, Inc., New York.

Mbiti, John S. (1969), *African Religions and Philosophy*. Heinemann Educational Books Ltd., London, Nairobi.

Runyan, William McKinley (1984), *Life Histories and Psychobiography*. Oxford University Press, Oxford, New York.

Tucker, John T. (1933), *The Blacksmith Prince*. World Dominion Press, London.

Vansina, Jan (1969), *Kingdoms of the Savanna*. University of Wisconsin Press, Madison.

From Jugum Press

The Sky High Road by Moses L. Howard
How to keep hope kindled for a brighter future?

> Jason, a teenage soccer player in a Ugandan village, is worried about his O-levels and grieving his father's death from AIDS. His grandmother sends Jason and his sister Katura on a journey to her home village. That unwanted chore turns to catastrophe when they are enslaved as child-soldiers in the Lord's Liberation Army.

Accidental Heretics Series by E.A. Stewart
Lost in the Languedoc Crusade

Bone-mend and Salt (Book 1)

> Fight or beg for mercy when enemies turn an unjust war against you? Three ruined crusaders battle conspiracy and disaster while trapped in the new war against the Cathar heresy. Swords and grit must defend against deceit.

Trebuchets in the Garden (Book 2)

> How do you prepare for the dawn of the Inquisition? In the Languedoc, three embattled crusaders seek justice and respite amidst terror, siege, and conspiracy—as zealots prepare to ignite the next heretics' pyre.

Personal Voices in History Series by Ralph Buckingham

Journey Into Gold Country: Memories of a Forty-Niner

> Three wild years in the California Gold Rush, remembered in tranquility sixty years later by a New England younger son of a youngest son who went to seek his fortune.

Find print and ebook editions
and sign up to receive notice of new books:
www.jugumpress.com

Jugum Press

CPSIA information can be obtained
at www.ICGtesting.com
Printed in the USA
LVOW11s2335201017
553233LV00001B/48/P